The
GLAMOROUS
DEAD

The
GLAMOROUS
DEAD

SUZANNE GATES

KENSINGTON BOOKS
www.kensingtonbooks.com

KENSINGTON BOOKS are published by

Kensington Publishing Corp.
119 West 40th Street
New York, NY 10018

All Kensington titles, imprints, and distributed lines are available at special quantity discounts for bulk purchases for sales promotion, premiums, fund-raising, educational, or institutional use.

Special book excerpts or customized printings can also be created to fit specific needs. For details, write or phone the office of the Kensington Sales Manager: Kensington Publishing Corp., 119 West 40th Street, New York, NY 10018. Attn. Sales Department. Phone: 1-800-221-2647.

eISBN-13: 978-1-4967-0813-7
eISBN-10: 1-4967-0813-X
First Kensington Electronic Edition: November 2017

ISBN-13: 978-1-4967-0812-0
ISBN-10: 1-4967-0812-1
First Kensington Trade Paperback Printing: November 2017

10 9 8 7 6 5 4 3 2 1

Printed in the United States of America

For Jeanette and Joanne

Paramount Pictures

"The Lady Eve" Preston Sturges, Dir

Extras Production Schedule   Final Draft October 30 1940

Show up ON TIME. No lipstick provided.

Date/Location	Time	Type/Wardrobe		Scene
Thurs, Oct 31 Stage 9	8am	All	Hats	Wedding
Thurs, Nov 7 Blue Sky	8am	All	Hats	Horse races
Wed, Nov 13 L.A. Arboretum Meet at Admin	6:30am	All	Wardrobe provided	Amazon
Fri, Nov 15 Stage 9	8am	All	Leisure	Exterior ship
Sat, Nov 16 Stage 10	8am	Wallflower: Glasses All	Evening Dress	Ship dining room
Mon, Nov 18 Stage 10	8am	All Evening Dress Wallflower: Glasses Career Girl: Cigarette Holder		Ship dining room
Tues, Nov 19 Stage 10	8am	All Same Evening Dress Wallflower: Glasses Career Girl: Cigarette Holder		Ship dining room

Date/Location	Time	Type/Wardrobe		Scene
Wed, Nov 20 Stage 10	8am	All	Same Evening Dress	Ship dining room
Mon, Nov 25 Stage 10	8am	All	Cocktail or Evening Dress	2nd Ship dining room
Tues, Nov 26 Stage 10	8am	All	Leisure	1st Ship breakfast
Wed, Nov 27 Stage 10	8am	All	Cocktail or Evening Dress	2nd Ship Standby
Sat, Nov 30 Stage 10	8am	All	Leisure	2nd Ship standby
Tues, Dec 3 Stage 10	8am	All	TBA	Standby for retakes

Paychecks issued at Payroll after week's shooting completed. Do not ask for advance pay. Miles Abbott signs all timesheets. No paychecks issued without his signature.

Are you LOST? Map on reverse.

Questions? Dial Paramount Publicity Department
HOllywood 2411

MA:mb

CHAPTER 1

So you've envied *those* girls out in Hollywood with all
the screen heroes to choose from.

—*Photoplay*, November 1940

Someone buried a girl in the narrow pass behind the Florentine
Gardens. Two sailors dug her free and a crowd of us watched, late
night, still in fluff costumes from our Hail the Indians dance.

Stany hit my arm. "Might not be her. Rosemary's across town,
think of that. She's out dancing, and here we're all worried. Didn't
you say she always comes back?"

"I can't see. Let me go."

One sailor lifted a handful of dirt. "I need a flash," he said,
and a flash appeared in his hand. He switched it on, and the light
beam made his handful of dirt glow. He shook dirt between his
fingers until a chunk remained, and then he yelled and dropped
the chunk. It bounced and settled by Stany's shoe: a thumb.

Funny how long we can stare at one thumb. I knew it so
well. Who wore pink polish when red was the thing? Who bit
that polish and scraped it with her teeth to a pink oval? And
next to the thumb my friend Stany's open-toed pump, bone
leather, toes painted red, little ankle strap leading to her calf,
her linen skirt, and around us the feathered colors of Apache
Girl, Navajo, Chumash, still costumed for the night's second

show. We heard sirens then, and my eyes stung from mascara and false lash glue.

Stany hugged my shoulders. Stany, who two weeks ago heard Rosemary went missing and said *let's be friends* but gave me no reason. Movie stars don't say to Farm Girls *let's be friends,* but she did, and tonight she hugged me, and tonight nobody recognized her. Tonight she was one of us around a dirt pit and a thumb, and Rosemary was the center now because it was her thumb, her pink polish. Stany leaned into me, and my breath wheezed.

"Clear out," said a cop voice. Girls moved inside the club's stage door. The two sailors clapped dirty hands over the grave and pointed to what they'd dug so far.

I watched like my real self circled above the alley and all Stany held close was a skin sack. I'm describing it now, and I still don't want to feel. Stany told me it's shock, and that's what shock is. Stany was wrong. I knew about shock. I was circling. I saw streetlamps and cars down Hollywood Boulevard, scrolled front doors of the Florentine Gardens with its neon flashing *Nightclub Nightclub,* red velvet rope, and line of couples waiting to dance, square building, then its pitted rear walls. The stage door open enough for a long yellow triangle to cut light through the alley by trash cans, between dance hall and dorms. Three cops, two uniforms and one in a suit, and sailor hats I could see the tops of because I circled the air and pretended I couldn't feel. Stany's rolled hair.

It's November in Hollywood, and the Florentine Gardens is the town's best revue, and nothing I say can make you feel how I felt, sucking air, me in a short feather skirt. I was Cree Girl, and Barbara Stanwyck hugged me, I smelled my best friend in the dirt by my feet, and I thought, *Keep that cop away.*

CHAPTER 2

Says Joan Bennett: "It's of great importance to have one's hands blend with one's personality."

—*Photoplay*, November 1940

The suit cop raised a notebook and smiled. A detective. He made me sit on a bucket he'd turned upside down, he gave me his coat, and Stany tucked it around my shoulders. My headdress wobbled, and Stany unpinned it. She never moved, not when the detective told her to. We stayed outside so the detective could watch us and still see his cops dig up Rosemary.

"My best friend," I said. "Rosemary Brown."

"You know without seeing the face?" Burned brown skin and round eyes. A fat Mexican.

"Who needs a face?" Stany talked for me. "Look at the thumb."

It lay on the dirt, no blood, nail bed white around the pink oval.

"You are—"

"Barbara Stanwyck," Stany said.

"Like the actress."

"Just like."

The detective wrote in his notebook. "Barbara Stanwyck, your friend doesn't talk?"

"She's terrorized. She's asthmatic. She—"

"I talk." I hardly heard myself. "I live there"—I pointed at the dorms—"with Rosemary."

"You dance at the club?"

"Not really dance," Stany said. "She's in the girl revue. They *parade* is all. In costumes."

"I can't dance," I said.

One uniformed cop had a shovel now. He dug around Rosemary's shoulders, and the loose dirt built into a pile between me and the body.

"Why did you bury your best friend?"

"I didn't bury her. I walked over a little hill, I didn't know it was her, we all walked over her body for days before the hand got free. Then those sailors dug up her arm."

"You walked on your best friend."

Everything said to a detective sounds bad. Say a girl walks the hard, flat dirt from backstage to her dorm, and she does this again more times each day, then the next day a hill comes and she walks over that, but she doesn't have time to think about the hill. She has to get somewhere, a studio or rehearsal, to dinner or bed, and she doesn't think where she's walking. Other girls do the same, all day, and we never think it's a body we're walking across. We have somewhere to get to. We have to make money.

"I guess so," I said. "I walked on her. I didn't know it was her."

"You didn't smell her."

"Nobody smelled her," Stany said. "Look at the garbage cans. Who can smell a body over that?"

"I smell her now," I said.

"You parade at this club."

"She's an extra at Paramount," Stany said. "She works on my set."

"Sure," he said. "We all work there."

"So did Rosemary," I said.

"Sure, all of us. When did you start walking on her?"

"Two weeks? I can't remember," I said. "I know Rose went missing on Halloween." But I'd wished Rosemary gone every day since we'd moved to Hollywood. I didn't tell the detective that.

If not gone from the city, then missing, so each casting call the directors would look at me instead of beautiful her. She was the girl stopped by tourists, the girl handed free drinks, with a small nose and Hedy Lamarr eyes. She was taller than me. She had gold hair that I hated because mine was light blond, boring. She had movie star breasts.

The cop with the shovel stopped digging. "We have a face. Don't let the ladies see."

Our detective turned, and his body blocked the view.

Stany nudged me with her elbow. "The cop digging. I know him," she said. She talked soft, so her voice didn't reach the detective. "He works security at Paramount. A lot of these guys moonlight. Jim? Joe? Joe. Security. Good news for us."

"Why good news?"

"Information, Pen. Joe's our link to the case. I'm having a look."

She left me and stood by the digging cop, both watching something I couldn't see. I heard mumbles and some words—"damage," "chin"—and inside the club, drums beat the beginning of the second show.

Maybe Stany was right. Maybe I was in shock. I couldn't move from that bucket, and my skirt feathers stuck to my sweaty skin. Under the sweat I felt cold, and the detective's jacket didn't help. My legs shook, I think because they understood it was Rose they'd walked across and stomped on and smashed. In my head I got stuck on little things, like, *where's our rent, what's my schedule tomorrow.* I didn't think about why Stany looked excited instead of scared, how many times did I walk across Rose, or why did Joe the cop stare at me. Those are the questions that come now, as I'm telling you.

I didn't answer them. I was still on the bucket, and the fat detective shifted so the light from the cop's flash shined past his body, and I saw in that light Rosemary's beautiful yellow face with her eyes open and dirt-clogged. The cop was holding her head, and she was staring through me. I heard Stany say, "Why is her neck green?" and I vomited.

"Let's finish our talk," the detective said. "Forget what they're digging up. We don't see them. Where do you really work during the day?"

I wiped my mouth on my arm. "I'm an extra at Paramount."

"Sure," he said.

"I met Stany there. Hank Fonda, too. Rosemary and I got the job on Halloween, with a group from Central Casting. We work the club nights. Rose and me."

"And I'm her friend," Stany said.

"Not really," I said. I looked at the detective's dark eyes. "She says she's my friend, but I don't understand why."

"You are *worth* having a friend like me," Stany said. "Is that guy supposed to move the thumb? I'm sure it's a clue."

The detective said, "You work at a dance club where you don't dance."

"Right," I said. "We've been Indian Girls since we moved to Hollywood. That was last April. Rose and me."

"Last April. So that's, what, seven months you've been in town? Seven and a half months? How old are you?"

"She's twenty-two," Stany said.

I said, "I am?"

The detective wrote in his notebook and closed it.

"I saw her last at the Palladium," I said. "We went to the grand opening on Halloween. Can I have some water?"

"If I get you water, will you tell me the truth?"

"Sure," I said.

He tucked his notebook under one arm and disappeared behind the stage door. I stood and dropped his coat on the bucket. "I'm tired," I said. I watched Stany watch me. "Early call tomorrow."

"You're in shock," she said.

I stood two feet from Rosemary's body. A couple feathers drifted from my skirt to her yellow chest. The flash cop brushed dirt from her ribs. I stepped around the cops, the dirt pile, the hill of Rosemary, and I crossed to the dorm.

I must have gone in and climbed the stairs. I remember lying on our mattress in the room we shared with two other girls, but I don't remember the girls coming home.

I slept, then I woke, and I recalled the night through waxed paper, all smeared except for her body. I thought and thought about Rosemary's body, and why I should remember it so clear. Then I knew: She didn't have clothes on. Someone cut off Rose's thumb and killed her, and buried her nude in a place I'd have to walk over all day.

CHAPTER 3

"Get out and live!" That's what the old maestros in the opera houses and the theaters used to tell those they were grooming for fame. "And if your heart gets broken, be glad! It'll make a better actress of you!"

—*Photoplay*, March 1940

"I'm going to Hollywood," I told Rosemary. This was last March. We sat under an old Washington navel that waved branches over the Knotts' farm. Their berry canes stuck through the barbed wire property line. On my family's side, the orange trees grew in rows for twenty acres and stopped at Grand Avenue. Rose and I sat two acres up and couldn't see all the people in line down Grand, but we could hear them. Rose stretched her legs in the dirt, and we both breathed in orange blossoms. We lived in Buena Park.

"Hollywood," she said. "Hollywood! What changed your mind? Oh, who cares, we're going, who cares. We'll be stars by next year." She stood and twirled with her arms out. Her skirt became a bell. "I'm Ann Sheridan, I'm—no, I'm Alice Faye, I'm anyone but Joan Fontaine, who mopes like she's dead, bless her, I'm Rosemary Brown—"

"Rose."

"We'll rent an apartment by MGM. The studio makes the girl.

We don't want anywhere but MGM. I'll meet a director in three days. No, two."

"What about Will?"

"We're not married, Pen. He can visit. It's not that far. I'll need new earrings. I've just these, and look at them. And a dress."

I could see her think up her options. She tilted her head, and a gold hair fringe covered her chin. Hair stuck to her lips. She twirled a circle, she danced in her dream Hollywood.

"I've saved eight months," I said. I wore dungarees and red lipstick. "I have to leave here. I'm going. In Hollywood I'll be somebody else."

"Eight months? You saved and you didn't tell me? I need money from somewhere. I've made forty dollars at Godding's and I've spent it all. Why didn't you tell me?"

"Rose, are you listening? I want to go on my own. I can't stay here. These trees, all those people . . ." I meant the line of people I heard beyond the trees, their mutters that reached me as claps and chirps of sound. I breathed and couldn't quite get the air in.

"You're selfish," she said.

"I'm selfish, then."

"What about Will? Your mom and Daisy?"

"Two minutes ago you said Will could visit. I won't be far away. Mom doesn't need my help with Daisy any more than she needs your help."

"Now you're selfish and mean." She sat again in the dirt. "Look at me. I belong in Hollywood."

She did. The sun skipped tree leaves and settled direct on her hair. The wind blew just those parts of her that looked better in motion, her skirt hem and two curls by her cheek. If it rained like it rained two years ago, to a flood, Rose's wet blouse would drape her waist like a Greek statue. Perfect for film.

"It's not the trees," she said. "It's that date. One date. You go on one date with an old friend and you keep thinking about it. I don't get you."

"So I can't forget." Across the barbed wire, through canes, in front of his barn, Walter Knott lifted a hand at me. A sort-of wave. He wanted to buy us out. I lifted my hand back.

"It was my idea to go to Hollywood," Rose said. "For years I've dreamed it, and now you'll go alone."

"You never dreamed it. I'm sorry. You said you don't get me, and it's true. I'm not like I was."

"Don't I know," she said.

"Please. Let me have this. Let it be mine."

She lifted a twig and made it a wand, tapping her feet and knees. "I need trousers"—tap—"and stockings"—tap—"and another skirt."

"Rose—"

"I'm going. You're not the only one with bad luck. So he forced you a little. What do you think a date is?"

I could shift, lean on my side, and see down a tree row to Grand and the line-up waiting for chicken dinner. Through branches and thick trunks and leaves, I saw them: dollhouse families who didn't care if the wait to be served was three hours. Before the flood, just a few people had stopped at the Knotts' roadside stand. And now Mr. Knott, in a black town suit, walked with a clipboard from his barn to the back of the restaurant, where Cordelia Knott fried her chicken and served it with stewed rhubarb and goddamn boysenberry pie. He looked at me again and nodded. He knew he'd have our orchard within a year and a half.

Chapter 4

We Cover the Studios: If you like the livelier things in life, this is your meat—some authorized eavesdropping on the sets.

—*Photoplay*, November 1940

I walked Rosemary's hill for more than a week before she was found. After the cops dug up her body and smoothed the dirt— after it was flat again—that's when I stepped around it. I came and left by the club's side door, and I entered the dorms through the kitchen, but I'd gotten that dirt on my shoes, and dirt like that doesn't wash off. I already had blood on those shoes, and now dirt, too.

The next morning it didn't matter. I didn't need shoes. We shot *The Lady Eve* on location in the Los Angeles Arboretum, by a pond edge with a skiff and Hank Fonda balanced inside. I was wedged between leafy cannas and a queen palm, behind a wood box that Paramount publicist Miles Abbott said held a snake but sat with lid open, empty. I wore full body makeup and a bandeau top. I carried a spear, and through pepper trees I could see the horses run at Santa Anita. Deep hoof thuds from the racetrack next door rose in the arboretum through my bare feet.

". . . and I want that snake back, *now*. You—Amazon Girls. Eyes off Seabiscuit. Bet horses on your own time."

What snake? I stood in a line of ten Amazon Girls. We all watched Hank in his Amazon gear. Khaki breeches, pith helmet. A beautiful man. Something moved at my feet, and I looked down.

That snake. My grass patch. Little snake flecks stuck dull on the grass at my feet. They caught sun and sparkled. Emma the snake slid by the cannas and disappeared into a fern bank.

From the skiff in the pond, Hank shouted, pointing. "Left, left! Here, Abbott—behind the rock." Abbott ran to a rock, and I saw Emma's quick tail flash. Hank called from the skiff, "Abbott! No, stage right. Go slow—she's shedding. Or molting. What the hell it's called."

Then I saw Joe the cop. Sun shone off his black hair. He wore shades, and his cheekbones looked high and shiny, like the Indians I've seen on street curbs in Tijuana. Joe wasn't a cop today. He wore security brown and a Paramount cap.

"Why are you here?" He stopped two feet from me, too close. "After last night. You couldn't take a day?"

"You think Abbott would give me a day off?"

"Your best friend died."

"Yeah. Step back, I'm on my mark here. I can't move. A little more." I pointed at Hank in the skiff. "You block my view."

Joe, night cop, thought I didn't care about Rose. He thought last night was nothing for me, a missed show, no tips. He thought I woke this morning excited to ride the Paramount van from Hollywood to almost the mountains, one girl whispering to another, all looking at me without really looking. He didn't see that Rose was beside me on the van. She stood next to me in the jungle. Her green neck sputtered blood, and when I turned to her, she vanished.

"Why do you act strange?" he said. "The other girls hate you. These other girls." The extras, he meant. The Amazons beside me. "If their best friend died, do you think they'd be here today?"

Yes. Maybe they all had dead friends beside them. I couldn't tell. I knew not one would miss film time and the chance to wear a bandeau in front of Hank Fonda. And what if she did miss? Back to Central Casting and cattle calls and crowd scenes in Air Corps training films. Better to be haunted than looking for a job.

Preston Sturges, director, sat in his chair at the pond. He drank from a flask and yelled to actor William Demarest, "Bill! Before she throws the spear, kick her."

"Kick her? I won't kick a woman!"

"She's not a woman, she's an Amazon. It'll be funny," Sturges said. "You kick her and growl, you know how you do, and say, 'I've got enough woman trouble.' Then Sweetie puts the wreath on your neck."

"I'm not kicking a woman."

"Don't really kick her," Sturges said. "Just half-kick her. Then say, 'I've got enough woman trouble.'"

"Sure, and who picks me up when the Amazon kicks back?"

"Growl like that, Bill. Perfect. Where's the snake?"

Lost snake in the Amazon. Joe leaned in, bent so his lips touched my ear, and his touch made me shudder and wheeze, and he whispered, "I'll arrest you for murder. At the end of the murderess hall is the door. You only go through that door once. The gas *clicks* on."

"There's the snake."

"Where?" He jumped.

I'd left my shoes twenty feet from my mark. I had blood on those shoes. Rose's blood, from what happened on Halloween. Joe would arrest me and take my shoes and find Rose's blood. He'd match the blood type. He'd take my fingerprints, and he'd match my prints to the room where Rose bled. I'd touched the room all over. Glass, window frame, ladder. Fingerprints and blood. They didn't mean anything yesterday, before Rose was found. They didn't mean much this morning, when dead Rose followed me on the van and floated behind cannas and palm trees. But now, if they led to a hall and a gas chamber at the end, the shoes and prints said I was her killer.

Get rid of the shoes. The blood wouldn't be noticed unless I wore the shoes. They were black, and Rose's blood had seeped into the crease between leather and crepe sole. I could see the stains if I looked close, and if Joe arrested me, he'd look at everything I'd worn to the Amazon. I couldn't wipe my prints off the glass and the ladder, too late, but I'd get rid of the shoes.

And then what, walk out of the Amazon barefoot? Joe would find the shoes.

Buy more shoes with no money?

I'd have to steal.

"You're pushing," said the Amazon on my left. She hit me with her spear. "You're blocking Hank. Where's your mark?"

Through trees in front of me I saw the parking lot, trucks and vans, a pile of stuff we'd left at the edge of the pond trail. A line of shoes, ten pairs, mine with blood in the cracks. My throat had closed, my chest forced little breaths out and in, fast. I'd steal another girl's shoes.

Not the Career Girls'. They'd know it was me right off, because they hated me. And they never wore black shoes like mine. Their shoes always matched their skirts, like they both dyed their shoes in a big Career Girl pot.

I dropped my spear and hunted for Emma, pretended to hunt for Emma, in back of the Amazons.

Amazon: "Get to your mark."

Amazon: "He'll see you."

Amazon: "Let her get caught."

They hated me. Stany was my friend, no one knew why, and now a dead girl floated around, so they hated me more. I cut through the trees at the far end of the Amazon line, through two scratchy bushes and rocks that made me hop on each leg. Down by the clearing, Abbott ran between shrubs and palm trunks. *Snake here? Snake there?* Preston and Bill Demarest argued. And Hank floated in his little boat. Joe. Where was Joe?

I crouched by the pond trail. Each girl had a handbag or sack, a brush, lunch maybe, a pair of shoes on top.

Shoes! It was like a street market. Femme Fatale? Her shoes

had fat heels and a buckle with rhinestones. I needed shoes like mine so I could exchange, not steal exactly. Shoes like the Wall-flowers' or Old Maid's.

No, not the Old Maid's. Her shoes sat like gray boxes. They hooked on the sides. No man would marry those shoes.

Wallflowers, then. They both had black shoes, one with an-kle straps like mine but cuter than mine and newer, and that Wallflower wore glasses, so she'd see half what she needed to. I checked the Amazon line, all girls with spears up, heads down, on snake watch. I lifted my shoes in one hand and duck-walked the shoe line to the Wallflower's pile. I squatted and grabbed her shoes. Nice shoes, shiny. It hurt to hold them because I had a long, red scab on my palm. A hurt palm, from Halloween.

"The snake's over here?" Joe stood behind me. I hadn't heard him come. "Snake in your shoes?" Joe asked. He squatted be-side me. He put one hand on my back, above the bandeau, on top of brown makeup base, over two deep scars that rose and sank in skin globs. I have two scars on my back, souvenirs from my one date with an old friend, and Joe rubbed each of them with his hand. Tears hit the brown base at my eyes, and I wiped them. Now my eyes stung. My chest burned from wheezing, and I had tight skin. My skin stretched under Joe's hand until I thought it would split, from Joe's hand out, to each shoulder and around.

He took the Wallflower's shoes and flipped them. He showed me their insides. "See? No snake. What's the big *C* written in here? What are you doing with two pairs?"

"Hold it." Abbott's voice, close. "Don't move. I got her. Farm Girl, out of line. Don't *move*, I said. Here—nice Emma, here—Preston, I got her. *Got* her."

I dropped my old shoes on the Wallflower's bag and I stood. I pretended I could breathe.

"Goddamn snake," Abbott said.

Across the clearing Preston Sturges waved a hand to the pond. "Hanker," he said. "Ready to shoot?"

Hank waved from the bobbing skiff. All ready in the Amazon.

In front of me, Abbott unwrapped Emma from his arm. He knelt and coiled her in the empty box by my feet. I shifted, and one of my feet hit the box. Abbott kept one hand on Emma and looked at my foot, then up my brown leg, the split skirt, then tummy, bandeau, hair snood, hot warrior face. He frowned. "Don't move again. Bad enough I have to run after a snake."

"Ladies!" Sturges yelled into a megaphone. "Lift those spears. You're getting kicked."

Through the palms, through the grass, I saw my bag trailing ankle straps. New black crepe wedgies, smudged from the arboretum walk.

Back at the Gardens in my dorm room, my new bedmate, Madge, answered the hall phone. I had a new bedmate one day after Rose was dug up. No weeds growing here, no sir, not at the Florentine Gardens. We replace girls every day.

I recognized the new girl from the Amazon. She pulled double duty, Paramount and revue line, like other girls at the Gardens. In my room Career Girls shared the second mattress, and a Wallflower slept somewhere downstairs. Now Madge complained, "I get the bad luck bed where a goddamn dead girl slept. Stany's on the phone. I won't be your secretary. It's *Stany*." She rubbed Amazon base off her hairline. She pulled the Amazon snood off her hair. She'd told me she was brunette, but I saw puddle brown. I picked up the phone in the hallway.

"Are you standing or sitting down?" Stany's voice was still new to me, low and smooth.

"Standing," I said. Every time Stany called, I felt sick and nervous.

"Sit on the floor then. There's news."

"Okay, I'm on the floor." I stood on the hall linoleum. At the hall's end was a door, like in Murderess Hall. This locked door led to a third floor deck. Someone stood outside on the deck, rattling the knob.

"You're sitting?"

"I said so."

"Rosemary was strangled."

I leaned on the wall. "How do you know?"

"I told you to sit down. Now you're all weak, aren't you? Penny, if I suggest that you do something, listen."

"Strangled?" My hand rubbed the wall. Cracked plaster, cold. Beige paint I could flick off with my nails. *Rattle rattle*, the doorknob at the end of the hall.

"Maybe wire. Cut her bad. There's more. I wasn't on the schedule today, so I thought, hey, make use of my time. What's the most interesting thing that's happened this week? Last night, right? And how can I follow that up? I went to the cop station and talked to Detective Conejos. He's the guy—"

"The detective."

"Good for you. I talked to him and do you know, he believes me now. He knows who I am. Our friend Joe the cop told him about me. Conejos politely asked if I'd like to watch the autopsy."

"He let you watch?"

"Perks of a film star. I'll tell you about it on the way."

"What way?"

But she'd hung up.

In my room Madge had kicked off her shoes and sat Indianstyle on the Career Girls' mattress. She had fingers in her mouth, ripping off cuticles, little blood pearls around her nails. "Stany wants something from you. Aren't you worried?"

"What choice do I have?"

"No choice at all. You've got to be friends with her. I just think you'd be worried."

"I won't tell you," I said.

"I know. But you're worried, right? I would be. Downright fucking scared." She talked odd. Her mouth opened wide, and she made city sounds between sentences: little snorts at the back of her throat that sounded like a car low on gas. She was still talking when Stany parked on Hollywood Boulevard and honked. We heard the horn clear through the walls of our building, third floor, through peeling beige paint, a good two hundred feet from the sidewalk. Nobody told her to stop honking because they saw who she was. Perks of a film star.

CHAPTER 5

Before that pearly freshness of the American girl's face came an enduring tradition of fastidious care of her person.

—*Photoplay*, November 1940

Stany kept her left foot on the gas and her right foot on the brake. She didn't have a third foot for the clutch, so she wiggled the stick between gears. She drove a Ford coupe with the bonnet down, cream-colored, like a good blouse. Her hair looked red against the car's paint. She leaned across and pushed out the passenger door for me.

"Conejos is waiting, we've got to move." Car in gear, horn honking, gas revving the engine. Stany in traffic. "Preston called, I heard this morning went well. How'd you like Emma? She's cute, for a snake. Tomorrow I play a scene where I scream because she's a snake. I told Preston how silly that sounds—me afraid of a snake, imagine. We had garter snakes in Brooklyn and I cut them in chunks and sold them for fish bait. Pretty good bait if you cut them small. But I told Preston I'd scream. It's his script. What's that shit in your hair?"

"Brown makeup from the Amazon. It won't brush out."

"Sprinkle talc on your hair, wait one minute, and brush again. Talc sticks to the makeup and it comes right out. That way you don't have to wash."

By now she'd turned off Hollywood Boulevard and drove toward
Los Feliz. I kept my arms crossed because wind came over the
windshield and the afternoon was cool, not quite seventy degrees.
Stany wore a wool jacket over chinos and didn't notice. She wore
sunglasses too, big, round ones, and I could look across and see her
eyes trapped between the lenses and her face.

"Where's Conejos?"

"Meeting us at the morgue," she said. "He's cute, have you noticed? Except he's fat. That little hair curl on his forehead. Almost handsome. We're late, but I called him from the studio so he
knows we're still coming. I ran overtime with the dialect coach."

"Why?"

"Because I can't speak with a fucking English accent. I definitely sound like something, but it's not English. I told Preston
if Cary Grant were my dialect coach I'd learn a lot faster. Oh, you
mean the morgue? For the autopsy, like I told you."

The air got colder. "I thought you went this morning."

"No, it's going on now, or will go on, when we get there."

"Then how do you know Rose was strangled?"

"Conejos says it's obvious," Stany said. "Cut through the neck.
He'll show you."

"Stany, I don't want to see. I'm not watching Rose cut up on a
table. I can't stop seeing her anyway—"

"Here we are," Stany said.

The morgue smelled funny. You know how put-up asparagus
smells when it's left on the shelf too long, maybe a couple of years?
Then you open the jar and all the spears mush together when
they're poured out. The juice stinks. That's the smell, some rooms
worse, some the light asparagus smell. We walked through room
and room and room, led by a kid in blue work clothes who stared
at Stany and couldn't say her name right. Then we walked down a
long hall with bulb lights hanging from cloth-covered cords. One
spat at us and flicked out. The kid knocked on a door and Conejos
opened it. He smiled at Stany, and then he saw me.

"Why is she here?"

"I brought her," Stany said.

"She's a suspect. I'm not letting any suspect watch."

"I'm a suspect?"

"No," Stany said. "He's a kidder. You can watch."

Conejos set both his hands on the doorjambs, like a brace. "She can't come in." Under his arm I saw the room, white enamel table with a white-sheeted lump on top. Two white-coated men stood beside the table.

"I'm a suspect?"

"Stay here," Stany told me. "Sit on that bench. Relax. I'll tell you everything."

The door closed, and I was in the asparagus hall alone with the stammering kid, who shut his mouth now that Stany was gone. He left me there, by a wood bench.

The autopsy took two hours. I could have left, I wanted to. Madge was right, Stany's friendship made me jump at small sounds. Downright fucking scared. I should have left. I even stood up and thought, as a suspect, I should disappear like most come-and-go girls. They show up with a suitcase in Hollywood, stand in line, smile and con drinks from sailors, dance in the all-girl revue at the Florentine Gardens, or if luck's really down, at one of those burlesques on Century Boulevard where all the girls wear are balloons and guys buy straight pins at the door.

Pop!

And every Monday they're at Central Casting with an arm out to push the girl in front. They grab a studio call or they don't, at the back lot they get picked or they don't, they stand hopeful on Hollywood and Vine, and when they leave, because most of them do, nobody remembers. Someone like Madge the Amazon steps in to fill the dorm room. If I left, by tomorrow Madge would have a new bedmate.

But I didn't have anywhere to disappear to. I listened to voices for a while, not through Rose's autopsy door, but upstairs. I guess the ceiling above me was thinner than the walls. A woman's calm voice, a man's, another man yelling the only words I could understand: "Stop yelling at me! Stop yelling!" Then that faded, and a door slammed and took all the voices somewhere else. I stood,

I stretched, I wiggled my toes in my new shoes half a size too big; I walked the long hall and got bored doing that, and nobody else seemed to walk the long hall, so I tried doorknobs until one turned. I went into Posting Room Five.

I stood in another white autopsy room with an enamel table and a white-sheet-covered lump. In back of the lump I saw a sink, a hose, cupboards, and no windows. A folding chair sat by the table. I walked to the chair and pushed it so it moved and the legs scritched. I looked at the white sheet. I knew whatever lay under that sheet wasn't Rosemary, but inside me I didn't believe it. It's possible to know something for sure, like I knew Rose was in a room down the long hall, but still feel like I was looking at my best friend's body and all I had to do was take one corner of the sheet and lift it and there she'd be, dead but *there*. I needed her. I missed her so much. My hand reached for the sheet but didn't touch it.

I let my eyes follow the sheet lumps, because now that I stood close I saw not one lump but lots of little ones, little rises and falls of the sheet. I saw where the cotton skimmed ankles and settled high on dead toes, then fell around the table end. I saw the fabric lie flat on a stomach, up for ribs, and then mound at the side like a woman's breasts when she's sleeping. It wasn't Rose but it could have been, and that's probably why I lifted the sheet from the top edge of the table and pulled it away from the body.

She had no face. I saw bloody hair and a neck, and in between was a skin jumble like someone put the puzzle together wrong and gave up, then messed with the pieces. But her body was fine, beautiful, not Rosemary's movie star breasts but someone's. I had that feeling again like Rosemary stood beside me, the feeling I had in the Los Angeles Amazon, Rose looking with me where the face had been. I didn't turn this time so she could disappear. I made myself look at the dead woman and think of Rose, and I started to cry.

Twelve days before, we'd both danced to Tommy Dorsey at the Hollywood Palladium and Rose laughed when a guy dipped her backward on the huge dance floor, with the Pied Pipers singing "I Wouldn't Take a Million" and Rose spinning into another guy's arms. She leaned toward me, away from him, and yelled, but in the noise it sounded like a whisper: "I've got a secret."

Nothing good can happen after someone says that. Look at the woman on the table, where her secrets led her. Now Conejos called me a suspect and I couldn't tell Stany the secret, and I had to find, on my own, what happened to Rose, or I knew Conejos would blame me for her murder.

"Here you are," Stany said.

I pulled the sheet over the woman's messed face.

"Don't worry about that, I'm a tough broad from Brooklyn. I've seen worse in a street fight. I have loads to tell. Are you ready to go, or do you want to visit the posting rooms and stare at all the corpses?"

"Just this one."

She linked her arm through mine and turned me toward the door. "We'll have a good cup of coffee and we'll talk. You know what I said about your hair? Don't use talc after this place. You'll never get the smell out until you wash. Here's my plan. I tell you everything, and we decide what to say to Conejos."

"Stany, I'm a suspect. He's not going to be all nice and question me like I lost my best friend. He's setting up the lights right now for a grilling."

"He wouldn't do that with me around." Her hair looked brown under the sharp lights.

"No?"

"First I tell you what I know. Then you tell me. We'll solve this together."

No, I thought, but I didn't say it.

CHAPTER 6

How to Get a Raise Without Asking: Tips the stars wish
they'd known when they were struggling wage earners!
—*Photoplay,* October 1940

"I've got a secret," Rose said on Halloween night. I barely heard
her.

"Just one?"

"Oh, catty."

"Tell me the secret." I caught her arm before she danced away.

She danced and danced. She lifted the sailor cap from her partner's head and swung it above her own. He laughed and dipped
her, then held her close and sang so loud I could hear him above
the Pied Pipers, above Connie Haines's lovely, deep voice, above
Dorsey's orchestra on stage, his trombone. Rosemary slapped her
sailor light on the mouth, and instead of singing, he hummed.

She wore green crepe with a peplum and a skirt that split up her
thigh. She'd pinned a fresh orchid against a side roll of gold hair,
and she'd painted her lips pink, extra wide lines.

I looked dull beside her: black rayon dress with a front drape
that nobody saw because ten thousand people stuffed the Palladium. I had red lips, but every girl had red lips. I looked like every
girl, but Rose—she looked like a star.

Rose dumped her sailor and danced now with a carpenter from Paramount. I recognized him from the back lot. I danced all evening with the same guy, who watched the stage instead of me and who held me so loose I tripped and he didn't notice. He yelled to me when skinny Frank Sinatra came on stage, but that's all.

"We're going," Rose said in my ear. She pulled my wrist, and I don't think my dance partner noticed. Rose weaved me through people, bodies, noise, through the huge, round room with its ceiling of a circle, then another circle, then another, all connected at the stage like wrist bangles and then flaring above the dance floor to the galleries, where the real stars sat and ate roast beef. I didn't want to leave.

"The guy you danced with," Rose said. She stood by the hat check and handed her receipt to the girl. "He's out there dancing by himself."

"Naw, he's got Frank Sinatra."

Rose laughed.

"And you'll tell me this big secret?"

"We'll go there now. The secret isn't a place, but it's happening at a place."

"Where's the place?"

"Just follow," she said. She took our coats from the hat check girl and handed me mine. I took my coat and my handbag and tucked both under my arm. I was too warm to wear a coat.

Outside, the air felt breezy and cool on my arms. Midnight, too late for trick-or-treaters but early for a Hollywood Thursday, so traffic buzzed on Sunset, and Rose raised her hand at the curb. A cabbie pulled over.

"I don't have money for a cab," I said.

"I've got money. We're not going home yet."

I got in the cab with Rose. I didn't hear what she told the cabbie. He angled his rear mirror to stare at her, and he'd drive, stare, drive, stare. I'd had three gin and sevens, and I watched buildings blur through my side window: Sunset Boulevard, past the Trocadero and Ciro's and The Players, all lit from the fifty klieg lights that scanned skies for the Palladium's opening. The street became quiet and leafy past UCLA, and then the cabbie turned at Beverly Glen. One block up he stopped at a corner park.

"What are we doing?"

"We'll walk from here," Rose told the cabbie. He asked for her phone number instead of a tip, and Rose just laughed. He left us by a small triangle park. Ahead, a Beverly Hills street of big houses and yards that looked black in the dark but I knew would be perfect and green in daytime, every bush and palm frond vibrant. Houses here looked unnatural from the front. They were stage houses behind high hedges where nobody lived and nobody needed to sweep the front stairs because no dirt settled on them, ever. They had narrow drives hidden on one side where the trash cans stood, where people parked cars and hid their dirt.

We walked past them to a short street, turned right, and up a bit to North Faring Road.

"You know how I've been short on money," Rose said.

"Not anymore."

"Well, yeah, not anymore. Don't you like how I pay my part now? Rent?"

"I appreciate it like you can't know." My shoe hit a rock, and I stumbled. "Couldn't you show me this secret later? I wanted to stay at the dance. Celebrate! Paramount, Rose. A major production."

"We're Farm Girls."

"I don't mind being typed. We're on the back lot. Would you rather be at Central? At least we're not the Old Maid."

"I wanted to be the Femme Fatale. We turn here. Is this Faring? Turn left. Up the hill."

"Why do rich people live on hills? My feet hurt. Plus, they have to curve streets."

"Shh," she said. She stopped in deep shadows and put a hand on her chest. She breathed fast. "I'm nervous. I didn't tell them I'd bring you."

"Bring me," I said.

"I needed money, Pen."

"What?"

"I didn't save like you did. If you'd told me in time, if I knew we were moving, I'd have saved too, right?"

"Bring me where? Who didn't you tell?"

"I'd have saved, right? You know I would."

I faced her but I saw only her outline. Her shoulders, the orchid's petals a small black flare that stuck to her head. The lamppost across Faring lit me, but she hid in the dark. I felt wrong, I felt stuck to the road. "Rosemary, what is it?"

"It was a joke, to start." Her voice was low, flat. "I'm small, and upstairs windows are small, and nobody locks their windows here, Pen. It's not like at home. These houses, the second floor sashes lift right up and I can fall in, then run down the stairs and unlock the kitchen door. Nobody sees. The kitchen goes to the driveway all along these roads. Nobody sees! It's so easy. If we cut right through there, we'll be in the backyard."

"You're robbing them," I said. "You're robbing them." A car's engine revved and sped toward us, past us, me in the street's light.

"You could say it that way," she said. "Or you could say it different."

"How? How is it different? You sneak into people's houses and rob them. What do you do with the stuff?"

"I don't do anything. They have a fence."

"They? *They?* The people you're meeting? Who are *they*, Rose?"

"Don't yell at me, Penny. I didn't have to tell you or bring you here."

I closed my eyes. Holmby Hills on Halloween, past midnight, witches' hour. My mom used to call Halloween "snap apple and candy night," but I don't know why. I've never heard of a snap apple.

Another car drove past us. Rose tugged at the coat over my arm and pulled me into her shadows.

"You can't be seen. You have to learn to dodge headlamps."

"Right, and the cabbie that asked for your number won't remember you. Rose, you're in trouble."

"I'm cold. Hold my handbag, I'm putting my coat on. Aren't you cold?"

"Where are you meeting these people?"

"Just up Faring. There on the left a little ways—see the cut in those bushes?" She took her bag. "Okay, we can go."

In Beverly Hills and Bel-Air, anywhere rich in LA, it's hard to judge distance because the roads aren't set in city blocks. I can't say we walked two blocks or three because the road curved with high bushes and gates, and once in a while a house was set so far back that the driveway became its own road. As soon as we'd passed into Holmby Hills, old-fashioned lanterns on poles lit the streets. We walked until Rose stopped at a narrow opening between bushes. A brick path ran between them to a solid wood gate.

"This is the house," she said. "The guys should be here."

"And you know where you're at."

"Sure," she said.

"You know whose house this is."

"Someone rich."

"Oh, Rose. We both took the tour. Past Hank's house, down the hill. Pickfair is somewhere close, I can't remember. Johnny Weissmuller's long pool. We took the tour."

"I remember the bus gave me a headache. All those fumes. You don't know whose house this is. You couldn't find Pickfair, especially in the dark. It's a maze up here."

"But I know Faring." I looked past Rose to where the nearest driveway started and curved up and around to a house out of view. "Up there is Claudette Colbert's house. There's no missing it. I remember. That means this is Robert Taylor and Barbara Stanwyck's house, right here."

"No," Rose said.

"It is."

"You're trying to scare me."

"Are you scared? I am," I said. "I just walked nearly half a mile uphill to watch you rob my favorite movie star's house. We'll be kicked off the back lot, and I haven't even met her yet! At least let me meet her before you ruin it all. Two cars just passed me and probably are calling the cops right now."

"Lower your voice. I don't pick houses, one of the guys does."

"Guys? How many guys? How many houses, Rose?"

We stood on Faring. We hadn't moved. Rose stared up the driveway like she could see through the dark to who lived in that house but wasn't home. Like their names were painted on a sign: THE ROBERT TAYLORS LIVE HERE.

"Stany, huh?"

"How many houses, Rose?"

"Voice *down*. Don't yell. Fifteen in Beverly Hills. So far. Nine in Bel-Air."

"God. Oh, Jesus God."

"I climb a ladder and try windows. All they'd have to do is lock them, Pen, but they don't."

"We're leaving." I grabbed the sleeve of her coat and walked her so the driveway disappeared from us and became all tall bushes.

"I'm not leaving, Pen."

"It's Barbara Stanwyck's house. You understand?"

"I'm not stupid."

"You're witless."

"Let go of my arm. You talk to me like I'm stupid. I know where we're at."

My body hit an ice wall. Not a real wall, I hit the kind that pops from the ground when I see a truth I should have seen before. It's an invisible ice wall, but feels real. "You knew. You pretended you don't know who lives here. You knew and you brought me along. Oh, my God."

"*Shh*, quiet. I don't know why people think I'm stupid when I plan all the time. I'm not stupid. I didn't have money so I made a plan."

"You have money now, though. You have two jobs—"

"—that pay almost nothing. I'm not talking hairnet money, I'm talking bucks. I love Will, I do, but I can't be a Farm Girl here or at home."

"How about in prison? You'll go to jail and so will I, for not turning you in."

She stopped pushing against me. "You, too?"

"Well, yeah."

"No, you won't. You didn't do a thing."

"Except follow you to a robbery. Hear you confess that you robbed all these houses. Stand in the street so I can be recognized once Stany calls the police and tells them someone broke in."

She fell against me, and I hugged her. I hugged her tight, and I hated her then for being witless and more like my kid than my best friend. *I* was witless. I never asked where she got her money. We needed it, and there, she'd open a hand and spread out dollar bills. I took them, and I didn't know whose fur, or necklace, or diamond-drip earrings got cut up and resold downtown. I didn't think, on North Faring Road in the dark, of Rose's anger, so big she had to bring me along while she robbed Stany's house.

"You can't rob Barbara Stanwyck. We work on her *film*."

"Okay," Rose said.

"We'll go to the backyard and tell your guys."

"I'll go. You stay here so they don't see you."

I said okay, I wouldn't move. I believed her, and she believed me. I waited for Rose to pull herself up the wood gate and swing her legs over. I set my handbag and coat on the bricks and followed her, hands on the gate top, pulling with my arms until I could swing over one leg. I don't know how Rose did it so fast, with a coat on. I scratched my leg on the swing-over.

At the other side I couldn't see anything in the dark. Then I saw her scuttle from shadows like a bug. I followed like another bug: Run into shadows, wait, look around. Run to the next shadow. I was witless. On Faring we'd stood in the street, where old-fashioned lamps showed me to passing cars. Here on the service path where nobody would come for hours, I hid my whole body and ran from light like a roach.

The path was paved with loose rock. I didn't have to watch Rose now, I could hear her shoes sink and scatter gravel while she marched along. I tried to match my steps with hers so she wouldn't notice the extra rock shifting behind her. She wouldn't have listened. She thought I stayed on Faring like I'd promised. Another girl would think, *I'll bet she broke the promise and followed*, but not Rose. I said I wouldn't move, and she believed me.

But then, I believed Rose when she agreed no one should rob Stany.

I heard male voices. I couldn't tell who spoke, or words. They came from beside trash cans at what I thought must be Stany's property, because that's where Rose stopped kicking gravel and ducked behind a hedge. I crouched about two feet from Rosemary's hedge. I saw two figures, one short, one tall, both talking in whispers, both wearing black or brown and on their faces, too: Rose's guys, the guys, *them*. Arguing enough so the whispers gave off their real voices. I might have known them, but I couldn't guess. I knew tall and short guys, ones who yelled but pretended they whispered. The ones here could be them, or anyone else.

Rose left the hedges. She disappeared from me then, and one guy, then another, disappeared, too.

I kept crouched on the path. Nothing, no sound for ten minutes. Then glass cracking, glass hitting, *clink*, Rose's yell and some other yells, two assholes running from Stany's backyard past me and down the loose rock, and after that, no sound.

I couldn't move at first. I tried, but I shook. My legs and my arms shook. I couldn't stand, so I put both hands on the gravel. I crawled, hands and feet, knees up like I was squatting, to the grass edge by the trash cans. I saw the part in a hedge that led into Stany's backyard. Through it, I saw lawn chairs and a table, a huge, quiet pool, a ladder against the back of two stories, and at the top, under a Spanish tile roof, a window frame with no reflection because the glass was gone. Rose was gone too, fallen into Stany's dark house.

CHAPTER 7

LANA TURNER ... bright spot of M-G-M's *We Who Are Young* is a plaid-picker, turning to forest tones for a smart little green, rust, and brown wool frock that blouses softly above a snugly tied waist, then dips into a slimmish buttoned skirt.

—*Photoplay*, November 1940

Stany said, "She's been dead one to two weeks."

I traced my finger over little pigs in the wall tiles. They all played tiny flutes. Tile pigs at the Pig 'n Whistle. "One to two?"

"You saw her on Halloween, right? Okay, then, the doctor said anywhere from ten days to two weeks. She must have been killed on Halloween or directly after, and that's why she never came home."

"She liked to stay out sometimes. She wouldn't come home for two or three days. If she did that, then she died way after Halloween."

"Yes, but—are you contradicting me? I'm trying to find out what happened. You eating that olive?" She reached across the table to my plate. "You want to hear everything, right? My memory's excellent. I can repeat every word."

"Tell me."

"You want dialogue? Or the story line, or just the high dramatic points?"

"I don't know," I said. "The whole thing." Our waitress set extra napkins on our table. Stany smiled at her.

"You know the room where I found you and the dead face? Our posting room was like that, but longer. More exam tables and a long counter across the back wall. You could lay out an entire feast on that counter. The whole room looked like the kitchen of a fancy restaurant. If we walked to the back of Chasen's right now, we'd see a setup just like that autopsy room."

"But without Rosemary."

"Well, of course. And my room had two bodies, Rosemary and one other. I don't know who the other was. I didn't see the body, just the sheet over it."

"Nothing to do with our case?"

"Not at all," Stany said. "I mention the other body because it sets the scene. Conejos stood right by me. I've decided he's definitely handsome. Then some secretary sitting next to the other body, she's taking notes. So the surgeon, he's a short guy with no eyebrows—looks like he lit his cigarette with the lighter too close to his face and the eyebrows burned clean off—his name's Dr. Weiner, something like that. He pulls the sheet off Rosemary and she's nude."

"Describe her to me." I'd know my own Rosemary. This one could have been someone else's.

Stany cut her meat loaf and watched me. She seemed sad. "Beautiful, Penny. Dr. Weiner had her cleaned up, and except for the dead-looking parts, like her neck cut completely open, of course, you'd never know she was dead. Her skin fell apart a little. Her eyes were closed, and her mouth a little open—I could see her teeth, like this—and you already know she was strangled. Her neck's cut all smooth on the outside. Her arms, they're pretty cut up. And she had little cuts and dents up and down her body and arms and legs, too. Probably those happened when she got walked on."

Dents.

"A bruise, size of a breakfast plate, on and below her ribs, here." She pressed her left hand to her jacket, beneath her heart. "Dr. Weiner says she was alive then and got kicked or punched. He looked for needle marks, too. Used a magnifying glass. None found, you'll be happy to know. So many come-and-gos get hopped up, I don't know why. Thank God our Rosemary didn't fall into that.

"Then he opened her chest with a sharp little knife, and some ribs were broken so he lifted those out. Oh, don't worry about the ribs—they got broken after death, when she got walked across. Pen, don't chew with your mouth open. You're not looking great. Why don't I stop now and tell you stuff about Hank? I'm half in love with him, and I know he's been dying for me for years. I'm not saying anything's happened, but then I'm not telling you everything. You know that, right?"

"Please tell me about Rosemary's thumb."

"Cut off, that's all. You know about Hank's first wife, right? Tragedy."

My right hand wrapped my water glass, and inside the glass, water shook side to side. My anger, shaking inside a water glass. I lifted the glass off the table, then smashed it down. Lift and smash. Water flew and sprayed the table. Stany shut up.

"I broke those ribs. *I* did it. I walked on her and dented her body. I broke her ribs and look at me, *look* at me, Stany. Should I look great? I don't know, should I? She's my best friend, and now her skin's falling apart. You knew her half a day. You've only known *me* two weeks. Why do you like me, Stany? Why do you care that Rose is dead, and maybe I did kill her, what do you know about it? Why me? Why help me?" People across the Pig 'n Whistle turned to watch me bang the glass on our table.

Stany lit a cigarette and blew smoke at the ceiling. She waited for quiet, and it was hard to give it to her. I wanted to keep yelling and then turn those yells into screams and spill all the plates on our table. She waited.

"You done now? You done? I can wait. Okay? Then listen. I have three friends. I work all the time. When can I see friends? Oh, and four, my husband. But it seems he'd rather fuck Lana Turner than come home, so let's say I'm lonely, okay? Let's say it's good to stay busy."

"You have a son," I said.

"Yeah. Huh. What do you know about kids. Oh, Pen—I forgot— I have to tell you, about Rosemary—"

My Rosemary.

"She'd been pregnant. Dr. Weiner said at some point she was pregnant. Did you know?"

"Yeah," I said.

"Oh, here's a surprise."

"No surprise to me. I knew about it."

"Are you going to tell me about Rosemary's pregnancy?"

"It was two years ago."

"Did she keep the kid? Is it your brother's?"

I wouldn't answer her. She kept trying: My brother's? Was that why I wouldn't talk?

She tried everything. She tried to tie Rose's kid to what happened on Halloween, she blamed my brother, she nearly called Rose a whore. I wouldn't tell her about Rose's pregnancy. Rose had mentioned the child to me once, the day I told her I was moving to Hollywood. Even Will didn't know she'd been pregnant. I wouldn't bring it up now. Besides, her pregnancy had nothing to do with her murder. How could it have? She'd had that child two years before her death, had held her baby once, and now someone else called that child *daughter*. I knew part of what happened to Rose on Halloween, and it didn't have anything to do with a child. Not Rose's child, anyway.

"Your brother, was he at the Palladium on Halloween?"

"No."

"Was he at the Palladium?"

"Stany, he wasn't there."

"Ten thousand people, crowds at the door, are you sure?"

I stared her down. She must have seen the Amazon in me.

"Fine, but use logic. Did she meet anyone new at the Palladium?"

"Yes," I said. "She danced with them all."

"Anyone special?"

"No."

"Whatever happened to her happened on that night. On Halloween."

"She wasn't buried on Halloween. I don't know when she was buried, but I would have noticed."

"You walked across the grave and didn't notice," Stany said. She pulled an ashtray toward her and ground out her cigarette. "She could have been buried from the first of November. But she wasn't buried that deep. Since she got so much traffic someone was bound to kick her loose. Are you going to eat at all?" She reached across the table again. "I'll just eat half of this. I don't usually like egg salad, but I skipped breakfast. And then . . ." She bit the sandwich. "And then there's the neck wound. Whoever did it had to be strong, stand at the back of her, hold the wire like this." My egg salad became Rose's neck, and Stany circled her thumb and forefinger around the eggy middle. "Strong. A guy, taller than her."

"Did the doctor say that?"

"No, but I saw her neck. I was standing toward the top of the autopsy table by her head. The cut goes in, and then about half an inch inward it curves up. I figure someone had to be taller than her, because pulling his arms back he'd naturally lift them a bit, and the wire would pull up, too."

I looked at her: Barbara Stanwyck, across from me at the Pig 'n Whistle, where nobody noticed her because she ate there a lot. "You figured that out, and the doctor didn't? Does Conejos know? Stany, how smart are you?"

She grinned. "Not smart enough to divorce my husband. The bastard."

She'd married Robert Taylor, not a bastard. I'd never seen him except in the movies, and I loved him, too. Every girl loved him.

"It's easy," she said. "Strong, to pull that wire through. Tall, to make the cut angle up. It's a guy. That's what I'm telling Conejos. We'll take you off the suspect list, and that'll give us more time to look for the real killer. Next we look for a guy who has cut hands, because pulling the wire would make his hands bleed."

"What if he wore gloves?"

"Hmm."

"I need to go. I can't miss Indian practice."

A waiter stopped at our table and held out a caramel sundae. "Miss Stanwyck, your usual dessert?"

"I love it here," she said.

CHAPTER 8

Lucille Ball will make you sit up and take notice as the burlesque queen of doubtful virtue. Maureen O'Hara is the "good girl" dancer and Louis Hayward a millionaire playboy.

—Photoplay, November 1940

I called my brother Will from the dorm phone. He usually woke early, and I woke early on Thursday to catch him.

"She's dead, Will."

"No."

"We found her body two nights ago. Oh, Will, I'm sorry."

"No, if she were dead, you would have told me right away. If she died, you wouldn't have waited. You'd call me. Why didn't you call? Don't you go telling me she's dead, Pen. Don't you tell me."

"I'm sorry," I said. I couldn't cry, couldn't do anything but hold the receiver in two hands and keep it pressed to my ear. I heard my brother breathing, long breaths, then fast breaths, and then his breathing stopped.

"Oh, my God," Will said. He hung up.

Will didn't want to give us a ride, me and dead Rose, but he couldn't afford a hearse trip from Los Angeles to Buena Park. Neither could I, but Conejos released Rose's body and she had to go somewhere.

Will arrived at ten a.m. with a long, wood box already in the bed of his pickup. He looked straight out the windshield until I climbed in and shut the door. His face had the profile of old concrete, hard and grimy.

"Don't talk to me about it, don't talk to me," he said. Rose's casket slid each time he shifted a gear. Inside Rose's casket her sewed-together body shifted, too, must have slid front to back.

Will loved her, but different than I loved her. He'd proposed until we'd stopped counting, and that's a lot of proposals, when they begin in third grade. *When we grow big we'll get married. Why not marry me now, before prom? Don't go to Hollywood, Rose. Stay.* She loved him, too, loved his proposals. Yeah, love: We all loved each other.

I sat in the pickup with Will and said nothing, not at all. I didn't talk, and we listened to Rose slide for a good fifty miles.

I had two mothers, both in the same body. The first mother grew Will and me. She laughed when the orange pickers told nasty border jokes she didn't understand, or she brought them johnnycake and cold city water. And sometimes, with work done, she'd play cat's cradle with me, using long colored yarn from old sweaters. I hardly remember that mom.

The second mother came in 1938, after the Santa Ana River pushed water two feet high over Buena Park. This is the mom I remember: She sets my dad's ashes on our mantel but won't let me dust the urn. She steals Mrs. Knott's chickens. She hugs Daisy and won't let her play. The second mom thought Rose a tramp but let her move in with us. Rose had just moved back from Pomona. She had nowhere to go. Will and I told Rose how sorry we were, her old Aunt Lou dead, her only family. But the second mom said to Rose, "If the old whore had charged for it instead of giving it away all these years, you'd be rich."

True, but not what you tell a girl whose last family just died.

The second mom stood on the bottom porch step when Will and I parked by the barn. We let Rose's casket wait in the pickup.

"Don't you talk about her," Will said.

Mom snapped a rose hip from the bush by the steps. "I wasn't saying a goddamned thing. She looks better than last time I saw her."

"I told you to shut up."

"I didn't say a goddamned thing."

The second mom talked that way. She didn't talk to me at all because I'd moved to Hollywood. All tramps live in Hollywood, or end up there. If I wanted proof, Mom said, look at that tramp Shirley Temple. What kind of parents let a girl dance with a colored man?

We went in the house because there wasn't anything else to do. Will couldn't work in the orchard, not with Rose's body parked between house and trees, pickup at an angle so we could see the box. Will and I sat on the couch. He scratched fingernails on his blue jeans, *scratch scratch,* his foot kicking the underside of a hacked-up stool my dad had said was a coffee table. Will's nose, his half-closed eyes staring through the living room window, the dot-to-dot stubble on his chin and cheeks—he should have cried. I wished he'd cry. We'd stopped at Rancho Los Coyotes Mortuary on the way into town, and we'd both climbed from the pickup to introduce Rose and take her box inside. I pressed on the back buzzer, and we looked at the squat stucco building, up at the tile overhang, then around by two failing magnolias in a sand yard, and the note taped to the door that read:

Closed until 4 PM.
We value your business!!!

I started to cry, but Will didn't. We both climbed back into the pickup and Will drove Rose down Second Street to Manchester, past Buena Park High, where we'd all graduated but Rose nearly didn't, past Godding's, where Tim Godding took a rowboat from his store to paddle me and Rose home in the flood, past the Blue & White, Lily Creamery, Mitchell Brothers garage. We passed everything. Every fucking thing in that town, we passed: oil derricks, Buena Park Woman's Club, and I really cried now, past the Masonic Lodge, Wilkerson's Grill and the sheriff's station beside it, me slurping tears and Will driving a steady twenty-five, on to Grand Avenue stretched forever with eucalyptus each side, sky cloudy but hot, the Knotts' fields, their new ghost town and restaurant, into our dirt-and-gravel drive to the barn, home to our bungalow and the second mom.

Rose's casket sat in the pickup, and from our couch we watched her out the window. Will watched her. I watched him, and cried and thought, *Now, is now the time to confront him?* But it wasn't.

I knew I'd seen Will on Halloween. I'd seen him run by me. In the dark, sure, but I saw my brother. I'd crouched on a gravel path waiting for Rose, but she didn't come. Then glass breaking, then two men running by me. I knew what I saw. I couldn't tell Stany and I wouldn't tell anyone else, and I had to ask Will if he cut Rose's neck with a wire. Only not now.

Will wore his cement face, and mine was all snotty beside him. In the kitchen our mother banged cupboards and sang: "Before you left, I had hope, I had love." Through the picture window Rose baked under clouds that broke and mended. The mortuary opened at four, but it was only 11:30 when we got home, and clouds broke again. The sun hit a board on Rose's box so the board looked solid purple for a long time.

Backstage that night I powdered and feathered. Beside me the orange Chippewa suit wasn't Rosemary's anymore, Madge wore it now. She spread her arms, and Cree came alphabetically behind her. I spread my arms, too, and the orchestra at the Gardens built the horns until we moved in one line through the Zanzibar Room.

Applause, hail the Indians, step-touch, step-touch. Dinner served on round tablecloths to a roomful of clapping hands and heads that wavered in front of me. My head grew hot under the feather hat. I stepped, dizzy, out of line, Madge and Cherokee

CHAPTER 9

If you can close your eyes for a few seconds without missing any action on the screen, do so once or twice.

—Photoplay, October 1940

On Halloween, in Stany's backyard, shards of glass balanced on ladder rungs and twinkled. More glass scattered the lawn. I crunched some when I ran. Up the ladder, top rung, I saw glass shards lean out from the window frame. I had sturdy shoes, closed-toe Woolworth's flat-sole shoes that could climb a ladder, but not this ladder. Tiny glistening glass shards lay on each step.

My hands shook, and my arms, and I held each side of the ladder as hard as I could, and the shaking passed through my arms to the ladder. I climbed and swayed, climbed and swayed, felt shards cut through my shoes and feet, looked up at the window that kept stretching farther, looked down, and then closed my eyes because looking down was a mistake, climbed, and at the high window, the ladder stopped shaking.

"Rose?"

Something rustled far in the room.

"Rose?" A little louder.

"Penny, I'm cut."

"Where are you?"

"On the floor, there's blood and I'm woozy. . . ."

I got cut, too, when I climbed in the window. Little cuts from the window frame on my forearms and thighs. They stung. I rubbed my skirt over my arms to knock out any stuck glass. The window led to somebody's bedroom, with a mussed bed and nobody in it. Rose lay curled on a wood floor.

"Can you walk?"

"I'm woozy."

"What's cut?"

"My thumb, here, look . . ."

"God. Take your coat—where's your coat?"

"Outside. I couldn't climb with my coat on. I tried to open the window. I don't know why it broke. . . ." She lay curled on the floor except for her hand with the cut thumb. She held up the hand and blood pulsed, ran down her arm to the floor, and Rose's head rolled back and forth like she said *no*. "It doesn't hurt, but I don't feel good."

I tried to rip the front drape off my dress, tried again with my teeth to tear threads, then I cut the drape with a big glass shard. The glass slipped and cut both my palm and the dress. A deep cut clear across my palm, first a white line and then blood bubbled through the white line and ran down my wrist.

My palm stung, but nothing like Rose. Her whole thumb wobbled. Her blood ran hot on my arm where I held her hand. I wrapped my dress piece around and around the cut, and I heard our breathing loud, like someone pounded the floor. Blood seeped through the cloth.

"Hold it here. Tight, so the bleeding slows."

"Your dress—"

"I hate this dress. Can you stand?"

"Woozy," she said.

"Shake it off. You need to stand, then you need to climb down that ladder."

"I can't climb the ladder. I can't stand."

I shook her. "You can stand. You'll get down that ladder and run—you're going to run—to Sunset. Got that? Then you're flagging the next car. You need a hospital."

"You go and I'll wait here."

"Rose, stop it. I don't need help. I need to clean this floor and hide the ladder. Both guys left."

"You saw them?"

"I saw them. They ran. Let's not talk about it now."

"I'm sorry, Pen. I should have—"

"Later. Here, stand. That's it—slow—move your feet a bit—lean against the wall."

"Is this Stany's room? Nice colors, hmm?"

"I'll hold your arm. Lift that leg. Can you balance? Do you know what to do?"

"Climb down. Run to Sunset. Hospital." She stood on the ladder outside the window frame and rested her cut hand on a rung.

"Go," I said.

"I hate you. I get so mad."

"Don't be stupid."

"You hate me, too. Don't you? Don't you?"

"Go down the ladder, Rose."

"I've got dust inside me. I miss my tiny girl. She was in my arms, Pen. Do you know what it's like?"

"Get off the ladder."

"I hate you for not understanding. Admit it, Pen. I'm not going until you admit it. You hate me, too."

I broke. I wanted to take that ladder and push it. Through the window frame, pressing her forehead against the same rung as her hand, Rosemary cried, and we both watched blood seep from her bandage. Yes, I hated her. The force of it made me hold my stomach. I wanted to fly out that window. I wanted the ladder to fall.

"I hate that you're bleeding and you're still beautiful. God, I hate you," I said.

She nodded. That seemed to be enough, what she'd wanted to hear. She climbed down the ladder and waited on the grass, good hand still gripping a rung, then she let go and ran across the yard to the pool and beyond it, to the hedge and beyond it, and I heard gravel crunch, her kicking the wood gate to get over, then nothing.

I stood in our blood. I'd knelt in it when I'd ripped my dress for a bandage. I had a crazy thought: I'd clean so well that Stany would come home and see a window broken in this room but not know why. A bird? Maybe. Or kids playing baseball. The street had kids, didn't it? I could find a baseball and toss it in.

I'm sure I could find a baseball at one in the morning, in a neighborhood that did everything to keep me out except lock their top windows.

Witless.

I needed a towel to clean the room. Nice colors, like Rose had said, yellow, or would be in daylight. A bed and nightstand, dresser, the usual bedroom stuff. The unusual part was the little boy on the far side of the bed, staring at me, pulling his pajama arms to cover his hands. Red hair, or would be in daylight.

"I have a girlfriend," he said. He looked about seven or eight. "Her name's Joan."

CHAPTER 10

The Jack Bennys are wild with joy that a new baby of their very own is on its way to keep their adopted daughter, Joanie, company.

—*Photoplay*, November 1940

Stany sat in the studio commissary with Paulette Goddard, both of them drinking coffee and knitting for England. She didn't invite me, so I ate lunch by myself and watched other girls eat and pretend not to stare at Paulette Goddard's hand. They wanted to see the scar where Rosalind Russell bit her. Behind Stany's table, mirrors tiled the length of the wall and reflected a row of two women holding knitting needles and skeins of yarn. A whole row of Paulette Goddards and Barbara Stanwycks. I could reach my hand and touch Paulette Goddard getting smaller until her mirrored head became a tiny dark spot.

"Penny, come here. Set down your tray. Aren't there waiters to pick those things up? Meet my friend Paulette. Paulette, this is Penny. Penny, Paulette. Now that we're all good friends, let me tell Paulette your secret. Penny's a Farm Girl."

"A Farm Girl? Really? You must know a lot about farms."

"*Knitting*, Paulette dear. Farm Girls have to know about knitting. Isn't that a prerequisite? Knitting and farms? Penny, where do I place my needle after I've purled?"

"I've never knitted in my life," I said.

"You're a dirty little liar." Stany tapped me on the nose with her needle.

Paulette said, "Can't you pretend? We're dropping stitches all over." She smiled at me and held up her needles and yarn. On her hand I saw a curved row of red dots: teeth marks. She said, "I pity the poor Englishman who gets this sweater."

"Why don't you just buy a couple of sweaters and mail them to England?" I asked.

"She's a kidder," Stany said, and she turned back to her knitting. Paulette began counting her stitches. Around the room, extras had stopped eating. They all stared at me, at my new friend Paulette. I picked up my tray and left.

Stany joined us later on set, and Preston had to pick yarn fuzz off her white crepe. He laughed and smoked and picked fuzz, and we extras watched him from the bow of the *SS Southern Queen*. Today we were passengers on a ship and our job was to peer over the railing, look down, and pretend the ship floated on an ocean. That's all: look down and pretend. While all this pretending went on, Edith Head tied white chiffon around Stany's hair and pulled the knot to the right. Then Stany leaned on the *Southern Queen*'s railing beside an old man I'd seen in movies but couldn't remember the name of, and since nobody introduced him to the extras, we all looked at him and shrugged. Nobody could remember his name.

Our afternoon went on with Stany and the old man talking, Preston posing Stany's hands on the railing this and that way, and the extras looking from fake ship to fake ocean until I thought I could see water there below the floor's cement blocks, there beyond where the ship's rail ended and other sets in Stage 9 wavered like foggy islands. One Wallflower got seasick and had to sit. The other Wallflower kept hopping and complaining her shoes were small. During our break, a coffee girl handed me a note. Inside, the slashed, slanted writing of Barbara Stanwyck:

Afterward *wait* for me.

I thought about that note all afternoon. I kept fingering it in my pocket. At four o'clock the *SS Southern Queen* docked in Stage 9, and Stany left for her dressing room. I left, too. I didn't wait for Stany. She had plans for solving the crime. I had plans, different ones, and I walked past Stage 4 out to the Bronson Gate and stood at the bus stop on Marathon. Any minute it would rain. My hair had gone curly, and every dark cloud in the sky looked ready to drop.

I'm not selfish. Not really. I didn't want to get jailed for Rosemary's murder, but more than that, I didn't want Will jailed. I knew he probably killed her. He hated her for leaving Buena Park and hated me more, for taking Rose and for leaving him with the family. So he killed her and made me walk on the grave. I understood his reasons. I could make Conejos understand them, but then I couldn't stop the series of things that would come of it: Will arrested, so there's no one to organize pickers, and the crop doesn't get in or get sold, so no money, and then Mom sells to the Knotts. Okay so far, but then Mom and Daisy go where?

Will could rot. He could get jailed for murdering Rose, and I wouldn't care. But then Mom and Daisy . . . I'd have to go home, and Teddy Marshall lived there. He showed up all over, he walked the town. I wouldn't date him again. I wouldn't live in Buena Park.

I saw my bus down the street. Quick stop for two guys, then motoring onto our block, a swerve to the curb for the Paramount stop, then the bus horn and burning, squealing brakes when an old Dodge cut it off. The car squeaked and stopped and barely missed a good clip from the bus. My bedmate from the dorms, Madge, leaned across the Dodge's passenger seat and rolled down a window.

"Get in. Don't let anyone see you."

"I'll take the bus."

"Get in," she said. She pushed the passenger door open. It squeaked. I slid into a saggy, squeaky seat.

"Shut the door hard, will you? Harder. It has to click. Where to?"

"Nowhere you're invited," I said.

"I've got a quarter tank of gas. You're planning shit or you're mad at Stany, whichever. Right or left?"

"Turn right."

"Stany looked for you. She came out of her dressing room and asked where you'd gone. All those girls who hate you? Get this. Stany asks the question to nobody, to the air, and girls jump up and down to answer. That fucking Career Girl—the one with the nose, sniffy—she *hits* Wallflower and pushes her back, then sniffs to Stany how you've already gone. She's probably sucking Stany's tits right now."

"You've got a foul mouth."

"Which way, right or left?"

"Turn left."

"Reach in the glove box, will you? Hand me my flask." She took it from me, unscrewed the top, and drank, then passed it to me. Bad whiskey, but I drank.

"How far up Sunset?"

"Keep driving," I said. It was cloudy out, late afternoon. Close to rain. On Sunset cars honked and stopped. At the corner of Gower a man waved an American flag and a sign: DEPORT GERMAN SERVANTS! Lots of honks, lots of folks with servants.

Madge honked. "Fucking Germans," Madge said. "Can't the studios do something about Germans? Don't look like that. Let me guess," Madge said. "I'm a good guesser. Stany wants something from you. Why else would she be your friend? I mean, who are you? But you have something she wants. Or your friend did, but she died. I don't know what you'd have. You're a fucking Farm Girl. Pass the flask. So it must be something she'll learn, something she'd learn now or later on. You remind her of someone she used to know, from her stage days. That's it—you remind her. So she wants to keep you out of trouble. How am I doing?"

"Turn right at Beverly Glen."

"My, we're in fancy town now."

"Park anywhere. Can I trust you? Can you keep a secret?"

"No and no," she said. "Fucking Germans."

"I need to find out what happened to Rose. It's going to rain, so I've got to find out now. Last I saw her was around here, and I'm looking for clues." I opened the car door. It squeaked.

"What clues?" Madge stretched herself out of the driver's seat and pulled her skirt down in the back. Her puddle brown hair looked dull and her pin curls frizzed.

"Blood. Any drops of blood, a trail of blood or bloody fabric. You want to help? I'm looking in bushes and grass, along the road, here and on Sunset, both ways."

"Blood? Don't tell me. I don't want to know."

"Look for blood fast, before it rains."

"Bring the flask," Madge said. "Hell, open the trunk. The whole bottle's in there."

CHAPTER 11

Important point to Jeanette MacDonald is a good speaking voice, clear, crisp, but never shrill.

—*Photoplay*, October 1940

Stany had a son. On Halloween I saw him. I'd never thought of him, hardly heard about him, maybe in *Photoplay* with a spread of stars' kids in Hollywood, or the big custody trial a couple years back, but that was more about Stany and her drunk ex than about the kid I saw in Stany's yellow room. She must have wanted a kid, she'd adopted him. All the women stars adopted except for Dottie Lamour, and look at her hips.

"Are you here to kidnap me?"

"No."

"Because you could, then make my mom pay you to get me back."

I tried to cover the blood with my hands. I measured space to the bedroom door, first bed then kid then door. Then whoever was downstairs, because this kid wasn't in the house alone.

No, that wouldn't work. Okay, I'd go down the ladder and leave this mess. It wasn't my mess. I should still be dancing at the Palladium.

I backed to the window, and glass cracked under my shoes.

"I'll write the ransom note," the kid said.

I felt behind me for the window frame. My fingers touched putty, then a chunk of glass that tipped free and hit a ladder rung. I jumped but didn't turn. I couldn't stop staring at the kid. He stood behind the bed and never moved except to pull his pajamas and talk. He didn't look scared. I could see him better now, the room wasn't so dark to me, and if I hadn't heard running outside the room, feet hitting a wood hallway harder and louder, each hit nearer and closer, I might have talked to the kid. But I couldn't make my mouth do anything.

I lifted each leg through the window, and the ladder shook again, faster than when I climbed up. I made my feet do what my mouth wouldn't. I slammed each rung loud, but not as loud as the yellow door banging a wall, someone running to the window through glass and blood and then at the window frame, a woman's voice yelling down, "I called the cops. Run, you bitch, I called the cops!"

CHAPTER 12

Blackmailers, kidnappers, unscrupulous servants, shrewd lawyers, opportunists of all kinds, demented people of every description always have been the stars' natural enemies.

—*Photoplay,* November 1940

It hadn't rained for over two weeks, since before Rose disappeared, before Halloween. Rose dripped blood that night even with my torn skirt wrapped around her thumb. She'd been bleeding bad and fast. Say the wrap on her thumb held for two blocks, if she ran. Then blood would drip, because rayon doesn't suck up liquid like cotton or silk. She'd be running and dripping, and it hadn't rained since then, so somewhere I'd see her trail and know where she turned, which way on Sunset, where she flagged down a car and got in. And from there—I didn't know.

I should have come as soon as Rose disappeared. I felt sick that I'd stayed away, and sick to be here now. If I'd come to Sunset after Halloween, if I'd looked for blood on the roadside, that would have meant something bad happened, worse than getting her thumb cut. To stay away had meant hope that she'd return. I'd stayed away, and she'd died, and now I felt sick.

"Look everywhere. Madge, right? Look for blood on leaves. And you're looking for dried blood, not red."

"I know," Madge said, and we looked on Beverly Glen by a triangle park I'd only seen once before. Now it held a mom with a baby carriage and umbrella and dog, and two boys smoking by a king palm. It doesn't change, does it? Rich or poor, the boys find a park to smoke in.

"Part branches and look at the ground. She could have hit a fence or that ivy."

Madge kicked a rock at me. "You want me to look or not? You through with the lecture? *Look on the ground. Look in the air. Look on the fucking sidewalk.* It's getting dark."

We looked. We split and walked the triangle, through the park, to Sunset. Cars passed us both ways. This far east on Sunset, through Beverly Hills, through Holmby Hills and Bel-Air, there were no sidewalks. Sunset was paved and narrow with inches of gravel on each side. Then high hibiscus bushes and hedges or iron meant to keep out people like us.

"Here," Madge said. "Is this blood?"

"Tar." A car sped by and honked. We'd be easy to hit, so close to the road.

"Is this blood?"

"Tar, Madge. It's tar."

A few minutes more, cars passing close to the gravel, one car swerving toward us to make us run, then: "Is this blood?"

"Tar," I said. "Or oil or dried skunk or"—I bent over the tar— "blood. Maybe it's blood. I don't know."

"Feel that? Rain. It's too dark. I can't see the goddamn road until a car comes by. You'll get us killed out here. I see more tar. There, too." She opened her handbag and pulled out a lighter. She flicked it, and I saw where she pointed: splashed on the gravel maybe two feet apart, small, dark brown circles that could have been blood. I wasn't sure. Madge lit a cigarette with her lighter.

I knelt and touched a brown circle. Rain wet my hand. Not many people bleed this far up Sunset Boulevard. If the circle was blood, then it had to be Rose's blood. Her blood, under my hand. Shielded from the rain by my hand. I touched the last tiny part of her to live above ground. I scooped the gravel into my palm, rocks, sharp bits, squeezed in the hand that was sore already from a Halloween cut. I squeezed so tight I cried out.

"You can't make her come back." Madge crouched and scuffed along the gravel. "You can hurt yourself all you want, but she's gone. Nothing makes her come back. You're left with nothing. You don't know that yet? You can't even save the blood. You save that blood and it'll be used against you. I'm not saying drop it. Do what you want, but if you keep it, and the police arrest you, well, what have you got? Her blood from the last place you saw her. Sounds guilty to me. Wait. Here's another."

I dropped the gravel. I felt something mess up inside me, like I'd dirtied a room, like I'd made a choice between holding Rose close and keeping myself out of jail.

"We've got a bunch of drops here," Madge said.

"So she stood. This is where she tried to flag down cars."

"No. If she'd stood, all the drops would be round, like the first one. These along here are a mess. See the rain, how a drop makes one round circle? Now look. These drops are long. They look like sperm. Yes, they do! You know they do. We all saw the same slides in fifth grade." Madge held her cigarette to the ground so I could see by its coal a cluster of dried brown drops, some wet again from the rain.

"So she didn't stand," I said. "She was hurt and panicky. She jumped and waved at a car. Oh, God, she must have been scared."

"And then ran the opposite way?" Madge looked at me, and I followed her face to her hand, then followed her hand as it pointed through glare from a passing car, past the mess of stains at my feet to a trail of drops nearly hidden at the edge of the gravel. The drops weren't two feet apart. They were one after the other, a little blood chain that stretched down the gravel into the darkness. Rain fell on my hair and my face. The car's lamps lit the gravel and then were gone, the car gone, the gravel all dark again.

"She couldn't have her hand wrapped and still bleed like that. What happened to the fabric?" Madge flicked on her lighter until it got too hot and she tossed it hand to hand.

"She did have cuts on her arms. Maybe she got cut on these bushes. That's what the blood's from."

"On this hedge?" Madge tried to stick her hand in a juniper hedge, and she couldn't get her fingers in more than an inch. "Gardeners trim these hedges ten times a week. Do you see sharp twigs sticking out? She wasn't cut here. I say the blood's from her hand. She dropped whatever wrapped her hand."

We couldn't find fabric anywhere—the drape of rayon I'd cut from my skirt with a glass shard. We shook the hibiscus and looked on both sides of the tall gates lining Sunset. We woke a dog that jumped on his side of an iron fence nearly to its top spikes, trying to bite us. No drape, just the few round drops of blood where Rose had walked Sunset west of Beverly Glen, then the mess of blood where something happened, then the blood chain that led fast the opposite way. By the time we ran back to Madge's squeaky car, nobody smoked in the triangle park. Rain fell hard. The blood chain had washed off the gravel, and Sunset was clean, with no sign at all that Rosemary had run from whatever chased her.

That night in the greenroom, Madge fought with Apache Girl. The Gardens manager, Granny, had to stand between Madge and Apache. Granny is a man, not a real granny. He looked huge and gray between them, a rock between two feather clumps.

"This is the thanks I get," he said. "'Oh, thanks for hiring me, Mr. Granlund, I promise not to fight before showtime or tear your beautiful costumes.' And you're out there with smiles, right? Charlotte, where's your headdress? Fighting over lipstick. Do I care about lipstick? Here." He grabbed Madge's. "Now you've got lipstick. Christ. Any more fighting and I'll throw you in the back of my car and dump you in the ocean. Full house tonight, girls. Someone help Charlotte with that headdress, will you? I've got . . ."

That was Granny. A nice guy in a middle-aged thin-hair way. He was Granny to most of us and Uncle to a few, with a different niece every month. But he could send a girl places. He could lift a girl to MGM with a phone call. We knew it, and tried not to fight.

"It wasn't your color," I said.

"I know, but I hate her."

I tossed Madge my lipstick, and I leaned on the wall near the greenroom door. The greenroom wasn't green. It was a pasty white with old dirt scuffs near the baseboards.

"Look at her. Watch her swing those hips at Granny. She's got no troubles at all. I hate her."

"We probably imagined the bloodstains."

"Sure," Madge said. "Oil drips like that all the time. Drip, drip, then splash all around with little sperm tails, then drip-drip-drip the other way down the road. It's oil."

"So it wasn't oil. Something else, then."

"You want to go back and see? You can't. They're gone with the rain. Watch Apache. You watching? Somebody sent her carnations."

"Here's what I think happened," I said. "Rose walked along Sunset and waved at a car. When she waved, the cloth fell off her hand and she bled on the ground. Then the car pulled up and she ran to get into it. Nothing bad at all."

"Then next we call hospitals. Somebody picked her up and drove her to a hospital."

"I like it," I said. "I was worried out there, on Sunset. I thought—I don't know what I thought. What happened to the bloody fabric?"

"Don't be simple. You thought what I thought. And if she dropped the cloth when she waved down a car, do you think she'd pick it up before she ran to that car? Do you really think she'd re-member to bend down and pick it up? The cloth's already a bloody mess, right? Wouldn't she leave it and run to the car? We didn't find any cloth."

"The wind blew it away. An animal took it. Raccoon. Or a coyote."

We lined up alphabetically by Indian. Madge shoved around until just before curtain, when she stepped into line in front of me. She shook her orange Chippewa bodice. The name sparkled in orange sequins across her breasts: CHIPPEWA.

"Here's what *I* think happened," Madge said. "She walked along Sunset and the cloth around her thumb dripped. Just a little, every now and then. She saw a car and waved. She waved her good hand because her bad hand hurts, right? She waves her good hand. The car pulls over and stops close to where she's standing."

The orchestra in the Zanzibar Room began our overture, drums and a long, low clarinet wail. More jungle than Indian.

"I'm not sure about this part," Madge said. "If the guy was driving east he might have been alone in his car. He'd cross lanes, then pull up to Rose and open his door. The driver's side, that'd be next to Rose, if he's driving east. If he's driving west, there's two guys in the car and the guy in the passenger seat is next to her. Either way, door opens, guy tries to pull her in, she fights him, he grabs at her and gets the cloth from around her thumb, but she's free. She runs—and the car follows. The car's moving forward or back, depending on which way it's facing. The car catches Rose, maybe cuts her off. We didn't see where the blood ended so we don't know what happens after that. But I think he pulled her into the car."

The music grew loud, the greenroom door opened, and we all raised our arms in feathery *V*s.

"Did she know him? The driver, did Rose know him? Is that why she ran?"

We all smiled wide. Madge had to talk through her teeth. "I don't know. How the hell do I know? I have no idea why you were on Beverly Glen with your friend, and don't tell me, I don't want to know. Watch Apache, goddamn her. I pulled most of the pins from her headdress."

We step-touched into the Zanzibar, semicircle in front of the bandstand, and turned toward the audience at their cozy tables. Arms down, then reaching side to side, step-touch, sway. Step-touch, sway.

During the second sway I spotted Stany at a front table close to the bandstand. Third sway, and I saw who she was with: Joan Crawford. Fourth sway to swallow all that, Joan's eyes and jet gown, to see Stany light a cigarette and finger-wave and smile, and fifth sway I faced the other side of the room, tables close to the kitchen swing door.

Small table, crappy, but perfect for Detective Conejos and Officer Joe in his cop uniform. I saw Conejos's trilby. I saw Joe's badge. I couldn't see the gun on Joe's belt, but I knew it was there.

Our headliner walked to the mike. Tonight she was just in from New York. They always came just in from somewhere terrific, like New York. Before the ships stopped running they came from London, too, and from Paris or Monte Carlo, or said they did. Now they all came from New York, perky with manicured nails and gardenias tucked in their hair rolls. They smeared petroleum jelly on their teeth but didn't share with the revue girls. If I turned to look at our headliner, I'd see her mouth sparkle under a gold spotlight. The drums beat her cue, and she sang.

Transition for us: no step-touch now. We wove between each other, in and out. I'd step out of the weave and see Stany and Joan and then I'd turn, see Joe and Conejos watch me from their crappy table, step into the line and weave, and faces disappeared into colored feathers. Purple for Cherokee, pink for Paiute. Tomahawk and beaded shawl, we love them all.

My third weave I saw Granny pull a chair next to Joan and sit down. I said Granny could lift a girl to MGM, right? That's what he did for Joan Crawford. One phone call, two, and Joan had her screen tests and publicity shots. She was just a revue girl and then *whoosh*, lifted up.

We Indian girls turned and held hands. We faced the headliner, lifting clasped hands and swinging them down.

> *From our mighty plains they come*
> *They fish in our lakes and streams*
> *They weave with hands strong and worn*
> *They live in America's dreams*

We turned, one girl at a time. Cherokee, Chippewa, Cree. And I saw someone else at Stany's table, across from Joan, someone I'd seen before on Halloween night in Stany's backyard. I didn't know his name, never saw him in light, but he was a thief. He ran past me on the path from Stany's yard to the road. He left Rose in a hundred glass shards. I'd thought my brother killed Rose, but it could have been this guy, who used hair pomade and unbuttoned his tuxedo jacket to settle in. Did he have cuts on his hands? I couldn't see.

My legs went numb. They moved without me. They step-touched. The guy watched me from Stany's table. He lifted his hand and scratched his nose. Elegant fingers. He couldn't recognize me, not as Cree Girl. Not in green feathers. My throat swelled. It started shallow, in my mouth, so I had to take air gulps. Then way down my throat I felt tight. I wheezed. My chest lifted high with each raspy breath.

Next to me, Madge hit my arm. "Watch Apache."

I could wheeze and follow directions at the same time. I learned it in Hollywood. I lifted my arms, step-touch, eyes blurry, and ahead of us, Apache stuck one hand to her feathery headdress, which tilted forward and shook over the tables next to the dance floor. Granny saw, too, and ran to help. Behind us the headliner held her last note and we bowed, except for me, because I couldn't breathe, except for Apache, because her headdress fell into a guy's T-bone plate. The crowd clapped, except for Conejos and Joe. They weren't at their table. I looked for them, I looked for Joe's uniform. I wheezed. I didn't know they stood behind me until they pressed me on each side and Joe said, "You're arrested for murder."

CHAPTER 13

Like a fortune-teller peering into the future, the beauty camera's lens is focused on YOU! And, let us add, it doesn't miss a single line, wrinkle, or blemish on your skin.

—*Photoplay*, November 1940

The Hollywood Division police station was a brick building on Wilcox with a receiving hospital next door, kind of pretty, but out of place in a town that doesn't use brick. In the dark it looked sad and heavy: a guy whose girl has shoved him into a deep lake.

I held my vaporizer and kept squeezing that rubber bulb to get medicine in my throat. Then the vaporizer was gone, and I wore a city-issue orange shift, and a matron pushed me through Hollywood Division with rooms of cops sitting and talking, standing at telephones, no exact words but just talk, and once in a while a woman's sobby cries somewhere down the hall. Across the linoleum, above a long counter that held up talking cops, cigarette smoke floated past two hanging lights.

A murderess doesn't get the big room with the long counter. I got the corner room with no windows and the two-hour wait. I got the wood table scored with initials and swear words. When Conejos came in, he stood in the doorway and turned his head toward the hall, like he'd come to the wrong room and he'd stored his own murderess somewhere else.

He yelled to the hallway, "Water in here!" He turned to me and asked, "You thirsty? I'm thirsty. It's a hot business. What happened on Halloween?"

"The Palladium. I told you before."

He stood across from me, in front of the door. He'd taken off his hat. His brown hair stuck to the sides of his head. "Yeah, you told me. Tell me again. Pretend I'm deaf and you've got to yell. Tell me about the Palladium."

"Dancing. Tommy Dorsey and some singers. We went."

"And you got there . . ."

"About ten," I said. I kept laying my palms flat on the wood table and then curling my hands. Curl, and then flat again. The fingerprint ink on my hands made nice smudge marks. "We got a ride from our dorm. It's not far, it's—"

"Yes, and what happened at the Palladium?"

"We danced."

"And you left together?"

I curled my hands tight. The ink had left finger ghosts on the table. "No. It was crowded. I lost Rose in the crowd and I walked home. Alone."

"Time?"

"Maybe midnight?"

"Funny," he said. "That's the time a cabbie swears he took Rosemary Brown for a ride. Described her, too. Hard to forget, a girl like that. Fancy ribbons, a big flower in her hair. Green suit that fit pretty good. Oh, and our cabbie swears Rosemary Brown had a friend with her. How did he describe the friend? 'Not as good looking but okay on a dark night.' Does that sound like you? Blond hair rolled a lot like yours right now. You breathing okay? Because I want you to keep breathing. We're just talking here. Hard to be friends with a glamour doll, right? She gets the wolf calls and what do you get? You ever angry about it? You ever think she didn't deserve all that attention?"

"Sure, but I didn't kill her."

"It's hard to be friends with a girl like that, is what I'm saying. Where did the cabbie drive you?"

"What cabbie?"

He smiled. He unbuttoned his suit jacket and nodded, like he agreed with me. "Miss Stanwyck—Missy—says she'll invite me to a premiere. How do you like that? Me at a premiere." He didn't look at me. He sat half his butt on the table and took a knife from his pocket to shave his pencil. Everything hit my ear loud: the creaky wood when Conejos shifted weight from foot to hip, his knife flipped open and attacking a pencil, *scrape-scrape*, shaved curls falling to the table in light poofs, his finger pushing them into a pile. When a detective doesn't talk, every sound in the room talks for him, and they're not *good* sounds. They say, *You filthy liar.*

"Tell me again about Halloween."

I'm a filthy liar. Filthy. "I couldn't find Rose. I looked, but so many people—I couldn't see her. I stood on the gallery stairs and looked for her hair in the crowd, how bright her hair was, but so many people, I couldn't . . . couldn't see her, so I left. Got my stuff from Hat Check and left."

"The cabbie's wrong? Is he a liar?"

"Maybe Rose took that cab. Maybe another girl went with her."

"Some girl who looks like you," Conejos said. "Your height and hair color, your brown coat."

"Sure."

"Some girl who wasn't wearing her coat at midnight in the cold." He pushed and pushed the pencil shavings on the table, a line of wood curls and lead. They popped and flew over carved words and gouges. *Liar.*

"Tell me about Rosemary's friends. She have a lot of friends?"

"Girls didn't like her, but yeah, she had friends. Guys, mainly. I don't know them all."

"She have any guy friends at the Palladium that night?"

"No. I mean, she danced, but not with one guy."

"Okay, what guys?"

"Sailors and some flyboys. A guy with freckles. One guy in a suit." All true. I could see them dance in a big clump around Rosemary. I could hear Tommy Dorsey's horn from the stage.

"Guy in the suit. What did he look like?"

"Blond hair. A little short and wide through the chest. His jacket pulled at the shoulders. Tight."

"And the freckles?"

"Different guy. Freckles and brown hair, that's all I saw. Oh, and he bought Rose a drink."

"The drink?"

"Just a gin fizz."

"How do you know?"

"What?"

Conejos stood, and the table creaked. "The room's crowded, right? Packed like a cheese crock. You can't find your friend. It's late, you're tired. You even climb the stairs and look down on the crowd to find her. I've got this right? You did this, right?" He sat in the chair across from me and shoved his knife at the pencil bits. "Then how come you know who she danced with?"

Rose would know what to say. Rose would open her mouth, and words—none true at all—would sail past me through the pencil dust, over scratched initials and foul words from all the liars who'd sat at this table and panicked. Rose would know what to say. Me, I didn't know. I didn't say anything.

"Where did the cabbie take you and your friend?"

"Don't you know? Didn't the guy tell you?"

"I know," Conejos said.

"You don't need me, then."

"Sure I do. You just admitted you were in the cab. You stuck by your friend that night enough to know who she danced with. Then she and you got in the cab and drove—"

"I'm leaving."

"—to Beverly Glen. Sit down. Your friend paid off the cab. You hated her. I mean, look at you. Of course you hated her. You know she won a speaking role on that movie you're in? Yeah, I thought you didn't. One day on set and she's noticed. Your big group of extras, and she's the one. She didn't even know. Kind of makes you feel ordinary, doesn't it? You feel small? Your director told me—what's his name? Stargill? Real character, him. Gave me a tour of the back lot and wore two hats the whole time. He says Rosemary Brown looked too good on camera and he was trying her in a speaking role. He'll have to reshoot the wedding scene she was in, that's how much she stood out. And I was thinking—sit *down*—how angry you'd be. Your first movie and here's that god-damn Rosemary hogging the camera.

"You watched her. You knew how you looked next to Rose-mary. A doll like her, who'd notice you? So you're angry. Hell, I'd be angry. I'd say, *Hell, I've had enough.* I'd see her dance all over one guy then another, and I'd drive her somewhere quiet. Beverly Glen. I'd pick up whatever I found—wire, maybe—and I'd say, *Hey, Rosemary, look over there*, and she'd look, and I'd take that wire and pull it tight in my hands and loop it on her neck and *pull*—I'm so angry I'd *pull*—and she'd drop and bleed, and I'd pull until my arms gave.

"I'd pull that wire and then see I'd pulled so hard I strangled my own hands. I'd cut the wire through my palm. So when I danced in the line revue later, a couple weeks even, I'd show my scabby palm to the crowd. I'd have to. And if a detective sat in the crowd and watched me, what would he say? He'd see that long cut on my palm. What would he say, Penny?"

I slid my hands off the table, and Conejos caught my right wrist. He turned my hand over and squeezed my wrist so hard I couldn't keep my fingers curled. My hand opened.

"You know what he'd say? He'd think of the rotting dead girl you buried close by so you could kick her. Stomp on her. He'd think of what this world lost because you hated real beauty. I saw you prance in that line tonight, and I pushed my steak with my fork and thought what a racket, a line of showgirls so we don't notice tough meat at four dollars a plate. And I thought maybe I'd leave.

"Then you turned your hand to me. Not a lot, but enough. I saw the gash real plain, like I'm seeing it now. Deep cuts heal slow, don't they? So I hit Joe with my fork. Oh, you were dancing your little Indian heart out, and that cut on your palm danced right along. I stopped thinking about the goddamn dry steak. I told Joe, I leaned over and I hit him with my goddamn fork and I told him, 'Fuck me deaf and blind, Joey, I've caught myself a killer.'"

CHAPTER 14

I Want a Divorce: Tragedy is sometimes the surest road to happiness.

—*Photoplay*, November 1940

Years ago—this was when Mom was the first mom, before the flood—she'd take Will and me deep in the orange grove to rake branches. After the Santa Anas, branches would kick loose and scatter, and here we'd come, Branch Patrol, ready to rake and tug those branches to the end of a row. Hot work, dusty afternoons. Mom saved all the twigs with blossoms, and when we got home she'd stick them in a vase and set the vase upstairs in my room, on my dresser. I'd be cut and scratched from dragging branches. I'd be tired and mad. Here I'd done Branch Patrol when I could have jumped double Dutch with my friends. Then I'd get in bed, with the window open and no light, no breeze. And I'd smell them.

The things a girl remembers when she's locked in a room. Conejos left me alone a good hour. Me and my jail dress, my autographed table. Me crying about orange blossoms. I couldn't explain to Stany. She thought I cried about the arrest, and I let her think it.

Joe unlocked the door and let her in. He didn't look at me. He held the door wide, and while Stany walked past him, he stared at the ceiling. The door stayed open, but Joe left. It was late, after midnight, maybe more. Stany came around the table and knelt in front of me. She gave me a hankie.

"Wipe those tears. I mean it, stop crying. Christ, I can't stand a woman who cries. See me? Am I crying? Well, shut up, then. When I cry you'll know there's something to cry about. Where's that nasty little man?"

"Joe?" I rolled her wet handkerchief into a ball.

"No, the nastier one. He charged me for your godawful prison dress. You'll need to schedule with him to get your feathers tomorrow. Their—what do you call it?—oh, hell, their *wardrobe* is closed for the night. Can't think of the name."

"How long does Conejos say I should sit here?"

She stood, and the hem of her gown fell nearly to the floor. Almost touching, but not quite. A spray of sequin roses covered her bodice, all cream-colored, and the gown cream, too, in rayon. She could kneel all she wanted, and when she stood, no wrinkles. "I paid your bail," she said.

"I'm a murderess. There won't be any bail."

"Not for you, maybe. But for me . . ." She winked and smiled. "See this hand? I've got your handsome detective's balls right here. I can tug to the left and he'll turn left. He'll do anything I want. And I just met a judge who thinks I'm Stella Dallas. He watched the picture three times. I didn't get you for free, but I got you. I promised you'd stay in town. You will, won't you? You cost me the goddamn horse I was going to buy this weekend."

"Stany, I can't—"

"Shut up. And I found you a lawyer. Marty, come in and meet our charity case. Don't move, Pen, I'm just kidding. It's not charity. Marty's charging me the other horse I was going to buy."

I wondered why Barbara Stanwyck talked a judge into bail. I wondered why she paid the bail, why she came to the station and paid a lawyer to come, too. She believed I didn't kill Rose, but how much can someone believe when they've only known you a couple of weeks? Two weeks. I wondered, and I yawned, and

Marty the lawyer stood there in his tuxedo, the same black-haired guy who'd sat with Stany and Joan Crawford at the Gardens, the same guy I'd seen in Stany's backyard on Halloween.

"I'm a divorce lawyer," he said. "I might not be able to help."

"The absolute best divorce lawyer." Stany pulled out the chair where Conejos had sat and let Marty the lawyer sit down. "He took care of Joan's divorce from Franchot, and she couldn't be happier. And divorce is a kind of murder, when you think about it. Yes, they're not far off, not really. Marty, you're what Pen needs."

Marty pushed Conejos's pencil shavings to the floor with his clean hand, short nails, cuticles pink and soft. His hand looked like the rest of him. He didn't look like a guy who rubbed ash on his cheeks and forehead and then let a girl climb some ladder into a stranger's house. I couldn't imagine him holding the ladder. He was the guy I saw on Halloween, I knew it, but he wasn't, too. Joan Crawford's divorce lawyer sat across from me, not a thief.

"Penny? You there?" His forehead reflected light from the ceiling bulb. His wide, clean face leaned toward me.

"Here," I said.

Stany slapped the back of my neck. "Wake up. Act outraged. You're innocent, so act it."

"She's tired," Marty said. "Look at her eyes. How about this. For tonight, tell me what you told the detective, and we'll meet again tomorrow."

"She can do that," Stany said, but I couldn't. I didn't have much to tell, simple stuff like the cab ride, guys dancing with Rose, me with a wire at Rose's neck, and none of it came out. I wasn't tired. I was scared. I stared at my new lawyer, and my knees bounced. I didn't know what I should say.

"We'll talk tomorrow," he said, and then didn't leave but stared at me, too, and Stany got bored, I think, because she said, "Fuck this" and grabbed my arm, and we left.

"Life shoves a stick in your ass. *Hard.* We get to roll around and cry, *Oh, I've got a stick in my ass*, or we get to ignore the fucking stick. Act professional." Stany hitched her cream gown to her knees and drove that way, fast. She pressed the brake with one foot and gas with another, and her car whined. Her wipers thumped rain off the glass. Roads empty, she ignored a red light on Wilcox. "Men, they get whiskey or a slut and it's aaaall better. Nothing's changed but they've got their whiskey and their slut and it's *better*. What do you and I get? You know the last time I saw my mother? I'm on the sidewalk, and I look up, and here she's getting shoved off a streetcar. *Slam*, Mom on the street. And the sidewalk. She's pretty much all over me, too. Am I crying?"

"No." I needed to tell someone everything. I needed help.

"I learn my lines. I fight for my roles. I tell Jack Warner I'm the one to play Pioneer Woman, or Stella Dallas, or Eve. I'm on time, and I'm grateful."

Not Stany, I couldn't tell Stany. Not Will, either. The lawyer, Marty—he'd want to know what I'd told Conejos. He scared me. Maybe I'd talk to Granny, he seemed nice and hadn't fired me yet, and didn't blame me for the body dug up behind his nightclub. Or Madge, I could talk to Madge. She'd already helped me find blood. Yes, I'd tell Madge.

"You listening?" Stany pulled up in front of the Florentine Gardens. She kept her foot on the brake and the car running. She geared into neutral. "I'm telling you, the only morals we've got are how we work our profession. You get a role, you practice. You get a lawyer, you talk. Now, get out. We've got early call, and you're going to be there. You'll stand around and do what you're told, then you'll visit Marty and tell him the truth, and on Sunday you'll come with everyone else to my house and act perfectly normal. Get out of my car, Penny."

"I'm grateful," I said, and I said it again when the doors to the Gardens were locked and I couldn't get in. Stany didn't wait to see me home safe. She was in second gear before I closed her car door. I stood in the dark between the nightclub and Hollywood Boulevard. Ten steps through rain to the left, and I turned down the building's side. More steps, and I stood in back where Conejos thought I'd buried Rose.

But if I'd done what he'd said, strangled her on Beverly Glen

CHAPTER 15

Recently Wally Beery was fortunate enough to outwit
a gentleman who might have grown considerably richer
at his expense.

—*Photoplay*, November 1940

I found Marty's office from the card Stany gave me:

MARTIN MARTIN, ESQ.
DISCREET FAMILY LAW
SUITE 302 6391 WILSHIRE BOULEVARD
LOS ANGELES, CALIFORNIA
FITZROY 5212

An elegant card. A card matching the man I'd seen at the Gardens.

I had taken the bus downtown. Marty worked in an office building next to two lots for sale, and I could see Bullocks Wilshire
from the lobby. I had to stretch on tiptoe and look over the fence
past the two empty lots plus the junk sticking up from those two
lots: rusty metal, a couch tipped on its short end. Over the fence,
past the two empty lots and a NO DUMPING sign, Bullocks rose
in green copper cake layers high to the clouds. I'd been in that
Bullocks but never bought anything. The shopgirls can tell who

has money and who wishes they did. Someday I'll buy a dress at Bullocks Wilshire, and I'll have three shopgirls trail me with live mannequins: "This one? The gown with the tulle peplum? It will show off your skin."

I stood in Martin Martin's lobby a long time. I didn't want to see him. I knew he wanted not to help me but to find out if he'd been seen at Stany's on Halloween night. I waited past my four p.m. appointment time, and the elevator man sat on his stool watching me each trip down when the elevator doors shoved open. I could walk in an autopsy room and lift a sheet, but I couldn't enter an elevator.

"The ride's free," said the man. "You don't have to pay." An old guy with a bell cap and a big wad of gum. "What floor? We've got more than the lobby, you know."

"Martin Martin," I said.

"Third floor. I told you it's free, right?"

I stepped in. The doors shut in my face, and I listened to the operator gossip. The best gossip is from elevator guys. If you want to know what goes on in this city, ride an elevator. Ride a few of them. I don't know why, but people pretend elevator guys don't exist. They get in, the doors shut, and life stops until the doors open again. People should listen to elevator guys, because what happens between floors makes party gossip for a week. My guy today had some good stuff.

"—gets in with her dog, Miss Swanson, I mean, and the dog's bigger than she is, right? One of those racing mutts, I don't know the name, skinny as hell . . ."

"Greyhound?"

"Naw, not the racers. Not a greyhound. Big like that, and skinny."

"Great Dane. Dalmatian, wolfhound—"

"Hound, that's right. Some kind of hound. Skinny as hell. She's got a pink collar on this dog, and I can see it's a male, it's got the business hanging on his behind, and a thin dog like that, you can't hide the business. So she ignores me and ignores the dog, and that dog smiles right at me and backs up to the corner and does you know what, all the while she's pretending she can't see a thing, can't smell a thing, and the door slides open. I say, 'Miss Swanson, your dog just shat in my elevator.' I say it that way, 'your dog shat,' very formal. Here you go. Third floor."

"What about Miss Swanson?" Outside the elevator a sign listed tenants and numbers. MARTIN MARTIN, ATTORNEY AT LAW, SUITE 302.

"Half a story on the way up, half on the way down. The ride's more exciting that way." He grinned and let the doors close. I knew I'd have to tip him if I wanted the end of the story. Elevator men make good money around Hollywood.

I knocked on Suite 302. I knocked right on Marty's painted name, twice, then I opened the door to a reception room. His secretary could have gotten up, opened the door for me, but she didn't. She'd sat waiting for me to come in.

"Penny Harp? You're late. Mr. Martin may have to reschedule."

Mr. Martin probably had a house to rob. Probably all the stuff in this room came from a home in Bel-Air: two Chinese dogs on a mantel, fire burning in the fireplace below, white chairs, one wall all mirrors like the Paramount studio commissary, white tables with oriental vases and plants, and in back of the secretary, a short wall covered with tufted white silk. The wall looked like a headboard, with the secretary sitting in bed instead of at her desk. Her sweater looked to me like a bed jacket.

"I'll see if he's still available." She got out of bed and knocked on Mr. Martin's office door. She opened the door wide enough to stick her head in.

I heard Marty's voice. "Penny? Of course I'm here."

I'll admit, my voice cracked when I talked to him. At first I wheezed. I sat down across from his round desk.

"Start with your arrest," Marty said. "What did you tell Detective Conejos?"

"I told him the truth."

"Which is . . ."

"The truth."

"Right," he said. "What I mean is, tell me the truth, too."

"We were at the Palladium, and I lost Rosemary. I looked for her, and then at midnight I went home."

"Home is . . ."

"The Florentine Gardens dormitory."

"Do you share a room with other girls? Did anyone see you come home?"

"I shared a room with Rosemary and two other girls, but we don't talk to each other. Those girls have one side of the room, and we have the other. I mean, we had. Now I share my side with someone else."

"Do you like my desk?"

"I . . . what?"

"My décor."

"I guess. White's hard to keep clean."

"Styled after Louis B. Mayer. Have you seen his office? What am I saying, of course you haven't. L. B.'s desk is huge and round like mine. Much bigger. I had the whole thing scaled down, to fit the room. I have several clients from MGM, and it makes them feel comfortable. It's extremely important that I make clients comfortable."

"I'm comfortable," I said.

"White is hard to keep clean, but that's the point, isn't it? If I can keep this desk clean, I must know what I'm doing. Is your seat comfortable?"

"Sure." A white chair, slats on the back that looked like huge chicken wire. I kept squeezing the armrests.

"It's extremely important that you're comfortable, Penny. The more comfortable you are, the more you'll trust me."

"I trust you," I said. Lying's not a sin if you want to be an actress.

"Tell me again. What happened on Halloween? Everything you can, from the beginning."

Some people are too clean. Like this office. He said if he kept his desk clean, he knew what he was doing. Liar. He didn't clean that desk, his secretary did. She had to wax the thing every night,

I could tell by looking. If I bent my head I could see fingerprints in the wax.

"And remember to call me Marty," he said. "Like we're friends."

"Marty," I said. "I lost Rose at the Palladium. I looked for her, but no luck. I went home." In my head, I saw Gloria Swanson's dog squat and strain in the elevator. "Okay. I'm sorry. You want more? I can fill it out some. You want a *lot* more? I'll try. We were at the Palladium. The people. The crowd! You've never seen so many people. Ida Lupino wore the most darling shift, sort of a wrap-around thing that tied here, above the hip. Rolls in her hair like you'd think she owned a bakery. And the dancing—"

"Penny. Don't fuck with me." This was a new Marty Martin, both hands stiff on his desk. He wanted me to be comfortable. He wanted me to tell him the truth, trust him. He smiled, and his hands stretched white on his white desk. White cuticles under his buffed nails.

"You want to know if I was there," I said. "Not at the Palladium. Somewhere else. You want to know if it's possible when you ran out of Stany's backyard, running away from breaking glass, a little noise, was I that thing you ran by on the path. It's what you want to know, right? Was I the thing?"

"You're babbling, sweetie. I want the truth. I want the best way to represent you. It's a murder case. You're up for murder."

"You want to know if I saw you. From the path, when you ran by with my brother. Is that enough said, or do you want the whole story? I can tell you what happened when you left and Rose was bleeding. We didn't have a car. She was bleeding hard, and we didn't have a car. I keep thinking, maybe if those guys hadn't run by me and driven off, if one of those guys had been *brave*, Rose would be alive. You want to know why? Why we needed a car?"

He swiveled in his white leather chair. Where he'd lifted his hands, I saw two wax handprints on his desk, deep, like spoon rests on a stove. "You've said enough, Penny. You stayed at the Palladium until late. You lost sight of Rosemary, but as you said, the crowds. People get lost and found all night long in those crowds.

It's not your fault you couldn't find her. Stop blaming yourself. Any sane woman would give up and go home while she could still get a ride; streets aren't safe for women at night. You did the right thing."

"I did," I said. "The right thing."

"How did you and Rosemary get to the Palladium if you don't have a car? Did you take the bus?"

"A girl at the dorm gave us a ride. I don't know her name. Navajo Girl. Granny—he's—"

"I know Granny."

"Well. Granny canceled our second show. The Gardens was dead. Thursdays aren't packed, but we usually have more than two tourists for an audience. Granny canceled the show, we all ran to get dressed, and the girls with cars began selling their extra seats. Most everyone at the dorm wanted a ride, so Navajo took the top bidders. Rosemary got us in with pearl bob earrings and twenty-five cents."

"We should talk to Navajo Girl," Marty said. "What do you know about her?"

"She wore blue feathers. Royal blue. There's a new Navajo now, so the new one wears the blue feathers. I don't know what happened to the old one who gave us a ride."

"Better for us," he said.

"I don't know why. It's not better or worse, because Navajo wouldn't remember us. She'd know the earrings, but not who gave them to her. Were you looking for a witness?"

"The fewer witnesses, the better for us. When I say 'us,' I mean you, of course. Right now Detective Conejos has a cab driver who can describe what Rosemary was wearing on Halloween night. He can describe you a little bit, but not as much. Pretty vague description of you, if you ask me. With no other witness to confirm Rosemary's clothing, we're better off."

"I can describe her clothing."

"You're not a witness. You're a defendant, and you keep your mouth shut. You're Helen Keller. You understand me? Now, when you left the Palladium, did you take a cab back to the dormitory? You left at midnight."

"Midnight, right. Yes, I took a cab."

"No."

"I didn't? You said streets aren't safe for girls."

"I know it's hard to remember, emotions and all, such a difficult night. Do you remember now? You saw the line at the cab stand, all those people, it'd take an hour if you stood in that line, so you walked home."

"My feet hurt," I said. "I'd been on them all day."

"Nonetheless, you walked. How far is the Palladium from the Florentine Gardens?"

"Not too far. Four blocks maybe. Big ones. I wouldn't walk it alone at midnight with sore feet."

"Except for that night," he said. "That one night you walked. Halloween, lots of costumes, the packed bars up and down Hollywood Boulevard, it's not your average night. You had to decide between standing in that cab line or walking a few blocks, and like you said, your feet were sore."

"Okay, I walked."

He stood. "I feel good now. Damn, this is shaping up. We've got it all nice and shiny. So glad you came by. I'll tell Detective Conejos your story is solid. He won't believe me, but that's why he's a detective. Our great state pays him to distrust people. God bless California. Let's see that terrible cut on your hand."

I held up my palm. "It's healing now. Hardly sore."

"And you got it . . ."

"Cutting an orange?"

"Excellent. Orange it is. Next we'll take care of that cab driver in Beverly Hills. Let me think on it. We have the grand jury in December, but if that cab driver, say, is in Waikiki in December, on a trip with his ailing mother who may be dead come the new year, who would think it anything more than unfortunate timing? Why are you still sitting? We've covered the basics." He walked a half circle around his white desk and moved my chair as soon as I stood. He didn't move it much, a few inches, so the chair faced his round desk exactly. A wood row from desk to chair to office door. "Tell my secretary to bill Missy for two hours. Penny?"

"I heard you," I said. I'd almost reached the door to the outer office. I'd stopped wheezing. Marty didn't kill Rose. A guy like him, with his waxed desk, no. He was a coward. He left Rose at Stany's, but nobody with a white office can store a bleeding girl. Too messy. His secretary wouldn't clean that mess.

"Hear this, too," he said. "Keep to your story and we'll be fine. Palladium. Cutting an orange. That's what the grand jury hears. If you change it—are you listening to me?"

"Yes."

"You change your story, and I'll walk you to the gas chamber myself." He smiled. "Oh, that's right—wait—I have something of yours." He walked to a white cabinet and used two fingers to pull on a crystal knob. The door sprang open, and he pulled out a paper sack. He tossed it to me. "Yours. I brought it from the police station."

I unfolded the sack, and green feathers popped out. Cree Girl in a bag.

Marty kept smiling. His teeth looked yellow in the white room, but even with the teeth, anyone would look at Marty Martin and say, *There's a fine man. There's a man with taste.* I was saying the same thing to myself when I stood in the hallway outside Marty's office, waiting for the elevator.

The elevator doors shoved open. "Third floor," said the man with the bell cap. He'd stuck the wad of gum in one cheek. A gum tumor. I stepped into the elevator, and he worked his buttons. Bigger smile than Marty, yellower teeth. He waited. The elevator jerked up, then down.

"I don't have much money," I said.

He shut the elevator's outer doors.

"I have enough change to get home, and that's it. I'd tip if I could."

He shut the inner doors. The elevator bounced downward.

"Will you tell me the end of your story?"

"What story?"

"Gloria Swanson and the shitty dog."

"First floor," he said. The elevator hit bottom and jumped, then settled. He sucked spit from the gum in his cheek. "Watch those doors. They snap."

CHAPTER 16

Magnificence itself, modeled by Claudette Colbert . . .
Chantilly lace and black net are designed by Irene in
the season's newest silhouette (slimmed to the knees
and flounced below) with a cowl that can become a
hood.

—*Photoplay*, November 1940

I stole a hard-boiled egg from the fridge for breakfast. I don't know
whose it was. I stood outside to peel the egg and then buried the
eggshell in a dirt hole I'd scuffed with my foot. Eggshells are good
for soil. I've had vegetable beds at home where I bury eggshells
under tomatoes or peppers and the plants grow strong, with lots
of buds.

Sundays are calm at the dorms. Girls sleep, and there's no yelling, no throwing bottles or keys across a room, no running to get
somewhere first. Girls do laundry and shopping on Sundays, and
nobody goes to church, nobody I know. God understands we only
have one day for laundry and errands. The dorm sinks are high
with suds, and pans line the kitchen counters, every one full of
stockings. By Sunday night, clean stockings hang all over the
dorm. They drape across beds and the stair rail, clothes hangers,
backs of chairs, doorknobs.

I figured Madge would wash stockings and cover our bed with them, since I'd left the bedroom and I knew she was up. Madge was a girl who would cover a whole bed with wet stockings and not apologize.

I was wrong. She hadn't washed her stockings. When I reached our bedroom, she stood at our shared closet and thumbed through the hangers.

"You smell like farts," she said. "You know those Career Girls on the other mattress? One threw a comb at my head."

"What are you doing?"

Madge held a dress in front of her. It was Rosemary's dress. "You haven't cleaned your friend's stuff from the closet. I need room. What will you do with her clothes?"

Her clothes? I hadn't thought about it. To be honest, I'd made myself not think about it. Rose had so many clothes that the closet was stuffed with them. I kept my few things folded in one of the dresser drawers, a few dresses on the closet's left side, but Rose—I didn't know where to start.

"We can wear them," Madge said. "Don't throw them away. Have you seen what's here? Have you taken a look?"

"I can't wear Rosemary's clothes. It's not right."

"She's dead," said Madge. "Of course it's right."

I couldn't look at the closet. Not that side, anyway. Not Rose's side.

"Who else will wear them? What'll you do with them? I need these clothes. My life will be better with these clothes. They're hanging in my side of the closet. You know what that means? I get to wear whatever's on my side."

"No," I said. "I'll burn them all."

"You're going to burn this?" She lifted a hanger and held velvet in her hands. Soft burgundy velvet with a silk gusset pleat and the most lovely puff sleeves I'd seen. "God will send you to hell if you burn velvet," Madge said. "He sends people to hell for murder, doesn't He? Murder's just one step below burning a dress like this. God wants you to wear this dress. This, too," she said, and out came a black wool gabardine with patch pockets and white embroidery at the neck. "Where did she find these clothes? How'd she afford them? I'll take that suit with the lace cuffs."

"Put them back."

"I won't. They're beautiful. You know what we could do with these clothes? Nobody buys stuff like this at Sears and Roebuck." She kept pulling them out, hanger, hanger, hat box.

Caramel net and organdy. Red chiffon. Roses on a black poke hat. Round pockets, peplums, wool trousers with pleats deep enough to stick your whole hand in. An evening gown with a drop waist and full chiffon skirt, all bright pink, stunning.

"See? You could wear this gown tomorrow. Look at the neckline. Have you ever seen anything like it? Try it on."

I was crying. Madge unhooked the gown and held it out to me. Long, sheer sleeves, sweetheart bodice, sheer yoke to the neck.

"Touch it, for God's sake."

I couldn't touch it. I'd spot the bodice with tears, and my life would be over. Dresses like that, they were worth more than any girl at the Florentine Gardens. More than all of us. Those dresses had stitches so tiny a needle couldn't have made them. Those dresses weighed nothing, they floated when you put them on. I couldn't touch the gown.

"Where do you think she bought it? What am I saying— stupid—had to be Bullocks, don't you think? Or I. Magnin. Why are you crying? It's only clothes."

"Rose's clothes. She bought them with robbery money. They're not real. There, I've said it. Rose was a thief. You want to know why she was in Beverly Hills? Robbing houses. My best friend was a thief."

"Hell with you. I'm wearing them," Madge said. "Let's see how this blouse fits. What size was Rosemary?"

"I feel sick."

"You must have seen these clothes. She wore them, right? You knew they were here. You're in this closet every morning."

"I don't know. I try not to look on that side. I put my hand up to keep from looking. Maybe I knew. She never took me clothes shopping, so how could I know? Oh, God. That gown used to be some old rich woman's necklace. Everything in that closet used to be something else."

"Hogwash. They're clothes." The blouse fit her perfectly, little darts lining up under her breasts. She tried on the jacket with the lace cuffs. "I'll have to do my hair different, but it works, don't you think?"

"Weren't you listening? I just told you Rose was a thief."

"I heard you. Robbed houses. And had great taste in clothes. I'm sorry for your friend, but we can use everything in this closet. People make mistakes, I've made a few, too. So your friend robbed houses. I don't blame her for it."

Madge looked nice in lace, like she'd laid down her city skin and picked up a new Madge suit. "You look nice in lace," I said. "Softer. You're not worried that Rose stole someone's china or diamonds for that outfit?"

She laughed. "Can you imagine your friend stealing a china set? She staggers into a pawn shop carrying the whole set. Dinner plates, dessert, bowls, cups, all of it. A teapot's balanced on her head. *Here's a service for twelve, Mr. Pawnbroker. How much?* She didn't lug any china, Pen. Stick to the jewelry. Diamonds bought this suit."

Madge wore the diamond suit and kept searching through Rosemary's clothes. "I'll wear the suit tonight. Oh," she said. "Oh, yes. I know what I'm wearing on set tomorrow." She held a sea blue gown at her neck. Bias-cut satin with a striped dimity skirt. The cap sleeves had dimity, too. "A flower in my hair, and I'm set. Are you wearing the pink gown?"

"I'm not wearing Rose's clothes."

"I wish I could wear pink, but it dies on me. You're lucky. We'll pull your hair up in pin curls."

"No pin curls. No gown. I'm not wearing Rose's clothes."

"And tonight? Stany's party?"

"I'll wear an old sheet."

Madge unbuttoned the suit jacket. "I can't wear this today, not for what we'll be doing. Too fancy."

She kept up her talk, unbuttoning, hanging Rosemary's beautiful clothes, and I watched her. I watched the clothes bend and fold themselves onto hangers and racks.

"We need a city directory, so we'll ask Granny for his. I don't have much gas in my car. Do you have money for gas?"

"Gas? Why?"

"Penny, what have I been going on about? Our plans. Today. The hospitals."

"What plans?"

"To search the hospitals. Find out where Rosemary went."

"Take off the blouse. I don't want to see it. If we're searching, we start with the ones close to Sunset," I said. "It's most likely that whoever picked her up took her to a hospital close by."

I knew Rose didn't visit a hospital. She sat in the wrong car and got killed. The car never went to a hospital; it didn't have to. A killer drove the car, and killers don't drive their victims to hospitals. But what else would I do today, wash my stockings? That would take fifteen minutes, a few more to lay them around, and then I'd have the rest of today to wander the dorm and think of how Rose's clothes changed the color of Madge's skin. They made her look lighter, even the pink she couldn't wear. Every piece of clothing Madge had held against herself made her skin turn smooth and shiny, mother-of-pearl. I couldn't do it. I couldn't think about Rose's clothes all day. I couldn't think about how the clothes looked on Madge.

"We'll be hungry," I said. "We should take a couple of eggs for lunch."

We made a flyer and copied it on the Gardens mimeograph. I'll skip details about prep work, how Granny gave us paper and added the cost to my rent, how Madge snuck to Woolworth's, and while I was writing the damn flyer, she stole thumbtacks. I won't discuss how I yelled at her, I'll skip that part. Just know I was mad.

When we were done, we laid flyers on the bar in the Zebra Lounge, and Granny said the flyer would bring us information or jail time.

DID YOU SEE ROSEMARY ON HALLOWEEN?

TWENTIES—BLOND—GREEN SUIT

CUT RIGHT THUMB—BLOOD (REAL, NOT COSTUME)

AT YOUR HOSPITAL ABOUT 1:00 A.M.

SHE IS MISSING AND HER FAMILY NEEDS HER

CALL PENNY AT HOLLYWOOD 4423 OR 4425

"Someone will call," Madge said. "Dorms or Gardens, they'll call."

"Yeah. Woolworth's security will call."

"You ready, then? I'll drive. I'm thirsty. Open the trunk, would you? I've still got that bottle."

CHAPTER 17

Read about Arno, Errol Flynn's dog, who is practically
human.

—*Photoplay*, November 1940

Tacking up flyers made us late for Stany's party, but I didn't mind.
I didn't want to go back to Faring Drive and walk into Stany's
house like I belonged there. But I did want to see the upstairs yellow room and look for blood. I wanted both, to stay away and to
go. I stood by Madge's car, deciding.

"Robert Taylor," Madge said.

I got in her car.

She stopped at a gas station on Sunset and pulled a five from
her handbag.

"I thought you didn't have money."

"No," she said. She leaned her head on the steering wheel. "If
you'll remember, I asked if *you* had money. I knew I had some, but
why should I pay for the gas to hunt down your friend?"

"You're drunk."

"Thank God."

She looked good, though. She wore Rose's black suit with lace
cuffs. I'd curled her hairline with a curling iron I borrowed from
some girl. I forgot to put the iron back in the girl's room, but that
was okay. Madge's hair fit the nice suit, and that's what mattered.

And me? I didn't touch Rose's clothes. I wore a long checked skirt I'd made myself, in high school, and the same white blouse I wore with trousers and coveralls. I'd hid a pocket stain with a rhinestone brooch. I'd tied my hair with white ribbon. Parties shouldn't be fashion shows, should they? A party's a place to meet friends and enjoy food and gossip, wander Stany's house a bit, find the room where Rose bled, and sit in that room to honor the last time I'd seen my best friend alive. If I happened to meet Bob Taylor, fine, but I wasn't betting on that. I kept my autograph book in my purse.

We parked on Mapleton and climbed the hill. Rocks in my stomach grew bigger the closer we came to Faring Drive. Sharp, mean rocks. Gravel. I wanted to tell Madge everything. I needed to tell her. I was walking the same street I'd run down that night, after I'd jumped off the ladder in Stany's backyard.

"Don't you wonder," I said, "why Rose and I were close to here on Halloween?"

"You told me. Rose robbed houses."

"Don't you want to know which house? Aren't you dying to know?"

"This is where you confide in me, isn't it?" She stopped and pulled her lighter from her handbag. She lit a cigarette and blew smoke to the hibiscus that hid a rich house. "Where you make me listen to your awful story and how bad your life is. I'm going to Stany's, Pen. I'm going to drink and dance and eat all the food she sets out. I'm not carrying your trouble with me, I won't do it. I have my own. I don't think you killed your friend. You're too weak to rob houses, you don't have the guts. Therefore, you either followed your friend to Beverly Hills to stop her, or you came with her and didn't know what she planned. Either way, you're innocent. Can we go to the party now? Damn. Which is hers?"

"Faring Drive," I said. "Left side. Like a Mexican villa. Tile roof, hedge. Nice pool in the back. You have to climb over a gate to get there. Madge, I really need to tell you this. I need you to know. If you lean a ladder against the upstairs, you can break a window and fall right in. You might cut your thumb on some glass."

Madge let her eyes glance at me, but not her face. She kept her face toward the corner of Mapleton and Faring. She smoked. "Goddamn you. I knew it. I hate you. You just ruined my goddamn night."

"The Career Girls are here." They walked toward us on Faring Drive. They came from the direction of Claudette Colbert's house, but they didn't know Claudette Colbert. They must have just parked by her house. The girls saw us, ignored us, and turned onto Stany's front walk.

You might think it's strange we didn't talk. I'd shared a bedroom with two Career Girls for months and never talked to them. Not a *hi*, not *get your clothes off my side*. A Wallflower lived downstairs and we didn't talk, either. It's because they weren't always Career Girls or Wallflowers. Before the Paramount job, they were just Nez Perce and Sioux and Paiute, and who cares about them? I don't mean to be cold. They thought the same of me. None of us could do the others any good, so we didn't talk.

Besides, friends are messy. First you learn real names and then you're buddies at cattle calls, you both go to clubs and pictures, and soon you think of a girl as herself, a person. Then the day comes when you and the friend both get callbacks. It's the same role and only one girl gets it. If you get the role, then it's your fault she's the loser. If she gets the role, you hate her. Either way, the friendship is over, and ignoring a friend is harder than ignoring a Career Girl.

I've never been in the situation where a picture role was between me and a friend, but it could happen. We hear stories like this all the time.

"Stany's house isn't as grand as it should be," Madge said. "I'm disappointed. This house could belong to anyone rich. I expected more, you know? The hedge needs a shave. Think she'll recognize me?"

"She'll know you're part of the cast." I got swallowed by trumpets. Stany had a small band instead of a table in her dining room. We walked into a dance hall. Stany must have had regular house furniture like a couch and love seat, but not right then. The furniture in her house was gone, and a few chairs and small tables held people and food. Couples danced, maids served plates of nibbles, and roaming between cameramen, gaffers, assistants, sound guys, and assistants to the assistants was Stany. She wore black trousers and a red silk blouse, black bangles on her wrist. I remember the bangles, how they clanked on each other when Stany wiggled fingers at Ed, Preston's secretary. He held a plate of meatballs.

A cast party, except the cast wasn't here. Hank didn't come, or Eugene Pallette or Abbott or Preston or the guy whose name we didn't know. This was the other cast, the one that wasn't seen. Robert Taylor wasn't here, either.

Madge was right, though. Stany's house wasn't grand. The inside wasn't marble or anything, just Mexican tile. I've never been in a marble house, but I've seen photographs, and the staircases always curve. There are chandeliers, and the movie star—say, Carole Lombard, because that's who I've seen in the photos— stands on a marble stair in a belted silk dressing gown. She has one hand on a handrail, and she could be going up or down the marble stairs; you don't know, up or down. Anything less than Carole Lombard's marble is a disappointment. At Stany's, the doorways are arched like Rose's Aunt Lou's. A plain staircase with tiled stairs. No furniture and no rugs, and people eating. The house looked like a church basement. No wonder Robert Taylor was gone.

"It's like Abbott said that first day on set," Madge said. "See the Femme Fatale? We're exactly like our types. Femme Fatale. See her? I expected more. I wanted different." Then Madge was dancing, and her brown curls bounced on the shoulders of Rose's suit. She let a guy twirl her. I climbed Stany's tiled stairs.

Bathroom, with tile and soap. Bedroom. Another bedroom, a study. All full of clunky Mexican carvings and headboards, dull reds and orange.

Middle of the hall, on the left, I found the yellow bedroom. The room was dark. I walked right in before I knew it was the right room. I stopped when I saw the bedspread. Yellow walls that looked brown in the dark, open closet with suits that smelled like cigarettes and a screen star. Closet with suits, not dresses.

Rosemary fell into Bob Taylor's bedroom. She'd have loved that. She'd have danced in his room and touched his sheets if she'd known. With new window glass and clean floors, I had to think hard to remember the room on Halloween, with glass pieces all over, cuts on my arms and calves. A slash across my palm. No blood on the floor now, no stains.

I backed to the doorway, my hand on the wood frame. I rubbed the scar on my palm. I guess I was looking for *something*—a left-over bit, a glass chunk not swept from the baseboard. A souvenir like we bring home from vacation. Everyone does it. Go to the Grand Canyon, bring home a rock. From Monterey, a crab shell. From this room—nothing. Yellow drapes, matched bedspread and walls, ashtray, pottery horse on the bureau, and all of it fine, like it hadn't seen me slip on Rose's blood and crouch beside her and rip my dress to press on her hand.

I moved into the dark room to look at the floor, a close look at the wood slats. Rose's blood leaked into these cracks between planks, and mine, too. Stany couldn't have cleaned it all up, she'd have to replace the floor to get rid of us. We still lived in the seams of Bob Taylor's bedroom. I couldn't see much in the dark, but if I switched on the light, I would have seen dried blood in the cracks.

"I knew you'd break in again." Stany's kid stood in the door-way. Dion, her little boy, her son, her freckly baby. He wore kid blue jeans and a checked shirt.

"Don't tell," I said. "Don't tell it was me. Our secret. It's fun to have secrets."

"You should have broke in downstairs. You should have walked in like you went to the party, then waited all night until we're asleep."

"I didn't take anything," I said. I was stuck in the room, in the spot with the bloody wood floor. And then he walked closer, like he expected something. He looked at the window and its new pane. He was between me and the door, and my eyes were flicking around.

"I'm packed," he said. "I knew you'd come back. I've got my own suitcase."

"I'm sorry," I said.

"You're not good at planning. We have to wait until everyone leaves." He reached an empty hand to me like he was already passing over his suitcase, his *packed* suitcase, and I couldn't touch him. The room was dark except for the light from the hallway and the light from the old-fashioned lanterns on Faring that stretched over the hedge and shone into second-floor rooms. I didn't know what he expected with that hand. And I peed a little.

Then I heard feet on the stairs and saw Madge in the doorway. A guy was with her.

"This is Kenny," Madge said. "He's half-French and half-something."

"Hiya," Kenny said. "I've got hiccups."

"Come meet Uncle Buck's dog," Madge said. "He can do tricks. You hold up a cracker and the dog bows. I'm not kidding! Maybe it's a curtsy, I don't know. Who's in here with you?"

"Nobody." It was true, sort of. The room was dark enough that it was true.

"Well, come see. Did you try the shrimp dip? Who can afford shrimp? I'm eating as much as I can."

All I had to do was leave the room and walk down the hall, but it was the hardest thing, a simple turn to the door, with Madge saying "shrimp dip, shrimp dip." Yellow bed, yellow walls, and the window. The ladder. A gash on my hand, a little boy. Rose cold, because she'd left her coat on the ground and climbed the ladder without it.

I hadn't picked up her coat. Did she pick it up? Would she have remembered to grab her coat? I told her, *Get down the ladder. Run to Sunset. Wave at a car.* I didn't say, *Remember to pick up your coat.*

Now I tried to imagine the ladder and me climbing down it, fast. The woman yelling. Yes—at the bottom, a dark pile of coat that I left in Stany's backyard like I left the ladder when I ran to the gravel path. Or was I making it up now, and hadn't seen the coat at all? I couldn't remember.

"Shrimp dip," Madge said. "And big mushroom caps stuffed with cheese and sausage, served hot. Only they might not be hot anymore."

"*Hic-hic,*" said Kenny.

"Why are you standing there? Pen?"

The hardest thing, that turn to the door. The step past a short kid in shadows with his hand still out. Then: "Mushroom caps? I'm starving. Where are they?"

Madge pulled me back to the party. I watched a Career Girl dance with Uncle Buck, dance with Uncle Buck's dog, dance with some guy. The Jack Bennys came for a while and then left. Some neighbors stopped in. Nobody could talk with a trumpet and drums, so we smiled and ate and watched each other. No little kid came downstairs.

Then Stany's red blouse danced toward me. I saw the red blouse and then Stany, because I was drunk. She yelled in my ear. She led me through her patio, into her backyard. It took a while. People stopped her to yell hellos, or yell how lovely, how delicious, with Stany smiling and yelling back. Each time she stopped, I waited and looked at the pool. My stomach hated that pool. I didn't want to go outside and stand where I'd stood on Halloween. I knew I'd get out there and look for Rosemary's coat. Or that was exactly why Stany wanted me outside, to confront me, because she knew I'd climbed into her house. Her kid had told her I was the Halloween thief.

Oh, hell. I went outside with her anyway.

"You all right?" She stood at her pool's deep end, and the house lamps lit water, then lit Stany and turned her hair swimming pool blue.

"Yes," I said. One thing about trumpets, you can hear them from anywhere.

"You having fun?"

"Oh, sure."

"You are? You don't look like you're having fun."

"Such fun," I said.

"Well, good. Are you drunk?"

"No, I swear."

"You can be drunk if you want. I was just asking."

"Your blouse is nice."

"Yes, it is. Well. So you're having fun. That's good. Penny, I want to ask you. Can you talk? Do you have to go? If you can't talk . . ."

"What is it?"

"I'm a little embarrassed," Stany said. "A little, oh, you could say embarrassed. Tell me about your friend."

"Madge?"

"Who's Madge? I meant Rosemary. Tell me about Rosemary."

"That's your question?"

"Sort of," she said.

"Rosemary," I said. The night air was chilly. I didn't see Rose's coat in the backyard.

"Who was she? I mean, why was she here, what did she do for fun?"

"Why was she here? Why was she *here?*"

"In Hollywood."

"Oh. Rose was here for the jobs, same as me."

"She was very beautiful," Stany said.

"She was. Everyone says she would have been a star. She had the looks and—"

"The tits," Stany said.

"Yeah. I meant personality, though. She had the kind of spirit that made people notice her. She was excited to work on your picture."

"She was?"

"Oh, yeah. Rosemary was excited," I said. "The first day on set she said it was the best that could have happened."

"You told me she wanted to sign with MGM."

"I know, she did. She did. But you should have seen her. When security first let us past the gate, she pushed a girl to get in front. The girl sprained her knee and security called a nurse. Rose was that glad to be at Paramount. Not Paramount exactly, it was you she was glad about, that we'd be in a picture with you. At Central Casting she begged for the job. She promised the clerk she'd date him if he got us to Paramount."

"You're lying," Stany said.

"All right. Not date. She took him in the back room for a while. When they came out he gave us the job. He wanted to see her again but she said no."

"She fucked the Central Casting guy to work with me."

"I don't know, but yeah, she did it for you."

"I should be flattered," Stany said. "I think I am flattered. What? Why are you looking like that? What aren't you telling?"

"Shrimp dip," I said. "It'll be gone, and I want some."

"Liar."

"I like shrimp, I do."

"I'm sure. I'll send you a crate of the fucking dip. Nobody cringes because they like shrimp. You're leaving out something big. What is it." Not a question, a command.

"Stany—"

"I'm perfectly capable of using my fists."

"That *hurts*. Don't hit me. Don't touch me."

"I want the truth, damn it. I'll hit you again."

"Fine. She said you're not glamorous. You can act, but that's it. She said in a race with her, you'd lose. That's why she wanted on your set. Because on film, Rose glowed like a goddamn klieg. She'd drown you out in a crowd scene, in a speck of film. If Rose was there, it didn't matter where you stood, what you said or did. She'd get the audience, her, not you, and she was right. Conejos told me Preston noticed her. The wedding scene has to be scrapped. Did Preston tell you he scrapped the scene?"

I'd given Stany the wrong truth. She didn't like what I'd told her. Rose's coat didn't wait in the backyard. I hadn't come tonight to steal a kid and his suitcase. Rose didn't idolize Stany, although I

stood in a houseful of folks who did. A houseful, in a church basement. Yet they didn't matter. They weren't the reason Stany knelt
by the pool with her face away from me and scooped water in her
hand, then splashed the water on her face and silk blouse.

"Bob Taylor has his own bedroom? You take the keys, I'm too
drunk."

"That's what I thought, too," I said. I unlocked Madge's car,
and she crawled into the passenger seat. "I thought, why don't
they share a bedroom? But now I know. I think he has a room for
his suits."

"I'm tired. I'm so tired. That Kenny's a liar," Madge said. She
hit her head on the back of her seat. She kicked the dashboard.
"He don't even speak French."

"Ooh la la," I said.

"Fuck you. Fuck your 'ooh la la.' All Kenny's good for is rumors. He says Edith Head's teeth are rotten and that's why she
never smiles. He says Zukor's cook is a Nazi spy. Well, of course
she is. Isn't she German? He says there's a secret tunnel between
Paramount and that building across the street. A camera guy told
him. He says that's where the bigwigs meet their girlfriends, right
in the middle of the day. I don't feel good. And those guys are all
married."

"You said Kenny's a liar."

"Ah, who knows. We probably walk on top and don't even know
it's there. I'm tired. That Kenny's a goddamn liar, I told you. And
you're going to believe him? Are you going to let this guy follow
you?"

"What?"

"Joe is following you. Studio Joe. That's his name? Joe?"

"Now you're the liar."

"Then why is he following?" Madge asked.

Joe in his squad car, engine idling, middle of Mapleton, waiting
for me to pull out.

"He's a Hollywood cop. What's he doing in Holmby Hills?"

"Following you," Madge said. "Are you stupid? I keep saying."

"He might've went to Stany's party." In his squad car, on duty for Hollywood.

I drove Madge's car downhill to Sunset, turned left, and Joe's car trailed me. I shot corners, stopped and started again, pulled to the curb, and Joe did the same. Madge kept talking, probably drunk talk, none of it true.

CHAPTER 18

Ginger Rogers and Ronald Colman in an unusually so-phisticated comedy which has stretched several points in the matter of plausibility, but is good entertainment nevertheless.

—*Photoplay*, November 1940

"I lost my parents," Madge said.

"That's terrible."

"I mean they're *lost*, not dead."

"I'm trying to drive here," I said. "I'm trying to lose this cop."

"That's what I mean. I lost my parents like that."

"You drove and they followed you?"

"No, that's not what I mean." Madge was drunk. Her head rolled back and forth against her seat. "I mean I *lost* them."

"Okay," I said. "Tell me."

"Aw, you don't want to hear it."

"You're right. I don't. You're drunk and you're making stuff up."

"Probably."

"Okay," I said. "Tell me."

"If you turn this corner you can lose the cop by Bing Crosby's house. I spent the night in his bushes once. See it? You can lose anyone at Bing Crosby's house, it's a fact."

"And that's your story? Bing Crosby's house?"

"I'm trying to *help*," she said. "Let's hide in those bushes."

"Sure, he'll never see your car."

"Let me know if you need my help. Otherwise I'm just talking here. So, my parents," she said. "My mom and dad. A few months ago my dad says to my mom, *Honey, I've got a surprise.* And out pop these tickets for the Queen Mary. It's stupid, really. He never takes her anywhere. He waits for a war and then says, *Let's go.* He says, *We've got to see Paris.* Who doesn't, if you think like that. So they go."

"I can't lose him," I said. "He's right behind us."

"That's okay," Madge said. "My story's done. That's my story."

It wasn't exactly her story, just part of it. Her dad had said, *Honey, we've got to see Paris,* because Hitler had just crossed Belgium to France, and when troops reached Paris, nobody would see Paris ever again. Not even Americans. Sounds stupid, run to see Paris before Hitler bombs the Eiffel Tower. Most people would stay clear of Europe in wartime, but consider this is Madge's dad speaking. Plus the boats were still running, from New York to London to Marseille. Consider also that Madge's mom said, *Yes, honey, let's go right now.*

They left Madge in Riverside with plenty of money to last six months. Madge got beautiful postcards: Hello from *Westminster Abbey!* Greetings from *the fish markets of Marseille!* Toasting you from *the vineyards of Burgundy!* From the world's most beautiful boulevard, *the Champs-Élysées!*

Then nothing. Not a thing, no letter or postcard. German troops reached Paris in April. Americans were told to get out, and most did. But not Madge's parents.

Their ship docked in Long Beach in early July, and Madge was there waiting. She saw Charles Laughton get off the ship, she swears it was him with his ugly wife. But where were her parents? Lots of crying and hugs, other moms and dads home at last, glad to be home, thank God for America, have you read the papers? Poor souls, and those evil Germans! What will happen now?

Madge said the worst part was listening—all those parents telling their kids how they'd nearly died, they'd heard jackboots behind them, it had been *that close*, and their kids crying because Mom and Dad were back safe, fuck those people in Paris and Dunkirk and Versailles, at least they had Mom and Dad, and let's go home now, let's get your trunks and go home.

Madge went home, to hot Riverside, where it hadn't rained since December. She let her maid go because the money had run out. Then she locked the house and moved to Hollywood, because who had more power than studios? Not the bank, where a guy told her the house was her father's, sorry, no loan. Not the State Department, where a guy told her that maybe her parents would cable. The studios, though, they had power. Nazis watched movies, didn't they? Jews ran the studios, but after a long day of war, didn't Nazis say, *Let's catch that Cagney show at the Bijou? That Laurel and Hardy, that Mickey Rooney comedy? What a kick, that Mickey Rooney.*

Madge went to the oldest, wisest studio head: Adolph Zukor at Paramount. He could do anything. He was the Wizard of Oz.

"He promised to help," Madge said to me.

"When did he promise? How long ago?"

"He says it takes time. He gave me a job, see? He's the Wizard. I work for him, and he'll help me. You know what I really want to do? Here's what I really, really want to do. I want to get on a highway and keep driving and driving until I get there."

"Where?"

"What are you talking about? I want to throw up now."

I pulled her car to the curb. Behind us, Joe braked his squad car and we both watched Madge open her door and vomit shrimp and mushroom caps on Bing Crosby's grass. Then we drove back to the dorms, the three of us, me and Madge in her squeaky Dodge and Joe behind us, braking close at red lights.

Once I'd heard Madge's story, Joe didn't bother me. Joe wasn't nearly as scary as Nazis. I waited for my asthma to rise and drown me, I waited for my lungs to suck in on themselves, my panic to take over. I couldn't shake Joe, but I didn't care. I waited—and I breathed. Madge cried and wiped her mouth. Joe followed all the way to the Gardens, and my throat never swelled. I saw his windshield in my rearview mirror, his red bubble light on the hood, and still I kept talking to Madge and breathing. I never got asthma. It was my favorite thing that happened all day.

I didn't always hate cops. I never baked cookies for the squad or sat cold hours waiting for cop parades, but I thought cops were okay. I still do. Conejos called me a murderess, but he was okay. He dressed like a normal guy. He didn't wear one uniform in the morning and another at night, like Joe Flores.

Or Teddy, my old friend, who never took off his uniform. He'd worn trousers and old shirts in high school because then he worked with his dad fixing cars. But the minute he joined the sheriff's department, he put on that uniform and hasn't taken it off, not even to wash. He wore it the day flood waters sank in the ground around Buena Park, and rolled back to Coyote Creek, Brea Creek, wherever they came from. He stood with Daisy and me at a sinkhole to the far right of our orange trees. Far, far right, past the orchard, almost to Orangethorpe Avenue. The rain had stopped. Daisy's boots slid in mud, and if I hadn't held her hand, then her arm, she'd have fallen. I could hear her make little throat noises, like a kid does when he's sick. Teddy stood on my other side at the sinkhole. It was almost night. Teddy said, "Is this him?" and I said yes, and he threw his coat over the drowned face of my father.

CHAPTER 19

Irene advises: "All brides should remember that half the beauty of the gown lies in the way it is worn. Don't slump. Learn to walk well and stand as if you were proud of yourself."

—*Photoplay*, November 1940

The skirt and blouse worked so well at Stany's party that I wore them to Paramount Monday morning. When I arrived on set, Miles Abbott yelled at me.

"You look like fucking Daisy Mae," he said. "You could plow a field in that skirt."

"I'm a Farm Girl."

"You know what I mean. We'll have to hide you in back." He wore a brown wool jacket with huge shoulder pads and a tie that had little Paramount mountains on it, each mountain surrounded by twinkly gold stars. He was as short as me, and he never smiled at the extras or crew. He only smiled at Preston and Stany and Hank. "I ought to send you home. Do you know what *ship dinner dress* means?"

Then, swooping in like a bird, Stany said, "Here you are, Pen. I brought that gown I told you about. I'm not too late, am I? Hello, Miles, just outfitting our girl for the day. Won't take half a minute. Is Preston on set? Good. We have time. Penny, let's go. The gown's in my dressing room." Abbott smiled at Stany, frowned at me, and walked across the set to yell at Madge. Stany pulled my arm.

"How did you know?"

"*Sshh*," she said. "Let's get outside. We don't want anyone to notice."

No notice, except the extras wandering the ship's big dining room. If Stany were a bird today, then these were the mean bird-watchers, all in ship dinner dress with fox stoles, fingertip veils, gowns from J.C. Penney or Woolworth's. Then there was Madge in blue bias-cut satin with a dimity overskirt fresh from the stash in our closet, but she wasn't watching us. She argued with Miles Abbott and leaned against a ship rail, back arched so her breasts stuck out. She waved around one arm.

Stany passed a long buffet table set with real food, dinner on the ship. She stole some grapes and tossed them into her mouth. "I didn't eat breakfast. Might as well eat this stuff today, because tomorrow it's going to turn and we'll smell old meat all day and never want to eat again. Hurry up."

She'd already left by the stage door. It's not that she could move faster than me. People moved out of Stany's way. They let her eat grapes and gave her a path without feet or equipment. Then came me, and the path closed behind Stany, so I had to squeeze between a wheeled boom mike and a Wallflower who spit on my skirt.

"Did you steal my shoes? Those look like my shoes."

I kept walking and pushed her with my shoulder.

She yelled at me, "I'm limping. I'm wearing shoes that are *too small*."

My feet slid inside the Wallflower's shoes, comfortable, and I ran out, past the tin shed, past the high security wall that separated the back lot from Hollywood Cemetery next door. When I reached Avenue P, I saw the back of Stany turning into the alley. Her hair flashed coppery gold. I ran toward her with my skirt bunched in my hands. I followed her into her dressing room.

"Let's see what I've got," Stany said. "Polka dots. How do you look in dots?"

"That Wallflower's feet hurt."

"She'd better get new shoes, then."

"I should feel terrible for her."

"Oh, Penny." She hit my shoulders with her hands. She made me look directly at her. "I know what this is. You're feeling guilt about last night."

"I'm not. I can feel bad for a Wallflower without feeling guilty about you."

"I don't believe you. Dissolve the guilt. Get rid of it. Although last night, you did hurt me deeply."

"Okay."

"Why don't *you* buy that Wallflower new shoes? Wallflower, right? At least she's not in England. Do you think they have shoes in England? We all have something to be thankful for. Here we are," she said. Her hands lifted from me, and she turned. Behind her a wardrobe had both doors open; beside her a cream velvet couch and cream curtains made the room airy and cozy. Hanging in the wardrobe was a lovely embroidered black column dress with peplum and bodice in navy blue. Stany's hand reached out, paused at the dress, a long pause with her fingernails scraping the hanger, then pushed that hanger to the side and lifted the next hanger off the closet rod. She let a gown fall off the hanger and handed the gown to me. "No time for gawking. You're not a tourist, Penny. Try on the dress."

I tried it on. Gray taffeta with a split skirt and a gray chiffon train that looked like a tail. The dress stopped four inches up my ankles. "I'm a tall squirrel," I said.

"Nonsense. It's perfect." She wore a black crepe skirt with a beaded top that showed her tummy. Red beads clacked on her wrists. Any dress she held against her own outfit would look old. "Walk around a bit. Now turn toward me. Okay, you could use some inches at the hem, but otherwise, perfect. Let me see . . . let me see . . . I've got . . ." She pulled a purple chiffon driving scarf from the foot of the wardrobe. "Tack this on the bottom. I have thread somewhere, not me but my dresser, and she has pins, too. We'll pin the scarf at the bottom, and you can sew during breaks. We'll pretend it's a flounce. You'll look great on film."

"What about your dresser? Can't she sew?"

"Do you see her around? Is she hiding? Honestly, Pen, I wonder about you. Did you find needles? Look in that drawer."

"I'm sorry about last night," I said. "Sorry I upset you."

"I asked for the truth, and I got it. What more can one friend give another? Don't move, I need to pin the scarf."

"I can't move and not move at the same time."

"First law of acting," she said. "Make each move on purpose. That's how you move and not move. Body stays perfectly still, and then your arms move. Just your arms. Yes, like that. Good. Now reach for the needles."

Stany taught me the first law of acting: move and not move. She says she learned that more than one body part in motion means the audience follows your body and not your words. Fine, if you have no dialogue and want to be noticed. But if you're speaking, Stany says, move and not move. She learned the trick on Broadway. I'd never noticed her moving and not moving in any of her pictures, that's how well it worked.

"And you'll sew during breaks," she said, and on set, Abbott placed me at a table with two extras hired for this scene, an older mom and pop couple, my parents for the day. We all had to stare at one spot in the dining room. The most interesting invisible person stood at that spot, invisible to us, since we stared at an empty booth. Imagine the set: ship's dining room with tables in tiered circles around a few booths and a buffet table heavy with roasts and ham and a waterfall of fruit, and we sit at tables and watch not the food but an empty booth. Not many extras eat breakfast, and ham has a powerful smell. Preston should have stuck that ham in the booth, then we wouldn't have had so many retakes.

"Cut," Preston said. "Vic, angle the shot to that corner table. I want the look on her face." The ham look.

During breaks I tacked the scarf to my hem and watched the

Wallflower limp in my shoes. Stany sat outside the ship and played five-card draw with Hank and some sound guys. On stage we were supposed to be staring at Hank, that's who would sit at the empty booth, but why use the real Hank when we've got an invisible spot to stare at and a good ham to smell? Let Hank rest.

I've held back one part of the scene. Imagine again: We're staring at an empty booth, and above the booth are more tiers with tables and extras, and they're staring, too, so I can stare at the invisible Hank, and right above him is a table where Madge sits. I lift my eyes a little to stare at Madge, sitting across the set in her blue bias-cut.

It was a beautiful gown. Even Madge looked pretty inside it, though a little upset because she'd fought with Abbott and her parents were lost in Paris. My Rosemary would have looked stunning in sea blue. She'd have pinned white hibiscus in her gold hair to match the dimity's trim at her hips, and the bias would swirl and settle over those hips when she walked. Rose would have shown me a gown like this as soon as she'd bought it. She'd come home and try the dress on, twirl in front of me to show off.

She didn't, though. She didn't show off the sea-blue gown or the pink one with yards of chiffon. She never showed me any of the clothes Madge had pulled from the closet, not the jacket with lace cuffs, not a blouse, nothing.

Why wouldn't Rosemary show me her clothes?

She bought them with cash from robberies, that's why. She'd have to explain how she got the money, and she couldn't explain, not for all those clothes, a fortune hung in a closet.

No, that wasn't right. Rose could have made up a story and I'd have believed her. *A man bought me this dress,* she might have said. *I've decided to build a wardrobe. Each guy I meet, I'll get him to buy me a dress.* I'd have believed that story because it could have been true. I'd seen guys buy Rosemary all sorts of things. Never something from Bullocks, but expensive dresses meant she'd have to meet rich guys, that's all. In Hollywood, rich guys jump up and down and wave their arms. They're not hard to find.

"Cut," Preston said. "Where's my coffee? Eddie, track down

the coffee. Add a slug of scotch if you find some. Do I look like I'm kidding? Would I kid about scotch? Take a slug for yourself. Ten minutes, everyone, we need coffee."

I stuck a needle through the chiffon scarf into my taffeta hem. Every two inches I sewed a tacking stitch. Across the set, Madge stood and stretched her arms in Rosemary's gown. She yawned and didn't cover her mouth. A girl at the next table—Femme Fatale?—watched Madge's dimity hips when she stretched. Jealous. Such a beautiful gown. Rosemary didn't buy that gown. If Rose wanted to, she could have lied about the whole wardrobe—stacks of dresses—where they'd come from and who bought them. She didn't lie. And she would have lied, if she bought them herself.

A gift? Someone gave Rose the clothes. *You can have it all,* someone told Rose, *I'm buying new, this stuff must be six months old and besides, I've worn most of it once.* But if someone did give Rose her wardrobe, a rich socialite maybe, a star, Rose would have told me right off. She'd gloat in an attractive way and tell me I could borrow whatever I wanted. We'd both be wearing the clothes.

I couldn't see it. Women hated Rosemary, and a rich woman wouldn't want her clothes worn by someone so beautiful. A rich woman would give her clothes to an ugly girl and then feel smug, like she'd fed the English.

Rosemary didn't buy the clothes. No rich man or woman gave her the clothes. The only choice left was the one I hated.

Rose took those clothes from a house. She stole them, she snuck through each house with armfuls, she layered them over her own clothes, she stuck them in sacks and cases and baskets each time she robbed a Beverly Hills house.

"Find your marks," Preston said. He held a huge coffee cup and smiled. "Vic, what do you think—shoot across the buffet table? All that ripe fruit and a girl staring beyond it. Doesn't even notice the food with handsome Hank in the booth."

Stany touched me on the shoulder. "Who are you watching? Isn't she an Indian at your dorm? Tom-Tom Girl. Nice gown for an extra. I know someone who has a gown like that, but I can't think who. Looks like an Irene. Claudette Colbert? Ah, well, it'll come.

Pen, you look fine. I told you the flounce would work. What's happened to our little gray squirrel?"

"She's now a squirrel with a purple flounce."

"That's gratitude. I give you a nice dress and you notice the defects."

"Thank you for the squirrel dress, Stany."

"Fuck you and you're welcome. Find your mark, Pen. Move and don't move."

CHAPTER 20

Lucille Ball's farewell to Desi Arnaz was touching and sincere. Make no mistake on this romance.

—*Photoplay*, November 1940

At the Florentine Gardens, the dorm had two bathrooms to serve sixteen girls, so we broke bath nights into rounds. Bedroom Three, that was us. We bathed on Tuesday nights, no more than twenty minutes each. Bedroom Four bathed on Mondays, Bedroom Two bathed Wednesdays, and nobody bathed Thursday through Saturday because those nights we worked a late show at the Gardens. Bedroom One, first floor, took Sundays. We all hated Bedroom One. The Sunday girls took two-hour baths and brought books inside with them before they locked the doors. With four girls to a bedroom, eight to each bathroom, that meant no toilet in the house for at least four hours and no hot water after that. All stockings had to be washed before Bedroom One took their baths. Those were the rules, they'd been the rules for ages, they wouldn't change.

Madge didn't like the rules. She said Sunday girls used to be Granny's nieces: "They're like old horses. When he gets a new niece he puts the old one out. Except we don't have a pasture so they get Bedroom One." She sat on the Zanzibar bandstand before rehearsal. She helped me button a new costume that looked a lot like the old costume, with ruffles instead of feathers, and a short skirt.

"I tell you, I'm going to be Granny's niece. Hold still. At some point he'll get tired of Apache, and here I am."

"She won't be Apache soon." The new routine was on bullfighting, *Hail the Bullfighters*, something like that. We'd all be picadors and carry spears to stab the poor bull.

"Whatever her name is, she's headed for Bedroom One. It's my turn. There. You look great. Except your hair. Why don't you try pin curls? Here's Granny," she said. "God. He's got the bull hat."

Granny set a big box on a table. A couple Picador Girls followed Granny onto the dance floor, and more girls walked in from backstage.

"Take a spear, take a spear." He waved his lit cigarette over the box, then put the cigarette between his lips and kept talking. "Not you, Charlotte. You're my bull. Tie that cap so the horns don't slide. Christ, are those your ears? You look like Clark Gable. Take off the hat. I don't know, pass it to someone, anyone. Yes, she'll do. Penny, tie it on. Straighten those horns. Pull your shoulders back, the horns tilt. You're top-heavy."

Some girls laughed. The hat hurt my head.

"Now, here's the deal. We're filming a simple, three-act talkie at the Gardens, along the lines of *Broadway Melody* but different. A look at what goes on backstage at Hollywood's most famous revue. Warners will shoot everything at their back lot. They've got a cast, and no, you're not in the cast, just a few background scenes of the Zanzibar and the bull revue."

Aha. Nobody laughed now, with me wearing the bull horns. I'd get film time. Nothing like film time to make the horns beautiful. They'd all be picadors, but where would the camera look? At me. At the bull trying to stay alive.

Granny clapped his hands. "Is there a problem? Now you all want to be the bull? Too late. Charlotte, you can't be the bull without surgery on your ears. Listen up. When the matador flips her cape a third time, the picadors circle and raise their spears waaay up, waaay up—picadors, spears waaay up—that's fine, let the ribbons trail—here, bull in the middle. You're trapped, see? You're angry. Picadors, move in. Bull Girl, you're surrounded. Picadors ready to strike. What'll you do?"

I snorted. I dropped my head, and the horns wobbled and weaved right and left. On the bandstand behind me, musicians wandered in from the kitchen and watched me spin circles in my tiny picador jail.

"Striking, striking—stab those spears—"

And the phone rang. It sat on a table next to the kitchen swing doors, and Granny answered because mostly the calls were for him.

"Penny? No Penny here."

I said, "Granny, it's for me."

"We're in rehearsal. We have no time for phone calls."

"Please. Just this once. Then I'll do the bull better. I'll be a great bull. Just this once?"

He passed me the receiver. "Four minutes. Not five. Hear?"

I snorted my bull snort. By the stage the Picador Girls watched me until Granny turned them away. "That's not a stab. You stab roast duck that way, not a bull. Circle up, let's try it with music. Matador, where's your cape? Christ, I leave for one second—"

From the receiver, an old man's voice spoke in my ear. "Penny Harp? Hello?"

"Yes," I said.

"I'm calling from Hollywood Receiving Hospital."

I couldn't think a minute, with picadors in the room. I hadn't tied my cap tight, and the horns slid.

"Hello? You're looking for a missing girl?"

"Yes," I said.

Madge drove me the next afternoon. I'd been there a few days earlier and hardly noticed the receiving hospital. It sat next to Hollywood Division on Wilcox, they were both made from the same brick. Pretty handy, when you think how many criminals get shot or beat up. Stitch crooks at the hospital, then cops push them next door to get booked, then on to jail right there in the division basement. It's a fast process. It's like making a Ford.

Madge parked near the end of the block and got out of her car. She lit a cigarette and waited for me. I didn't open my door.

"Right place?"

"Yeah, but I hate to get out. There's the cop station. Conejos could be around."

"Anyone could be around." She picked tobacco off her tongue with her fingernails. She ignored the pretty fountain that made the grass strip between the police station and the hospital look like a tiny park. "We're around, how about that? Get out of the car."

I did, and held up a hand to block my view of the station. What a coward I am. One arrest for murder, one night in an interview room with Conejos yelling and my new sneaky lawyer digging for what I knew, one cab driver on a Hawaiian trip to avoid testifying, Stany paying for the whole mess, bail and lawyer and ridiculous sunbathing cabbie, and I couldn't look at the building. I kept my hand by my eyes until I stood in the hospital's lobby. Even then I had trouble. The lobby seemed hollow, like the police station. One reception desk by the door, far-off sounds of crying, like the police station. Women's League volunteers instead of cops, but still.

We waited in reception off the surgery ward. One other man sat on a bench but didn't notice us. He leaned forward with elbows on his knees, no tie, hat on the seat beside him, cigarette passing mouth to fingers, mouth to fingers. He tapped both feet. Madge raised her eyebrows a couple times, and we sat with the man about twenty minutes until a nurse banged open the door and stared at Madge and me. I think the nurse wanted us to talk first, but we didn't talk, and she stood there waiting. She was *skinny*, the kind that scares old ladies and makes them bake prune cake. Her uniform sank on her.

"Who's here for Dr. Frith?"

I raised my hand.

"Both of you?"

Nod. "You're Agnes the nurse?"

"I'm Pam."

"We're supposed to wait for Agnes."

"Agnes was his wife. He was the best doctor in this hospital. He's tired. He's here all night sometimes. He shouldn't see you. But does he listen to me?"

"No," Madge said.

The nurse turned and walked down the hall. We followed, up stairs, down another hall, to a small office.

Dr. Frith was an old, wispy-haired guy with a cigarette holder and a hanging skeleton. Through his one office window he had a nice view of the police station. He rocked in a chair behind a metal desk, and his hand shook. Dust sat on his desk, the file cabinet.

"Agnes," he said to Pam the nurse.

How could you keep from hugging him? A weak doctor who loves his dead wife so much he sees her in every girl. I wouldn't want him near me with a bone saw, but if he called me Agnes, I'd answer him. I'd make-believe I was Agnes so he'd smile and eat his afternoon snack.

"You called me," I said.

"Maybe. Why would I call you? Why would I want to?"

"You saw my friend on Halloween."

"When was that?"

"Last day of October."

"When?"

"Two weeks ago," I said. There are no other ways to say it. Halloween is always Halloween.

"Blond, she was. Like you, but pretty."

"That's her."

"I never called. Open the window. Agnes, tell this girl how I like things."

Agnes shook her head at me. She moved her lips: *No window.* She raised her hand and walked her fingers across air, then ran her fingers and lifted them up and then falling, fingers falling out a window. Not fingers, she meant a person. *Don't open the window or he'll jump.*

"She was pretty," I said. "What else?"

"What else what?"

"The girl you saw on Halloween."

"Are you still here?" He chewed a cracker.

"The girl," I said.

"Agnes?"

"Not Agnes. The girl on Halloween. What did you see?"

"Oh, the *girl*. She was blond. Listen, you see that bottle in my equipment case? Bring it here."

No bottle, said Agnes's hand. Behind Dr. Frith, her hand waved at me.

"It's empty," I said. "How about tea?"

"Goddamn it to hell."

"We're going," Madge said.

"No, Madge, wait. He saw Rose. He did. He can tell us."

Dr. Frith looked at Madge. Maybe he hadn't seen Madge until now. He got big eyes and set his cigarette holder on his desk. Wispy white hair slid from his forehead. He said, "Goddamn. How much for a tickle?"

"I'm gone," Madge said.

"Tickle in the tunnel," said Dr. Frith.

"Madge . . ." I ran into the hallway after her. "He could help us. Be patient, I'm sure he'll—"

"Pull out a huge knife?" She walked the hallway fast, each step a little bounce in her rubber soles. "He's a *nut*, Penny. He's every nut in the nut dish. If he were forty years younger he'd have us tied under his desk."

"He loves his wife—"

"And they'll never find the body. I'm leaving."

We passed the room where the nervous guy still sat, elbows on his knees, feet tapping. He looked up when we crossed the doorway, paused, then dropped his head.

"We'll try again," Madge said. "We can visit the hospitals this time instead of posting flyers. Posting was a bad idea. You should have listened to me. We make a list, we go to each hospital, we check to see our flyer is on the bulletin board. We can bring more flyers and post them. The trick is to post and ask, do both. This time we'll steal paper from Paramount. There, are you cheered up? Where's that smile, Bull Girl?"

"He knows something, and you want us to walk away."

"Not walk, more like a quick trot." She pushed the hospital's front door and the air smelled great, clean, wind and sun in my face. Inside the hospital I couldn't think, with the air full of bandage smells, tape, and infection. A guy tapping his feet, bouncing his knees, waiting for bad news. If Rose came here, she was scared. She'd have smelled the same things I did. If she was here, someone saw her. Someone checked her in.

"Oh, I've got it. Oh, yes. Yes! I've got it, Madge. Where's the ambulance entrance?"

"In back probably," Madge said. "Why?"

"That's where emergencies go. If someone brought Rose here, they'd go to the ambulance entrance."

"Rose wasn't here. You're going to believe a nut?"

"Madge, he knew she was blond and pretty. She was here. Dr. Frith's office isn't that far from the back of the hospital. What if he saw her? I don't mean as a patient, I mean he happened to see her walk by or he passed a room she was in. Don't do that with your eyebrows. It's possible."

"Our flyer said she was a blonde. He never saw her. He read her description on the flyer. What a mess."

"I'm going to the ambulance entrance."

"You'll ruin your shoes, walking through that grass. At least take the sidewalk."

"You coming?" I started to ruin my Wallflower shoes.

"Goddamn you," Madge said, and she followed me.

CHAPTER 21

Don Ameche, who was glum and blue all through the shooting of *Down Argentine Way* while his wife lay so ill following the birth of his new son, is all life and fun and pep again, now that Mrs. Ameche and the baby are home.

—*Photoplay*, November 1940

The ambulance entrance was more like a doctor's office, with a few people sitting around holding their arms or elbows, whatever hurt.

"You can't see Dr. Ostrander." A nurse checked off names on a list. She sat at a desk by the door and wouldn't look at us. "These people are waiting, and besides, he's with an emergency." No, she hadn't seen Rosemary. No, she hadn't worked Halloween. Only the doctor and the surgical nurse worked that night, but we couldn't see them because we didn't hurt anywhere. Could we please go now so she could help those in need?

"I know plenty of girls like you," Madge said. "I've met them all. You wear a little hat and that makes you important."

"That's right," said the nurse. "I've got the hat."

"I've got five bucks," Madge said. She handed a bill to the nurse. "We won't take more than a tiny minute."

"He's behind this curtain," said the nurse, and she pulled the curtain so we could step behind. She slid the five into her blouse.

The curtain divided a big room. On the nurse's side, the nurse with the hat, was the reception desk and chairs for people holding what hurt them. On our side was a row of beds with smaller curtains between, and at the back, a long counter full of books and medical things, pill bottles and jars of cotton or throat sticks. A man in a doctor's coat stood at the counter reading a book. People lay on the beds, curtains open or pulled shut.

"There he is. What's his name? Asslantern? Go ask him before he cuts someone open and we have to smell it. I already smell sour milk. A whole sour refrigerator."

"I can't pay you back," I said to Madge.

"The five? Sure you can. There's always a way. My feet are wet from that grass and I want out of here. Go ask him."

I did. I walked right up to him, and he heard me and turned, and he sure wasn't Robert Taylor, but close. He had the brown hair and eyes, but this doctor's smile was bigger than Bob Taylor's, really big, so his lips stretched beyond his cheeks. It was a beautiful smile until the top of his face sat on his smile and weighed it down.

"We're looking for a young woman about my age who might have come here on Halloween night."

"A young woman," the doctor said. "Is she missing?" He kept flipping pages of the book. He kept smiling.

"No, not missing, no. We need to find out what happened to her on Halloween."

"Why?"

I couldn't think why, at least no reason I wanted to tell him. I shifted a bit. The doctor found the page he wanted and started to read.

"Gangrene," he said. He turned the book toward me, and I saw the ugly picture. Gangrene. "Smell that?"

We all smelled that.

"I don't have time to wait for your answers." He closed his book. "Why?"

"What?"

"Why do you want to know about a young woman?"

Gangrene, that's all I could think of.

"She might've skipped out," Madge said. "Didn't pay her hospital bill."

"Ah. And who are you?" He meant me.

"Her sister," Madge said.

"Ah," again. He smiled. "Maria, bed four is the amputation. Bed one can wait. Where's our ether? Sorry," he said to Madge and me. "You can talk to our billing office. They'll know who skipped payment." He tried to leave; he had to amputate someone's gangrene.

"Not the bill," I said. "It's her. Something happened to her on Halloween. Please, she was blond, taller than me, looked like Lana Turner only not those thighs, green dress, bad cut on her hand."

I could see him decide. He took a pencil from his coat pocket and bit on it. He looked at Madge and me the way a doctor does when he's deciding to tell you the bad news. Without his smile he was lovely to watch. He put the pencil back in his pocket.

To Maria: "Have her phone her husband. We need his consent. Do you have the form?"

To me: "She was here." He held up his right hand and with one left finger he fake-sawed the soft skin between his right thumb and finger. "Sliced, through tendon and muscle. She told me she'd cut her hand on broken glass, but then she also told me her name was Glinda the Good Witch." He smiled, and his face sank to his chin, like a rock on a stretched rubber band.

"How deep?"

He sawed again, then pointed to his hand. "Tendons cross here below the thumb's second joint. The radial artery runs beneath. She nicked the artery."

"You fixed her hand?"

"I would have. She needed stitches. I left her in that bed"—he pointed to a bed with a woman in it whose leg twisted funny—

"and told Maria here to clean her up. We were busy. Your friend's hand wasn't the worst I saw that night."

The woman in Rose's bed cried into a telephone: "I prayed all morning, I'm sorry!"

"Time to go, girls."

"The cut, was it serious?"

"Yes, serious, a cut to her radial artery. Not as serious as it could have been, and certainly not as serious as others. I had many patients. When I came back, she'd gone."

"What do you mean, she'd gone?"

"Maria," he said, and Maria came over. She had towels in her arms and a leaf print scarf tied over her mouth. Maria set her towels by the medical book. When she talked, her breath floated the leafy scarf. A mouth sail.

"You girls need to leave right now," she said. "You've got your answers. Dr. Ostrander, permission granted."

"You cleaned her?" I asked Maria.

"Your sister? No. She stood and left. She didn't say anything. I tried to clean her, and she left."

That wasn't Rose. She'd always been full of words. "Why would she leave?"

Dr. Ostrander to Maria: "Husband on his way?" And to me: "It's all I know. I wasn't her doctor. I never treated her. So," he said to Madge, "no emergency bill."

"She left when, around two thirty? Did you see who she was with?"

Maria said, "The man who brought her had gone, I think. I don't know who gave her a ride."

Madge, beside me, grabbed my arm. "A man?"

"The man," I said. "Who was he?" It didn't matter, because anyone could have picked her up along Sunset. That's what I'd told Rose to do—flag a car. So she did, and a nameless guy took her to the hospital, helped her inside. Then he left. The guy didn't matter, he was the ride.

"Smooth-looking," Maria said. "Dirty face."

The only smooth-looking dirty face I'd seen on Halloween was

Marty Martin, but he'd run off. He'd have been far away when Rose reached Sunset.

"Black pants, black shirt," Maria said. "I think it was a costume. He wore blackface."

But he'd run off, hadn't he? Marty with a sooty face and black clothes, scared off, wouldn't wait to see if Rose was okay. If he'd waited, he did so for another reason, and I couldn't think of many: to see what Rosemary would do, or to see what Rosemary would say. Either reason, they were to keep Marty safe, not Rose.

Dr. Ostrander wheeled Bed Four from the room. More voices, a phone ringing. Maria lifted her hands at us: *Will you leave?* Patients groaned in their line of beds, the air smelled like shrimp dip. Rose had been here. Marty Martin had brought her. She didn't wait to be cleaned, she got up and left, and all I could think, all I could feel, from my crawling skin to my fists, was that my lawyer had killed her.

Madge bought me dinner at Tick Tock. We sat in a booth and ate chicken pot pies and drank big Coke floats with foam so high we had to lick the tops. We had to wipe foam from the table. Madge used her fingers to wipe foam and then stuck her fingers in her mouth and sucked. She didn't know about Marty Martin, and I couldn't tell her that he was more than a lawyer.

"I was right," I said. "The ambulance entrance. Dr. Frith must have wandered like he does. Agnes said he stayed at the hospital all night sometimes. Why not Halloween? Say he stayed the night. He's eaten dinner, Agnes brought it before she left, but he forgets. He's hungry again. He doesn't realize it's the middle of the night. Empty hallways, and the lights buzz and flicker. *Zzzt. Zzzt.*"

"A horror show," Madge said.

"Exactly. Shadowy corners. The stairwells are gaping black holes. I can see the poor doctor in the hallways. Wandering, calling for Agnes."

"Poor doctor, my ass. We'd have to view him from behind so

we don't see him ogling patients. The camera follows him so we don't see his face. That way we notice his feet shuffling and how his jacket's too big. The jacket hangs. Then a close-up on his feet. I think Wally Beery should play Dr. Frith."

"John Gilbert."

"He's dead." Madge twirled her Coke float with a straw. Her ice cream bobbed. "Though he shuffled pretty good toward the end. Lionel Barrymore would work."

"Yes. Lionel Barrymore. Shuffling the hallways. He calls for Agnes."

"*Agnes! Agnes?*"

"He calls and calls," I said. "No Agnes. He's wandered across the whole hospital to the emergency room. He hears a noise and thinks—"

"*Tickle your tunnel, little girl?*"

"You're ruining it."

"Sorry. *Agnes? Where is my Agnes?*"

"He's closer," I said. "He sees light through a doorway. He looks beyond into a room with a bunch of hospital beds, all full, but his eyes turn to one bed."

"She's sitting, holding her cut hand. His Agnes." Madge raised one hand like it hurt her.

"Yes, his Agnes with gold hair. He hasn't seen her in so long. He misses her so much."

"We're still viewing the scene from behind. The camera trails Barrymore through the room, and we can see Rose's face as she waits for a doctor to help her. She's not Agnes."

"No," I said. "Not Agnes, but Barrymore thinks she is."

"Are you eating that foam?"

"Don't touch my foam," I said.

"All I have left is Coke."

"Get your hands off my foam."

"*Agnes, here you are, at last.*" Madge sucked a plop of my foam into her mouth from her fingers. "Mmm. *I've been looking so long, my darling. I've wandered the world.*"

"Rose is in shock. She's shocky, but she knows she's not Agnes."

"She's not Agnes. She's Glinda the Good Witch. Lionel Barrymore scares her. He shuffles near. Close-up on Glinda, eyes wide, mouth wide. Blood smears her cheek. She forgets her cut hand and knows only that she must run, get away from the shuffling monster."

"The shuffle's important, isn't it?"

"Essential," Madge said. "Monsters shuffle. Think of Lon Chaney."

"Glinda flees."

"*Come back*, says Barrymore. *My beloved. What about our ten children?*"

"Ten?"

"Anyway," Madge said. "That's how it happened."

"Then later Barrymore sees the flyer posted on the hospital board, and he remembers he'd found his Agnes."

"Heartbreaking," Madge said.

"It is, isn't it? That poor man."

"At least now we know."

Yes, now we could picture the truth, except when Glinda left the hospital: Who did she meet, what happened to her? That part was a different movie.

Madge drank the last of her Coke. She looked in her glass, empty but thick with ice cream smears. "I didn't want you to be a friend."

"I know." I looked in my own empty glass.

"I hate friends."

"Me, too. Especially when they steal my foam."

Madge looked from her glass to me. She laughed. "I'm thirsty for something real," she said. She paid for our food, and we left.

I loved that Coke float at Tick Tock. The restaurant was stuffed with people, but they didn't count. We didn't see them. We had our horror show.

If you asked me to point to a time in Hollywood when I felt

I belonged there, when moment and place came together and I'd remember them perfect and right, I'd tell you, *The dinner at Tick Tock. Madge stealing my foam and us laughing. How we built our movie and believed in it, and a radio by the cashier played "Sing My Heart."*

CHAPTER 22

Says Linda Darnell: "The person who lacks poise often manages to preserve a certain calmness of expression."

—*Photoplay*, November 1940

It was past twilight by the time we got back to the Gardens. Bath night for me. Madge parked on the boulevard behind an old pickup. I didn't know it was my brother's pickup until he yelled.

"He's calling you. That guy." Madge pointed at Will.

"Penny. Pen!"

"You ignoring him?"

I wasn't sure. I might be ignoring him, I hadn't decided yet. Will got out of his truck.

Madge watched him. "You have a date?"

"Go take your bath," I said. "Leave me hot water."

"Joe's following you. Now you've got two guys."

"Where?"

"Across the street. Past the traffic light," Madge said. "How do you get two guys and still dress like that?"

"Take your bath," I said. In front of Will's truck, across the street, and beyond the traffic light, I saw Joe in his squad car. I saw his cop hat, shiny above a face I could barely separate from shadow. I would have missed him except for Madge, who could spot any guy near her. I hardly saw him now, even though I knew he was there.

"Penny," Will said. I looked at Madge.

"I know," she said. "Hot water." She ran the alley between buildings. She'd gulp a drink first, a big whiskey drink, then take her bath, where she'd use all the hot water and the Career Girls would yell. With Rose it had been the same, minus the whiskey.

"Who was that?"

"A friend," I said.

"You have friends here?"

"No."

"Can you talk?"

"Will. Why are you here? I'm tired. I'm not coming home to help pick."

"Talk for a minute. Just one minute. Here, sit down." He sat on the curb, and I sat next to him. I only sat down because Joe couldn't spy on me when I sat between cars. I was too low, and he couldn't see. Cars drove past and couldn't see us, either. We were part of the street.

"Mom's okay?" My feet crunched on trash.

"She's fine. She wants to know if you're coming for Thanksgiving."

"That's why you're here, to ask about Thanksgiving?"

"Are you?"

"No," I said.

"I'm sorry you got arrested," he said. The streetlamps near the curb sputtered and lit. Even with streetlamps Joe still couldn't see me, not from inside his car. I saw Will, though. I could see him without turning my face, through the streetlamp and sifting, floating dust that swarmed the light like no-see-ums. He looked speckled. "Your best friend murdered and you're arrested for it," he said.

"I didn't kill her."

"I know."

"I couldn't have."

"I know."

"You came here to tell me about Halloween," I said. "Not Thanksgiving, that's not why you're here."

"I guess," he said. He rolled a pebble in his fingers. He reached for a bigger chunk of rock. "Navels are up, over twenty-five cents a pound."

"You robbed Stany's house on Halloween," I said. "I thought you killed Rose."

"I didn't kill her."

"I know. I didn't know then, but now I do. You're still a bastard. You ran out of that backyard. I saw you, and you saw me. Except you left, you left her in that house, and she was bleeding. I helped her, and I'm arrested. What do you think about that?"

"I love her," he said. He threw his rock at a passing car. The rock hit a fender and bounced. "I'm a bastard."

"Are you here because you feel guilty? Don't talk to me then. I don't care how guilty you feel."

"You want me to leave?"

"Why would you break into houses? God, Will. Bel-Air. Holmby Hills. Those people breathe and a cop comes running. God. Did Rose talk you into it? Where's the stuff? What happens to Mom if you're caught?"

"Pen."

"What happens to Daisy, or me? What happens to Mom?"

"All right, all right." He looked toward me—looked into the streetlamp glare—and I saw him crying. "We lose it. The house, everything. But how's that different from me hiring goddamn pickers for a useless crop? We're losing everything anyway. You see what Knott's doing? He's plowed under half an acre to build that goddamn ghost town. Maybe you'd see if you came home. People don't want fruit, they want something to do. They line up to watch each other, not for some chicken dinner. Nobody makes chicken that good. Christ, they're all in a line over there staring at each other. And where are we? They're not standing in line for oranges, Pen. We have another year, maybe."

"Did Rose talk you into it?"

He shook his head. "You don't listen."

"I listen," I said. "Here's what I heard: You have to rob houses because Mr. Knott wants to buy our property. Poor Will, trying to hold the family together. So Rosemary meets the wrong guy and they decide, *Hey, let's rob movie stars,* and Rosemary talks you into it because you're a sucker for her, and you become this night bandit who runs when Rose gets in trouble."

"I didn't know you were there. I panicked," he said. "We ran right by you, and I saw you, but I didn't know it was *you.* I couldn't figure it. I mean, I was scared. Later I kept thinking, did I see Pen or not? I didn't know what was real."

"What's real?" I was angry, but I understood, because I'd felt the same a year ago after my date with Teddy. Even with thighs that hurt when I walked, I still thought: *Did it happen? Did Teddy shove me against that wall until the paint chipped and nails wedged in my back?* The bad things we never imagine happening to us still seem like they couldn't happen, even after they do. I wasn't pushed in a room and forced until I bled. Will didn't see his sister when he turned coward and ran out of Stany's yard.

"You're wrong," Will said. "Rosie didn't talk me into it. She wouldn't have done that."

Right, because afterward it seemed like she couldn't have, even if she did.

"I went to her. I had the idea, but I didn't know where, you know? Rose knew where people lived and she had guts, but she still didn't want to. I told her that Mom and Daisy depended on it. I said Daisy was near homeless."

"That's a lie."

"How do you know?"

"You didn't go to her. You wouldn't do that."

"I did. My idea, Pen. Besides, it's not so far from stealing cantaloupes or tomatoes. How often did we sneak into somebody's field? Houses are just a stretch more. Not much of a stretch."

"We had rules."

"There's always rules! Any field without cars. Tomatoes and squash and watermelon—"

"I don't remember those rules. We only stopped at company-owned fields."

Will threw another rock at a car and I heard *ting* when it hit. From the car came a voice: "Hey! You throwing rocks!" But the car was moving past us, down the street.

"You're something, really something," Will said. "You know? You want to think Rosie's so bad she talked me into robbing houses. You've changed her already, in your mind. You don't remember who she was. And you want to think I'm bad because I left her there and ran off, and you're the good girl because now you're charged with her murder. Yes, I ran off. I heard the glass break, and God help me, I didn't think of Rosie. I should have. I kill myself in my head every day because I love her and I ran. I *love* her. You know what happened to me when the glass broke?"

"No."

"You don't. You were sneaking around the bushes. The whole house I didn't like, the way the pool sat in the backyard. Any stuff we got we'd have to run around the pool with it. That took too much time. Some of the houses up there, the pool is set off from the house, to the side or by the master bedroom. There's always a back door so we can haul out stuff in a straight line and pass it guy to guy. We had that scheme down. But at that house, we had to go all the way around the pool with every trip. I already felt nervous."

"Guy to guy? Teddy, right? You and Teddy steal stuff, pass it guy to guy."

"Shut up. You want to hear this or not? Did you see the streetlamps that night? Christ, I'd never pick Holmby Hills."

"Rose picked it?"

"Some guy. The slime. Rosie knew him. How do you think we picked houses? The slime told us which ones. But Holmby Hills with all that light, Christ. So yeah, I was nervous. I held the ladder and Rosie climbed up. That window was painted shut, I swear it. I said stop, because I saw the window was stuck. I couldn't yell it, but I called out loud as I could. She must have heard me. I swear she heard me. She kept shoving the frame with both palms, and

I thought of how Mom's always doing that, always pushing something that won't give, you know?

"And I'm at the ladder seeing Rose bang at that goddamn window, and I'm getting scared, and all I can think is me in jail and Daisy with Mom, all alone. Then the glass cracked. It happened *slow*. Rosie hit the glazing, and I could see the crack start in the corner and crawl up. Rosie lifted her hands to hit again, and I called 'Stop!' I know she heard me.

"Then it all shattered, and I hid my face and chunks of glass hit me, and I heard glass crack on the ladder, and when I looked up again Rose was gone. The window was just a frame with shards stuck in the glazing, and goddamn it, I didn't think of Rose or where she'd gone. I saw Daisy's face. I ran."

"Did anyone see you?"

Will had thrown all the little rocks. He felt on the curb and brought up a three-inch chunk of concrete. He bounced it in his hand. "Besides you? No. Maybe. Probably not. I didn't see anyone. I'd come in my own pickup just in case. I didn't see anyone drive off. I didn't go home. I drove to Santa Monica and parked. I felt awful and so glad to get free, and I couldn't stop shaking. The only thing in my mind then was Rosie."

I didn't believe him. I thought the only thing in his mind was Rosie, but Daisy, too, and himself already changing how he remembered it: *Did I really run because of Daisy, or am I thinking of Daisy now? I can't remember thinking of Daisy, but I must have. I wouldn't run otherwise. Would I? I wouldn't leave Rose.* What Will told me, his thinking of Mom, I didn't believe him. I still don't know if it's true. I believed him about Rosemary hammering a crack and the glass breaking, but in my mind I've changed it a bit. Now I have a new memory, even though that night I only heard the glass shatter and I didn't watch it happen.

In my new memory I can tell what Rose is thinking. She hits the window frame with her palms, really hard, because she's mad at me. I've just told her she can't rob this house, not this one, not ever. She hates me and I hate her. We hate and love each other. She hits the window. The frame doesn't move. She hits it again, and gets madder at me because the frame doesn't move. She hears Will call to her from the ground, but she ignores him. She thinks of me and hits the glass, not the frame. She sees herself in the glass, cracked now, and the crack slides right through her reflection. She pulls her hands into fists and doesn't hit the glass. She hits herself *within* the glass. She hits the reflection of herself.

"I'm going in." I stood and stretched. Across Hollywood Boulevard, Joe watched me from inside his dark squad car. "Early call tomorrow," I said. "Give me that rock."

"What, this?" Three inches of concrete in his hand.

"See the windshield of that car? What'll I get if I hit it?"

"The cop? One buck. I'll give you one whole dollar and a picture frame. I took the frame from Errol Flynn's house."

A pretty good windup, solid release, and the chunk sailed from my hand toward a windshield that reflected all the lights of the street. If I'd thrown the rock from in front of Joe's car, I'd have to watch myself do it—throw the rock at my own reflection. I'd be like Rosemary pounding a hand on her glass face. But I threw at an angle, and I missed. The chunk hit a fancy blue Packard on its fancy door. It rang like a dinner bell.

"You still can't throw a goddamn ball." Will tugged my skirt. "Thanksgiving?"

"Why not come here? Bring them here. I'm under arrest. I shouldn't leave town, I'm being watched."

He answered no or yes—I don't remember. I don't think I heard. I was seeing Rose see herself in a window.

CHAPTER 23

Technicians at one of the big studios have developed the echometer, a device that pursues elusive sound rebounds to their source so that they may be put to death.

—*Photoplay,* July 1929

When I was twelve, I didn't like kissing games. Rose called me silly. She said kissing is good, especially when you're twelve and it's July and dark and firecrackers sell a nickel a string on 4th Street. She bought three strings, then stole matches from her Aunt Lou.

Here are the rules: Light a firecracker and throw it. If it explodes in the air, nobody gets kissed. You pass the match to the next player. If it hits the ground first and then blows, you get to choose two people and they have to kiss. If it's a dud, you have to kiss someone. The game is fun with a lot of people. The game isn't fun when there's me and Rose and Will and Teddy, a heat wave, a hot night, airless, and we're playing in Aunt Lou's yard so Will and Rose can kiss without getting in trouble. That meant I had to kiss Teddy every time.

Aunt Lou yelled out the screen door, "Rosie, you seen my matches?"

Rose held the matches in her right hand, a firecracker in her left. "Where did you set them last?"

"Hell, then. It's hotter than a good French whore. I'll try the bedroom."

She'd look for another ten minutes, easy. Rose lit the firecracker. In the glow I saw the outline of mounds across the street. A watermelon field. Rose aimed the cracker for Will. "If this were a snowball, I'd hit your eye out."

When you're twelve, it's how you flirt.

Will laughed, Teddy peeled crackers off the string, I watched Rose, and Rose threw the lit cracker far over us. It fell on the ground and then blew. Teddy tossed the string to my brother and pulled me by the hand into the mock orange. We shoved between bushes and porch, and he kissed me hard on the mouth, no tongue, because he couldn't work his tongue and his hands together. One tooth jabbed me. His face dripped and smelled like the watermelon we'd broken an hour ago. Hot watermelon vines. His hands felt up my shirt to my chest.

"Time," Will said. Will had to call time twice to get Teddy from the mock orange. "Time," Will said. "Above the waist only. What are you doing?"

I pushed down my shirt.

"Why don't your bubs get pointy?" Teddy asked me.

"I don't know."

"Rose has—"

"Kiss Rose then." I left the bushes. I bent a branch so it snapped him.

Aunt Lou stood on the porch in her housecoat, rocking on fat ankles. "You lighting those firecrackers with my matches?"

Rose lit another. "If this were a snowball, I'd take out your whole eye."

"You've never seen snow," Will said.

Rose threw the firecracker and kissed Will quick, in front of everyone. He didn't pull away, so Rose pushed on his chest because she'd thrown the lit cracker straight up. She pushed him. She probably saved his face. Instead, the cracker blew by his ear and he fell.

"That's what you get," Aunt Lou said. "That's what you kids get for swiping my matches."

"He's bleeding," Teddy said.

Rose on her hands and knees, screaming. "Willie," she said. Her shirt parted, and I saw her breasts and how Teddy was right. I stared at her breasts. She held my brother's head and screamed and wiped blood off his ear with a finger. I saw the whole picture like my eyes were a telescope and I watched them in the distance, at the far side of a field. My brother's ear trickling blood, him not moving; Rose's shirt; Teddy kneeling, too. Rose's screams, across a field. I smelled sulphur and hot melon. I was twelve with sore breasts and telescope eyes.

"What are you doing? Don't stand there, get your dad." Teddy grabbed my ankle and shook me.

CHAPTER 24

Kidnappers always have been one of Hollywood's most horrible menaces.

—*Photoplay*, November 1940

"We'll play golf in the morning with Jack and Mary," Stany said, "then a dinner party at Zeppo's. A small group, nothing fancy. Zep and his wife, a horse or two. I'm kidding about the horse."

"Tomorrow," I said. "You're sure."

"Eugene's going duck hunting. He'd better shoot enough to share. And, let's see, Hank's staying home with the family. Oh, here's Preston. Preston! Bill wants you in Stage 9. Emma's decided to hibernate. First the shedding and now this. Are snakes bound by contract? No, don't answer." To me: "Okay, I wasn't kidding. Zep lives on a ranch, so several horses are invited. What's Thanksgiving without a horse? You don't have plans?"

"I think so. My family's coming. Are you sure Thanksgiving's tomorrow? I don't know what to do with them. Where will they stay?"

"Your wardrobe's improving," Stany said.

"I borrowed from Madge." Madge borrowed it from Rose. And Rose borrowed it from—who? Who had money for wool gabardine with thick gold braid? Lavender wool so thin and smooth I crunched the skirt in my hand and it never wrinkled.

I wasn't going to wear Rose's clothes. I meant it at the time. When Madge first picked through Rose's clothes I'd wanted to burn them. Then Will and I talked, and I slept and woke, and in the closet the lavender dress started humming. *You've never*, it said. *Never in your life.* I tried on the dress. I had a list of things that I'd never, all girls do, and I didn't want the dress to be on that list.

"I'll wear the squirrel dress on set," I said, and I did. I sat by my fake parents. Madge sat by hers. We all sailed on a ship that didn't exist, and in its dining room that really was Stage 10 at Paramount, the buffet food began to smell. The fake chefs sliced prime rib that smelled old like I'd worn it for days.

Preston signaled, and Stany became Jean the gambler, who looked at her compact mirror, and what she looked at was us: Farm Girl and Femme Fatale and Wallflowers and Career Girls and Old Maid. We all tried to get Hank's attention while he sat in a booth. We'd been coached: look coy and friendly. Not *too* friendly. Don't overact or get up. Don't *move*, Farm Girl.

Jean, not Stany, studied the room through her mirror. She talked to herself, like perfect girls do when they see the rest of us. How we all wanted Hank but couldn't get him. Stany, I mean Jean, of course, in the most beautiful gown on the set: her black sparkling shortie and a crepe skirt with a split that showed her leg each time she stuck it out to trip Hank. He walked past Stany's table, where—oops!—she tripped him and then blamed him for it.

Take four. She stuck out her leg and Hank, fourth time, didn't know it was there. He tripped.

"Lunch," Abbott said. I changed out of the squirrel dress and stood on 11th Street looking for Madge.

"Wait," Stany said. She was still dressed like Jean the gambler. I waited and watched her watch Avenue P. I couldn't tell why she watched. I looked down Avenue P and saw three armored knights dragging a wooden horse to a sound stage. I saw a security guard hitch his crotch.

Stany watched the wrong avenue. She should have watched the corner of Avenue L, because that's where Detective Conejos and Joe marched around, onto 11th Street, where we stood.

Conejos reached us and shook my arm with his hand. "Is this her?"

"Yes," Stany said. "Her."

"Me?"

"Nobody kidnaps my son," Stany said.

"Your—"

"He told me," she said. "Do you know the mess I cleaned up that night? You have any idea?"

Joe pulled my arms behind me. I heard the rattle of handcuffs. "You're arrested."

"Why?"

"Breaking into my house," Stany said. "Trying to steal my kid. Leaving your blood on my heart pine floor. I had to refinish that wood, and I'm not happy."

"What? I didn't break in. Your kid—"

"My kid saw you on Saturday night," Stany said. "At my house, where you ate all the shrimp. He comes to me, he says, *Mommy, the lady. I know her.* I say, *Why aren't you in bed, you little fuck?* And he says, *I know her, Mommy. The ugly skirt lady. I saw her on Halloween, she was here.* I'm no idiot, Pen. I don't believe a half cup of what the kid says, but this time—"

"I didn't—"

"This time—"

"Fingerprints," Conejos said. "It's great luck for us that you're a murderess. We matched your booking prints to ones found at Missy's on Halloween."

"Detective Conejos called me this morning to say the prints matched. I'm so mad at you. You left a mess in my home," Stany said. "I should write you a bill. One broken window and a whole wood floor. Plus the towels Harriet used to sop up blood. She used every towel in the house plus a mop. Do you understand the mess?"

"Not kidnap, it was robbery . . ." I couldn't stop. I kept yelling. There's a rule that says the worse trouble you're in, the more you need to yell. It's not a very good rule, but there we were, me and Stany, on the Paramount back lot, yelling.

"Robbery," she said. "Sure. That's why nothing was taken. A Tang horse on the dresser, and it's still there."

"A horse?"

"Shut up," Conejos said. "Shut up, Penny Harp. You and your lies. We put together what happened. We reasoned it out."

"Great," I said. "Let's reason in private and not with the whole cast." A few girls clapped. Stage hands, Wally the makeup guy. Preston stood with his gallon coffee cup, happy, planning his next script. He took a flask from his jacket and sprinkled his cup. Preston-style thoughts rose from his head: *A girl tries to kidnap a movie star's son and botches it, then fate makes her the movie star's friend.* Yes, he could see it. Yes, he'd make them yell, too, but funnier, more bouncing around.

"You must have known Missy'd be gone," Conejos said. "You met her on set that day and heard her talk about evening plans. You went to the Palladium, then you took a cab. Rosemary Brown insisted on coming with you. I don't think she knew your plans, not Rosemary. She came with you and when she saw what you planned, she tried to stop you."

"She what?"

"Tried to stop you," Conejos said. "We found her prints at Missy's, with yours. Anyone with a heart would have stopped you. For one woman to take another's child—Miss Brown couldn't allow it. And you couldn't allow her to interfere."

"I get it," I said. "I killed Rose and then climbed the ladder."

"No," Conejos said. "Get it right. We found Rosemary Brown's prints *inside* Missy's house, which means you killed your friend after she climbed the ladder to stop you. She fought and you pushed her against the window."

"You're saying the window broke and cut her neck?"

"You picked up some glass," Stany said. "In your right hand. You shoved that glass into Rosemary's neck. Poor you, the glass cut your palm at the same time."

"This is garbage," I said. "Stinking garbage. If you want truth, how about this? Rose climbed that ladder. She broke the window. Stany, the blood on the floor was mostly hers."

Stany didn't like my version. She shook her head and the beads on her top bounced, but not enough to make Preston notice. Not enough bouncing at all. Comedy has to move quick, snap-your-fingers fast, dialogue spinning. Time for a pratfall. Someone has to slip, hard.

"Why would Rosemary Brown want my son? She had no reason. You told me yourself she'd landed a speaking role."

"Oh, God," I said. "If I took a cab, how did I bring a ladder?"

Joe pushed me then, down Avenue P, and I walked. I kept yelling at Conejos, "Did I *find* the ladder? Did I steal it from someone's garage? Did you think about the ladder?"

We all walked—Joe, Conejos, Stany, Preston, extras, stage-hands, cows, Egyptians, whoever and whatever was on the lot, and me handcuffed—down the long Avenue P to the security booth at the Bronson Gate. A parade, led by me in lavender gabardine.

"Did I carry Rose's body? Did I put her bloody corpse in a cab? Where would I hide a stolen kid? Who is thinking here? What happened to Rose's clothes? Are you all dumber than me? Stany? You said you were my *friend*."

"Oh, not that *et tu* stuff, Pen. Nobody does Shakespeare in Hollywood."

Anyone who watched from the front would think me a star. They'd see a blond woman on a stroll, hands behind her back and all her followers, her *people*. If you'd stood at Paramount Pictures outside the Bronson Gate, that's what you would have seen. It's what my mother saw, and my brother, Will, and Daisy, waiting on the other side.

"Where did you get that dress?" Will asked. Not *hello*, not *Why are you in handcuffs leading all these people, and who are the idiots in the cow suit*, just his face stuck between the gate scrolls and *Where did you get that dress?*

Joe unlocked the Bronson Gate, and it creaked and swung.

"You know exactly where I got it," I said. Conejos squeezed my arm and walked me past my family. "Why? Why did you bring Mom? And Daisy?"

"Thanksgiving," Will said. "You told us to come. What's the

surprise? We wanted your dorm key. What did you expect? Were *you* going to cook?"

"So Hollywood has brought you to this," Mom said. "Hand-cuffed in front of your mother." She wore her best hat and gloves. Her shoelaces dragged, untied. She held Daisy's hand. I think Daisy was crying. She had her eyes squeezed hard, and no crying sounds, not from our Daisy.

Conejos sat me in his car. If I hadn't been handcuffed and shifting to sit without cracking an arm bone, I could have waved to them all. They stood inside and outside the Paramount gate. Friends and enemies and family, a good crowd scene for Preston.

The heroine is arrested unjustly. She waves to her family from the police car, hoping for a sign of support, but none comes. Her mom and brother stare but don't wave. She's crushed. Then Stany lifts a delicate hand in friendship.

No, make it betrayal. Scratch that last. The friend shakes a delicate fist.

Scratch again. Move instead to heroine's sister. Two-shot on Mom and little sister. The silent little sister lifts her arm to the police car. Cut away to heroine sobbing, unable to help her sister or herself. Then Mother begins to sob. Perfect. The heroine has to hurt when her mother hurts. Cut to heroine's face, extreme close-up on heroine's face. End of scene.

CHAPTER 25

Paulette's new Mexican coiffure is a Hollywood sensation. The center part continues down the back, and the side braids are interwoven with velvet ribbon that ties in a bow.

—*Photoplay,* November 1940

Mexican hookers are mean. They're beautiful, sure, they all look like Dolores Del Río. But they sleep in their makeup. They carry knives in their girdles, and they file their hairpins to points. They wear an extra layer of clothes to cover their bruises. They've been thrown out of their homes. Not even their mothers speak to them. It's true; everyone knows it.

The three Mexican hookers in my jail cell made sure I sat in a corner. One stood in front of me, one to my right side, and one to my left. I could draw a dot to dot and make it look like a wall of hookers cut me off from the world. They spoke Spanish and laughed a lot, and the middle one, in slinky red rayon, lifted her skirt to show me she didn't have on underwear. Oh, they laughed! *Show the girl how you can squeeze your thighs and make whistle sounds. Show her how far down your throat you can suck. Use her finger.* I don't speak Spanish, but sometimes I could tell, depending on what followed their talk.

I lived in a jail cell for four nights with the hookers. I didn't wear an orange shift like the first time I was arrested. I kept my lavender dress, but I wished I hadn't. There's not much you can do with wool gabardine after three Mexican hookers and four nights on concrete.

The hookers slept two at a time, I think so I couldn't attack them. Once when the two side hookers were stretched on the concrete, sleeping, the middle one sat on the flat cot and cried. Her hands shook, and she rubbed them together. I pretended to sleep, but my corner was dark, and I had my eyes open. I watched her scratch and rub her hands. I had made my mom cry and watch me get arrested, and my insides felt like I'd been swept with a sharp rake, my eyes swollen and raw, but I think this hooker had it worse.

I liked her then. She had something wrong with her hands, and she didn't want the others to know. She couldn't eat much, but neither could I. Oatmeal in the mornings, for lunch chicken or meat loaf sandwiches, and stew at night, every night. Turkey stew for Thanksgiving. The night guard would walk by our cell and make kissy noises, and the hookers all waggled their fingers or shoved out a hip and answered in Spanish I didn't understand.

The hookers thought I was funny, how I pushed myself into the corner and pulled up my knees. I tried not to cry in front of them. They got bored with me and ignored me, but never slept three at one time. On Sunday morning they left the cell, and the guard stood in the doorway and winked at me. He asked me, "What did you learn from the Mex whores?"

I knew what he meant. His wink told me.

"Your turn," the guard said and switched on the hall light. The hookers had been gone all day. In the hall I saw shadows, shadows all over, shadows of bars that crossed the hall floor and hit my cell at an angle. The guard unlocked my cell. The hallway clock read five thirty p.m.—between sandwich and stew time—and the guard pushed me in front so I walked the hall before him, then down a flight of stairs to another hall. He knocked on a door, and when it opened he hit my shoulder with his hand. I went in.

After the dark cell, the light made me squeeze my sore eyes and look through my eyelashes. A small room. Stany was there, and Detective Conejos, and Marty with one swinging lock of hair that had missed his morning Brylcreem. They sat around a long table, smoking. I didn't see Will until the guard shut the door. He sat in a chair behind me. He wore a blue jacket that didn't match his work pants. He didn't look at me straight on. Instead, he picked his fingernails and leaned forward, elbows on his knees.

"Why are you here? Mom's all right? Will?"

He wouldn't talk or look at me.

"What is this? Why do you have my brother?"

"I've met your whole family," Conejos said. "Sit down, please. You look like you slept on the floor. How's your breathing? We've got your vaporizer. Need it?"

My breathing was fine. I sat on the only empty chair, beside Will.

"Okay, then. Your brother has told us a story. It's a good story. Not the best I've heard, but he doesn't have the practice you do. Brother, you want to tell your story again?"

Will shook his head.

"I understand." Conejos tapped his cigarette on the table corner and turned pages in his notebook. "I'll tell it for you. The story starts last April. A young man in need of money. How'm I doing, Missy? I want the right touch of drama."

"Shut up and talk," Stany said. She lit a cigarette with the butt of her last one. Through the layers of smoke, her hair was dull, like shelled walnuts. She'd tucked her curls into a snood.

"April. Your brother and Rosemary Brown cook up an idea between them. She moves to Hollywood and lets her beauty open doors. Ciro's, Earl Carroll's—you ever been to Ciro's?"

"No," I said.

"Me neither. Did you know Rosemary Brown had?"

"She didn't tell me."

"Hmm. Good story. But you've got practice. Anyways. You live here a while, it doesn't take long to figure out the social agenda. Go to a few nightspots, read the columns, pretty soon you know where people are going to be. A party at Ciro's, you show up. Say MGM needs girls to fill a room, you show up there, too. Rosemary Brown knew how to do this. Why didn't you?"

"I don't know."

"What do you know?"

I shook my head. This wasn't my story.

"Rosemary was smart. She discovered that she could be seen, get a free meal, just for showing up to these places. Meet studio guys, get noticed. And she discovered something else: If certain people were out at the clubs, that meant they weren't at home. All those beautiful homes. Right, Missy? Bel-Air, Beverly Hills—empty. Oh, maybe a maid or two, but that's all.

"Now, your brother says he came up with the burglary idea. His idea. But say that's true. I still believe it was Rosemary who figured out who to target, and when. She'd go to a fancy party or she'd read a gossip column that gave the invite list for that fancy party, and she'd call up your brother here. Brother drives to town, brings a ladder in his pickup—yes, he showed me his pickup—and we've got ourselves Bonnie and Clyde."

"Cut it out," Stany said. "Penny's brother is not Clyde. Look at him. He's crying, for crap's sake. Cut your goddamn drama and keep to the story."

"The story," Conejos said. "We don't know all the story. According to Clyde here, that's the end of it. Rosemary Brown used the ladder to get into houses, then opened a door for Clyde. He'd drive away with the goods. Did I get it all? That right, Clyde?"

Will hadn't raised his head. His shoulders shook from crying. The tears fell from his face to his lap.

"What about the kidnapping?" I asked. "What about Rosemary following me up a ladder?"

"That was a good story. I liked that story," Conejos said. "But Clyde here told us a better one, and he showed us a few items from a long list. Then I found a few more items in your bedroom at the dorms. Maybe you're Bonnie, *hmm?*"

"Conejos," Stany said, like a warning.

"What I can't figure is, where's all the other stuff on my list?"

He shook an envelope from his notebook and opened it, then slid out some pages. "Inventory. Fur coats, cash, jewelry, little statues and artistic shit people set on their mantels, some clothes. But we already know about the clothes, don't we?"

The hem of Rosemary's dress waved to me from under the table. I could see it if I leaned my head back and looked down. It wasn't Rosemary's dress, though. I didn't know whose it was. I could be wearing Dottie Lamour's lavender tea gown, or a cocktail number sewed for Claudette Colbert by Irene. Movie stars have designers so famous they don't need last names. I could be wearing Irene's design, and I'd slept in it on a cell floor and been kicked twice by a hooker whose hands shook.

It didn't matter. The kicks and the dress, they didn't matter. Will had turned himself in, and I knew he did it so I could go free. I wanted to cry since he was crying. I wanted to hug him and make him stand up, not hear him sniffing and swallowing beside me. I loved my brother right then. I wanted to hit him for telling the truth, but I loved him.

But I couldn't decide about Marty. I didn't know why he sat at the table. Thief or lawyer? Which was he today? I couldn't ask him, and when he looked my way he did just that—looked my way but not at me.

"The stuff," Conejos said. "Where is it? Your brother gives me a couple of ashtrays and says he sold the rest but won't tell me where or how. Don't watch him, Penny. I'm the one telling the story."

"That's enough," Marty said. He sounded like a lawyer now. "You've got your burglar. Let Penny go."

"Nothing of mine was stolen," Stany said. "I've got a question for Pen." She raised her eyebrows and pointed her cigarette at me. "You didn't break into my house to steal my kid?"

"No." My voice shook. "I didn't break into your house at all. I *fell* into your house. I tried to stop Rosemary."

"Irrelevant," Conejos said.

Stany pushed back her chair. "My ass. You bet it's relevant. Your story stinks, Detective. I've seen better scripts thrown out the window. What happened to Rosemary Brown? Where'd she go? Who met her and killed her? Penny says she didn't kidnap my kid, I believe her. Marty, we're leaving. And Penny's coming with us. You"—to Conejos—"lock up Clyde if you want, or throw him back."

I can't really explain; you'd have to watch her. When Stany's mad, the whole room is full of her, and the walls nearly crack. She talks fast, and each word is solid and spit out. The madder she gets, the faster she talks and the more she wants to say. Even Will had to raise his head.

"It wasn't just Will and Rosemary," I said.

"What do you mean? Pen, what are you saying?"

"Yes, it was," Will said. "Just me and Rosie. Nobody else. Pen, shut up."

"But it wasn't," I said. Marty had been there, and probably Teddy, too.

"That's enough," Marty said. "Penny, shut up."

"Just me and Rosie," Will said. "Pen didn't know anything. Get me out of here. Lock me up. The only other one guilty is Rose, and she's dead."

"You'll tell it all to me," Stany said. She sat in her personal chair—*Stany* stenciled on the canvas back—at Stage 10, Paramount. I sat, too, on a fake staircase. Stany had clicked on one table lamp. Marty wandered the set, picking stuff up like he was in Woolworth's and he'd find a price on the bottom.

Stany felt cozy here. She said it was more home than her own. Any set, any movie, any studio—Stany could live in it. She could pick up her chair and walk next door to RKO, she could unfold her chair and move in. That's why she drove us here, at night, and made security unlock the gate.

"Everything," she said. "Tell me every tiny thing."

My back was sore from the concrete. I wanted to sleep. My brother had just confessed and I felt relieved but dull inside, empty. I told her my story. I started with the Palladium, fifty klieg lights down Sunset, and how beautiful Rose had looked. I told her about Tommy Dorsey's orchestra, the crowd, and how at nine p.m. Dottie Lamour had walked onstage and together she and Dorsey cut a ribbon. The Palladium, officially opened. Dottie's hair, parted and rolled on each side. I told Stany I wanted the steaks couples ate in the gallery, but I couldn't afford to eat. I drank, though. Rosemary bought me drinks.

Stany frowned when I told her I'd seen Franchot Tone. He shared steak with a girl a lot younger than me. Claude Rains, Ida Lupino—I saw them, and George Burns, and Mary Astor sitting on some guy's lap. Like MGM, I said. More stars than in the sky. Then Rosemary on the dance floor, whispering: *I've got a secret.*

The cab ride, the hike into Holmby Hills, lanterns on Faring. Glass breaking. I told Stany and it happened again for me, like I was crouched on gravel and the glass exploded a ways off, about where Marty tapped keys on Preston's piano. Panic in my chest and shoulders. It was only Marty in the dark sound stage, not glass, but the telling and the dark made it real.

"So the glass broke," Stany said. She was a good director.

"Broke, right. So I ran. Not away from the sound, like I should have. I ran to the glass." Marty stopped tapping the piano. He waited for me to tell Stany I'd seen him, and seen Will, running out of the yard. I told Stany, but not everything. I didn't tell her about two men who ran past me.

"How bad was she cut?"

I held my scarred palm out, so Stany could see. "The glass cut my palm, but that's nothing. Rose's cut made me want to throw up."

"Who brought her to the hospital? Do we know him?"

We do. "Some guy," I said. From across the sound stage, *tap-tap* on the piano keys. *Tink-tink.*

"But you don't know who it is? Did anyone recognize this guy?"

"Described him to me, but no—the nurse didn't recognize him."

"Not at all? How old was the nurse?"

"Why?"

"Just—how old?"

"An average age," I said. "Not too old."

She nodded. Her chin circled around. "Not too old. So she'd probably know who she saw. She'd recognize somebody famous."

We weren't talking about Marty anymore. We weren't talking about Rose, either. I didn't know what we were talking about.

"Stany, who's famous?"

"Just a minute. Marty, stop playing that goddamn piano!"

"Stany, don't cry."

"Let her," Marty said. His dress shoes clicked on the cement floor. He pulled a handkerchief from his jacket and handed it to Stany. "If she needs to cry, then it's best she do it with us, and not in front of him."

"Him?"

Stany blew her nose.

"Him—her husband? Him—Robert Taylor?"

"It's stupid," she said. "He didn't do it, I know he didn't, but I couldn't stop thinking, and my mind kept playing the scene over. What if he did, what if . . ."

I had that rock in my stomach—the one that gets thrown when I finally understand a thing—that big rock—and I said, "You thought your husband killed Rosemary."

"I knew he couldn't have, but I kept thinking."

"Your husband is Robert Taylor."

"He wasn't even in town," Stany said. "He was off playing *vaquero* in Palm Springs. He was on a *horse*. He was gone five days with loads of other men—Jackie Cooper, for God's sake—all riding horses. He couldn't have killed her. God, I hate it. I hate that I love him this much. I'd kill him myself if I could."

Marty stood behind her and rubbed her shoulders.

I said, "How can you think your husband's a killer? He didn't know Rosemary, did he?"

"Shut up," she said.

"He knew Rosemary," I said.

"Shut up," she repeated.

"Didn't you hear her? Shut up," Marty said.

"Are you really that jealous of a dead girl? Why would he know Rosemary? They never met."

"They did," she said. "I was there. I didn't know who she was, but you don't forget someone who looks like that. Christ. We see beautiful girls all the time, they crawl off every bus that comes through. But *her*. I know Bob, and I know anyone who looks like that whore Lana Turner is trouble for me. Fucking Sweater Girl, my ass. We went to the Troc a couple months back and there she was, Rosemary Brown, just like Conejos said. Cadging drinks from some guys. Only I didn't know her name. Bob followed her all fucking night. Like a fucking sniffing, drooling dog.

"Then Halloween I show up for work, and there she is again. She's one of the new extras on set. I got sick. I wanted to kill her."

"Marty, did you know any of this?"

"No," Marty said to me. "But I know Bob and Missy, and I could fill a truck with all the pain this town brings."

The man sounded good. I was convinced. He'd helped Rose, and he coddled Stany. I could hardly remember that he also would have taken whatever Rose stole from Stany and hocked it for cash.

Stany rolled her head so Marty could dig into her neck. "I had this idea. I'd get to know Rosemary, or at least get close enough to warn her off. Something like that. It wasn't a full idea yet. I don't know what I would have done. It doesn't matter, because that night Rosemary went missing." She laughed. "I was sure Bob ran off with her."

"He was on a horse," I said.

"I know! A horse, and he called me at night that whole trip, and it's all wonderful except I was sure he'd snuck back to town, picked up Rosemary, and then holed up with her somewhere."

"Relax," Marty said.

"Shut up, Marty. Goddamn vulture." She hit his arms away from her neck. "What if he came back to town? What if he wasn't on a horse? He came back to meet her and then something bad happened. He wouldn't kill her on purpose, would he?"

"He didn't kill her," Marty said.

"I knew you had a reason for being my friend," I said. "All the girls hate me because of you."

"I'm sorry. No, I'm not sorry. I'd do it again. I needed to know about the case, who Conejos suspected—"

"You got me out of jail."

"Well, come on. You didn't kill Rosemary. She didn't take your man like she tried to take mine. Am I irrational? I'm feeling crazy inside."

"Bob didn't drop Rosemary at the hospital."

"No?"

"No," I said. "The doctor described a man who wasn't nearly as handsome as Bob."

Marty winked at me. Goddamn vulture.

"Think about it," I said. "If Bob had a date with Rose, she'd stay away from your house. I mean, yes, she'd go after Bob Taylor. Who wouldn't? Excuse me, Stany, but that's the truth. Bob Taylor, there's nobody like him. So say Rose and Bob have a date. No, I'm saying what *if*. Marty, keep rubbing her neck. Just if. I was with Rose on Halloween, and I know what she did. No Bob. So if they had a date, they'd have to meet later. Except that later she was breaking into your house. If she'd arranged to meet Bob later than that, she'd call off the robbery. She wouldn't risk breaking into the house where Bob lived. Bob could be anywhere: at home, at a club—"

"I was at the Cocoanut Grove, and he wasn't with me."

Marty chop-chopped on her neck. "That's because he sat around a campfire singing trail songs. He played *vaquero*. Missy, you've got to trust that if Hedda Hopper says thirty men are riding circles in the desert for a week, then that's what's happening."

I got tired convincing her. Marty didn't look tired, but he did this a lot. Stars paid him to do this. I said, "If, just if, Rose knew she'd see Bob on Halloween night, she wouldn't have broken into your house. She wouldn't risk it."

Stany believed me. She stared up at the catwalks. Finally: "Then who killed Rosemary?"

"I don't know," I said.

"No idea," Marty said. "Why don't you ask another question: Why bury her at the Florentine Gardens?"

"For me," I said. "So I looked guilty."

"Do you know that for sure?" Marty asked.

"Who cares, if it wasn't Bob?" Stany brushed her hands on her trouser legs and stood. She'd had her moment and her ideas, and she was done.

"What about me?"

"You?" Stany looked at me like she'd just noticed a grease stain.

"I need my job. Am I still on the set? I can't be fired, Stany. I need to work."

"Well, how do I know? I can tell you, Preston's fed up and Miles Abbott's furious. He said—what did he say? He said if you showed up at the back lot he'd arrest you himself. Does that mean you're fired? I've never been fired. I wouldn't know."

"You're the one who had me arrested in the back lot," I said.

"*You're* the one who left blood in my house. Did I mention that we had to strip the floor? All right, all right. I'll talk to Miles. I'll tell him your brother's the thief. That'll make him happy. Can we get out of here now?"

The wondering, trying to see why I was given her friendship— I could stop thinking about it now. I can't compare it to much, but imagine a movie star visits you, takes you to autopsies, lunch, digs you out of jail, and pays for a lawyer. She saves your job at the studio. She loans you a gown. Wouldn't you wonder? Wouldn't you walk around all day thinking, *Why? What does she want? How am I special?*

You would. You'd think, *how am I special*, and you'd think maybe you weren't. Maybe it was a mistake.

CHAPTER 26

What Happened to Hepburn? Is she really different, as some say, from the hard-to-manage gal she used to be?

—*Photoplay*, November 1940

Marty dropped me at the Gardens. On the street, the lampposts had become Christmas trees, and I didn't stand on Hollywood Boulevard anymore. Yesterday it had turned into Santa Claus Lane, and it would remain Santa Claus Lane until after Christmas. I was in jail and had missed the Santa Claus Lane Parade, Roy Rogers, Rudy Vallee singing, everything.

"You might make your second show," Marty said. The second *Hail the Indians* show. I heard the orchestra from the Zanzibar Room as soon as I opened the car door.

"No revue on Sundays. I'm tired. Sleeping on concrete is tiring."

"We got you out as soon as we could, but Thanksgiving—"

"I know. Thank you, Marty. I'm tired." I swung my feet from the car to the sidewalk.

"Penny—"

"What happened to my mom?"

"Huh?"

"When I got arrested, this second time, I mean, my mom and sister were there. Where'd they go?"

"Nowhere," Marty said. "Missy gave them a studio tour. I wasn't there, of course. I'm repeating what she told me."

"She had Conejos arrest me and then she took my family on a tour." Inside the Zanzibar Room, horns bleated Paul Whiteman. Horns and a bass thumped, loud enough to make me pull my legs back inside Marty's car and shut the door.

"She's on your side," Marty said. "Missy, I mean, not your mom. Sure, she'd drop you if it saved Bob, but that's all cleared up now. You've got to realize how hard it is for someone like Missy. Her entire life is ruled by studios, so she's going to protect the one thing she can control."

"Bob."

"Well, yes—as far as Bob and MGM will let her."

"And in a few years you'll handle the divorce." The car was too dark to see Marty blush, but I hoped he did. The Christmas trees on Santa Claus Lane didn't give as much light as before, when they were streetlamps.

"If she allows me the honor of representing her, yes, I'll handle the divorce."

"I mean," I said, "you've handled Joan's already, and Stany and Joan are best friends."

"You can call her Missy," he said. "Everyone does."

"You're disgusting. You're like lice on a cow."

He waited a bit, then: "Get out of my car, Penny. I was going to thank you for keeping your mouth shut earlier this evening. Now I realize you have no control over your mouth. Don't slam the door. I hate door slammers."

I shut his door. I tried not to slam it, to show him my perfect control. He gassed the car and the motor roared, then he was gone, and I saw I wasn't alone on Santa Claus Lane with the Gardens orchestra leaking sound. Across the street, between traffic, I saw a squad car. Hollywood Division. Joe Flores in the front seat, watching me. He might have parked there for hours, waiting for me to get home.

I could have left him parked, ignored him, but I didn't. I was tired and filthy. My hip was sore where one of the hookers had kicked me. My back hurt. I wanted to hit Joe Flores, who sat clean and awake in his squad car. He watched me until he saw me run toward him, then he faced the windshield and wouldn't turn.

I pounded a fist on the window. I pounded two fists. I yelled, "Open this window. Roll it down. I'm not leaving until you roll it down."

He rolled down the window about four inches, face toward the windshield, not looking.

"I hate you. Understand? I hate you following me everywhere, looking at me, thinking, *She's a killer, I'd better follow her all day.* I see you at the studio. What did you find out? Am I a killer? Bastard. You're a cop bastard." I hit the window again and then I left him like that, staring at the windshield.

I entered the Gardens by the side door, straight into the Zebra Lounge. Two black-haired headliners drank at the bar. Other people sat in the lounge, a few at tables, nobody I recognized. I was looking for Granny or Madge. I limped from my sore hip, and my knuckles hurt from banging on Joe's window.

"Finally," said a city voice. Madge sat behind me, in a booth. A Career Girl sat beside her, crying. Madge wore a winter white cape from the right side of the closet. She slid out of the booth. "How is jail? Same as you left it last time?"

"Now you're making Career Girls cry?"

"Naw. They don't need help. Crying comes naturally to them."

"Is she okay?"

"She'll be dandy."

"Where's Granny? Do I still have a job?"

"You're still Cree Girl, goddamn you. At least, I think so. I think Granny likes you. He must be attracted to jailbirds. However, I don't know about your job at Paramount, because Abbott was pissed almighty when Joe dragged you off again. Even Zukor heard about it. You'd have a better chance of keeping jobs if you could time your arrests."

"I was looking for you," I said.

"Granny said you'd got out. I have to talk."

"My brother took my place in jail. He confessed to the break-in at Stany's. And my lawyer, he should have confessed. He's a bigger thief than Will. Oh, and Stany thought Bob Taylor killed Rose."

"*Bob* is it now? *Bob?* Sit down. I'll kick out the Career Girl. I need that drink. Do you have any money?"

"Not a cent."

"Goddamn cops. They probably searched your bag and took everything. Sit down, you look awful. Oh, and guess what I borrowed from Apache? A bottle of gin. It's nearly full. We'll have drinks here and then go to our room for real drinks. Your dress is ruined. We can try vinegar on that bloodstain, but I'll bet it won't work. That's a damn shame. Who beat you up? Don't you get baths in jail?"

"Are you sure I'm still Cree? I need to make sure. Where's Granny? Is he around? Let me look in the Zanzibar. Get the drinks."

"Detective Conejos was here on Thanksgiving. He searched our room."

"He searched? What for?"

"The closet. Your side, to be exact. He tried to search my side. He said the clothes were stolen, can you believe it? I tried to tell him they'd been passed down from our good friend Rosemary."

"Then why are you wearing the cape?"

"You're lucky to have me," Madge said. "Lucky I was there, able to tell him which clothes were stolen and which were mine. Rosemary didn't steal much. A few items, a blouse and hat. I pointed them out, he took them, and the closet's still full." Madge pulled the hood of her cape up and over her hair. She looked like a huge moth. She looked pretty, a little mysterious, her face shadowed from the dim bar light. The two headliners at the bar had turned to watch Madge in her hood, and Madge knew they'd turned to watch her, and she loved it. She winked at me.

"Drinks," she said. "And I need to talk."

"Did Zukor find your parents?"

"Zukor. I hate him. I read that Nazis are releasing ten thousand French. But what about Americans? I've been calling Zukor all day. Have you seen him?"

"No. Just my slimy lawyer."

"Your lawyer? Here? God, I miss Riverside. I miss my bedroom. You know how good this cape would look in my closet?" She grabbed my wrist and pulled close. "See Granny. Come back fast, okay? I'll get rid of the Career Girl. Promise me. Come back fast."

I left Madge in the Zebra. I promised her, and I left. I opened the connecting door between Zebra and Zanzibar and searched for Granny. He stood by the lobby door talking to a starlet I recognized from some movie—Charlie Chan, I think. She might have been cast as a victim. She wasn't important. The victims die pretty early in Charlie Chans. Granny saw me and waved.

"Please, Granny." I started talking before I'd made it through tables and across the room. "I need the job. I'll be the best Cree."

"I didn't fire you," he said. "I should have." He squeezed my arm, and I followed him away from the starlet. "Breaking into Missy's house, what were you thinking?"

"I didn't break in," I said, but the orchestra began "I'll Never Smile Again," and Granny couldn't hear me above the trumpets. I could barely hear him, and he was yelling.

"Missy called twice. First she told me to kick you out in the cold, no paycheck, nothing. I was quite prepared to do it, too, but she called again and said she'd changed her mind. If she weren't Barbara Stanwyck I'd kick you out anyway, and I still might if you screw up the routine again. Madge told me you stole hairpins from the Apache headdress. Yes, she told me, no denying it now. You know how much those headdresses cost? I need more girls like Madge and a few less girls who steal and cause trouble. Come with me."

Madge said what? We cut through the Zanzibar, through tables with diners who glanced up, watched me and my filthy dress and hair, and sawed at their roast beef. The starlet sat with whatever single man 20th Century Fox had forced her to date. She watched Granny and me cut through the room, and I watched her eat chicken and boiled potatoes. Some chicken fell from her fork, and her date said something I didn't hear and didn't have to hear because I knew it exactly. *Is that how a star eats? Dear God, do I have to be seen with a pig?* It's what any guy would have said. The girl should stab her chicken instead of scoop it.

In the Zanzibar's corner, Granny opened the greenroom door. "Start with the clothes rack. All those outfits need to be rehung and then alphabetized. And why the hell is Charlotte's skirt on the floor? Get the costumes done, and then wipe the counters. I can't walk through the room without face powder all over my suit. Why the look? You're not pouting, are you? You want your job? You missed Thanksgiving night, huge Indian night, you should have been here. I had to dress a barmaid as Cree Girl, and she didn't know the steps. Plus she kept burping. You know how embarrassed I was? Clean this room."

"Madge said it was me? *Madge* said it?"

"Thank God I can count on her for the truth."

He left me in the greenroom. I could have gone back to the Zebra, gotten the drinks and Madge, and then cleaned the greenroom while we drank and talked. If Madge hadn't blamed me for the headdress, I would have gone to the Zebra and fetched her. I should have. But I was mad. I hadn't touched Apache's hairpins, and I knew Madge wanted to be Granny's new niece, and being a tattletale is like a niece without sex. Madge wasn't about to tattle on herself, so she used me. I was in trouble anyway. I'd been arrested as a murderess and thief. Therefore, I probably sabotaged the Apache headdress. Sabotage was one step worse than murder, as far as Granny was concerned. *Kill my girls—I can replace them—but don't fuck with my costumes.*

I alphabetized the Indian costumes. It's not hard to do when each tribe is sequined across the chest, Apache to Zuni. Then I wet my dress in the sink and wiped the counters with it, still wearing the dress, using the skirt as a rag. All that lovely lavender gabardine. I pulled off the gold pocket braid so the counters didn't get scratched. I'd ruined the dress in jail. I was filthy already, and the dress made a fine dusting rag.

I worked on the greenroom for about forty minutes. Granny never came back. I'd added dust and cosmetics to my skirt and attractive sweat to the armpits, so I left by the stage door, out the back of the greenroom to a hallway, and then outside to the alley where Rose's body was found. The dust in the greenroom had made me start wheezing, not bad but enough to notice. The chill outside made me rub my arms.

I circled the Gardens to the Zebra Lounge door again. Madge wasn't there. She'd gone; she'd drunk both drinks and bought more, drunk them and waited for me, and waited, and then bought a shot of whiskey, then left, the bartender said. She'd walked unsteady and forgot her nice cape, the bartender said, then came back for the cape and wrapped it tight. Good thing, he said, those girls at the bar were eyeing the cape and one had moved close to it, but then Madge came back for the cape. Too bad I didn't have a cape, he said. Cold outside at the end of November. I'd freeze in two hours the way I was dressed. I needed a blanket and coat. Didn't girls on the street know how to get by these days?

I was wearing my Girl on the Street dress, pockets torn, slept in, collar ruined by the hooker who threw me at a wall. In the Zebra Lounge, the black-haired headliners sat at the bar and dreamed of Monte Carlo. The Career Girl was gone.

I'd find Madge and apologize. I'd wake her, and we'd drink Apache's gin. She'd talk, because that's what she'd wanted, to talk to me, to see me listening. After all, her parents were lost. She was homesick. And who cared about hairpins? I wasn't mad anymore. The Zebra was still and empty, the headliners sad, bartender tired. I felt my heart knocking around for no reason. I went to the dorms.

Once, I don't know when, the dorms had been a family house with three floors, shingled and boxy, one family living there with farmland around them instead of busy Hollywood Boulevard.

They didn't know the boulevard would run west and east along the side of their house, with the Florentine Gardens in front, so they planned their main door facing east. Their front door now faced nothing, faced the brick side of the next building. The farmhouse's backside squeezed another building, but once, I don't know when, it faced farmland there, too, so the family had built an outside deck off the third floor.

They could sit on warm nights and look at their farm. They could climb stairs directly from outside to the deck, to a door, so Mr. Farmer could come from the fields straight upstairs and get changed instead of tracking mud through Mrs. Farmer's clean floors. Thoughtful of Mr. Farmer.

I tell you this so you'll know what I saw. No night is dark on Hollywood Boulevard, not even when it's Santa Claus Lane. The Christmas trees make the night gray, not black, and shadows are larger, and so are the dark corners where Christmas trees don't reach. There's always an orchestra on the other side of a door. Most evenings klieg lights pass over and about, drawing people to Hollywood to a premiere or opening, and if you're not there, you're nothing, you might as well leave town, that's what the klieg lights say. Drunk flyboys sing on the boulevard, strolling from bar to bar. Long Rolls-Royces drop off fur coats with people inside them. Those people don't know they're on farmland. I wonder if Madge knew.

I saw her on the stairs at the back of the dorm. She faced downward, sprawled, one arm over her head and the other touching the dirt at the stairs' base. The white cape covered her body and most of her legs. Her feet, what I could see of them, looked wrong, like she'd gotten in a fight with her feet, like she'd been headed downstairs but her feet kept going up. And her head, face to the stairs and turned enough my way to make me scream. Her mouth hung open, and all that dirty brown hair, thrown free of her wool hood by the fall, stuck to her mouth and tongue. Blood dripped out of her right eye.

I kept thinking, *I wonder what crop they planted here.* Was it corn or summer melon or—what did they see, those farmers, when they

CHAPTER 27

Woman-skin owes its witchery to that tender *look* and *feel*, so different from a man's.

—*Photoplay*, November 1940

"You could have pushed her," Joe Flores said.

"We all could have. Maybe it was you."

"You're not crying," Joe said. Behind him, Detective Conejos stretched a measuring tape from Madge's feet to the top of the stairs. A cop stood on the deck with the tape end.

"I'm sorry. I'm probably too tired to cry. I tried to get teary before you got here so I'd look how I feel, but I'm dry inside. I'll try crying tomorrow."

"It makes you look guilty, not crying. And now you're sarcastic. You say you found her dead, but she's your friend and you can't get one tear out."

"Tomorrow," I said. "See me tomorrow."

"About thirty feet," said Conejos. "If she fell from the deck to where she landed. She might have slid or rolled down the stairs. You didn't touch her?"

"No," I said.

"Bartender says she was drunk." Joe Flores was the first cop on the scene. Not hard to be first when you're parked across the street waiting for something to happen.

"How about you two?" Conejos asked.

In the crowd of people around the stairs—most of the Gardens staff and a few revue girls—the two black-haired headliners nodded. One said, "She drank by herself in the bar. We thought she was crazy, ordering two drinks. She'd drink hers, then the one for her invisible friend."

A laugh, agreement from the other headliner. "Her invisible friend threw her down the stairs."

Conejos looked at me.

"No," I said. "I am not her invisible friend."

"She was crazy, then," he said. "Climbs these stairs and throws herself down."

"She was in the bar waiting for me."

"And you were—"

"Cleaning the greenroom." My stomach and throat folded inside me. She was my friend.

"I'll bet you were alone," Conejos said. "In the greenroom alone, no one to watch you, with a back door so you could sneak out, run to the dorm, throw Madge down some stairs, sneak back to the greenroom and finish cleaning. Every mess you've been in, you're sneaky."

"I was alone," I said. "Granny left me alone in the greenroom. I was there about forty minutes, used the back door just like you said." And came out here, and found my friend. My drunk and wonderful friend.

Conejos climbed the couple of stairs from dirt to my friend's body. He lifted the cape, lifted my friend's head and twisted it side to side. "Feels like rubber in here. Joe, hand me the flash. No, don't hand it. Point here, at her chest. See? See what I'm seeing?"

"A bruise," Joe said. "Could be a bruise. Hard to tell."

"She fell or was pushed," Conejos said. "An argument and some hitting, she could have stepped back, been too close to the stairs and fell. Someone in the dorm might have heard arguing."

"I've never seen her on that deck until now," I said. I couldn't say her name, I'd folded that inside me, too. "None of us have a reason to climb the stairs. What's there to see from the deck?

Garbage at the back of these buildings? Why would she climb the stairs tonight? It's cold out."

"She has that wool cape," one of the headliners said. "We noticed the cape right off, in the bar. She was warm in the cape and talking with her imaginary friend. Maybe the friend wanted to climb to the deck."

Conejos looked at me.

"No," I said. "I am not her imaginary friend. I'm her real friend. I mean, yes, I met her in the bar and we talked for a bit—wait, Detective, let me talk—and then I looked for Granny while Madge bought us drinks. Two drinks, one for me, one for her. Granny sent me to the greenroom. Forty minutes later I ran from the stage door to the bar. Madge had already left."

"You were her imaginary friend after all," Conejos said.

"I've never been on that deck. She wasn't crazy. She was drunk, but what's odd about that? She was drunk most of the time. Why would she pick this night to climb to the deck? Joe, you were watching the Gardens. Don't shake your head. I know you watched, you sat in your car. Did you see her leave? Who else did you see?"

Conejos looked from me to Joe. "You watched her from your car? Who told you to watch her?"

Joe pointed the flash at me, in my face. I heard his voice but could see only glare from the flash, so I squinted my eyes.

"You think she was killed," Joe said. "You could tell Detective Conejos some nutball story about how she drank too much and fell and we might buy suicide, we might, but you're saying someone killed her." His voice sounded different, not mean anymore but like he'd discovered something, like he was trying to understand. "You don't know how to save yourself, do you? If Madge was killed, you're a suspect. You know that, right? You don't have an alibi, and you're talking yourself right into jail again."

Conejos, still looking at Joe, said, "I want to know why you're watching her."

"I'm tired," I said, and I started to cry, the flash glare making my eyes hot, my face hot. My legs curled beneath me, and I sat hard on the dirt by the stair rail. My friend's arm hung about five inches from my head. I leaned and touched her arm with my forehead, and although she was empty, I knew she was empty, I was glad to touch her that way. I made her arm rock by pushing it with my head and then pulling back. Her arm swung and hit my forehead, little smacks that woke me and made me cry. I know I can't make people come alive again. Madge was killed and she'd stay killed, and I could rock her arm and pretend she was thumping me in the forehead. *You're stupid,* she'd say. *You're fucking stupid to let me drink alone. I waited for you.* All while Joe's flash burned my eyes.

"My coat," Joe said. His coat wrapped my shoulders. Joe didn't seem there, I barely heard him. I'd left the Gardens. I was with Madge, and somehow I was with my dad, too, because he'd understand why I needed to move Madge's arm and how badly I needed her arm to hit me. I was with my dad and his little brother. As kids they'd played ball on the same team. Afternoon practice, dad at bat, brother in right field, the ball leaves the bat and shoots straight to his brother, hits him on the chest, and his brother falls before the ball hits the ground.

Three days in the hospital, my dad held the ball in his hands and sat in a hallway. Nuns carried towels back and forth. The ball had stopped his brother's heart. But what do you do while you're waiting, brother's heart confused, beating slow and then faster? Do you throw the ball out, hide it in the trash and sit with hands empty? Or do you hold the ball because, through that ball, you're holding your brother, and the only way he'll live is if you keep tight on the ball, not drop it, not let a nun complain and take it from you, keep holding the one thing, a baseball, that makes you guilty but frees your brother?

Dad understood. To feel guilty is to feel alive. I'd left Madge in the bar, and I knew she waited for me. I was angry. I let her wait. She'd told a lie and blamed me for a stunt that was hers, so let her wait. Damn her. All that happened next, her leaving the bar, her climb up the stairs and her fall, blame me. I held that ball in my hands. Her arm was more alive on my forehead than I'd felt in three days, *bang,* her arm hit me, *bang,* and when Conejos knelt beside me and caught Madge's arm, I leaned against him, I felt his hand on my dirty jail hair, and I rubbed Madge's cold hand and kissed her arm by the inside of her elbow.

I should tell you if my dad's brother lived, but you probably guessed. Baseballs don't have that much power.

CHAPTER 28

With unusual social implications, the picture tells of three youngsters banded together in business and friendship in a wasted country after the War.

—*Photoplay*, August 1938

Rosemary phoned me at the end of summer a few months after Dad died. I'd just seen her at Godding's, we'd worked the same shift, and I'd see her again tomorrow, same shift, our schedules the same all week. I didn't know why she'd call me now. I remember I stood at the telephone desk in our short hallway, more of a foyer, by the stairs, and I played with the light chain so the table lamp switched on, off, on. Each tug and the lamp gave a tiny *sst* of electric surprise.

"I'm leaving," she said.

"Where to?"

"Inland. It's best for Aunt Lou. She went to a doctor."

"You didn't tell me. What did the doctor say?"

"She needs drier air, the desert," Rosemary said. "We're too near the beach, and—"

"Nevada is good. Arizona."

"—tomorrow."

"What?"

"You heard me, Pen. We're going tomorrow. Aunt Lou sold her house."

I tugged harder on the light chain. The lamp rocked on the desk. "You didn't tell me. You put up the house and never said one stinking word."

"You know how I am, Pen. I'd cry, then you'd cry, then Willie would have all these questions, and we'd all cry, and I can't take it, Pen. You know I can't."

"Tomorrow?"

"You can write me." She gave me a post office box number in Pomona. "Tell me how Will does. I'll miss him."

"You're packed and everything? Did you quit your job?"

"We'll be gone early morning."

"For how long? When can Aunt Lou come home? If you sold your house, where will you live?"

"Write me, Pen. You can tell me the news."

"There's dancing this weekend. We have plans. What about your wedding? And peaches to set up. I'll need help with the peaches. What do I tell Will?"

"I'm sorry. I'm sorry, sorry, sorry, sorry . . ."

Our poor table lamp. It was old. Nobody much liked it. Rose wouldn't say, but she was four months pregnant. I didn't know at that point. You know those words that fall out of your mouth, like a lamp might fall, those words that have to be said and then later, maybe two years later, you think, why did I say them, why did I think them important, what if I'd just shut up?

"Selfish," I said. "You were born selfish. I'm sick of you. What about Will? You're leaving without telling him? He won't understand. What'll he say? Should he write? You're making me tell him you're leaving. You're taking Aunt Lou, and we can't tell her good-bye. Why Pomona, Rose? And you owe me five dollars. Fuck you, and I want my five dollars, Rose. Fuck you in Pomona."

I swept the tiny shards from where the light bulb smashed on the floor. I had to sweep a huge area because you know how glass flies. A few minutes later Will came in with dirt on his boots, and I swept that, too. Then Mom came home and said, "You learned to do housework? When you're finished with that broom there's groceries, don't let them rot."

CHAPTER 29

Then Love Came to Henry Fonda. He was 18; she was 17; and their great romance was kept alive by daily letters in which Hank excelled as a wordy wooer.

—*Photoplay*, November 1940

The day after Madge died, some girl stuck her head in my room without knocking. "A Mexican's here. He said you'd know who he was."

I only knew two Mexicans well enough for them to come calling. "What time is it?"

"I'm not a clock." The door shut, girl gone. The mattress across from me held two lumps of Career Girls. Madge's clock, when I found it under her clothes pile, read six a.m.

Bumps and creaks in the hallway, then a knock on my door. In the other bed, one lump rolled and groaned. I answered the door in my nightgown. I didn't care. I'd see either Conejos or Joe, and both knew me in feathers, an orange jail shift, a stolen, filthy tea gown.

Joe was in the hallway. I lied before; I did care. My nightgown was clean, but ugly like any cotton nightgown, good for wearing but that's it, no looking allowed. I closed the door on Joe.

"I'm checking on you," he said.

"Fine," I said. "I'm fine."

"Shut up," said a lump in the next bed.

"Did you sleep?"

"Yes," I said.

"Oh. Okay. I'll just—I was—"

"I'll come down," I said. "I'll meet you downstairs."

He was dressed in his cop suit, like last night only without the dirt that he'd added from sitting with me by the stairs. I was dressed in a stolen gown, one of the simple gowns Rose must have stolen to wear in dark restaurants. This one was ivory rayon with a sash that tied in the back.

"You're clean," Joe said.

"Last night I took a cold bath without suds. It wasn't my bath night." Girls moved around and in front of us, eating toast and pulling out curlers. "I didn't set my hair. I guess barrettes are okay. The main thing is the gown. I don't want Abbott to yell at me. Today's scenes are dinner dress."

"You're going to the studio after what happened yesterday?"

"I don't have a choice. I mean, I do, but it's not a fair choice. I mean, I might be fired at Paramount, but I won't know until I get there. Are you here to arrest me?"

"I'm here to take you to breakfast. Your call is at eight, right?"

"You know it is. You follow me around, you know my schedule better than I do."

"I'm sorry about that. I'm sorry you don't like me following you. No, I take that back. I'm not sorry."

"I'd like pancakes and ham and a Coke. No meat loaf. Can you promise no meat loaf?"

"No meat loaf, no handcuffs."

"Freedom? I'm not sure I'll know how to act. You better set the handcuffs on our table so I feel comfortable."

He took me to The Grotto across from Paramount. The restaurant opened before talkies, old place, and everyone ate there—stars and everyone else—because the food was cheap, and if you wanted to split a plate with someone you could, without getting in trouble. I wouldn't split my breakfast with Joe. I ordered my own pancakes, side of sliced ham, and a Coke. I'd eat it all. Every bite.

"I just came from the coroner's office." Joe plopped eight sugar cubes in his coffee. "I saw Chippewa."

"Her name is Madge."

"What's her last name?"

"Chippewa."

"Come on, Penny. What's her last name?"

"I don't know. She never told me. I don't know any girl's last name, except for Rosemary's. And my own. Why don't you know her last name? You know everything else."

"What do you mean? What do you think I know?" He lifted his spoon too fast from his cup, and coffee sprayed his shirt.

"You're dripping," I said. "Coffee spots. And I think you know everything. You follow me, you work with Conejos, and when something bad happens, guess where I see you? Oh, come on, guess. Don't bother wiping those spots. They won't come out without vinegar. You won't guess? I see you looking at me. Rosemary gets dug up, and where are you looking? At me. Madge vomits all over Bing Crosby's front lawn, but who do you watch? Me. Madge falls down stairs, Stany accuses me of stealing her kid, everything that happens, you're there, but what are you doing?"

"Watching you?"

"Just like right now. Why am I here? What do you want?"

"Your dress today is nice."

"Stolen," I said. A waitress set down my pancakes, and I wanted to swoon. My lips shook while I looked at those pancakes. Butter all over, syrup until it dripped off the plate. I'd been eating watery stew for three days. I stuffed my napkin in the neck of my gown.

"There you go again," Joe said, "acting like I've got something against you."

Pancakes, heaping, buttery mouthfuls. And here came my ham, fried and shiny.

"Penny, how much money have you got?"

I kept chewing.

"Can I look in your handbag?"

"What? No! Why, are you making me pay for breakfast? What are you doing? Hands off my handbag!"

"Fifteen cents? That's all you got? What if I told you that Madge had more, a lot more?"

"You're lying," I said. "We're living on apples and hard-boiled eggs. If she had money she'd tell me. Give me my handbag." I let syrup drip on my chin like old men do.

"Over two hundred dollars. Twenties, tens, some fives. Do you know where she'd get money like that? She bought drinks last night."

"But that's just drinks. A gin fizz, a couple of whiskeys. She bought drinks, not a fur coat. She wasn't rich. I know she wasn't. She couldn't afford to go home to Riverside, and she loved it there. She spent most of her money on bottles and she wore Rosemary's clothes."

Joe reached out, wiped my chin, and showed me syrup drops on his finger. He rubbed his finger on a napkin, but I swear he wanted to put the finger in his mouth. I saw his lips open then close, and I knew he thought about licking the syrup. "You make it hard to believe you," he said. "Wearing that dress, but only fifteen cents in your coin purse. If I'm watching you, it's only because you're suspicious. I'm around when bad things happen because of my job, but why do I see you every time? What's your reason?"

I finished my ham. I drank my Coke.

"Where did Madge get two hundred dollars?"

"I don't know. Do you want the rest of this Coke?"

"Where did Madge get two hundred dollars?" He reached for the Coke and I handed it to him, same time, and our fingers bumped.

"I said I don't know." My stomach was full. The pancakes had exploded inside me.

"Penny, I've decided I really like you. I just don't believe you, that's the problem."

"Your check," said our waitress. She handed the bill to Joe.

I took the napkin from my collar, dipped it in my water glass, and wiped my chin and hands. "I have to go. If you don't mind, I'll leave while you're paying the bill. What time is it? Thank you for breakfast." I already had out my studio ID and my mirror, and my handbag hung on my arm. I left Joe at our booth.

I sound cold, don't I? Frosty Girl. First Rose died, and next day I'm back at work. Then Madge dies, and next day same thing. Big breakfast, and I'm on time for my call. Nothing shakes me, I'm Frosty Girl.

Except I wasn't. I threw up pancakes on Marathon Street. I leaned at the curb and shook and cried and wiped my face. At the studio, nobody asked about Madge. Nobody missed her, not Abbott or anyone. I stood in a second ship with my ivory gown that had water spots from where I'd scrubbed off my breakfast, and next to me were my new fake parents, and Preston set up shots from all angles and had us watch another empty booth. The only people on set were extras and a couple of contract players; Stany and Hank had no scenes today. Just us, background shots and some staring, waiters with trays.

Inside me I was so quiet I disappeared. I hardly remember the scenes from that morning. I missed Madge. I was angry that nobody asked where she was. I missed Rose so badly my hand ached, between thumb and finger where she'd been cut. I had to rub the spot and press hard.

I said earlier that girls don't make friends because what if they're both up for a role. I had two friends, Rose and Madge. I knew Madge was a friend, and I liked her anyway. And Rose had always been my friend, my whole life. Now I had no friends, and my thumb ached. I'm not Frosty Girl. I needed my best friend, so when Preston dismissed us late morning, I went to find her.

After work I changed clothes, rode a bus, transferred, rode, and walked down Spring Street. My feet hurt. I skipped lunch and counted the dead: Rose, Madge. My dad. Madge tired of waiting for me. Drunk, climbing the stairs to the outside deck. Madge in a winter white cape.

From Broadway, the Hall of Justice looked dried out, like an old sandwich. Somewhere in the top five floors sat Will, in the county jail. He wasn't alone. Not many crooks got their own cells, so Will shared his with someone. I thought of the Mexican hookers and then of Will's cell, and all of them together in that cell, with the red hooker gagging on Will's finger and then mumbling Spanish at night.

I wouldn't visit Will. I needed the basement. I didn't know how to reach the coroner's office from the front, so I went in the way I did last time, with Stany, through the hearse doors. I had to wait for two hearses, but it takes a long time to unload and weigh one body, with paperwork, so when the second hearse backed in, I let the attendants pull a sheet-wrapped something out of the hearse and set it on a gurney. They hit the doors with their gurney, and I followed them inside. I saw two signs: RECEPTION AND COOLING ROOMS, with an arrow left, and CORONER'S OF-FICE, with an arrow right. The gurney guys must have wanted a cooling room. I turned right.

The halls again, a few benches and then swinging doors at the end. Through them a secretary and an office door beyond. The usual dark wood. It could have been any man's office, except for the vegetable smell.

"Here's Mr. Nance's noon appointment." His secretary with her guest smile, pretty except for her nose and eyes, puffy cotton scarf at her neck. Small scars that her scarf didn't hide, from her chin to her earlobe, little white scratches like somebody had shaved her face.

"Yes," I lied. Yes, the coroner's noon appointment.

"You're lucky. Mr. Nance likes his lunch, and it's not often he schedules straight through."

"I'm lucky," I said.

"I'll tell him you're here."

No, that wouldn't work, not if the coroner expected two gurney guys. I followed the secretary. "I'd like to surprise him."

She stopped. Her smile stopped, too. "What's your name?"

"Pen Harp. I want to surprise him."

"He's *married*," she said, and I knew why Mr. Nance liked his lunches.

From inside the office: "Whitey, is that my twelve o'clock?"
Whitey?

"Send him in, then."

I sent myself in, and his secretary pulled my jacket sleeve.

"Dr. Nance?" I saw round glasses and a round face sitting at a desk. Piles of paper hid the rest of him.

"Mr. Nance, she pushed me—"

"I mean Mister," I said. "Mr. Nance. I'm not your noon appointment, but I have a question. One little question."

I still wore my Paramount makeup, so I looked pretty. I smiled at him. He smiled back and stood.

Whitey didn't smile at all. She said, "I told her to leave, and she just—"

"It's fine," said Mr. Nance. His smile made his face rounder. He'd parted his hair on one side, brown on top and gray by his ears. He looked like an old baseball on top of a black suit. "One question?"

"A little one."

He pointed Whitey back to the door. "A little question, then. You are . . ."

"Penny. My best friend was killed a few days ago. May I please have a copy of the autopsy report?"

"That's your question?"

"Yes, Mr. Nance."

He smiled again. "I wish I could give you a better answer, but autopsy reports are confidential. They can upset families, and they hold information best left to professionals. You said your friend was killed?"

"A few days ago. Her name was Rosemary Brown."

"It's an open investigation, yes?"

"Yes. Her autopsy was held here."

"Penny, right? I'm sorry, Penny. I can't let you look at files during an investigation. Have you talked to the police?"

Of course I had. No, not really talked to them. They'd talked to *me*, questioned *me*, arrested *me*. That kind of talking doesn't hold much information.

Whitey appeared at the door. "Your noon is here. Your real noon."

Mr. Nance held out his hand, and I shook it. He apologized again and said something else I missed because I'd turned to leave. He wasn't the right person anyway. His office didn't have Rosemary's file. No filing cabinet in here, only a desk, lots of papers, some chairs, a little lean-back couch where Whitey and Mr. Nance shared their lunches and maybe dinners, too.

Out in the hallway, Whitey ignored me. She led the noon appointment into Mr. Nance's office. I saw her desk and behind it an open door, and inside I saw shadows and file cabinets, rows of them. Lots of people die in Los Angeles County and they're buried or burned, but they live on in Whitey's file room, locked in a drawer, alphabetically. Rose lived there, I knew it.

Whitey didn't move until I walked past her. "You heard what he said. You got your answer."

"Sure," I said.

The door to Mr. Nance's office closed, and Whitey sat at her desk. She took her lunch box from a drawer, opened it, and lifted out a wrapped sandwich. "Unless you like grape jelly, you should scram."

"I love jelly."

"Scram anyway."

"You could find out stuff about anyone, couldn't you? Anyone dead?"

"So?" She bit crust from her sandwich. She sat right in front of the file room doorway, framed in it like a publicity shot.

"I'll bet you find out about picture stars, how they die, stuff like that."

"So again," she said.

"Like Jean Harlow. You know stuff about Jean Harlow, how she died?"

She wiped a purple smear off her cheek. "I know stuff you'd die to find out. You'd kill your mother to know this stuff. Sure I know about Jean Harlow."

"You go to the pictures?"

"What is this? What do you want?"

"I have a friend," I said. "She's famous. Maybe you want to meet her."

"Who's your friend?"

"Barbara Stanwyck."

"You know Barbara Stanwyck? And in return I tell you about Jean Harlow?"

"No," I said. "Not Jean Harlow. Just a girl nobody cares about, not famous. Rosemary Brown."

"Barbara Stanwyck for Rosemary Brown," she said. "That's what you're trading?"

"It's a good trade. You dropped jelly on your scarf. It'll stain."

"Get out of here," she said. "I'm buzzing the cops."

All the way to the Florentine Gardens, on the bus, I saw the shadowy file room in my head, how the cabinets lined walls and made the center walk narrow, with barely room to turn and pull out a drawer. I saw Whitey and the grape stain that ruined her scarf. Cotton sucks up fruit stains, and you can't get them out.

CHAPTER 30

Hollywood has rarely dared to be different. And when it has, the result has seldom been profitable.

—*Photoplay*, November 1940

Joe said, "Listen to yourself. Do you know how you sound?"

"I shouldn't have told you my plan. I thought you'd listen, after what you said yesterday. You said you liked me."

"I like you, Pen, but I don't believe you. I said that yesterday, too. I don't believe anything you say, and I can't—no, I won't—help you."

"I'm not stealing anything. The file room is right behind the secretary's desk. I won't have to go in the coroner's office at all."

"That's because you're not going near the building," Joe said. "You're not doing it. Here comes Mr. Abbott. Break's over."

Outside Stage 10, a group of girls saw Abbott and took last puffs on their cigarettes before flicking them down the street. Paramount must pay one whole guy to sweep dead cigarettes each day.

"I should have kept my plans to myself. I know exactly where the file is, easy to reach, I don't have to break into an office."

"You're grieving. You're upset about Madge."

"I still want that file."

"Why is it important?"

"I should be allowed to read it. I'm the one up for murder.

Shouldn't I read whatever helps my case? I have a terrible lawyer. No, that's not true. He's a good lawyer, if you want a divorce."

"You can change lawyers. You don't have to use Stany's. Get a free one."

"I know. But I need to keep this lawyer. Don't ask me why, it's all confused. I have Marty, and I can't change him, but he's not trying his hardest to prove me innocent."

"You can request the report through your attorney. Have you talked to Marty at all?"

"About the report? Yeah, I have. He agrees it might be important. He says he'll ask for all the notes on the case."

"Well, then."

"I keep thinking of what Stany said. After the autopsy, she told me everything she could remember."

"Wait. She witnessed the autopsy?"

"Didn't you know?"

"Why would I? I'm just a beat cop."

"Stany said the cut in Rosemary's neck goes in about half an inch and then angles up. Stany's theory is that a guy killed Rose, because a guy would be taller and his first instinct would be to pull up on the garrote. See? In, then up. Stany said she noticed the angle, but nobody else did. If the autopsy surgeon described the angle in his notes, maybe it proves I'm innocent. How could I stand behind Rose and then pull up on a wire? We were the same height."

"She was flat on the ground, not standing. You were behind her. Then the natural action would be to pull up."

"You're saying I killed her?"

"I'm saying you're not breaking into the coroner's."

"You need to read the autopsy report. It will prove that I'm not Rose's killer. You say you don't believe me, okay, I might be lying, but that report tells the truth. You like me, right? At least, you want to like me. Then learn the truth."

"Hey, you," Abbott said. He stood in the Stage 10 door, boxy blue jacket with shoulder pads, Paramount mountains on his tie. He pointed to the unlit red bulb above the doorway. He yelled,

"Are you working for him or me? Fuck your boyfriend when you're not working."

"All I mean is, I won't let you make a mess," Joe said, but I'd already run toward Stage 10.

That night we sat in Joe's patrol car. Rain hit the car's hood, heavy drops, fast, so I couldn't see more than a few feet before the air turned silver.

"What if I get a callout?"

"You insisted on driving," I said.

"I could have followed you here, like before. It's simpler to be in the same car, that's all."

"Leave me. I'll go in, break the lock on the file door, steal the report, and then you'll pick me up when you're done. Five minutes start to finish."

"Five minutes. I can't believe I'm sitting here while you plan a burglary." He leaned his head back and shut his eyes.

"For information," I said. "I have a right to information about my own case."

"What time is it?"

"A little past one. Joe."

"*Mmmmrrr*," he said. He was falling asleep.

"A Mexican hooker. She said something to me in jail. The second night. I couldn't sleep—you know what it's like to sleep on cement? She didn't sleep, either, and she had the cot. She said, *Gabashya estubo*. What does it mean? She whispered it."

"*Mmmm*." He scooted around on the seat. "She's a *pachuca*. Any coffee left? Give it here."

He drank coffee from a thermos. Rain made a silver world outside the car. A guy could stab a girl outside Joe's window and we'd see tinsel thrown at Joe's car by the handful. Silver tinsel. Daisy and my dad in front of our Christmas tree throwing tinsel on branches. Daisy couldn't have been much past two.

"So she talks in slang."

"What?"

"Your *pachuca*," Joe said. Rain hit the car. "'*Gabacha, ya estuvo,*' that's what she said. 'White girl, I'm done.'"

All that silvery rain. This year I'd go home for Christmas. Mom in a housecoat drinking the Knotts' wine, the dog choking on ribbon, handmade presents that could have been sweet but weren't, tatted hankies and fudge made from marshmallow creme. I hadn't returned for a big day since I moved to Hollywood, but this year—yeah, I'd go. Especially this year, since Will was in jail. But first, at Woolworth's, I'd buy tinsel for Daisy. Five isn't too old to throw tinsel.

"I see someone," Joe said.

"You're lying."

"By the door. Look out my side. No, lean over. Lean more—there. Where the building ends, beyond the second wall. See?"

"Where? I don't see—" And then I did see an umbrella held by someone tall, and another someone pressed close so they both stayed dry. "It must be them. The tall one's Frank Nance. He's the coroner. Shortie's his secretary."

"Whitey?"

"Yeah, Whitey."

"They're leaving."

"A late dinner," I said. "On his couch. I'm going."

"Don't do it, Pen. I could arrest you."

"Then as soon as Stany pays my bail I'll come back. You can stay here if you want."

We ran and got drenched, those few yards to the hearse dock. Someone had sandbagged the little dock against flood. The hearse entry stuck out two feet from its swinging doors, two feet that weren't covered by roof. Sandbags propped the doors by a freight scale and lined up so the two feet open to rain couldn't wash the whole floor. Trickles of water ran between sandbags and wet the hearse entry hall. Joe stepped over the bags and then pulled me onto the dock at the start of the hallway.

"Let's leave."

"Go ahead," I said.

"Damn it, where do we go?"

"Left, I think. Left."

Down to Posting Room Three, trailing water. All quiet there, so on to Posting Room Two. We reached the end of the hall and heard a car's motor.

"Hearse," Joe said. "Stay here." He turned the knob of the posting room. "Locked. They shouldn't come down this far. You stay and I'll check it out."

He meant well. He tried to protect me, I think. He wanted to believe me, that I was innocent. Or maybe he thought I'd discover he was the killer. He jogged back to the loading dock, protecting me or himself. I followed a little, to Posting Room Three, and tried the door. Locked. Voices at the hearse entry: "You standing around? Give me some help, officer."

"Yes, sir," Joe said.

"I've got two corpses to weigh and a widow who left her husband's balls in bloody specks on her couch. You got something more important than that? Move your wetback ass."

Then Joe's *yes, sir* again and the sound I hated, the sound I closed my eyes against, wheels of a gurney on the linoleum, fast, rolling toward Posting Room Three.

I twisted the doorknob of the next room. Locked. I twisted another one. I tried all the doors, but they were locked tight. The one room I could open I hid in. Dark, and I bumped something soft on a table. I didn't open a posting room. I'd hid in the cooling room, with a table and a wall of refrigerated crypts. Cold air and cold metal. Full crypts, with leftovers stacked at the end like soft bricks. I didn't know this at first because the room was dark. I held out my hands and bumped a table, beyond that the crypt doors on each side, the wall of soft bricks at the end. I knew they weren't bricks. I knew they weren't bricks. Corpses: hacked, withered, dangling corpses in sheets, tagged and stacked in the cooling room.

I heard the cooling room door open, and I saw the wedge of light grow when the door opened wider, and I glanced around and then fell.

I became a soft brick. I snuggled close to the brick beside me and pulled its sheet loose so it covered me, too. The cold air made my shirt stiff.

Then I smelled them—the bricks—and then that voice: "Get the other corpse. You can hear, right? Get the other and bring it. Damn, look at those holes. You want holes like this? Use a shotgun, close range. What are you doing? You gonna listen to me or run get that corpse?"

Joe's feet in the hall, running, like he was told. Through my sheet I saw a bright, round globe on the ceiling and nothing else. I rolled against the brick next to me, and I shifted the stack. I hadn't meant to. The bricks pressed against me, hard, and I had to brace my feet on the wall so the whole stack wouldn't slide.

"Roll her in here," said the voice. "Put 'em next to each other. What are you looking at me for? Fill out the tags."

"Do you know their names?" Joe's voice.

"Fuck it. I've got to do your job, too."

Scratching sounds, sheets rustling, the loud voice yelling at Joe. I couldn't hold my feet on the wall. I tried. I lifted one hip so my left foot braced harder, then the other hip, then I kicked at something that touched my leg. My feet slid, the pile slid, and we all slid, one brick on another, rolling, thumping on the cold floor.

I needed them to be bricks, they had to be, because underneath all those bricks I breathed, and all I got was brick, brick, brick in my mouth and nose. They were heavy and solid, they pressed me down, and I had to open my mouth. I needed to scream.

"You standing there? Clean it up. Shit. I thought those corpses came alive. All I need is rotten bodies. You never know what'll happen in this fucking place. Fucking rain. Clean it up, I said."

Footsteps across the room, the stack shifted, and a live hand slid through the sheets to me. Joe covered my mouth with his hand. He waited, he pushed here and there to clean up, and more footsteps retreated to the hall, to the hearse.

"Don't move," Joe said.

"Joe? Don't leave. Oh, my God. Joe?"

"I'm here. I'm shutting the door. Okay? You're okay. Let me—

it's fine—follow my voice. I'm not leaving you. Now I'm locking the door, walking—let me roll off these bodies. Don't cry, Pen. They can't hurt you."

"You don't know that," I said.

"Grab my wrist. Can you stand?"

"All these people."

"Lots of people die, Pen. This is a big city. You're not breathing good."

"They covered me, Joe. They bounced on my chest. Some of them moved on their own."

"Let's go," Joe said. "Enough for tonight. We're wet, you're half-frozen—"

"No."

"We'll warm you up," he said. "Take this towel. Rub your arms."

I took it, a sheet, not a towel. The body underneath was nude and yellow, a woman, scrim wrapped thick around her head. She slid, arms first, toward the wall and hit a crypt door. I held the sheet in one hand.

"That's it," Joe said. "We're leaving."

"No," I said. I threw the sheet at the body. "I'm all right. We keep going."

"Buried under dead people, Pen. Some guy swearing his guts at me and you want . . ." I didn't hear the rest. I'd already opened the cooling room door and looked both ways down the hall. A warm hall, and I smelled rain and dirt and old tar, the way it always smells in LA when it rains. In the hall I could breathe and move arms and legs, my own arms and legs, past Posting Room Three, Posting Rooms Two and One, and I saw Whitey's desk at the end of the hall in front of the file room. Joe caught up when I turned the file room knob. Locked.

"For God's sake, use a glove. Put your hand in your sleeve. Wipe the knob off."

"It's locked." I felt in my hair, found a pin, and tugged it out. I pushed the pin flat and then shoved it into the lock.

"Where'd you learn that?"

"Ever live in a dorm? Push the tumbler for me. I can't get it."

He did, and I heard the bolt roll into the door. I stuck my hand in my sleeve and turned the knob.

"Fast," Joe said. He pressed on the light button and closed the door. "Faster than fast. Where's her file?"

The inside was as long as the cooling room, with wood file cabinets instead of frozen crypts. "*B* for Brown," I said.

"When I make the hat squad, I'm finding that guy. I hate that guy. I don't see *B* for Brown."

"You're afraid of snakes but you don't mind dead bodies."

"I never said I was afraid of snakes."

"It's funny," I said.

"*B* for Brown. I don't see it."

I looked for *B*, then I looked for *A, C, D,* the entire alphabet. Whitey hadn't learned the alphabet. Her filing system used numbers, with one letter at the beginning: N39203, N40051, like that, with numbers typed on neat little cards slid into frames on the drawers.

"We can't go through all these," Joe said.

"What do they mean?" I tapped a card: S40001-S40039. "Come on, Joe. You're a cop. You use numbers, right?"

"Not these. What? You think I know all these codes? Tonight's the first time I've been in this room. I wouldn't be here now except for you."

"We've got thirty-nine and forty. The first part must be a year. If it's the year, then we're counting within that year."

"I hear something," Joe said.

"No, you don't. Say thirty-nine's the year, then it counts up. The letters are—what? *H* could only be homicide. *S* has to be suicide. What's *N?* They're filed by type of death, year, then number. If we count from January, from the first homicide each year, the number goes up."

"*Shh,* someone's coming." He closed his eyes.

Shoes on linoleum, boots, more than one pair. I ran on tiptoes to the file room door. The boots echoed in the hallway, boom-

ing echoes, walking our way, toward the end of the hall. Only
two doors sat at the end of the hall: the coroner's office and the
file room. The coroner had gone, and it was the middle of a rainy
night, no reason to use that office. The boots headed toward us,
our room, the file room.

I grabbed the flat hairpin from Joe. My hand shook. I picked it
up with two fingers, then dropped it. I heard the boots stop. The
pin slid on the floor in front of me. I tried picking it up, but my
fingers kept pushing it around. I took both hands and scooped the
pin, then stood and reached my hand to the door. I saw the knob
turn. I stuck the pin in the lock, same time. Joe pushed my hand
out of the way and twisted the pin. The bolt slid.

The doorknob rattled on our side. Joe and I stood next to each
other and watched the knob. What happens when you've broken
into a coroner's file room, and it's rainy and late at night and the
room is more like a hall that stretches down, cabinets on each side?
And the rain slams through those cabinets and walls, on the outside of the building, where it pounds sideways because it's raining
thick and fast. What happens when the file room door locks, and
you're stuck in that room with cabinets full of stories, homicide,
accident, suicide, pending?

Joe reached for my hand. The doorknob rattled, and outside the
door I heard the voice from the cooling room: "Who's got the key?
Well, where is it?" Yelling loud down the hall. "Find that beat cop.
I don't care, find him. His unit's in the lot. I got to do everything?"
The voice, the boots, the echoing hallway got smaller, tiny, and
disappeared.

"Get your file. Now."

"I don't know where it is."

"He's coming back with a key."

"I can do this. A year, right?"

"Look for H40," Joe said.

"*H. H.* Where?" My eyes shook, same as my hands, and I
couldn't read the file cards right. They blurred in front of me. Joe
read the cabinets on one side, and I tried to read the other, fast.
Rain thumped the whole Hall of Justice.

"It'll be recent. High numbers," he said. "Where's the last file drawer?"

"Here," I said. "Don't—don't open it with your fingers. Wipe it off."

No time to wipe it. The drawer slid out and I rifled the folders.

"Start at the back," Joe said. "The most recent."

October. I had to lift each file and rifle through. Head wounds, arm cut off, something with poison, and then Rosemary Brown. I held her thick folder in my hands.

"You can't take the whole thing," Joe said.

"Why not? I need it all."

"And we need a file here when someone comes looking. They *will* look, Pen. It's a homicide. Grab part of the file. Grab one thing. Grab it, and let's go."

I squeezed the file together: at least a quarter inch of stuff. I didn't know what the file held. In my mind it held events that couldn't actually be there, about grade school and high school, about Aunt Lou, their move to Pomona, Hollywood, and me holding her cut hand, her blood tacky on my fingers. Silly. No file holds all that. Still, my arm shook. I couldn't choose. I slapped the file against Joe's chest.

"Lots of carbons in here." He slid out some sheets. "Put the file back."

Joe wiped off the drawer. He stuffed the sheets in his jacket. He unlocked the door with my hairpin and creaked it a little ways, then stuck out his head. He opened it full, and we ran through the hall, Posting Rooms One, Two, Three, to the hearse entrance. I jumped from the dock. I landed against Joe, and he knocked his body on a dark car that must have belonged to the voice from the cooling room. It wasn't a hearse.

We didn't see the guy who sat inside. Joe ran past the car, and I followed him. I saw the driver's side window roll down, and a hand stuck into the rain. "You two see my partner? Hey!"

Joe reached his squad car first and unlocked the passenger side. He yelled to me through rain, "I didn't close the file room door. I didn't wipe off the doorknobs."

"Doesn't matter," I said. Joe was already running to his side, unlocking his door, and we met on the front seat. I was soaked. Water slid off Joe's cap.

"What did we get?"

"Hold on," Joe said. "Let's get out of the lot." He pushed the ignition, the car roared, and he drove us to the street, then a block down to an office building. He parked at the curb. "We're lucky. You know that? We run out and some guy's in his car. We run by him. He won't see who we were through this rain. We're the damn luckiest people in town. Except for the file door. And he saw my car number."

"What did we get?"

"You're shivering."

"I'm shaking," I said. "There's a difference." I wiped my face with wet hands.

Joe pressed the ignition again and turned up the heat. He pulled soggy sheets from his jacket. "Carbons of something. Where's my flash? Hold it pointed down."

"You hold the flash," I said. I wanted to hold the carbons. We didn't get the autopsy report. We'd stolen the word-for-word autopsy transcripts instead.

CHAPTER 31

Fay Wray comes forth with this pointer: Always hold the hands in an upward position and they'll turn into lily-white attributes.

—*Photoplay*, November 1940

Office of the Coroner   Los Angeles County

Death Number *specify (A)ccident (H)omicide (S)uicide (N)atural or (P)ending*: #H40205
Rosemary Brown

Autopsy Notes Transcribed By: F. White

Date of Death: Found 12 Nov 1940

Identification confirmed: Miss Barbara Stanwyck (friend)

Conducted at: LA Co Morgue

Autopsy Surgeon: A. F. Wagner MD, Los Angeles County Coroner's Office

Dr. Wagner: All right it is two p.m. at the
Los Angeles County Morgue Posting Room
Three. Dr. A. F. Wagner, Autopsy Surgeon,
attended by Donald Olsen, Morgue Assistant.
Observing are Detective Louis Conejos, Los
Angeles Police Department Hollywood Division,
and Miss Barbara Stanwyck.

Miss Stanwyck: Also Hollywood Division.

Dr. Wagner: Miss Frances White transcribing.
All right. We have a female, weight 118
pounds, well nourished with blond hair.
Outward appearance, areas of discoloration
on face, neck, chest, and arms. Small
lacerations on face, neck, arms, and legs.
Amputated pollex.

Detective Conejos: Dr. Wagner.

Dr. Wagner: Sorry. I mean thumb. Don, help
me turn her over. Livor mortis on back and
thighs set and quite pronounced. Thank you.
Let us put her face up.

Miss Stanwyck: What is that at her neck by
the cut?

Dr. Wagner: Decomposition. The body eats
itself after death. What you are seeing
is normal. All right. Incised neck wound
transsects right and left carotid arteries
through epiglottis and hypopharynx. Left and
right internal jugular vein. This is easy.
Primary cause of death, transsection of
right and left carotid arteries. Contributing
cause, neck wound.

Miss Stanwyck: What is that inside her neck?

Dr. Wagner: The larynx.

Detective Conejos: What was she cut with?

Dr. Wagner: Don, give me that ruler. No, I
will stick my pencil in. Yes. This is not
a knife wound. Knife cuts in general are
shallow on one side, deep on the other.
Depending on left or right hand preference.
Whichever hand holds the knife. In this case,
it looks like someone stood behind her with
a garrote.

Detective Conejos: What kind?

Dr. Wagner: I'd say thin and flexible, like a
wire, probably. Had to be thin. Compression
cut. But these lacerations on her arms are
sharp and rough.

Detective Conejos: What about her thumb? What
happened to the thumb?

Miss Stanwyck: I want to see inside her
chest.

Dr. Wagner: Don. Pollex is in that tray. I
mean thumb. In the tray. Thank you. I see
two, no, three lacerations to the thumb.
First, a deep, transverse cut, smooth edges
made with a sharp, smooth-edged knife or
other sharp, smooth object. Then we have
jagged lacerations almost like skin is torn.
Let me see her hand. All right. Here we
go. Here we go. Contusions to both wrists.

Discoloration. Thumb missing from right hand.
Lacerations.

Detective Conejos: You are ahead of me, Doc.

Dr. Wagner: Somebody tied her wrists
together. Thin contusion line. Could be
wire on her wrists, and ankles, too. Look
at her wrists. She had this long transverse
cut first. The thumb. Bruising and clotting
at wound site. It looks like she had that
laceration a while.

Miss Stanwyck: And?

Dr. Wagner: Lacerations on her hand. Wrist to
hand. She struggled.

Miss Stanwyck: And?

Detective Conejos: Slow down, doctor.

Dr. Wagner: I need to see her mouth. Don,
grab her jaw. Hold it, will you? My God.

Miss Stanwyck: What, what?

Dr. Wagner: She chewed off her own thumb.

Detective Conejos: What the.

Miss Stanwyck: Chewed.

Detective Conejos: What the hell.

Dr. Wagner: Look, she has bone and skin in
her teeth.

"No," Joe said. He grabbed at the carbons.

"I'm not done. There's more."

"I've read enough."

"What does it mean?"

"You don't know? Pen." He switched off the flash. I couldn't see him.

"What?"

"Someone tied her up. Her wrists."

"Yeah, must be whoever she met after she left the hospital."

"She couldn't get loose."

"Right."

"Pen, stop it. Think. If you were tied up, if you had a cut thumb and your wrists tied together, you'd need to escape. Your thumb's already cut to the bone. Think hard, what would you do?"

"No knife? Nothing to cut me free?"

"The sharpest you've got is your teeth."

I thought. Teeth. Mine crowded my mouth. They knocked against each other. My face went hot, my hands too. I dropped the carbons on my knees.

"You understand?"

I did. My feet bounced the autopsy report to the floor. It stuck, wet, to my legs. I hummed.

"Wait a minute," Joe said. "What do you mean, she left the hospital? What do you know about a hospital?"

"Don't—don't touch me. You take it back inside. Pick it up, it's touching my feet."

"We don't need to return it. The thing's a carbon."

"Get it out of here."

"Let me—I've got it."

"Get it out."

He swung open the car door and disappeared in the rain. I disappeared, too, in my head. I pretended I never saw the transcript. Rose never sat tied up and scared, and she never, ever ground her teeth through her own bone to tear off her thumb and slip from whatever tied her hands. None of that happened, not when I disappeared. I couldn't go far—to Buena Park, for a moment, a few years before Daisy, with Will and Dad and Rose and me in the living room and the radio blaring Eddie Cantor, *funny*. And Mom brings in a plate: *Who wants lace cookies?*

"I tore it up," Joe said. The rain soaked him, and he looked at me through the driver's side window. He talked through the open vent. "Pen? Did you hear me? I tore it and threw all the scraps in a storm drain. The rain washes clear to the ocean."

"I heard you. The ocean."

He got in the car and sat there, dripping. "What now? Talk to me."

I shook my head.

He punched the ignition and the car's engine mixed with rain sounds.

"Take me home, okay?"

Joe wiped fog off the inside windshield. He drove me through downtown to Hollywood, to the dorm, without making me talk. Nobody else was out that late in a downpour. A silver world of rain and traffic lights. We skidded a little—deep puddles and hard stops—and the car got smaller the more Joe drove. Rosemary sat with bound hands beside me. She raised her fists to her mouth and bit down.

CHAPTER 32

Suddenly Carole Lombard was rushed to the hospital,
so the picture was postponed, and the wedding day set.

—*Photoplay*, November 1939

Last fall, when I still lived in Buena Park, Teddy asked me out to
a movie. Afterward, he said we should eat.

"Just coffee and maybe a pancake special," he said. I said okay.
He was my brother's best friend, I'd known him for years, and he
was a deputy sheriff. Our first grown-up date.

He didn't hold my hand as we walked past Godding's and Sani-
tary Laundry. He said, "I saw George Brent in a better show. I'd
give fifty bucks to see that Bette Davis close up. Here, I'll hold
that door."

"I liked the picture."

"If you like shows where every girl in the audience cries."

Silly talk. We sat and drank coffee, and I felt nothing for him,
and everything he said sounded stuffed together. "Then we stop
at that old ranch out Coyote Hills and the geez doesn't know his
own dog's been shot and the dog, he's on the front porch breeding
flies and panting with his mouth like this, *huh huh huh*, and I say
a sheep's missing next door and I can see sheep fuzz in the dog's
mouth panting, you want a refill?"

I might have seen him again. I might have dined out if he'd

asked me. We stood by the sheriff's station at the corner of Grand and Manchester, and he looked in the front window, slow and careful, then he pushed me around the corner and unlocked a side door to a private office. The room had a window and a desk and a smeary old wall lit by the streetlamps outside, hung with cheap prints of Christ and fishes, Christ in a boat, Christ leaning over a dead woman. Teddy pushed me into the room.

He swung his forearm at my breasts. I hit the stucco wall and Christ scattered, and then I hit nails. They cut into my back. I couldn't move, and my breath left. I heard Teddy unzip, and far off, someone's dog barked, and I thought, *sheep fuzz*, and he kicked me between my legs so I yelled, but I yelled in his mouth while he kissed me hard. Nobody heard. And if they heard, so what? He wore his cop shirt, cop pants, hat sliding off his head, hitting my head, one bounce, hitting linoleum, and my skirt up. Cop on a date.

It wasn't enough to throw me against the nails, tear my panties, pinch my inside thigh so hard his hand rose up bloody. It wasn't enough to shove whatever he could of himself inside me. He took one hand from my shoulder and pulled his gun from his belt. He lifted the gun and pressed it flat on my cheek. My ear was close; the loud pop when he cocked the gun; behind that, the slow talk and phone ringing in the station lobby, and on the framed side-walk outside the window, an old man holding his wife's hand and swinging it as they walked. They didn't notice a girl pinned in the room. We would have looked like a dark cave to them. I remember the man's hat, how it tilted forward, and I was afraid it would fall and they'd have to stop and his wife would let his hand go, and it was important to me that she held on to her husband's hand, not drop it, and the cold gun rubbed up my cheek, from my chin to forehead. The cocked gun on my cheek. If I cried, so what? Nobody heard that, either.

"You must have done something wrong," Rose said, after I told her about the date.

I held an ice chunk on my thigh where Teddy had pinched off skin. I bled on cheesecloth stuck in my crotch. "He forced me."

"What did you say to him? I don't get it." She held cotton and iodine, and my back was a splash of cuts, bruises, pink iodine dabs. Rose pulled out stucco and paint specks with her fingernails. "You act like it's the worst that can happen."

Rose could tape on a bandage, but she didn't get it. I believed she didn't get it because not one person did, not my mom or Will, who kept saying, "It's not like you're a virgin anymore. Christ, Pen, he's my best friend. What do you expect me to do?"

No, I wasn't a virgin anymore. But Rose should have known. She should have said, *Penny, I'm sorry. You can cry because it's the worst thing to happen, ever, nothing is worse, those cuts on your back will scar.*

That's what best friends are supposed to say.

I saved money for eight months. At Godding's I bought a gallon juice can and drained juice through a slot. I stuffed dollars and change inside. In town I'd see cops and start wheezing. I'd never had asthma before. Cops walked into Godding's, or I saw them drive by or they'd wave, and each time my throat stopped me breathing. I had to leave Buena Park, had to. I'd go to Hollywood. In Hollywood I didn't care who got it or who said I agreed to that date, so what'd I expect, a nitey-nite kiss at the screen door?

CHAPTER 33

The surprise of them all, however, is Basil Rathbone, who lives these days for his adopted baby. And when Cynthia needs attention, don't think Basil wanders off in search of help—he's Basil-right-on-the-job, reveling in her need of him.

—Photoplay, November 1940

I couldn't find Stany at Paramount. I walked the back lot and found all the people I didn't need: Abbott, two Career Girls, a script girl with typewriter ink on her shirt. Abbott took revisions out of the script girl's hands and didn't thank her, but a script girl doesn't wait for thanks. She's always running.

The two Career Girls stood by Abbott, and he stood by the publicity office on 6th Street near Avenue M. His office sat next to Preston Sturges's. Both offices had stucco fronts and short sets of stairs to the doors. They looked the same, except Preston's had a wide canvas awning that shaded his front window. Without an awning, Abbott's office looked bald. I'd never been in his office. No girl goes there unless she has to. I think the Career Girls had to, because they'd stepped out of his doorway and Abbott patted one—the Career Girl I'd seen talking to Madge in the Zebra—on the shoulder like she'd been upset.

No, she was *still* upset: I saw tears fall off her nose. She licked them. Abbott talked to her; I couldn't hear what he said, but he didn't fire her. If he had, there'd be no pat on the shoulder and no kind talk. She'd be walked out by Joe to the Bronson Gate, and we wouldn't see her again. So maybe her mother died. Her grandmother died. Her great-grandmother died. Maybe she misplaced her production schedule.

"You," Abbott said. He pointed at me. "It's eight-oh-seven. You're late."

I ran like a script girl down Avenue L to tiny 11th Street and our sound stage. Inside Stage 10, lighting guys set up reflectors and flipped bulbs on and off. Preston Sturges sat at the piano and played ragtime. The extras and actors smoked and chatted. Two guys moved a set wall forward five feet and then back. Forward and back. The wall flexed when they forgot to move at the same time, and a third guy cussed at them. Normal morning stuff. A whole five minutes later, Stany and Hank came in. I'd never talked to Hank. He scared me the same way that Bob Taylor did. When a man's too beautiful, there's an invisible girl line all around him, and only special girls can cross it, like Rose or Stany. I'd never tried.

"*Ssssst. Ssssst.*"

Stany didn't hear me.

"*Ssssst,*" I said.

"You're being called," Hank said. He took a match from his gray plaid suit and flamed it with one scratch on a prop table. He raised the match to his mouth and lit a cigarette.

Stany tried not to look at me. She saw Hank and Preston, and Eugene Pallette, who sat in a tux and played drums on two overturned pots, and a group of girl extras pushing each other close to Hank, but then she'd turn her head to me and raise her eyes up and over my body like I was a room she avoided.

"*Ssssst.* I have something to say."

"Say it, then." She watched Preston, who wore two hats, one on top of the other. *Clinkety clinkety*, ragtime.

"Not near *him*." I meant Hank, but I couldn't say *Hank* because he'd hear, and I'd never been introduced. How stupid—he knew everyone recognized him; he was costar of the picture. He was Hank Fonda, but I couldn't say his name. I couldn't say *Hank*.

"Hey, there's Wally," he said. "I need to ask him. Hey, Wally." He disappeared, so polite.

"What is it?" Stany said. She picked at her gold blouse. She watched Preston's fingers on the piano. She watched the two Career Girls come in the stage door.

"I read the transcript of Rosemary's autopsy."

"And?"

"You lied to me, Stany."

"And?"

"That's it. You lied. I asked you—remember me asking? We sat in the Pig 'n Whistle and I asked you right out what happened to her thumb, and you said it was cut off."

"So it was."

"Bullshit," I said.

She looked at me now. A mean look. "Don't cuss. Not at me."

"Or what? You'll get me fired? Look around, Stany. Nobody talks to me here. Not the extras or Preston. Abbott has it out for me. I'll never make contract player because I've got a record. You don't get Paramount contracts with a mug shot. So what do I care?"

"Your brother's a burglar."

"Another reason I'll never be hired. So he's a burglar. You never stole in your life? Miss Hard-Time from the Bronx?"

"Brooklyn."

"You knew Rose had been tied up. I didn't know. I didn't tie her up. I couldn't have. Where would I keep her? My dorm room? You knew, and Conejos knew, and nobody said a thing. I got arrested and fingerprinted and—and measured and turned side to side for mug shots, and you both knew I didn't kill her."

"I told you all along I didn't think you killed her. I never lied about that."

"Gracious of you," I said. "What a lady."

Preston banged the piano keys and stood up. He clapped his hands and his hats wobbled. Time to work.

"Listen," Stany said, just for me, under the shout and clang of cameramen. "What was I supposed to do? What if Bob really killed her?"

"God. God, Stany. You mean you'd see me go to jail to protect your husband?"

A lighting guy fixed a spot past Stany and clicked a switch. Stany's hair glowed orange. "You bet. I'd put myself in jail if I had to. I'd put anyone in."

Her face got tight. She loved him too much. She thought Bob might murder a girl, that's how much she loved him. She squeezed her lips together, and across the room, Wally yelled, "Missy! Your lip lines!"

Stany waved at him. *Sure, Wally. Anything for you.* "Besides," she said to me. "I got you a lawyer."

"A divorce lawyer."

"Well, I paid for him."

Here was the time I could have told her. Here was the moment to throw Marty up, to tell Stany about Marty's night job in the backyards of the famous. No reason to hide what I knew, with Will already in jail. Plus, I didn't need Marty now that I'd read about Rose. I didn't need a lawyer. Maybe right now Joe was telling Conejos to drop my murder charge. I could tell Stany about Marty Martin.

But I didn't. I opened my mouth, but that's all. No words or sound. I kept picturing Rose on Sunset with her good hand holding scraps of cloth on the cut hand, and the cars racing by. Dark out, except for those cars. She'd wave the good hand: *Stop!* Then she'd breathe hard and almost fall. She'd get dizzy. The cars racing by. Will already gone on the highway to Buena Park, bastard.

Then one car stops, and it's Marty returning to Sunset, and he calls to Rose, and she runs to the car. The blood's soaked through all the cloth scraps and drips as she runs. He drives her a few miles, passes some hospitals so nobody connects him with Rose, and Rose with the broken glass at the Stanwyck place. He's still Marty, after all. He wants distance. But he walks her into the receiving hospital. He helps her sit down, he finds Dr. Ostrander, and then—after she's safe inside, after she'll be seen by a doctor—he leaves.

"Extras are excused," Preston said. He stood on his piano bench. "Today's scenes involve Hanker and Barbs kissing, and I'm sure no one wants to stick around for that."

Groans and hoots. We don't get paid if we're excused, and we don't get to watch the kissing, either.

"Come to dinner," Stany said.

"She bit off her thumb. You didn't think that was important to tell me?"

"Your mark, Barbs," Preston directed from under his two hats.

"I have to work." Stany walked to her mark.

I followed her. "She bit off her *thumb*."

Across the set, people stopped: extras crowding the stage door, Wally and Preston and half a dozen cameramen, Hank and his cigarette. They gave the hush-hush of people who know something's happened. I'd followed Stany on set to her mark.

"And if I tell—"

"Shut up!" Stany grabbed my arm. "Everyone's listening."

"If I tell," I whispered. "The great Missy thinks her husband's a killer. What'll Bob say?"

"I'm not the one who robbed my house."

"I didn't, either."

"You were there," she said. "You lied about it. Get off my mark."

Then Hank said from across the room, "Well, look here. My shoe's in my hand. Gosh, it's heavy. I better throw it and break up this cat fight or we'll never finish our scenes." He tossed the shoe, and it hit the piano bench.

Laughing, and the talk started up and the whole sound stage moved again, toward the door and cameras and the spotlights.

"We're both liars," Stany said. She let go of my sleeve. "I've got to work."

"Both liars. Yeah, we are."

"We're even. You lied to me, and I lied to you," she said.

"But aren't you sorry you lied?"

"Are *you?* Of course I'm not sorry. I'd do it again. Get off my mark."

"I would, too, Stany. I'd do it again."

"I'd lie to you," she said, "but that doesn't mean we're not friends. Will you get off my mark?"

I stepped backward, out of the lights. Without Hank tossing his shoe I might have kept yelling and not understood that I lied, too. Both of us liars, like Stany said. Stany lied about one thing. I lied when Rose's body was found. Keeping silent is lying, in a way.

"Wait," she said. "Come to dinner Saturday. I'm throwing a good-bye party at Ciro's. Bob's leaving. No, not that kind of leaving. Utah, for filming. What is it—Wild Bill, Billy Goat—no, *Billy the Kid*. That's it."

"Saturday night I'm filming at the Gardens. I play a bull. It's a promotion."

"Oh, Pen. A bull?"

I joined the extras and set guys and the coffee girl at the stage door. We crowded 11th Street. No rain since last night, but the streets in the back lot smelled greasy and held little tidepools in cracks and drains. Bits of junk floated in them and stuck to the road. Joe waved me over from where he leaned against the back lot's rear wall.

"I had this dream," I said. Yelled, through people. "You sat in Conejos's crappy little office and told him how innocent I am. He has a crappy office, doesn't he? He must have."

"I haven't seen Conejos. I had to work here today," he said. "I do have news, though. Your brother's been moved to the Lincoln Heights Jail."

"How many bus transfers will it take to get there?"

"A lot. But not now. You're wanted in someone else's crappy office. I came to escort you."

I knew what came next. I held out both arms, wrists forward. Nobody in the crowd noticed. They'd seen me do it before.

"What are you doing?"

"Go ahead, put them on."

"Funny. No handcuffs, Penny." Instead he walked beside me down Avenue L, past Bing Crosby's long dressing room, and stopped in front of a building I'd never been in. From outside it looked like another sound stage; it looked like nothing, but a big nothing, as wide as Stage 10 and painted beige. No red lightbulb mounted over the door.

Joe set his hand on the doorknob. "You okay?"

"Sure."

"I mean last night. You were upset. Last night you mentioned a hospital. How did you know Rosemary was at a hospital? Which hospital? How did you know?"

"Fine," I said. "I'm fine. Really fine, thank you."

The knob turned, the door opened, and Joe stepped away. Abbott came out. He stopped when he saw me, but he didn't say anything. He frowned, like he does, and then he shook his head. He walked back the way we'd come, toward Stage 10.

"You need to watch him," Joe said. "He doesn't like you."

The door had shut again. I turned the knob and pulled it open. When I entered, a secretary smiled at me from her desk. This wasn't a sound stage, and Joe didn't come in. He waved at me from the street. I shut the door, and the secretary said, "Mr. Zukor's waiting for you."

Oak paneling, oak chevron floor, tall orchids, probably real, a second secretary typing on her old Corona from shorthand that looked like ink dribble to me.

The secretary glanced up, pretended not to notice me standing in front of her, typed more, and at last stood and knocked on a door in back. She opened the door, and inside Mr. Zukor rose from behind a huge carved wood desk. He looked like a nice grandpa. High collar, red handkerchief poking from a black suit. He had thin grandpa hair and a long face, cigar between fingers, and he pronounced his *W* like a *V*. He didn't look powerful, or maybe he didn't look mean. He ushered me in, then closed the door behind me. I liked him.

He sat, leaned back, and tapped his cigar in a plate. "We at Paramount are a family. Do you have a family, Miss Harp?" *Vee at Paramount are a Vaa-mily.*

"Sure."

"And in your family, do you take care of each other?"

Sometimes we did. Will sat in jail for me, so I guess we took care of each other.

"Sure," I said.

"We take care of each other here at Paramount. I'm prepared to offer you a two-year contract. One hundred fifty dollars a week."

"A contract."

"Do you have a boyfriend, Penny?"

"No," I said. "Not at all." Joe didn't count. He wore a uniform, just like Teddy.

Mr. Zukor swiveled his chair. "Please keep it that way. Lana Turner is a nightmare for MGM. I don't want a nightmare here. Do you understand?"

"Yes." I didn't understand. A contract.

"You'll be a studio player, scene-setting, like that. Small parts. Baby steps. You'll start small and see what happens. You'll need lessons. In everything, I understand. We'll train you to act and talk. We'll show you how to dress. Do you sing?"

"I can, but you won't like it."

"Too bad. We need a Deanna Durbin. Universal is cleaning up with her." Then he said, "When you work for my studio, I speak for you. People look at you, but what they see is this studio. They see me. They see Mary Pickford at nineteen and what she means to this country. Every time you are in public you are the best of Paramount Pictures. You are happy and gracious. If a dog pisses on your leg, you are smiling. You pet the dog. If you are the worst of Paramount Pictures, you are both a liar and in breach of contract. Do you understand?"

"Sure."

"I will insert a confidentiality clause in your contract, but I want all details clear."

"Details?"

"It's simple," he said, not a grandpa at all. "You forget what you saw at Miles Abbott's office this morning. You forget about Jim Ostrander and anything overheard at that hospital. That's all. You would do this, wouldn't you, for two years at Paramount Pictures?"

"Yes." My voice said it, not me. I still thought, *contract?* I couldn't say anything. My voice talked, not me.

"Stills next week," he said. "Have my girls set it up. And your hair. Yes, hair. Stop touching the sides. Can't you puff it? You work on the hair." He held up his cigar like it was a finger: *Hold on.* He pressed a button. "Shirley, who sets Dottie's hair? Good. Call him about the new property." To me: "You're off the Sturges set."

"Why?"

"You sign and you're no longer an extra. I don't want more scenes we have to cut. We'll call when the contract's ready."

"What's my job until then?"

"Stay off the lot."

I left Zukor's office, left his hallway and building, and saw Joe across Avenue L leaning against a vent room wall. Two Gower Gulch cowboys rode past him on horses. Joe flicked a cigarette into the street.

"I'm to walk you out the gate."

"Yeah, I have to stay off the lot. I have a contract," I said. "Mr. Zukor gave me two years at one fifty a week. Is that good, one fifty?" We walked down Avenue L, past the studio theater, past Preston's office to the admin building. Everywhere, all the streets had backed-up drains with mud and trash. Workers rode bikes and left little splashes and mud trails.

"A contract? What did you do?"

"I didn't do anything. He offered me two years to keep my mouth shut. Stop a minute. I've got to pick up my check. One fifty a week, imagine. I could buy clothes. I could buy shoes. Joe, I could buy *shoes*." I pulled the admin door. I stood in line at payroll and got handed my check from yesterday. The people in line were all extras, paid by the day. All in costume: *señoritas* and Air Corps flyboys and Chinamen wiping their drawn-on eyes. I'd stood in this line. I'd watched the costumes and people change. With a contract I'd get my check mailed, I'd get paid in costume or not.

Joe walked me toward the gate. "He must think you know something important. Mr. Zukor's a very smart man."

"He's wrong. It's easy to keep my mouth shut when I don't know anything. I've never seen anything to talk about. I've got a contract. Can you believe it? A Paramount contract. I wonder why I have to stay off the lot."

"We have too many people here every day. We don't want a bunch of people running around the back lot, it's not safe. If you don't need to be here, we lock you out."

"That doesn't sound right. Not if I have a contract."

On the lawn outside admin a couple guys in fedoras practiced their quick draw. A girl sat Indian style and read a book. None of them were locked out. Joe yelled to a security guard at the corner, "Open the gate. This one's leaving." To me: "What do you mean, that's not right?"

The gate squeaked and swung. On the other side, some girls waited with autograph books. "Did you see Nelson Eddy? Is he here?"

Tourists. "He's at MGM."

"Ladies, you have to move back. Don't crowd the gate."

"Joe," I said. "You don't have to look after me. You hardly know me. Two days ago you thought I was a murderess."

"And last night I discovered how nosy you are."

"I'll stay off the lot," I said. "But I still wonder. What does Zukor think I know? And what is he cleaning up before I come back?"

CHAPTER 34

Many of those who menace the stars' well-being un-
questionably suffer from delusions.

—*Photoplay*, November 1940

Nothing is like getting a contract. Nothing. Madge's car ran out of
gas on Olympic and I was nearly hit by Carole Lombard's DeSoto,
and still I was happy. I rode two buses to see Will, and the ride
took so long only ten visiting minutes remained. Then more time
pulling off all my hairpins, my wristwatch, earrings, ankle strap
buckles from my Wallflower shoes. I had five minutes to visit. I
was happy, and then I saw Will.

"Jail or army," Will told me. Will talked to me by telephone,
and we watched each other through the glass wall between. Next
to me on both sides sat another visitor, and another, in a row across
the dirty visitors' room. My voice echoed in the telephone and
bounced back at me. Other sounds—visitors, guards laughing, a
water fountain down the hall—bounced off the subway tile walls
and stained linoleum.

"Jail or army, I get to choose. Mom sent my draft notice."

"Nice of her," I said.

"Yeah, but she held on to it for two weeks. Two weeks! That's
way before Rosie died, Pen. She saw it in the mail two weeks ago
and never told me."

"Why would she do that?"

"Who the hell knows? I'm supposed to report for duty in two days. I already missed my physical."

"Does it matter? You're not going. Jail or army isn't a choice."

"It's not?"

"You know it's not."

He tapped fingers on the linoleum desk. He looked side to side. He scooted his chair. "I get a free lawyer. So I give the draft notice to my lawyer, right? He shows it to the deputy DA. And my lawyer says to me—get this—he says the DA phoned some publicity girl. Helen something. On account of it's Barbara Stanwyck's house, right? The next thing I know, the DA offers to release me to the army. All charges dropped."

"What publicity girl? From Paramount?"

"Voice *down*, Pen."

"He called Paramount? Who'd he talk to at Paramount?"

"Who the goddamn cares? It happened fast, I just got the draft notice today. I get the physical later tonight, and I'm gone. Day after tomorrow I'm gone."

"You're—wait. I don't follow. Your physical's today?"

A guard shouted from the door, "One minute. One minute left."

"Look," Will said. "You'll need to help out at home. Mom can't do it all. She can't do anything. There's not much money, and you'll have to organize pickers and all the crops. And for God's sake, don't let the oranges freeze. I've got new smudge pots in the barn. Listen to the news, will you? Listen to the weather. And Daisy's behind in school."

"She's in kindergarten. How do you fall behind in kindergarten?"

"She doesn't talk, Pen. You fall behind if you don't talk."

"I'll come see you tomorrow. Don't decide yet, Will. Don't go."

"And what, sit around? Go back home and watch the oranges grow? Nail more boards on Walt Knott's goddamn ghost town?"

"That's not what I meant. You won't pass your physical anyway. Don't go, Will. It's not our war."

"The thing about you," he said. "The goddamn thing about you is it's never enough. I confess my guts, but no, that's not enough. I have to sit in here while you're running around Hollywood pretending you're something. Everything I did was for *family*."

There it was. He'd said it. He was right, I'd run around Hollywood pretending. I'd left what was ugly in Buena Park, and that meant leaving our family, too, and now I looked through the glass at Will and felt my heart rip and scatter.

"Time," the guard said. Down the row people pressed palms to the glass between them: moms and sweethearts and sad fathers, and on the other side men in jail shirts with hands on the glass. A row of palm sandwiches.

Will leaned close to the glass, as if I could hear him better. He still talked on the phone. "As soon as that whosis—that Dr. Ostrich gives me the okay, I'm gone. I'm through with you and Mom and goddamn everything. I'm army and every kraut I kill is gonna have your face."

"Dr. Ostrander? Dr. *Ostrander?*"

The guard hung up Will's phone.

That night I asked Joe for a ride and he agreed, but I could tell he didn't want to. He drove me in his squad car to the Hollywood Division after my second *Hail the Indians* show.

"You promised a drink," he said. "I want beer." He was on police duty, in his uniform.

"We will. As soon as I see Conejos." I scooted to the edge of the seat, against the passenger door. I'd stopped wheezing around Joe, but that didn't mean I'd sit close.

"I'll get in trouble for driving you."

"No, you won't."

"Why do you think he'll listen? He still thinks you're a murderess."

"I don't think he does," I said. "When Madge died, he patted my head. Remember? He knelt down and let me kiss Madge's arm, even though I was a suspect."

"I don't like that he touched you."

"You'll stay outside in your car. I'll go in, talk to him real fast, and come back."

Except that I went into Hollywood Division, pushed through smoking cops, asked for Conejos, and found out he'd gone. He'd been sent to some murder scene. Someone had died, Conejos went. I hadn't thought about that, Conejos investigating one death after another. Conejos in the interview room grabbing another girl's scabby hand as proof she'd done it, a murderess.

I'd planned to tell him that Will couldn't go to the army. I'd ask for his help, and in my plan he'd say, *I was wrong about you. The studio has gone too far this time. Let's get Will out of jail.* Conejos wasn't under studio contract, was he? Paramount could get Will out of jail, but couldn't Conejos stop a phony medical exam? I'd liked my plan, but Conejos was gone.

Back to Joe's squad car, my hand on the door latch, my fingers squeezed, the door clicked. I glanced at the receiving hospital next door. My hand lifted. In the car Joe leaned to the side and looked at me through the passenger window. I shook my head at him. *Not yet.* Conejos was gone, but I knew someone else who worked night shift.

Through the grass to the emergency room, Joe said behind me, "Where are you going? Where's Conejos?"

"He's gone. Joe, I'll just be a minute. I know someone here. He can help."

"Who? Who do you know? Where are you going?"

"A doctor."

"What doctor? Stop, Pen. Stop right now."

"He did Will's physical. I'll tell him about Will. He's a nice guy, he—" I'd reached the emergency room door and turned the knob to pull it open. Joe grabbed my arm. He twisted, and the pain shot through me both ways. He twisted the skin on my upper arm, and everything underneath the skin twisted, too, up my shoulder and down through my wrist. My hand dropped from the doorknob. I leaned against him. He whispered in my ear.

"I'm sorry, Pen. When I say stop, don't keep walking. What if I think you're in danger? What if you're headed for an accident and I see it but you don't? When I say stop, it's for you. I'm taking care of you, so listen."

"Okay," I said, and he let go of me. He rubbed his hand on my hurt arm.

"Let's get that beer. I'm really sorry. We'll put some ice on your arm, no one will know it's swelling." He took a couple steps back and then held out his hand to guide me.

"Sure," I said, and pulled open the emergency room door. I ran in. I'd felt that kind of pain once, just once, last spring, and if I went with Joe, I knew what would happen after the beer. I'd been stupid to sit with him in a car. I'd been more stupid than that, letting my asthma tell me to trust him. My twisted skin burned and reminded me that when a man like Teddy, like Joe, is angry, it doesn't matter if I'm wheezing or not.

The nurse at the front desk didn't look up when I ran to her. The room was crowded and loud. A drunk guy slid against her desk, rolled his head side to side, and burped.

"Dr. Ostrander. Can I see him?"

"No," the nurse said. The pin curls by her white cap dripped sweat. "He's not here."

"Now. I need to see him now." The outside door began to open. I could see Joe's black shoe.

The nurse laughed. "He didn't show for his shift." Then the nurse tried to ignore me. She pretended to sign forms on her desk. She wiped her neck with her hand.

"Who's the doctor, then? Who's in charge?"

"He's a little slow, that's all. You want to sign in?" She pushed a clipboard at me, and I backed into a kid scratching red bumps on his face. The kid cried. Joe stood behind him, his face calm, shoulders relaxed. He patted the kid on his back.

"Tell me where Dr. Ostrander lives," I said.

She ignored me. She saw Joe patting the kid. She saw him watch me, calm cop face. "Thank God you're here," she said. She watched Joe watch me. "I called next door almost ten minutes ago. What took you so long? Get rid of this drunk, will you? The whole place stinks."

Joe kicked the drunk in his side—not hard, but enough so the drunk groaned and heaved. Joe tugged on his arm and waved to me. I shook my head. My arm still hurt where he'd twisted it.

"Help me with this guy, and I'll take you home," Joe said. "The doctor's not here, right? I'll take you home, Pen. How else will you get home? It's midnight."

"I'll wait for Conejos."

"You'll wait all night."

"I don't mind."

"I'm not mad, Pen. Is that why you're worried? Help with his arm. At least help me drag him outside."

"You twisted my arm."

"Do I look mad?"

"No. Why should I help you?"

"I can't drag him myself. He's going to throw up, and all these folks will get sick from the smell."

"Can't one of them help you?"

"Which one? The kid with measles? Please, Pen. Grab his arm."

We each took one arm and dragged the guy to the door. Behind me the nurse said, "Doctor, patient waiting in bed three." Then an old man's voice: "Line them up, Agnes."

"Push him onto the sidewalk," Joe said. He meant the drunk. We tugged the guy out the hospital door, across the few feet to the sidewalk.

"I'm really okay, Pen. I'm not mad. Roll this guy on his side so he throws up in the street."

"Joe, this drunk looks just like Spencer Tracy. Look at his nose."

"I'm dancing," said the drunk. Joe kicked him again.

"You're hurting him."

"Drunks don't feel pain. He's all right. He's dancing. Are you going to tell me why you wanted to see that doctor?"

"He gave Will a physical. Maybe he's still at the jail. I have to talk to him, Joe. I don't think my brother will tell him the truth."

"Hey, this guy's got a twenty," Joe said. He kicked him again.

My arm ached. Calm Joe, kicking the drunk. Empty Joe, kicking hard, again and again. I was watching Joe, arms in front if he tried to grab me, and I was thinking of Dr. Ostrander. If I could find Dr. Ostrander, if I could tell him about Will; I knew Will couldn't go in the army. Somewhere in his left ear bells rang all day, and birds whirred or flapped wings—tinnitus. Will might pass the physical, but his left ear would fail. Rose had given him that present one summer night with a firecracker. She didn't mean to, but she gave him 4-F.

Say Will's lawyer gave the DA Will's draft order, and the DA called Stany's publicity girl, like Will said. And at Paramount, say that Abbott had just met with Adolph Zukor, they smoked cigars in Zukor's big office and talked about me, how I knew something. I was a problem. The snotty secretary buzzed, *Helen Ferguson for you, sir. Something about the Los Angeles County DA*, and Zukor picked up the phone. More cigar smoke, the room thick with it now; Zukor thought about Stany and Preston Sturges and the money he'd sunk into *The Lady Eve*. He thought about me and my problem, how a convict brother would kill a girl's two-year contract. How Hedda Hopper would write it: *Stanwyck Accuses Paramount Extra's Burglar Brother, Chaos on Set of Upcoming Picture*. And my problem, what to do about my *problem*.

Time for another cigar. Give the convict brother a choice, and he'll take it. Send a doctor who ignores tin ears. Now we've got a solution: a contract girl with a soldier brother sells movie tickets, and she'll keep her mouth shut about the *problem* because she's signed her shut-your-mouth clause, and we're all happy, *puff puff*, spreading around cigar smoke.

Yes, we're all happy. Will was happy, and I could be, if I knew what the *problem* was—a big enough problem to send a thief with a tin ear to the army. The war wasn't ours, but it would be, we all knew it, and the new draft was proof. Will was happy, but he wouldn't stay happy. He'd be dead, because with tinnitus, he'd never see the krauts that looked like me. He'd never hear them coming. He'd be shot first.

When Zukor offered me the contract, I didn't care why. I saw the contract and nothing else. A hundred fifty a week and star lessons! How many come-and-gos get a real chance? How many times can Joe kick a drunk before the guy spits blood?

"Joe, stop it. Don't hit him. *Stop*." I held Joe's arm, and he shook me off. He pushed me, and I fell to the sidewalk beside the drunk's face. I had a close-up view when Joe kicked the drunk's nose. The drunk stopped moaning and blood squirted from his nose onto the sidewalk, and I screamed.

Cops ran from Hollywood Division next door. Then Joe was on the ground, too, with two cops holding his arms and another straddling his legs, and Joe looked at me—right at me—and his face held nothing at all. No anger, no breathing hard, although he'd just beat on the drunk, no hint that he even knew who I was. The Joe who looked at me was a flat paper doll, not a man.

"Christ, it's Spencer Tracy," someone said, and footsteps, voices, Dr. Ostrander running from an office door next to the emergency room. A stretcher appeared, and cops rolled Spencer Tracy onto the stretcher, and they all disappeared through Dr. Ostrander's office door. Then it was just empty Joe, and me, and Spencer Tracy's blood sprayed and pooled on the sidewalk, and the cops holding Joe, and then Detective Conejos was kneeling beside me, his soft hand on my hair, his soft voice saying, "Let's get you home."

"Don't think about it," Granny said. "Keep drinking that tea. At least your color's come back. Let me see those eyes. Yes, you'll be fine. Detective, help her sit down."

"Why would Joe beat up Spencer Tracy? Why did Joe hate him that much? He was mad at me. Why would he hit Spencer Tracy?"

The Florentine Gardens after closing is an ugly place. Chairs stack on bare tables, the lights are turned up, and you can see every crack on the bandstand. Conejos lifted a chair from on top of a table. He set it on the floor, pointed to it, and I sat next to the bandstand.

Granny chatted. "Why don't we talk about something nice? I

hear you had good news today. Is it too soon to look for a new name? You could be Sheryl with an *S*. I've always loved the name Sheryl. With an *S*. You'll have to change both first and last, of course. No star can be named Harp."

"If Dr. Ostrander was at work, why didn't he check in at the emergency room?"

"Drink the tea," said Conejos, beside me.

"If we find a last name with a *Y*," Granny said, "you could balance first and last names. Sheryl Mayfair. Something like that. The *Y* has to be inside the name, not on the end. Sheryl Layne. How does it sound?"

"Drink the tea," Conejos said.

"My clothes keep getting bloody." My skirt had dried stiff with Spencer Tracy's blood, and it crackled when I bent the fabric. Little blood bits flew off. "I should change my clothes before you question me." I tried to stand, and Granny leaned across to push my shoulders down. I sat.

"I'm not questioning you," Conejos said.

"Sure you are. I saw a cop beat up Spencer Tracy."

"I'm not questioning you, Penny."

"Okay, then someone else questions me. I have to be questioned. They'll take me to Hollywood Division. Change my skirt." I tried to stand again, and Granny leaned across.

"You're not going anywhere, Pen. Detective Conejos brought you home, and that's it."

I crackled my skirt and watched blood bits fly. Little bits of Spencer Tracy. "I don't understand."

"Pen, look at me. *Look* at me," Granny said. "Now listen. It's fixed. The situation, you're out of it. You never went to that hospital, not the first time, not tonight. The detective didn't bring you home tonight, because you didn't go out. You don't know any Dr. Ostrander. You never saw Spencer Tracy. What you're wearing, it's not blood, Pen. I know, yes, it's blood, but it's not. You'll change out of the skirt and give it to me, and it disappears. No blood. We'll sweep the floor—stop doing that with the skirt—and it's all fixed."

"Fixed? You can't fix what's happened. I saw it. I fell right next to him. Joe kept hitting and wouldn't stop, he was kicking, look at my skirt. How can you fix this?"

Poor Granny. He saw how slow I was. I didn't know that a studio could fix things. Sure, they'd fixed Will so he could leave jail, but that was different and took maybe money and promises, a phone call. How about a crazy cop who beats up a movie star? How can that be fixed? Everyone in the emergency room saw me and Joe with Spencer Tracy, including the nurse, and I doubted that money could fix her mouth the way a contract fixed mine. The kid with red bumps would remember me because I backed into him. I nearly broke his toe. As soon as the cops questioned that kid, he'd say, *Some lady came in here and pushed me around, then the nurse threw her out,* and he'd describe me, and the cops would visit me at the dorm. All those people in the emergency room, they saw me. Question those people, and . . . and . . . And. God, I was slow.

"You won't question me," I said to Conejos.

He shook his head. He didn't shake it, more a roll from right to left, a serious no.

"You won't question the nurse or the kid with bumps."

Conejos rolled a serious no.

"If nobody's questioned, nobody says they saw me."

Conejos nodded, a slow and serious nod.

"Studios can do that?"

Nod.

From Granny: "Why don't you get to bed, Sheryl? Think of that name. Doesn't it sound good? Smooth, like store ice cream." He lifted my teacup and walked with it toward the kitchen. "Take off the skirt right here. You won't be seen."

I unbuttoned the skirt, and it fell. A beautiful Celanese rayon with shirred pockets. A gift from Rosemary, after she died. I stepped out of the skirt, then kicked it toward Conejos. He picked it up.

Granny yelled from the kitchen: "Slip, too, I'm afraid."

I looked down at my slip where it stuck, red, to my legs. The skirt had dried, but my slip was tacky with blood. I unbuttoned my blouse, raised the slip over my head, and saw that my bra had blood stains. I stripped off the bra, too, and the girdle. I stripped everything. I gave him everything but my stolen wedgie shoes. I didn't care if Conejos saw me nude. If I wasn't here, if I hadn't watched Joe beat on Spencer Tracy and watched Dr. Ostrander run from a side office to save him, if I hadn't been driven home by Conejos and I hadn't sat shaking in the Zanzibar, blood dust in the air, then Conejos didn't see me undress. Right?

I wore my Cree costume to the dorm. I didn't sneak or try to be quiet when I climbed the stairs to my room, and I ran hot bath water with the door open. I stole some girl's bubbles off the counter and dumped a bunch in the tub. It wasn't my night for a bath, but who cared? Because I wasn't really there. I'd been fixed.

CHAPTER 35

If you want to get there, you'll stop, look and listen to
the most daring woman in Hollywood.

—*Photoplay*, November 1940

Friday morning, the day after Joe didn't beat up Spencer Tracy, I
went to see my brother in jail. By ten fifteen I'd walked through
the Lincoln Heights lobby. Morning visiting hours, ten to noon. I
took out my hairpins. My arm ached from where Joe had grabbed
me. I removed my shoe buckles, shook my purse for the guard, let
him pat my waist, gave my brother's name to the clerk, sat in the
chair on my side of the long glass row.

Other people came, mothers and sweethearts. They clacked
high heels across the dirty floor. Prisoners came to the other side
of the glass, talk and laughter and crying. I waited for my brother.
I held my hands in my lap, then on the narrow ledge by the glass,
then rubbed my sore arm, and finally, when I'd run out of things
to do with my hands, when I gave up saying my new name in my
head, *Sheryl, Sheryl,* I walked through someone's spilled coffee to
the clerk.

"My brother's not here yet. Hey? Where's my brother?"

"Just a minute." He sat at a little desk by the door. Little guy,
little desk, little bald spot that faced me when he looked down.

He shook a sack over the desk, and a pile of Green Stamps fell out. "I hate the taste of these little fuckers, but what can you do. You gotta lick to stick." He ran a sheet of stamps over his tongue and stuck the whole sheet in a collection book.

"My brother," I said. "I'm still waiting."

"Yeah, a minute." Lick to stick.

I'd waited a minute. My sore arm reached out on its own and swept across the little desk. Green Stamps scattered in the air, big, square bug wings that fluttered, then landed and stuck to the floor.

"Now, why'd you do that?"

"My brother's not come out, you understand? I've been waiting twenty minutes and he's not come out."

"No reason—"

"William Harp. William H. Harp."

"Fine. You spill my stuff, but fine, I'll look up your damn brother. What's the name? What's the *H* stand for?"

"Nothing. It's just an *H*."

"Harp. Harp. Funny name. I don't see it on my list."

I couldn't read upside down, but I saw the list in his hands. He held it over his Green Stamps book. "How old's your list?"

"Fresh each morning."

"And?"

"Well, what do you want me to do? He didn't come out. Maybe he doesn't want to see you. It happens, you know."

Every kraut I kill is gonna have your face. It happens.

"He's not on your list? Where is he?"

The clerk set his list down. "You come over here, knock my stuff to the floor—probably ruined some of those stamps—you start demanding things, making a fuss, want me to call a deputy? What do you think, you're a movie star?"

I had a couple seconds of standing in front of the little clerk, a couple seconds, when I knew the difference between Stany and me. Stany could wave arms and send Green Stamps flying and she'd get, *Yes, Miss Stanwyck. I'll look into it right now. I'll do it my-*

self. What, are you tired? Sit down, take my chair. I know how disturb-
ing a jail is. That was Stany. I had the arm-waving and not the
stardom, and the clerk tells me I'm making a fuss. In a year I could
wave a few arms and the clerk would say, *You're Sheryl, aren't you?*
Aren't you Sheryl?

One year. In two, he wouldn't ask my new name, he'd know it,
and he'd know me, and he'd say, *Sit down, take my chair.* All this
when I signed my contract. Yes, I'm talking about a jail clerk, so
who cares, but not really. Think bigger. I'm talking about every
clerk, every assistant, secretary, boss, big buildings and small ones,
every city and town. That's the difference between Stany and
me. And the jail clerk was right, Harp's a funny name. I needed a
star name. I needed to sign my contract with a real name, Sheryl
Somebody.

The clerk dialed his phone. "William H. Harp, *H* means
nothing, he's not on my visiting list. Where is he? William H.
Harp, I don't know. Yes. No, a visitor." He looked at me. "You
are . . ."

"Sister."

"Sister," he said. "Yeah. Well, where is he? *Where?*" He hung
up. To me, he said, "William H. Harp isn't here. He's no longer a
prisoner."

"He's free?"

"I wouldn't call it that. He's army now."

"No," I said. "He has a day. He doesn't go in yet."

"I don't know when he goes or doesn't go. He's army, left last
night, at some base by now, probably."

"Who can I talk to?"

"You're talking to me."

I grabbed the phone receiver and made to whack him. "Who?
You want to keep your head round?"

"Deputy. *Deputy!*"

From then on, I got more attention.

No, the deputy told me, my brother wasn't in jail. Passed his
physical yesterday. Signed release forms at three that morning,

left forty minutes later, all charges dropped as soon as he gets to Kansas and checks in at Fort Riley, two days maybe by rail. He might write from basic training, but maybe not. You know how that is, basic training.

Will was fixed. I was fixed. Paramount fixed both of us. We couldn't talk.

"You weren't there," Granny had told me last night. "You didn't see the doctor, you didn't see Joe, no blood. Madge wasn't pushed, no blood there, either, and of course there's poor Rosemary, bless her good soul, may she go to heaven and be with Our Lord, but she wasn't murdered. Accidental deaths, they're common in Hollywood. Take Madge. A few hard drinks, and look. She falls. She's a come-and-go girl, Sheryl. It doesn't pay to dwell."

Granny didn't mean the part about Rosemary, he was confused. I believed Granny, mostly. He was a nice guy. But I'd read the autopsy transcripts, at least part of them, and Joe read them, too. Not all Hollywood deaths are accidental.

I couldn't talk to Will anymore. Madge was dead, Joe was crazy, Stany at work, and who else to talk to but Rosemary? I'd talked to Rosemary all my life, all our fights and makeups and best friend pinkie swears. I'd been mad for months, both at Will and at Rose, for not caring when I said that Teddy forced me. He did. He forced me, he beat me up like Joe beat Spencer Tracy, he left scars on my back that matched two nails in an office wall at the Buena Park sheriff's station. And Rose had said it wasn't the worst that could happen.

She was right, of course. Everything that had happened since Teddy forced me was worse: walking on Rose's body, seeing her dug up, the autopsy notes, Madge's swinging, dead arm hitting me in the forehead.

I reached downtown by noon and walked through the main building entrance like I was Sheryl. Coroner's office, same as before, Whitey at her desk, same as before.

"Do you remember me?"

"So?" She wore a different scarf, purple dots, wrapped at her neck and tucked into a jacket. She'd hidden her neck scars pretty well.

"I wanted my friend's autopsy report. The coroner said I couldn't, and I understand, so I'm not asking for that. Not the report, I know I can't see it, but the transcript."

"What makes you think the transcript's less important than an autopsy report? Are you nutso? You get nothing from me."

"I'm a contract actress at Paramount. I'm Sheryl Lane." I deleted the extra Y in my head, it was too much.

"Paramount? Why not MGM?"

"Please," I said.

"Let me look."

She stood and walked to the file room. The coroner might have been in his office, or not. It didn't matter, except if he came out and said, *Hi, Pen Harp,* and I had to explain to Whitey that I wasn't anyone, I was between Penny and Sheryl and not quite one or the other. I wore Penny clothes, but soon I'd have Sheryl clothes and Sheryl hair, makeup, and voice inflection. *My brother's a soldier,* I'd say. *We're so very proud.*

"Your friend's name?" Whitey yelled from the file room.

"Rosemary Brown."

"Seven hundred, seven oh one . . ." Her voice came muffled through files. "Brown. Is it recent?"

"Yes, recent," I yelled back at her.

"Got it," she said. She held a thin file in her hand and waved.

Back to her desk. She looked around in case I'd messed with anything. "You have to sign to check it out. Sign this book."

I took her pen and signed *Penny Harp.* I'd never signed *Sheryl Lane* before, so I didn't know her handwriting. Whitey didn't look at the signature. She sat at her desk and watched me open the file and slide out one sheet of thick paper. Rosemary's death certificate. Most of it I knew: next of kin, funeral home, cremation. I skipped to the right side, to the good parts.

24. Coroner's Certificate of Death

I hereby certify that I took charge of the remains described above, held an ___*Inquiry*___ thereon, and from such action find that said deceased came to h _er_ death on the date stated above.

The principal cause of death and related causes of importance, in order of onset, were as follows: *Neck Wound, Exsanguination*

25. If death was due to external causes (violence) fill in the following.

Accident, Suicide or Homicide _____*Suicide*_____
Date of Autopsy _____*X*_____

Injured at City or Town of _____*Hollywood*_____
County and State of __*Los Angeles, Calif*__

Did injury occur at home, industry, or public place?
_____*Home*_____

Manner of injury ___*Cut own throat*___

Nature of injury ___*Neck Wound*___

26. If disease/injury related to occupation, specify
_____*X*_____

27. Signature ___*A. F. Wagner*___MD
Address ___*Coroner's Office*___

28. When required by law
_____*Frank A. Nance*_____Coroner
County of _____*L.A.*_____

"Suicide? What is this?"
"All the facts." Whitey kept watching me. She hadn't moved.

"She cut her own throat?"

"You're reading it."

"Who cuts their own throat?"

"Your friend, I guess."

"How? The cut's straight across. Who does this? Okay. Okay. If she did cut her throat, if she actually managed to cut, how could she cut straight across? Look. Look at me. I cut here, okay? I'm right-handed, like Rose. I start cutting and—oops—I'm dragging the knife up because I'm right-handed and I *have to*. I can't cut a straight line. Plus all the little cuts. Plus she'd be bloody. Oh, God. She'd cut halfway and blood spurting, and how could she cut the rest?"

"Suicide is hard," Whitey said.

"Where are the transcripts?"

"What transcripts?"

"From the autopsy. You have to have transcripts and a report. Where are they?"

"Did you read the certificate?"

I'd read the certificate. I read it again, again, and again, looking for what wasn't there. "What's this *X* mean?"

"We put the *X* when that line doesn't apply. Look at twenty-six, there's no relation to work, so we *X* it."

"But there's an *X* in the autopsy line."

"Right, inquiry only."

"I was there, at the autopsy, I sat in *that hall*."

She shook her head. A pin from her hair fell loose and swung, caught on a long curl. "You saw the autopsy, you saw the surgeon cut her open?"

"No, I told you, I was in the hall. I couldn't go in. You were there, too, at the autopsy, taking notes. Barbara Stanwyck was there. How could you forget an autopsy with Barbara Stanwyck?"

"Who are you? I didn't forget the autopsy because there wasn't one. Why would we? We don't autopsy suicides unless there's something to look for."

"Okay, the inquiry. Where are the transcripts? I want to see those."

"Transcripts."

"Yes," I said. "Inquiry transcripts. Let me see them."

"Currently unavailable."

Until you've stood at the desk of a coroner's secretary, until she moves to block the door of a file room, little neck scars poking from her purple dot scarf, you won't understand. The file room stretched behind her, and she could pull any dead person's file and read it or change information. A man hit by a car on Sunset dies instead in his home, alone. A girl drowns, but wait—she's not drowned, she choked on an ice cream. Whitey told me the coroner's in charge, what he says goes, but look where the file room is. She was standing in front of it, changing our stories. If you break into that room, you'd better do it like Joe and I did, before phone calls and favors fly and a girl cuts her own throat.

Joe and I had held the real transcript, a copy, at least. I read about the garrote and how she was tied up, how she chewed off her own thumb to get free, I read until Joe pulled it away and I told him to get rid of the transcript. I *told* him to. Now it was in pieces stuck to a drain.

"Suicide? How tragic, how sad," Granny said, in his office, backstage at the Gardens. "I mean, I knew she was lonely, maybe distraught, but to take one's own life—"

"Did she bury herself, too?"

"Don't poke around, Sheryl. You don't know why it was changed. You don't know the reasons." He shoved a *Hail the Bullfighters* mockup off a chair and let me sit down. "I guess you won't be our bull now. On to better things. But you don't have to leave the dorm yet, oh no, I care about my girls. Don't let it be said I kicked a Gardens girl to the street. You have two whole days to move out. I know, it's generous, since you can't be in the show while we're filming. Mr. Zukor would not like that."

"Right," I said. "I know exactly why it was changed. Why is anything changed around here? To protect the studio. My brother gets out of jail and that protects Stany, but in back of Stany is the studio. I get a contract with a shut-your-mouth clause, and that protects the studio, too. Why would someone change Rose's death to a suicide? I kept asking myself on the bus home, and you know what? I could only think of one answer. One answer, Granny. Someone at the studio killed Rose."

"Don't do this. Don't worry yourself. Think of the bright years ahead, what you'll do and see, the money. You can provide for your mother and sister. Maybe move them to Hollywood, hey?"

I'd never told Granny about my mother and sister.

"Granny, do you have a shovel?"

"What?"

"Do you have a shovel?"

"I—no, I don't think so. Hammers, yes, for set construction, and saws and nails. You're not looking for more blood on Sunset, are you? We have a broom and dustpan."

"That'll do." I found the broom and dustpan. I quit talking to Granny, because when he said *your mother and sister* I saw him clear, and behind him, the studio. I'd never told him that Madge and I looked for blood, so Madge must have told him. Behind Madge, the studio. Paramount has a big payroll.

Granny said more, but I didn't hear him. Instead, I heard myself at the Bronson Gate: *I wonder what Zukor's cleaning up before I come back.*

I carried my broom and my dustpan out the stage door to the alley, beside the full trash cans, next to stacks of bottles and boxes and laundry bags. I scared off a bum mooching food. In front of me was the dirt that used to mound over Rose, dug up and shifted around, rained on, walked on, hard as wood. Girls passed me, dorm and back, dark came, and I chopped at the dirt with one edge of the metal dustpan.

I made a pretty good pile of dirt chunks. By the time the Career Girls opened the stage door, I'd dug past chunks into soft dirt that scooped easy into my dustpan and rose in puffs, making me choke. I could smell her. I smelled Rose, and I guess that's why I'd dug, to be close to Rose.

One Career Girl didn't like it. "Besides making a mess, you've got a cloud of dust and everything's filthy. Look at my blouse. I bought this at full price."

The other Career Girl, the one who'd cried by the publicity office, didn't talk. I spilled dirt on her shoe, I blew dust toward her A-line skirt and she didn't notice. They both reached the dorm, and when one girl held open the front door for the other, in that borrowed light I saw in my hole something shiny. Sharp, too—it cut my finger. I scraped with the side of my dustpan, scraped more, and couldn't see anything now, but the dustpan hit whatever it was, dug around it, hit more of it. I'd dug deeper than Rose had lain.

Behind me the stage door opened. Granny said to me, "I'll have to tell him, you know. Mr. Zukor won't like what you're doing."

"I don't have a contract yet. I haven't signed anything. Can you move to one side? The light's blocked."

"Sheryl, stop digging."

"Give me your handkerchief, Granny."

"You're bleeding."

"Granny, your handkerchief." I took it from his hand and wound it around my fingers, then reached into the hole and pulled at something thin and sharp and springy. It didn't give. The dustpan again, banging away at dirt, freeing more of the thing, then a tug with my wrapped fingers. Didn't give.

"Let me try," Granny said. He propped the stage door and knelt. He took the dustpan and used its handle to break dirt from the hole. We both felt the release and snap of whatever it was, and I held the thing up in Granny's handkerchief: two spirals of wire.

"The garrote," I said.

"You don't know that."

"Right, because you use so much wire here at the Gardens."

"It could have been in the ground for years."

"With no rust?" I threw the wire at the garbage cans. "Doesn't matter now. Who would I tell?"

"That's my girl," Granny said. "Help me fill this hole."

CHAPTER 36

The domestic and parental urge seems to be sweeping all Hollywood these days, with those homes that aren't preparing for their own little ones getting ready for adopted babies.

—*Photoplay*, November 1940

I needed to wash the dirt and blood off me. In the dorm, upstairs, I knocked on the bathroom door. I rattled the knob. Down the hall, the door to my room opened and a Career Girl stuck out her head. She walked the hall in her slip and came up beside me.

"Cree." She called me by my Indian name. "Let her alone."

"I've got to wash up. I'm dirty all over."

"Use the first bathroom."

"With the nieces?"

"The kitchen, then. Use the sink." She slid one hand in front of me so her whole arm pushed me from the door. "You smell." She sounded like Madge.

"Who's in here?" I reached under her arm and rattled the knob again.

"Look what you did. Now the door's bloody."

"Who's in here, I said."

"It's Lorraine, okay? Let her be. She's had it rough. Use the sink off the greenroom."

We heard crying from inside the bathroom. The Career Girl's arm dropped. She turned to the door and yelled, "Lorraine, I'm here. Lorraine."

"I'm still bleeding," Lorraine said, through the door. I hardly made out the words. My face got cold. I knew why a girl bled, and where. I bled from my finger just standing there, but I didn't need to call out through a door. I didn't need to lock a door while I bled. A girl locks the door to bleed for three reasons. She has her monthlies, that's one reason. She gets pregnant and miscarries, that's two. She gets pregnant and spring-cleans, that's three.

I didn't go to the kitchen. I went to the greenroom, and on the way I put all the scenes together. One scene: Madge and the Career Girl Lorraine at a Zebra table, Madge talking, Lorraine crying, until I came in and saw them. Another scene: Abbott outside his office, patting the Career Girl Lorraine on the shoulder and yelling at me that I'm late. Scene three: the Career Girl Lorraine walking past my dirt heap while I'm digging out the garrote, letting me sprinkle dust on her clean shoes.

I did use the sink off the greenroom. I washed and thought, I dressed in my ugly checked skirt and thought. Tonight I didn't have to parade in the revue line. I was a contract girl now. I watched the Indian show from the Zebra doorway, a line of sequined Indians, step-touch, sway, and I thought.

What did Abbott tell the Career Girl outside his office? I hadn't heard him. Yesterday I'd run late, I should have been at the sound stage already, and I'd hurried past Avenue M. Wet streets. Little pools of rainwater and garbage. Career Girl crying, *I've got a secret.* Abbott in his doorway, his hand on the Career Girl's— Lorraine's—shoulder. Comforting. *We'll take care of it. At Paramount, we're family.*

And extras? Were extras family, too? Lorraine had no contract. The most she'd done was walk by Hank's table in a fake dining room of a fake ship. She did get camera time. If not lost in edits, she'd be in the picture and maybe have her name on the screen. *Career Girl played by Lorraine Someone.*

So the Career Girl might have a screen credit. Bad publicity if a Career Girl's pregnant. Career Girls weren't married, so they couldn't get pregnant. Lorraine must not have known the rules. She got pregnant.

Where would she have an abortion? None of us, except Madge and me, were from near LA. We came from everywhere else, Nebraska and Missouri, Stockton or Lodi, and we didn't know about illegal places except what we heard in the news. A Career Girl couldn't walk up to some house in the Hollywood Hills and knock on the door: *I hear you'll do abortions. Can I come in?* Plus, the house might be miles from Hollywood. It could be anywhere. We wouldn't know where to go.

Who would know? Abbott, he knew, because he worked in publicity. That's what publicists did: They herded girls and fixed problems. Once in a while they faked interviews. Stany's publicist faked an interview with *Photoplay*. How did I know? I read the interview. Stany discussing mothers in Hollywood, children in Hollywood, how they're raised full of values. The Hollywood child, beloved and guided. Except it wasn't Stany discussing, it was Helen Ferguson, Stany's publicist. Stany was at home calling her kid a little fuck.

Publicists fixed. Why else would Abbott pat Lorraine's shoulder?

That's what I saw yesterday, then. That's what Zukor feared I would tell. I didn't think it secret enough to buy me a two-year contract, but okay, I saw Abbott help a girl get an abortion. I could keep shut about that.

Lorraine—how did Lorraine know who to ask? Who told her, *Abbott can help you, he knows an abortionist, go to Abbott*? I didn't know Lorraine or her friends. Maybe one of her friends knew Abbott. How would she know which friend to ask? We didn't have many friends. We didn't talk to each other. When there are only so many jobs, you've got to be sneaky and willing to steal and lie. Sometimes I'd meet a nice girl, someone who wanted to be friends, but she didn't last long. She was gone by the next cattle call. Our friends were the ones who moved here with us, like Rosemary, and even she lied to me. Madge was a friend, but she'd lied to Granny about me.

Say Lorraine had friends, but that wouldn't matter. No unmarried girl goes around saying she's pregnant. As soon as we knew a girl's secret, as soon as the studio knew, she'd be fired. She'd ride back to wherever on a Greyhound bus. I didn't know anyone who wanted to go back to her past. That's why we were here.

Except Madge. She came to LA to get Zukor's help, and Zukor said he'd help and then gave Madge a job. I'd thought Madge meant a job as an extra, but maybe Zukor gave her a different job. I thought again of Madge talking to Lorraine the Career Girl in the Zebra Room. Lorraine had been crying. I thought of the three Lorraine scenes: Lorraine and Madge, then Lorraine and Abbott, then Lorraine crying through the door of Bathroom Two.

Then I added another scene, without Lorraine: Madge arguing with Abbott, the day I'd first worn Stany's gray squirrel dress. That day Madge was wearing the stolen blue dimity gown, and Abbott stood with her, and they argued. Why would Abbott argue with Madge? She hadn't been late to our morning call. She wore the best dress in our group, so why have words? Abbott and Madge, Madge and Lorraine, Lorraine and Abbott.

Lorraine talked to Madge. Or Madge guessed, if she saw Lorraine crying or throwing up. If Madge knew Abbott well, she might think Abbott could help. Or was I right, and Zukor had given her another job—the one where Madge watched for extras who got pregnant, and then directed them to Abbott?

I went to the greenroom and looked for the other Career Girl. Not Lorraine, the other one. I couldn't remember her Indian name. Nez Perce or Sioux. She sat at the mirror almost to the room's end and wiped her face with a tissue. I didn't talk to her. I pretty much knew that Madge was the one who had helped Lorraine, told her to talk to Abbott, and Abbott had sent her to an abortionist. But Madge didn't have any friends, like I already said, so I couldn't ask them. Instead I asked a girl Madge had hated.

Apache was pulling on stockings. She sat on a stool and tugged white gloves onto each hand, then crunched up one stocking to its foot so she could slip her leg in. I stood in front of her and she raised her face.

"You need something?" She'd drawn her upper lip too high. A lot of girls did that because it looked good on stage. Close up, her mouth looked like a pig snout.

"Tell me about Madge," I said.

"Madge."

"You know, the dead girl."

"Which one?" Apache snapped a garter closed and lit a cigarette in her snout.

"She stole your gin."

"Oh, her. Why do you want to know about her?"

"Because she's dead, I guess."

That made sense to Apache. She nodded. She hadn't taken her headdress off, so the feathers wobbled. "I liked her. Sorry she's dead."

"Really?"

"Of course not, stupid. I'm sorry she's dead, yeah. But she was something."

"Do you know anything about her?"

"You mean where she's from, what movies she liked, all that?"

"I guess," I said. I wasn't as good as Conejos at interviewing.

"No."

Conejos would ask something sneaky now, something to get Apache mad. When people get mad, they talk. They can't stop themselves.

"Madge thought your mouth looked like a pig," I said.

"Who cares? She's dead and I'm not."

I was a failure at interviews. Penny Harp was not a detective. Penny would go her whole life without making anyone talk. I wasn't sure about Sheryl, though, so I tried again as her. "You remember the night she took all your pins and your headdress fell off?"

"It was evil. I'll never forgive her for it. I had to buy new hairpins and everything."

"That day she helped me a lot. She drove me to where I last saw Rosemary, and we looked around."

"Who's Rosemary?"

"The other dead girl."

"Go on," Apache said.

"So we found Rosemary's blood. Madge helped me that day. Did she ever help other girls?"

"Wait a minute. What about the blood?"

"Nothing," I said. "We found the blood and then it started to rain. Now, there's nothing left."

"You don't know it was blood, then."

I was a failure as Sheryl, too. Madge didn't help girls get abortions. I was stupid to think so. The heels of my feet ached, my eyes hurt, my whole day was terrible, with no answers I could use. First my brother gone, then the phony death certificate, finding the garrote, Lorraine.

"You know about her side job."

"What?"

"I said," Apache said, "you already know about her side job."

"Sure," I said. I didn't know a thing. "Great side job."

"If you think so."

"Why? Didn't you think it was great?"

"Being a mole for Abbott? What's great about that? It's not like she got any good roles out of it. I don't know how much she earned, but if there's no camera time, what's the use?"

"Yeah," I said. "What's the use. Do you know what she told Abbott?"

"No. What?"

"I mean, what did she tell Abbott?"

"Only one thing, that's all I know. Her entire job was one thing."

"What thing?"

"You know, if a girl needs help."

"Yeah," I said.

"I wonder how much she earned. I could use a side job. I'm moving to Bedroom One. Did you hear?"

"No. Really?"

"I'll need a side job."

The nieces came and went. The girls came and went. If I owned the Greyhound bus line, I'd be rich with the money spent trucking these girls around. Some stayed a while, like me. Some needed help, like Lorraine. And there was Madge, stealing gin, watching for signs. She fixed girls for Abbott, who fixed messes for Zukor, who made the world go around. A moving picture studio is a world, it truly is. MGM and Warners and RKO, they're worlds, too. Every world gets dirty and needs a little tidy-up. See Abbott, he'll help. He'll send you to—not the usual abortionist, like a chiropractor or med student. He'd go top of the line, a real doctor. He'd have that doctor on contract. Like Dr. Ostrander. Disappear into a side office and come out when needed, to help the studio. Come out to drag away Spencer Tracy.

Granny stuck his whole chest through the greenroom door. "Sheryl, when you've changed, let's have a late dinner. I'd like you to meet someone." No one stopped dressing. It was Granny, after all.

"I'm wearing an ugly skirt," I said.

Apache hit my leg, hard. "Who's Sheryl? Does she get my bedroom?"

The one time I tried to wear honest clothes, and I was asked to sit in the Zanzibar. I couldn't do it. I ran from the stage door to the dorm, upstairs to my bedroom, to the closet. I knew I didn't own anything worth dressing in. All the stolen clothes on my side were gone, taken by Conejos. He'd searched through all my stuff with Madge. *This Penny Harp's? She buy it or steal it? This hers? She buy it or steal it? How about this?*

He hadn't touched Madge's stuff. He didn't know that Madge's stuff used to be Rosemary's. Her clothes still hung on the right side. I pulled out a couple of evening gowns that seemed too fancy for the Gardens. One crunched like good rayon and had a white sequin flower that started by one breast and wrapped around the waist, shooting sequined leaves over the opposite hip. If I wore that gown, the whole room would stare. It was a Rosemary gown, not a Penny gown. I hung it back up. Then there was the bright pink gown I'd loved when Madge had held it: sweetheart bodice, sheer to the neck. I couldn't touch its hanger. But Rose had a stolen silk suit that I liked, with an ankle-length skirt, wide satin lapels, and a peplum. I looked good in black silk, so I zipped and buttoned and tried not to stare in the mirror.

In the Zanzibar, I saw Granny wave. He sat alone. I'd expected a director, like King Vidor or Preston. If not a director, I thought Granny might have me meet another contract girl. I didn't expect Granny alone at a table on the kitchen side. I walked through dancing couples to his table.

"Was I too long? Did I miss whoever it was? I had to change."

"No, not too long. You did well," he said. "Do you want a drink? You sure? Keep your chin high when you walk. Every door you walk through, you're walking onstage. Even if it's to the farmer's market. You look fine. Your hair and makeup need work, but the suit is nice." He frowned, and his forehead wrinkled. He talked loud so I could hear over the orchestra. "The suit has an Irene touch. Where did you get yours?"

"Madge," I said. "Who am I meeting?"

"Nobody. Call it a test."

"Now you're testing me. Did I pass?"

"Yes, except for your hair and makeup. The way you walk, too. You need to work on that. And jewelry. Try to make your voice deeper. Do you smoke? That would help. I had a call from Paramount. You sign your contract tomorrow. Be at the studio by three thirty, that's in the afternoon. You're due at Zukor's office at five, but you'll need work done first. And for God's sake, don't go digging in dirt before you show up at the studio. Next time I babysit, I'm asking for combat pay."

"What work? You said I need work."

"Hair, makeup, jewelry. And clothes. Miss Head's office tomorrow afternoon, three thirty. She's going to comment on your eyebrows, so be prepared. You sure you don't want a drink?"

"Gin fizz."

Granny circled his hand in the air, and a waiter bent, took his order, and was gone.

"That'll put you back here by seven, and you'll need to rush to put on the horns, but thank God, your makeup will look good."

"But you said I wasn't the bull girl."

"Weren't you listening? Of course you're the bull. Mr. Zukor didn't like his new property fronting a Warners project, but I've changed his mind. Plus if you're gone, that puts us two short. I'm down a picador as well. Lorraine's sick."

Lorraine. A waiter handed me my gin fizz, and I drank. "Granny, if a girl needs an abortion, where does she go?"

"*Quiet*," he said. "Dear God, do you want people to hear? What are you saying, Penny? Are you in trouble?"

He'd called me Penny.

"If I were, if I were in trouble, who would I see?"

Granny scooted his chair and leaned across the table. "Wait. Don't get into trouble. No need to go into that now. Did you adjust that strap on the bull hat?"

"Yes. If I were in trouble, I wouldn't know who to see. Madge knew, though. She knew who to see because she told Lorraine, didn't she? Did you know Lorraine had an abortion? That's why she's sick. She's still bleeding."

"Dear God. Why can't you just worry about your hair?"

"I want to know. I need to understand. I think Madge worked for Abbott or Zukor. She kept lookout for when girls needed help, then told them to see Abbott. I understand that, because Abbott's a publicity man. He makes the studio look good. I also think I know where Abbott sent them. Dr. Ostrander, right? It's Dr. Ostrander. Maybe there are others, but he's one of them. I figure it's him because the studio hired him to give my brother his physical, and also Dr. Ostrander was the one who came running out and got Spencer Tracy after Joe hit him."

"You're reaching here," Granny said. "And Madge is gone."

"Dr. Ostrander was in his office even though he was supposed to be next door, in the emergency room. He must have been in his office working on something important, because the emergency room was full, and he didn't show up for work. But then he came out and got Spencer Tracy. He helped a movie star, but not those people next door. Did Madge know Dr. Ostrander? No, I know that one. I don't think so. We met Dr. Ostrander, and I would have known if Madge recognized him. The only thing connecting Madge to Dr. Ostrander is Abbott."

"Poor Madge. A sad accident."

"Right. We've got an accident and a suicide. Madge and Rosemary. And what does Rosemary have in common with Madge and Dr. Ostrander? Madge finds the girls, and Dr. Ostrander does the surgery. Then there's Rose. She cut her hand and went to the hospital where Dr. Ostrander worked. She saw Dr. Ostrander. What do you think it means?"

"Hollywood is a place where anything happens," Granny said. "A magical place."

"Right. Dr. Ostrander's nurse saw Rosemary leave the hospital, and that's the last we know."

"Do you want to be Sheryl or not? What are you saying?"

"Granny, Madge is dead because she knew something or saw something. I don't believe she fell, and there's no other reason to kill her. Why kill her unless she was a threat? She didn't have money, she wasn't a star. She wasn't threatening. Unless she knew something important that made her a threat. Her parents are lost in Paris, and she didn't know anything about them, either. The only thing she'd know is . . . who was pregnant? Who had an abortion? Besides Lorraine. Don't give me your mean look. Bedroom One is full of ex-nieces, and none of them hate you. That proves you're not mean. You know what I'm thinking."

"I have no idea. I don't want to know. My advice is to be Sheryl and shut up."

"Well, if Lorraine can get pregnant, anyone can. Big names. That happens, doesn't it? You don't have to say. I know I'm right. What if a big star is in trouble and Abbott arranges for Dr. Ostrander to help her? He'd keep it private, right? A private patient important enough to be treated on Halloween. The busiest night

of the year. What if she's leaving the hospital late at night so nobody sees her? What if Dr. Ostrander gives abortions in his office
next to the emergency room, and he's got a big star in there, and
he waits until late at night for her to go home, so nobody sees her?
But here's Rosemary, she's leaving the hospital, too, and she sees
Dr. Ostrander with this star, and now Rosemary is a threat. Madge
hears about it. What do you think?"

"Penny, you need to keep your thoughts to yourself. We tell
one story until it's the only one that counts. In six months your
name really will be Sheryl. Madge died in a fall. Don't you see?"

"Rosemary was a threat, so she committed suicide. What do
you think? Who was the star? Has to be someone on contract at
Paramount. Dietrich? Mae West is too old, otherwise I'd say it's
her. Dietrich, Lombard, Claudette Colbert, Ann Sheridan—"

"Girls used to do what they're told," he said. He swished his
drink with a finger and wouldn't look at me. "Ten years ago, five,
a girl would shut up and go with the story. Most of them still do.
You're going to make a scene, aren't you? In that case, you should
have signed with Louis Mayer."

He sucked booze off his finger. "You want to know what I
think? If your friend saw something she shouldn't have, I'm saying *if*, then the studio would pay her off. That's what they do. All
over town there are people counting money a studio's paid out.
Studios don't kill, Penny. They fix. They make phone calls, they
tap other guys to take the fall for a star, they do what they want.
They give anonymous girls like you a contract. But nobody here
kills. Not even Warners, and they're too cheap to pay out. That's
what I think. You're dreaming up an abortion ring to explain your
friend's death."

"You're saying Paramount doesn't arrange for movie stars in
trouble?"

Granny swallowed the rest of his cocktail and chewed the ice. I
sipped my gin fizz. The whole Zanzibar seemed thoughtful, like
we'd all paused to remember a sad day. The orchestra played "I
Surrender Dear."

"I love the Gardens," Granny said. "I belong in Hollywood. In

New York I stank, so I came here. Did you know that? New York hated me. Not the people, the city."

"Granny, what can you tell me?"

"You want to know how many abortions Dietrich's had? I don't know. Whenever she's not around for a few days, we say, *Marlene's taking a rest*, and when she pops back we forget there were days in between. Does Paramount arrange her 'rest'? I suppose they do. You've got to believe in the story, Penny, not the truth. There's no glamour in truth. Count on the story. This whole city exists because of it."

"I want to," I said. "I always believed when I was younger. I still do."

"You should get new shoes," Granny said. "High wedgies, with a nice strap. Did Madge wear your shoe size?"

I climbed the dorm stairs. Down the hall my bedroom door was half-open. I wasn't worried, because Lorraine was there and the other Career Girl, too, probably. Girls walked in and out of their dorm rooms, to the toilet, to the kitchen. I heard laughter and shouts in the hall. Other girls shut themselves in bedrooms and pretended they'd gone out. Not many of us wanted to admit we stayed home on Friday night.

I didn't notice the mess at first. In my bedroom I kicked at clothes on the floor, turned on a table lamp, and unbuttoned the black jacket. I would have hung it up except when I reached in the closet, I couldn't find a hanger. Nothing hung on the rod. No hangers or gowns. They all lay on the floor and on my bed, and my dresser drawers were pulled out. One drawer was tipped upside down on the bed. I hadn't made my bed that morning, but now all the sheets were stripped off and wadded in a corner. My hairbrush, hairpins, hair receiver, all hair stuff, a couple pots of rouge, all of it was on the floor. My stuff and Madge's. On the other side of the room, the Career Girl dresser and armoire stood like they always did. Only my side was tossed.

"Lorraine, what happened?"

Lorraine was in her own bed, asleep.

"Lorraine?" I stepped across clothes to her bed. "Did you do this?"

"Shut up." She pulled covers over her head and disappeared.

"Did you mess with my stuff?" I tugged a quilt from her face. "Take a look."

She saw the room with one eye. "No. Didn't you do it?"

"Why would I wreck my own stuff?" I kicked a foot, and one of Madge's hooch bottles rolled on the floor, empty. "Did you see anyone?"

"I don't know anything."

"Someone walks through the dorm, comes to our room, not to the nieces' room but to our room, *ours,* and messes my stuff. You didn't notice?"

"I didn't hear a thing," Lorraine said. "I didn't see a thing. I was asleep."

Sure she was asleep. Of course. She'd drunk the rest of Madge's gin.

CHAPTER 37

Joan Crawford hasn't been so happy in years as she's appeared introducing her friends to her newly adopted daughter, Christina.

—*Photoplay*, November 1940

All over the dorm I asked, "Did you see anyone?" I knocked on doors, and when girls didn't answer, I yelled through the keyholes, "Did you see anyone strange in the halls?" I wasted ten minutes. Another girl wouldn't be noticed, and a guy could sneak through the dorm because guys snuck through all the time. Some girls made money that way.

At the end of my search I leaned against a sink counter and hit myself, fists on thighs. Hitting through black silk feels just like hitting the normal way: It hurts. I'm the stupidest person I know. I sat with Granny half an hour and didn't ask why he "tested" me. Granny told me about tomorrow's signing time, but he could have told me that in the greenroom. I didn't have to meet him. He lured me—is that the right word? He said, *someone you need to meet,* and I ran to change clothes. My bedroom was fine then. It was a mess, but *my* mess, my bed unmade and dirty clothes in a pile. I'd piled them. Then I sat with Granny for a while, and what news did I get? Marlene Dietrich had abortions. I could have figured that on my own. Everyone knew she'd fuck a toothpick. Plus you can't be pregnant and wear trousers. Nobody can.

Granny set me up, then. He knew my room would be searched, and he didn't care.

I kept hitting my thighs. Then I climbed the stairs to get my handbag and found it dumped as well, on top of the clothes that were dumped on top of my bed. My money hadn't been taken. Only five dollars, but it was still there. Whoever searched my room wasn't looking for money. I shoved the five bucks, lipstick, a dime or two back in my handbag. On the clean half of the room, Lorraine snored and bled, with the quilt over her face to block the light. I turned off the table lamp.

In the dark, in my mind, I crossed off the people I'd normally go to for help. Will rode on a two-day train to the army. Rose allegedly cut her own throat. Madge allegedly got drunk and fell. Granny was alive and in town, but I couldn't trust him. Conejos had helped Granny fix me the night Joe beat Spencer Tracy, so I wasn't sure I could trust him, either. Joe, but I wouldn't call Joe. My arm still hurt where he'd twisted. Stany, I could call Stany, but where would I get her number? She'd never given it to me, and no operator would hand out a star's number. And then there was Marty. He was sneaky. Okay, he was beyond sneaky, but he'd kept me out of jail. I switched on the table lamp and found Marty's card in the jumble of pocketbook stuff. I called him from the telephone on the dorm's third floor: FItzroy 5212.

Ring ring. Ring ring. Click.
"Yeah? Yes?"
"Marty, it's Penny Harp."
"Oh."
"I need to talk. Can we meet somewhere? I'll buy you coffee."
"Penny? What time is it?"
"A little past midnight. Not that late."
"You woke me."
"But it's Friday night."

"Some people sleep on Fridays. Penny, right?"

"Yeah. Do you have a party line? Isn't this your office number? What am I hearing?"

"That's me preparing to hang up."

"Marty, wait. Wait. Someone just searched my room. What do I do?"

"Anything worth stealing? Do you have drugs, diamonds? Any plot treatments? Scripts?"

"No."

"Then who cares? Missy called me today. She says you're cleared, and I'm off her payroll. Aw, hell. I'm awake now, thanks to you. Go to bed, Penny. Or go anywhere. Just go."

Click. Buzzzzz.

Stany did a picture a few years back where she played a rich, single woman who finds a corpse. She screams, takes police to the scene, and—oh no!—the corpse is gone!

But I saw it, she says. *Right here on the floor.*

Nobody believes her. She calls all her rich girlfriends to help her search, and for a while all you see on screen are fur coats and ruffles.

And guess who plays a handsome detective? Hank Fonda.

It's a good picture, except for the girlfriends. They get in the way, and one keeps stopping to eat. They aren't very good at detecting. Lucky me, my girlfriends were dead. No Rose, no Madge, no fur coats. Just me, no girlfriends to get in the way. No crazy Joe. Not even a handsome detective. Both Joe and my handsome detective worked the Hollywood Division night shift.

I didn't need Marty Martin. He didn't hurt me by hanging up. I didn't squat by the telephone desk and hug my arms to my knees.

"Why are you here?" a girl asked me. "Don't sit on the cord. I can't use the phone when you sit like that."

I didn't stand and straighten the black silk skirt. I didn't smack the girl, either, so when she fell I can honestly say that I have no clue what happened.

I took a cab to Paramount.

* * *

At the Bronson Gate, I walked past the guardhouse. One security guard sat in the guardhouse: blond, scruffy face, flat nose.
Security guards at Paramount are used to girls trying to sneak
onto the lot. That's why the Bronson Gate is so high, because girls
used to climb the original gate to reach Valentino. Those girls ruined it for all of us. The guard looked down at some papers, but
every noise made him look up. A car drove by, and he looked up.
I kicked a rock toward the gutter, and he looked up. A worker on
a bicycle called from inside to open the gate, and the guard questioned him before letting him leave. If a real worker couldn't even
go home without a security check, the unknown Sheryl Lane,
who'd been told to stay off the lot, couldn't sneak by this guard,
coming or going.

The air was chilly now, with a little wind. My silk jacket was
stunning but thin, and I rubbed my arms. Claudette Colbert
would have a nice, thick Irene wool to wrap around her for when
she broke into movie studios in winter.

I crossed Marathon Street to the Gold Palms Apartments. The
building was a horseshoe curve that faced away from Marathon,
across the street from Paramount admin. The front door hid in the
horseshoe's middle, and that's where I went, where guards seated
in the Paramount guardhouse couldn't see me. The door to the
Gold Palms was locked. I waited. A guy opened the door to leave,
and he held the door for me, a gentleman, and I walked into the
lobby. That's what a good silk suit can do.

I've been in a few apartment buildings, and the staircases are
easy to find. This one sat right in front of me and the stairs curved
up, without a door, so I could stand underneath and see the land-
ing on all four levels. I didn't need those four levels. I needed
a basement. The only door in the lobby read LAUNDRY, so I
opened it and climbed downstairs. I searched the basement walls
for a tunnel that might let the studio heads meet their girlfriends
for lunch.

I listen to rumors. Most rumors are true, at least in the beginning before people muck them up with their own stories. Madge

had told me a secret tunnel ran under Marathon Street. A tunnel between here and Paramount had to be true, because who would make it up? Who would walk by the Gold Palms and think, *Oh, I wonder if there's a secret tunnel where high-paid studio guys cross over and visit a mistress?* Nobody thinks like that. The rumors I didn't believe were the add-ons: *I hear Zukor meets Edith Head at the Gold Palms each Tuesday. Watch, next Tuesday you'll see how her glasses are steamed.* You've got to be smarter than the added-on rumors. Go to the original rumor, trace it back, and that's where you'll find the truth.

The laundry, then. Washing machine, wringer, laundry press, two deep sinks. My dorm had the same setup. A clothesline stretched down the room: a few shirts, trousers, starch in the air. I rubbed my hand over the cement walls to find secret cracks and doors. I scooted the washing machine to see behind it. A girl came downstairs with a tub of clothes and a new issue of *Photoplay*.

"You won't find it," she said.

I ignored her.

"I said, you're not going to find the entrance." She ran water in the washing machine.

"Where is it?" In one corner, dusty wood pallets stacked four or five high. I rubbed the walls behind the pallets.

"Ten bucks."

"I've got four," I said.

"Deal. And the suit."

"This suit?"

"Do you want the entrance?"

"Deal," I said.

"Move those pallets. No, they're heavy, we'll both push. I hear Valentino used this tunnel to meet Mary Pickford. She was fifteen."

"Yeah, yeah."

"Maybe fourteen. Push on that side. I hear her own mother set it up."

"Her mother?"

"Mary Pickford's. How's that for a stage mom? *Meet The Sheik at the end of this tunnel, honey.* I wouldn't mind a mom like that. Here, you see? Lift the lid, and you're in. Everyone looks for a secret door in the wall. They don't notice the floor."

"I remember when Valentino died. We all sobbed."

"Imagine what Mary Pickford did. Watch those stairs. You have a flash?"

"No."

"Here's matches. It's all I have."

I took the matches and started down.

The girl tugged on my sleeve. "The money."

I handed her my four dollars.

"Your suit," she said.

"Right." I climbed out. We changed clothes, in a way. She took my suit—skirt, jacket with satin lapels—and I snapped off trousers and an Orphan Annie blouse from the clothesline. "I'll be cold," I said.

"Grab that cardigan over there. It's not mine. None of this stuff is mine."

"Keep this lid open, will you? I don't want to be in the dark."

"It's not bad," she said. "We use the tunnel a lot, to hunt around. I found Bing Crosby's snuff."

"Exciting," I said.

"I could sell it."

"Keep the tunnel lid up," I said.

About eight wood stairs brought me to a concrete and dirt tunnel under Marathon Street. I had to bend a little. Mary Pickford at fourteen would have run right through, head up, to Valentino. She wouldn't have met cobwebs. The tunnel then would have been clean. I hit floating strands of cobwebs every foot or so, in my nose, on my hair, long strings of broken dust. I'd gotten about ten feet when I heard *thump* and the tunnel went dark.

"I can't see in here. Hey! Keep the lid up!"

A scraping sound, pallets dragged over a tunnel mouth. Then quiet, and a car's muffled zoom overhead.

I scraped a match on the concrete wall and saw enough to keep going. Every ten feet or so I scraped a match. Scrape and walk, scrape and walk, until the matches ran out. The laundry girl had only given me three. After the last match died, I stood for a while and forgot which way I'd come. When I stepped forward, I hit concrete. I set my fingertips on the wall and used them to follow the tunnel.

I could hear rats, I'm sure of it. Rats and tunnels, they're partners. But Zukor wouldn't creep along tunnels from Paramount to the Gold Palms, kicking a rat or two on the way. I'll bet some studio guy had rat cleanup duty. Studios think of everything.

What do you do for Paramount?

Oh, I kill rats in the tunnel these guys use to visit their girlfriends. How about you?

Me? I don't do much. Just give abortions to movie stars.

Crazy world.

Beats the bread line. At least I don't sweep cigarette butts, like that guy there.

You want to know how I got from one end of a blackout tunnel to the other? My stomach and heart kept chasing me. I wanted to hug my knees and rock. Instead, I followed my fingertips along the concrete wall and I made up conversations. I thought of every dumb job at Paramount: elephant handlers for Mr. DeMille; nurses delivering Benzedrine; painters who zebra-stripe donkeys; one girl who can sing but not talk, and another who talks and has singing dubbed by the first girl; a diction coach who whacks a stick on her desk and makes both girls repeat vowels. Lots of dumb jobs, right to the end of the tunnel, another set of stairs to a hatch that lifted to a dark room.

In the room I felt for a light, bumped a wall, and traced fingers from the wall to inside a cool basin. I pulled against the basin to help me climb the last few steps beyond the hatch. Then a door opened, and someone pushed a button, and the room lit, white and harsh. The tunnel had ended at a men's room.

I stood halfway out of the hatch next to a line of urinals. My eyes hurt and narrowed, brightness after the tunnel. Both my hands pressed in a urinal basin, but I couldn't move them. I'd be seen.

I'd be seen anyway. The guy would see three stalls to his left, and he'd use one. He'd come out of the stall, look right, and see a sink, three urinals, an open hatch, and half a girl leaning out of a hole in the floor. Or he'd go directly to a urinal. Then open hatch, girl. Either way, he'd have to see me. I was leaning into a men's room with my hands flat inside a porcelain urinal. I squeezed my eyes shut.

Little footsteps, short, tapping footsteps, shoes with taps clicking on tile. Water sounds, trickles, silence. Silence, and out of it a hard panting, and behind the panting, silence.

He'd grab me. He'd pant close to my ear, and I'd feel my ear go hot, and everything white in this room would turn dirty. I knew what happened next. I waited for it. I felt it nudge my hip at the edge of the tunnel hatch. A hard nudge, and another. I held my breath. My eyes opened.

A dog, between me and the stalls, paws balanced over a floor drain, squatting. Black terrier against white porcelain, white tile, white paint, staring at me with round black eyes, open mouth, and wet tongue.

The door creaked open partway and a man's voice called in, "Toto, come. Let's go. No more pee time. You done here?"

The dog turned toward the door and clicked, paws on tile, furry tail. The man shut the door. I waited, then I left, too.

I was on 4th Street by the admin building. No dog, no man's voice. The studio was quiet this late, only a few people, mostly security strolling with hands in their pockets. Two workmen drove a truck past me. A third man stood in the truck bed and balanced a small airplane, wings up, then down so the plane cleared buildings. I'd been to Paramount at night. The trick was to walk like you're exactly in the right place, you're here on purpose. I walked the streets like I belonged, one thirty in the morning, two security guards at Avenue P, Stage 18. Somewhere, Toto walked with a man. Everything else, quiet.

I'd come because of what I'd told Joe after my meeting with Adolph Zukor: *What's Zukor cleaning up before I come back?* Zukor thought I saw Abbott fixing Lorraine, and he was right. I just hadn't known what I'd seen. *What does Zukor think I know, and what is he cleaning up before I come back?* I knew the answer to the first question, and I needed an answer to the second. I wasn't supposed to be on the back lot, so that's where I went, to the back lot, to find out what needed cleaning.

I belonged on Avenue M, by the publicity office. That's how I acted: *Oh, I just left something earlier, and I'm fetching it now.* I waved to a security guy. I waved to the guy in the truck bed leaning the airplane this way and that. I took pretend keys from my pocket and jangled them. *Move and don't move,* Stany had taught me. I jangled the pretend keys in my hand. I looked like I'd come from home, casual, my trousers and cardigan. Move and don't move. I stopped at the publicity office, I moved and didn't move to the door, I turned the knob.

Locked. Pretend keys wouldn't open a real door. No sound on Avenue M. I looked around me: no planes, no security, and Preston Sturges's office next door with its wide, striped awning. Two metal poles held the awning over Preston's window. The poles were nailed to stucco, and I knew how soft stucco was. Rose had pulled stucco chunks from my back after my one date with Teddy. Stucco crumbled. I crossed to Preston's office and leaned all my weight against one of the poles, then pulled back hard. I leaned, then pulled. Leaned and pulled. The nails holding pole to stucco loosened and gave, and I fell with the pole in my hand, the awning tipped like a loose eyelid, a truck turning at the corner onto Avenue M.

The airplane truck, without the airplane. Three guys in the cab. They stopped the truck in front of Preston's office.

"What happened? Are you okay?"

"I'm fine," I said.

One guy in coveralls jumped from the truck and helped me stand. "Are you hurt? Did this pole break off?"

"I'm not hurt," I said. "All I did was lean on it. I was looking for my keys—" I moved and didn't move. Just my head moved, looking for the keys. I'd dropped them when the pole broke, damn, where are they, here on dark Avenue M?

"There they are," I said, and I picked up my pretend keys. My fingers shook. *Make each move on purpose*, Stany had said.

"This pole is dangerous." The guy ripped striped canvas off the pole and leaned the pole against the building. "But you're okay?"

Fine, no problem, get in your truck, drive off. Wave, *beep-beep* of the horn, three guys waving. That's what should have happened.

"Wait, give me that pole." The guy tipped the pole away from the stucco wall of Preston's office. "We can't have poles falling on pretty girls."

"No, it's okay. The pole is okay." I grabbed the pole and tugged it toward me.

The guy tugged back. "What kind of Paramount man would I be if I left you with a pole that already attacked you once?"

"I'm okay. Plus," I said, "we don't want that pole getting lost. It has to get fixed to the building. I mean, look at this awning."

The guy looked at the pole, the awning, the stucco. "I have tools in the truck. Hey, guys." He waved to his two friends in the cab. "We're needed here."

"Isn't that nice," I said. "Aren't I lucky."

Three nice guys in coveralls. One said, "Looks like it got tore out."

"Recent, too. Where's security when you need them?"

"Knock that loose plaster. Here, hold the pole . . ."

They'd forgotten about the pretty girl. I backed toward their truck and then on down the street until I stood in front of Abbott's office again. I didn't have my pole to help me break into his office, but I did have my pretend keys. I took them out of my pocket and held them in my right hand and walked from the street up to Abbott's door, and I stuck a pretend key in the door. Still locked. I step-swayed to the right, to where my shoulders reached the bottom of Abbott's office window, and I looked over at the three Paramount workers. Paramount should be proud of workers like that. Here it was near two in the morning and did they slow down, did they sit in the break room and argue about who'd follow Toto and pick up doggie doo? No, they did not. They kept busy on Avenue M, reattaching a pole so I couldn't use it to bust open the publicity office.

I placed both palms against Abbott's window sash and pushed up. The window rose. It hadn't been locked. I'd broken the pole clear off stucco for nothing. I pushed the sash open as far as I could, and then pulled myself up so my stomach balanced on the window frame.

I'd done this before, at a different window higher from the ground, on Halloween. I'd climbed into Stany's window to help Rose, and there was an instant, just a flicker, when I balanced on Abbott's window frame at his office at the Paramount lot and I also was balanced on Stany's window frame, like I could bounce my legs for momentum and swing back to Halloween and climb down the ladder and go back, go *back*, to before Rose fell into Stany's house. But it was just a flicker, a quick there and gone, and I swung forward so I slid into the publicity office headfirst to the floor. When I sat up and looked out the window, I saw the three workers still making Paramount proud, one holding the pole, one a wrench, one a can of sardines. I could smell the sardines from inside, on the floor. The guys never looked at me. I shut the window.

The publicity office held a chair and a secretary's desk, a window seat and a wall filled with publicity shots in silver frames: Paulette Goddard smiling, Bing Crosby smiling, Dottie Lamour smiling, George Raft smiling, Carole Lombard playing golf and smiling, Claudette Colbert in profile and shadow, smiling. To the right, behind the chair and desk, were more chairs and desks, and behind them, a door with a painted sign: MILES ABBOTT, PUBLICITY.

The door was locked, for a while. I didn't have a metal pole, but I did have a metal letter opener I'd grabbed from the secretary's desk. A little wiggling in the lock, a lot more twisting than I'd done with a hairpin at the coroner's office, a big shove that cracked wood around the lock assembly, and I was in. Easy. I looked at Abbott's office, spread with lacy, dim light from a side window, and on top of his desk, through stacks of papers and files, script changes, press releases, carbons, and letters to and from that I could barely read in the dark:

To our friends at [enter name here],

Paramount Pictures rolls out the red carpet for Santa Claus and YOU on Saturday, December 21, at eight o'clock in the evening. Bring your favorite elf and your camera, because you won't believe who is helping Santa distribute gifts this year!

Cal,
Miss Davis remains with Jack Warner, but ooh la la, as the French say! You're right that something's up. In 1941 you'll see Miss Davis on screen with Paramount's most handsome star. Oh, and the French is a big hint. Sshh for now. You can bet you'll be the first to know!
Yours truly,
Miles Abbott

Hymie,
No offense taken on the *Movie Mirror* pics. You're absolutely right; we should have kept her from the punch bowl. But like I said, our studio will not be holding a Santa night this year, so rest assured you are not being slighted. If plans change, I'll ring you. You can bet you'll be the first to know!
Yours truly,
Miles Abbott

Miles,
Your job is to watch your people. Mine
is to write about them. The next time
you tell me to shut up about Charlie,
I'm putting Paulette with him in a
two-page spread. You asshole. You
know what I'm talking about.
                              Hedda

Worthless. The letters and scripts—worthless. I searched his desk, the cabinet at the side wall, telephone file, a box full of receipts and invitations. I needed a list of names, something that said, *In October, Madge referred five girls to me for abortions, and I sent them to Dr. Ostrander. Yours truly, Miles Abbott.* I didn't find a paper like that. I should have broken into the payroll office, because if Madge had an extra job, then she was paid for that extra job.

It wouldn't have mattered. I didn't know Madge's last name, so I couldn't look up her pay stubs. But Zukor had to be cleaning up something. Otherwise, why ban me from the lot?

The entire length of 6th Street was empty. Avenue M was empty. The publicity office was empty, except for me, and I lifted the receiver on Abbott's telephone. I thumbed through Abbott's telephone file. I dialed Stany.

Ring ring. Ring ring. Click.
"*Mmm hmm.*"
"Stany? It's me. It's Penny."
"Who?"
"Penny."
"Who?"
"I didn't kidnap your son."
"What are you doing? What's the time? It's—Penny, it's two a.m. Awww, I hate you so much."

"I'm stuck. I can't leave Paramount's back lot. How do I get out of here?"

"Oh, Penny."

"No lectures. What's another way out? I can't go by the guard-house."

"What are you doing at Paramount?"

"No lectures."

"I won't lecture, but you're not supposed to be at Paramount."

"Stany, help me."

"How did you get in?"

"The tunnel that leads to the admin men's room."

"That old myth. No, really, how'd you get in?"

"Just *help* me."

"Walk out, like I do. If the guard asks questions, just say who you are."

That works for Barbara Stanwyck, but not for Sheryl Lane, not yet.

"Okay, then jump the wall by the tin shed. Everyone does it. I mean, everyone trapped in the back lot. You land in the cemetery next door, you walk out to Santa Monica Boulevard."

"You've actually jumped that wall?"

"Of course not. I don't know anyone who's jumped that wall. When I'm at Paramount I'm *supposed* to be there. I'm not sneaking around, and neither is anyone I know. Except you."

"I'll jump the wall. Stany, pick me up, please? I don't have money for a cab. I've got a car, but it's stuck on Olympic."

"I hate you. I should call Adolph Zukor myself and rat you out. Twenty minutes. No, half an hour. I need to wake up. If you're not by the cemetery gate, I swear I'm leaving."

"I'll be there. Half an hour."

"Oh—Pen. Be careful on that jump. That barbed wire will shred your clothes."

I couldn't move my hand. I couldn't hang up the phone. It was cold in the office, and I'd never been so cold. Shaking cold. I thought of the wall behind the tin shed that rose high and ran the length of the back lot. That high wall. That barbed wire spiraling along the high wall that separated Paramount from Hollywood Cemetery. The wall I'd seen every day next to Stage 16, when I'd walked to Stany's trailer for the squirrel dress. I hadn't noticed the wire before, but now I added it to my memories: Joe leaning against the high wall, arms crossed, uniform pressed, cigarette in his mouth, barbed wire a long, thick, dull coil over his head.

Of course the wall had barbed wire. Of course it did. Otherwise, every tourist in town would find a way to hop that wall and land in the Paramount back lot.

And Rose's arms had cuts, jagged pokes and scrapes, and those wounds had bugged me, because how can a girl get cuts from plain old skinny wire? She doesn't. She gets cut through the neck when the wire is pulled, she spurts blood, and she dies, and that's all.

Barbed wire and a skinny garrote. I knew Paramount had barbed wire. Did the studio use skinny wire, too? Where would a killer get other wire, the thin, deadly kind, enough to wrap Rose's neck?

I couldn't think about wire. I had to leave Abbott's office, push the door, look up and down Avenue M, past three workers hoisting an awning, and—*now*—run in my Wallflower shoes to 6th Street. I hugged myself in the cardigan. I shivered. I wouldn't think of wire. I turned left, turned right, ran.

If barbed wire cut Rose's arms, the barbed wire coiling the Paramount wall, then Rose was here and she died here. How many kinds of wire does a studio use? Where do they keep it? The extra wire—spools of it, probably—how was it stored? Would they store it with supplies?

The tin shed. The long tin shed, stuffed full of supplies. Hammers and gaskets and stacks of pallets and trays of penny nails.

And I ran down Avenue L, I passed Zukor's office and Bing Crosby's trailer and the scoring stage where Dorsey was recording—I could *hear* the horns, see the red stage light flashing, he was there right *now*—and I passed that, too, turned left on 12th Street, turned right at Stage 16, and there, the tin shed, the flat, ugly tin shed. Next to it, one stretch of the back wall before it disappeared behind Stage 16. Shadowy, dark. Specks of steel caught light from RKO's kliegs next door, the gray of barbs twisted to a corkscrew.

Who else would pull Rose off the wall, pull her from a tangle of barbs? Who else but security, keeping people out and in. Protecting the studio.

If it was true, if Rose were somehow held here, tied up, panicking, chewing her thumb, if she got loose and climbed the back wall, if she fought the barbed wire, any Paramount security guard could have pulled her down. Any of them could have done it. Paramount had many security guards, and I knew one of them, and that one guard had investigated the death of Rose.

"Penny? Is that you? Penny?"

Hi, Joe. Yes, it's me. I'm cold and I've just run two baseball fields. Oh, my God, I'm cold.

CHAPTER 38

Marlene Dietrich looked like a breath of champagne, or
what every man wants but seldom can afford to pay for.

—*Photoplay*, November 1940

Joe held my wrist and walked me to the tin shed. His hand was
hot.

"We'll talk in here," he said. "No one will know." Joe squeezed
my wrist. He opened the shed door with a key.

I held on to the door jamb. "How often do you use the barbed
wire, Joe?"

"Go on in. The light cord's to your right."

"I'm not going in."

"Sure you are."

"Don't touch me, Joe. Do you have wire that's not barbed?"

"Fine, you have a choice. Go in, or have those guys locking
Stage 32 hold you and call Mr. Zukor."

The two security guards at Stage 32 faced away from us. They
hadn't seen me yet. I could yell. A quick turn, see me, call Zukor,
and I'd never be Sheryl. Sheryl hadn't noticed the barbed wire,
hadn't dug out a thin garrote. Joe yanked my wrist and pulled me
into the tin shed.

"Get the light cord."

Every part of me shook. I hit the light cord with the one hand I had free, but I couldn't grab it. Joe reached in front of me, caught the cord, and pulled. A bulb lit and swung over long tables with tools and metal parts, machine oil and pulleys and broken boom mikes and folding chairs and stacks of leather work gloves.

"Pen, are you all right? You're shivering." He led me to a work-bench and sat close, shoulder to shoulder, elbow to elbow, knee to knee.

It sounds peaceful, sitting together on a bench. I saw the barbed wire spools at the far end of the shed, where light barely reached. On top of them, smaller spools of wire, not barbed but smooth and round. Stacked spools. Paramount must use a lot of wire. And Paramount has stains, lots of them, even in the tin shed, little ones on the concrete floor and one big, dark stain under the bench where we sat, right under me. A stain so big I had to scoot forward to trace its edge with my foot.

"You're not here to see me," he said. "I wish you were here for me, I really do. But you didn't know I'd be here. I'm usually not here at night. No, don't say anything. Let me think. You're here to solve it. I don't blame you, Pen. She's your best friend. I under-stand. But some deaths don't get solved. No matter what you do, no matter what's done, you don't get an answer. Say you discover a killer," Joe said. He kicked at a bent nail on the floor. It hit my crepe shoe and bounced. "What then? Think about it. No, don't say anything. Can you call the police? Conejos doesn't care, he's on to other cases. People get killed in Hollywood, not just suicides but real deaths like murders. He doesn't have time to waste on a suicide. Can you call the newspapers? They never heard about Rosemary's death. They don't know who she is. They won't be-lieve you. Will you confront the killer? He'll either laugh because Rosemary's death was a suicide, or he'll kill you. Either way, I don't see a good result."

"I thought you liked me."

"Oh, I do," he said. "I like you too much. You look good in trou-sers. Are you cold? But I wish you hadn't come, Pen."

"I was looking for what Zukor was cleaning up."

"There's nothing to clean, Pen."

"What about the wire?"

"Wire?"

"All this wire."

"Are you listening to anything I've said?"

I was. He'd just said that whatever I did, whoever I told, Rose's death didn't matter. And all the while I was turning, turning, to one wall, then another, imagining Rose in this shed sitting on this bench with wire twisting her wrists and ankles, alone in this shed. She chews off her thumb. She chews and screams. The wire slides off her wrists, and she twists it off her ankles, too, she runs out, and her blood soaks into the concrete to mark her terror. She runs to the back wall. She climbs, her arms tangled in barbs and blood. Joe comes. He stands behind Rose, silent and staring. I'd seen him silent and staring before, not in my imagination but in real life, when he'd kicked Spencer Tracy unconscious. Anyone who can kick Spencer Tracy can kill a no-name girl and it won't matter, whatever I do, whoever I tell.

"What are you thinking?"

"You said you like me, you just said."

"I do, I like you too much," he said. "I don't think of the studio when I'm around you."

"That's good," I said.

He looked at the tin ceiling and then at me, at my face, my eyes. "No," he said. "You're still shaking. Why are you shaking, Pen?"

"Stany's picking me up. She might be there right now. I'm jumping the wall. She knows I'm here."

"Over the wall, through that big cemetery? That big, dark cemetery?"

"Dark cemetery, yes."

"Where anything can happen. Cemeteries are scary places. I'd never walk through there alone at night. Penny, you're going to sign your contract."

"Yes. Yes, of course."

"Well." He slapped my thigh and stood up. He stepped on the edge of the dark stain. "Let's get you over the wall. That barbed wire is tricky."

Tricky, yes. With RKO's kliegs roaming the night and two guards cussing each other by Stage 32:

You broke the lock.

You idiot, we've got the wrong key.

Say that again to my face.

"Hurry," Joe said. He took a dust mop from the shed and lifted the barbed wire with the rag end to make space between the wire and the wall. I climbed a step stool, then pulled myself to the top.

"Keep your head low. Where are those guys? Pen, pull yourself through. Fast, I'm throwing the mop down."

My hands scraped, my leg caught an edge of barb, ripping the trousers, a shallow cut on my leg from wire that had gouged chunks down Rosemary's arms. When I looked back, I saw my body slide over the wall, and the wire glinted and rolled along, a sharp tinsel strand in RKO's cast-off light. Barbs jabbed my leg and sprang free when I fell into the cemetery.

Joe stood on the Paramount side of the wall. I brushed my hands on my new, ruined trousers. My legs stung. Neither of us moved, Joe by the tin shed, me on somebody's grave, breathing fast.

I called to Joe on the other side. I put my hand on the rough wall between us. "Am I in danger?"

"Of course not," he yelled. His voice came over the wall through cold air, the other guards arguing behind him. "Not if you sign your contract."

CHAPTER 39

We drove some seventy-five miles out of Hollywood
into the ranch country to get a load of Mr. Power with a
wave in his hair and a glint in his eye and Linda Darnell
in his arms, and never were we more rewarded.

—*Photoplay*, November 1940

Valentino is buried in Hollywood Cemetery. His ghost is rumored
to walk the graves, but I wasn't afraid, not after the whole Mary
Pickford story. I felt safe thinking of Valentino in bed at the Gold
Palms and young Mary in the tunnel, trailing her hand on the concrete like I did, with a torch, with her mom waving her forward,
with Zukor floating above it all and passing a hand over them with
his blessing. Then Douglas Fairbanks came along to fuck it up.

No, Valentino didn't scare me. No ghosts scared me tonight.
I had a new fear that trailed me through the graves and pushed
me when my heels caught. One man with barbed wire: Joe. Two
men with a secret: Joe and Miles Abbott. I'd be all right when my
contract was signed. Joe said that.

I slid through the bars at the cemetery's front gate. I waited ten
minutes for Stany.

"You're annoying," Stany said. "And what happens if Bob wakes
up and I'm gone?" She'd reached across and opened her passenger
door. Her hair was in curlers.

"It's Joe. He killed Rosemary with wire from the tin shed. And I know why. Rose saw someone leave the hospital, someone famous."

"You're making no sense. Shut the door, you're letting the cold in. I just got the car warm and now you're letting in cold air. Calm down, will you? Are you bleeding in my car?"

"I don't mean to bleed." I told her about Madge's extra job and Dr. Ostrander's extra job and the silver garrote I'd found behind the Florentine Gardens. Stany pulled up at the Gardens on Hollywood Boulevard, I mean Santa Claus Lane, and the Christmas trees at every lamppost turned the street green.

"Madge and Dr. Ostrander, fine," Stany said. "Every studio has doctors on retainer. I could have told you that. MGM practically takes over Cedars of Lebanon. I don't know any other hospital with so many stars going in and out. So, sure, other hospitals do it, too. But how do you fit in Rosemary Brown?"

"The first part we know. On Halloween, Rose brought me to your house, and she broke a window and fell in. She cut her thumb, bad. I sent her to Sunset to flag a car. She was taken to Hollywood Receiving, and the room was packed full of Halloween people. Busiest night of the year. She left. That's her story, what we know. Let me link it to what I've found out."

"Link it," Stany said. "I'm wasting gas here."

"I'll talk fast. When I discovered Rose had been at that hospital, I kept thinking, where did she go? When she left the hospital, did she come home? Who drove her? But what if she didn't go anywhere? What if she left the emergency room and walked down the side of the building toward the street? She'd pass that door, the one Dr. Ostrander used the night Joe beat up Spencer Tracy."

"It was terrible," Stany said. "But I heard nobody hit Spence. He had an accident."

"Yes, an accident. Right outside Dr. Ostrander's door. On Halloween, Rose would have to pass the same door, and what if the door opened? Rose saw a woman who had come to Dr. Ostrander for help because she was pregnant, and a star can't be pregnant. Not if she's single. Rose saw who it was. Bad timing. If Rose had stayed in the emergency room, she'd be here now. She'd be alive. What I don't know—what I wish I knew—was who it was. Not the star. Who cares about the star? I mean who else, besides Dr. Ostrander, was there? Whoever it was, they recognized Rose. That person took Rose and locked her in the tin shed at Paramount."

"Why would this person lock her up? Who cares if Rosemary sees some star leave a hospital?" Stany said. "Even if there's a star, that doesn't mean the star had an abortion."

"No. You're right. Maybe she heard them talk. Yes, she heard them talk. She had to know."

"You mean she had to know in order to fit your theory. If Rose saw a secret abortion, why not pay her off?"

"Yes, that's what Granny said."

"Trust Granny. He's very smart." Stany looked at herself in her rearview mirror. Her lip line was smudged. The Christmas trees shone through the car and made her hair green. Her curlers sagged.

"Pretend Rose won't take a payoff. Pretend, okay? What would the studio do?"

"Offer her more money," Stany said. "Give her a job. A contract. They'd do exactly what they did for you."

I couldn't make anything fit. Dr. Ostrander and Madge, they had two things in common. Rose fit only if she knew how Dr. Ostrander helped Paramount. Three people with two things in common. First thing, all three worked for Paramount. Second thing, Dr. Ostrander and Madge, two of the three, were involved in illegal abortions. Rose saw someone leave, someone important. She had seen someone, or she just didn't fit.

"Stany, I'm so angry. My whole body is mad."

"You think your body is mad, but really you're tired. You've been sneaking around, and you're worn out. Oh, God, what do I do if Bob wakes and I'm gone?" She pressed the ignition, and the car died. We sat in her dark car on Santa Claus Lane. Trees flickered on the lampposts, and a single car drove by, the first since we'd parked. Stany shifted behind the steering wheel and faced me. "You know that squirrel dress?"

"Is this going to be a long story?"

"I hate it. I only let you wear it because I hate the dress. I don't care that you sewed a scarf on the hem. I never want to see the dress again, I'm throwing it out. My husband bought me that dress. Why would I wear gray? Why would he *think* I'd wear gray? And you know what else? I lied to you. No, another lie, an important one. Just—just don't interrupt me, okay? I told you I saw my mother fall off a streetcar. I didn't. Yeah, that's how she died, but I never saw it happen. Push in the lighter for me, will you?"

"I don't understand."

"Push. In. The lighter."

"Your mother. Why lie?"

"Don't be simple, Pen," she said. "You only get one story. Everybody gets just one, even me. If I'm there when she dies— that is, if I see her get pushed and fall and break apart—then that's a few more seconds I get to spend with my mom. I don't care what happens during those seconds. I just want them, is all. She's my mom, and I want every second."

"And your son? Do you want all the seconds with him, too?"

"You don't understand," she said. "You haven't gotten a word." She punched the ignition, and the car roared. "You need to know about Rosemary because you want every second, that's what I'm telling you. It's an analogy."

"And the squirrel dress?"

"No analogy there. I just hate the dress."

"I've got to make something *fit*," I said.

"I feel like that every day," Stany said. "Here's the thing. Once you sign your contract, nothing fits. You stop asking questions. *Nobody* gets to ask them. No more questions. If you want to make something fit, you have—let's see—about thirteen hours. Go in. Go to sleep."

CHAPTER 40

And so it goes, babies, babies, babies, soothing troubled hearts and bringing joy to movie homes.

—*Photoplay*, November 1940

I slept ten hours. Then I took a bus to Olympic and, at a filling station near Madge's old car, I spent my loose change on gas. I bought one canful. I poured gas on Madge's distributor cap, and another car pulled off busy Olympic and parked at the curb in front of me.

Conejos rolled down his window. "Let me help," he said. He stretched his legs, then his arms, and shoved his hat on. He left his jacket in his car. "You start the car, and I'll pour."

"Why? If you're arresting me again, I'll have to leave the car anyway."

"Just start the car."

I turned the key, pressed the ignition button, then *cough-cough, chuff-chuff-chuff.* Conejos walked to my window. I rolled it down.

"I've been waiting on the next block for the last three hours," he said. "I talked to Miss Stanwyck this morning."

"Miss Stanwyck? What happened to Missy?"

"I'm not happy with that name. It sounds impolite."

"Impolite, from the guy who called me Rose's killer."

"Nothing against you," he said. "I thought you were a killer at the time."

"Maybe I killed Madge," I said.

He looked at me, a round face, like Daisy's but bigger. It was almost four in the afternoon, and the sun hit his hair and neck. "I don't think so," he said. "I might be wrong, but I don't think so."

"Besides, Madge was an accident and Rose was a suicide."

"Yeah, I heard that. Listen, can I get in? It's hot out here."

I spread my hand to the passenger seat, and Conejos jogged around the car.

"So you talked to Stany—Missy—Miss Stanwyck," I said.

"Yeah." He shut the door, and the seat squeaked. He settled in, his neck sweaty. "She called me. I don't know how she got my home number."

"You don't?"

"All right, I might have given it to her."

"I'm late. Can you say why you're here?"

"Missy told me your theory. She doesn't believe the theory, of course, and neither do I. I'm not on the Rosemary Brown case anymore."

"There's no case. It was suicide."

"Yes, that's what I'm told. So there's no chance that Rosemary saw some big movie star leaving the hospital on Halloween. It's a far-fetched theory, don't you think?"

"Thank you for telling me."

"Just hold on, will you? Christ, I arrest you once and you can't find a kind thing to say."

"Twice. You arrested me twice. In public, and once in front of my family."

"I want to know why. Why do you think Rosemary Brown saw someone at that hospital?"

"Now you want to know. I can tell you and not be arrested?"

"There's no murder," he said. "You're no longer a suspect if there's no murder."

"Then everything you said about me was true. Except for the murdering part, and the kidnapping. That night, on Halloween, I went in a cab with Rose, and she brought me to Stany's house."

"I know."

"I lied to you."

"I know."

"So why are you asking me now? How can you believe me?"

He rubbed his sweaty neck, then rubbed his sweaty hands on his thighs. His face was a sunspot. Sun on his cheeks and chin, hat low on his head. I couldn't see him through sun and hat.

"Because it doesn't matter," he said. "Anything we do now, we'll swear later that we didn't do. I have questions. I know there's no case, but I have questions anyway."

"You have other murders to investigate."

"I'll always have other murders. It's Hollywood. Missy says you've got until this afternoon to get questions answered, and after that, the questions don't exist, either. You do have questions, don't you?"

"Yes," I said. "One big question."

"I'll admit, for a while my big question was whether you murdered your friend. It sure looked like you. I would have sworn it was you."

"What changed your mind?"

"If you killed your best friend, there'd be no reason for anyone to cover it up. The best proof of your innocence is me being told that Rosemary Brown committed suicide. So, there it is. The coroner's decision is final. I've been pulled off cases before, I know how it works. You and me, we know as much of the truth as we're going to. I can't say I trust you completely, but I believe you didn't murder Rosemary Brown."

"Thank you."

"Well, I was hard on you," he said. "I'm still not sure about the whole kidnapping plot. I thought I had you there. Aw, hell. Missy talked to a doctor at Hollywood Receiving. The doctor is waiting for us."

"I'm due at Paramount. I'm running late. I might as well be a little later. Do you have any money for gas?"

Dr. Ostrander wasn't happy. "I thought you'd be here three hours ago. I've been waiting."

"You're not busy," Conejos said. We stood in the empty emergency room. A nurse read *Movie Mirror* at her desk.

"It's Saturday. I'm busy, you just can't see it."

"We won't keep you," Conejos said. "Just one question."

Dr. Ostrander pulled aside the curtain and walked Conejos and me to his office door. He held it open for us and then shut the door so it was us, no curtains. It was me and Conejos and Dr. Ostrander, a metal desk and chair, metal clock, metal cabinet, metal hospital bed. At first I didn't notice the door to the narrow lawn and the street. It was hidden behind the metal bed. Conejos sat on the desk chair. His trousers bunched tight on his thighs, and he slid his hat off with one hand, then tapped the hat on his knee. He watched the doctor with his eyes nearly closed.

"I already know the question," Dr. Ostrander said. "Missy told me when she called. I wish I could help you. I'd like to know what happened to your friend. I'd like to know why she left here with that hand wound."

"You called her Glinda the Good Witch."

"No, *she* called herself Glinda. That's the name she gave. She was in shock. Aren't you supposed to be at Paramount right now?"

"How do you know? Who told you?" My shoulders felt tight, my stomach, too. I should have been in Wally's chair getting hair and makeup done. I should have been zipping a skirt designed by Miss Head. I should have looked forward to it all, but I didn't. Thinking about my contract made my stomach hurt.

"I'm not going to tell you how I know. Let's deal with your question, and then you need to leave."

"I think Rosemary left here and saw someone outside, maybe coming out of your office."

"You think. You don't know."

"Who was it? Who came out of your office?"

"Does it make a difference?"

"I don't know."

"I won't tell you who was here," Dr. Ostrander said. "I am on retainer. Do you know what that means?"

"You do whatever the studio wants," I said.

"Yes, that's about right. If I tell you, I will lose my job, everything. What you're asking me to reveal goes against every oath I've taken, not to mention the confidentiality agreement I signed with Paramount.

"I do, however, feel I owe you. I am very, very sorry that I approved your brother's physical. I had little choice. Now, given all I've just said, I won't tell you that Bette Davis was in my office on Halloween night, she did not have difficulty recovering from a procedure, and she wasn't picked up at three a.m. and driven home."

"Bette Davis."

"It wasn't Bette Davis. She was not here on Halloween."

"She had an abortion?"

"Of course not. Abortions are illegal," Dr. Ostrander said. "Besides, she wasn't here."

Bette Davis. On the metal bed, in the metal room. "Who didn't pick her up?"

"The usual driver who doesn't pick up movie stars after their private procedures. Police of some kind. Young Mexican. Good-looking, nice enough, I guess. I've never talked to him."

I looked at Conejos. "Joe."

"Maybe," he said.

But I knew. Beautiful Bette Davis, all eyes and deep voice, perfectly round vowels, the only star to wear red on camera, Best Actress, washed in klieg lights, *that* Bette Davis, blowing smoke from perfectly drawn lips, waiting at Hollywood Receiving for her ride. I knew it. I *knew* it. A huge star, Bette Davis. That's who left the hospital on Halloween. Bette Davis steps out of the doctor's office. Rosemary sees her. Joe drives up, Joe from Paramount, Joe from the Hollywood Division.

"Bette Davis isn't Paramount," Conejos said. "And Joe wouldn't pick up a Warners star."

"She's a star. Maybe he was told to pick her up."

"I can't stay here. I have someone waiting." Dr. Ostrander glanced at his metal clock. "I'm going. And you need to go, too. You belong to them now."

"Them?" Conejos said.

"I'm late," I said.

"But Joe wouldn't pick up Bette Davis," Conejos said. "This is the kind of clue I can't stand. A movie star, okay, I get it. Rosemary leaves and sees a movie star, then has to disappear. It's a stretch, but—okay. Why is Joe there? Joe is Paramount, and we've got a Warners star. It was middle of the night, so he'd be on duty at Hollywood Division. Everyone works Halloween, no cops get time off. He wouldn't risk his job as a cop to wait next to the police station while he's on duty and then pick up a star contracted to another studio. What's in it for him?"

I said, "The night of Stany's party he followed me from Holmby Hills back to the Gardens. He was on duty that night, too. He had the Hollywood Division squad car parked in Holmby Hills."

"But that's when you were a murderess," Conejos said.

"I'm late." No more questions. Joe did it. He waited for Bette Davis, he saw Rosemary come out of the hospital, and she saw Bette, too, and Joe took Rose and killed her.

"It's not enough," Conejos said.

"It's all I get. Let's go."

"You don't belong to them," Conejos said.

True, I didn't belong to them, but I would. In half an hour, I'd be Sheryl Lane with a wardrobe. Sheryl Lane, not Penny Harp. I'd be Sheryl Lane the actress, who had a little star power, not much but a little, maybe enough to get Joe fixed.

Dr. Ostrander opened the door to the emergency room. He began to walk through, but his hand kept hold of the doorknob. He stopped, paused, and looked back at me. "Now that you know the truth, what will you do with it?"

"Nothing," I said. "I'll get Joe fixed. Other than that, the truth doesn't change a thing."

Conejos stood and kicked his chair to the wall. "That's because you're missing a piece. Some piece of information that brings it together."

"I understand," Dr. Ostrander said. "I feel it all the time." He smiled the big, saggy smile that made his chin disappear. "You have to remember that Halloween was very busy. People hurt, screaming. After my patient left—"

"Bette Davis."

"Or someone. I didn't go outside. I handed her off, then came back through my office to the emergency room. I'm afraid I didn't see a thing. Go out the side door, please. You weren't here." He smiled, and his chin disappeared. He shut the door hard.

People hurt, screaming. The hospital busy. I had to remember people were screaming.

Something jumped in my stomach. Something trickled through my fingers and arms. I couldn't breathe. I saw Rose in my head, Rose at twelve, a hot July night, the air stinking, sulphur everywhere, in all our noses. Rose screaming by Will's side, his ear a ripped mess. Rose, in shock, who screamed and screamed. Rose, who wouldn't stop screaming, not when Teddy yelled at her, not even when he pushed her down.

No, I thought. Rose was twelve then, and she had a reason to scream. She'd just blown Will's ear off, and she loved Will. She screamed because she loved Will. She had a reason. Why scream now? What had happened to Rose, what big thing—as big as thinking she'd killed the boy she loved, that he lay there bloody and gone—had made her scream?

And then I knew. I'd known all along, but in Ostrander's office, I knew that I knew, I saw the whole thing like I sat there and watched it on film. I was the audience. I saw Rose in the emergency room, hugging her cut hand. I saw the helpful nurse come toward her. I saw Rose stand up and leave, I saw her walk outside, see Bette Davis, and scream. She wouldn't have stopped, not when Joe yelled at her, not if he pushed her down. He'd have to take her away from the hospital, he'd *have* to. He wouldn't know why she screamed, but I did. I knew.

"I can drop you at Paramount," Conejos said. "We'll get my car. If I use the siren, I can get you there fast."

"Paramount. Right." Star lessons and two years of paychecks. Hairstyle, makeup, movie star shoes. Film time. Night visits to Dr. Ostrander. And woven through it, too tight to separate, the reason Rose left the hospital, the reason she screamed. The worst that could happen. I knew why she'd screamed, the real story, a story that took place two years ago when Rose had just given birth and another helpful nurse came toward her and said, *Give me your baby.* That was a story Sheryl Lane would try not to believe.

"You want to drive yourself?"

"No," I said.

Conejos had his mean detective face. "Then let's go."

"I don't think I'm going."

"Why not?"

My cheeks went hot. My nose ran, I rubbed my eyes. "You'll think I'm a fool."

"I probably will."

"Rose had a baby a couple years back."

"I know. I knew she'd given birth. I didn't know when."

"Right, the autopsy that didn't happen. I can change the story of Rose's death, I don't mind, because I'll know what really happened. I can get Joe fixed. But I can't change why Rose screamed. I won't. Sheryl Lane won't like knowing, but I—me, *Penny*—I want to remember."

"You're no fool," he said.

CHAPTER 41

For girls who want to play sirens in their private life, we recommend Marlene's dress which she wears to the Navy dance on board a battleship, and the way she's done her hair.

—*Photoplay*, November 1940

Where does a girl go when she's missed her appointment with stardom? If she has any money, she might ride the elevator to the tea room at Bullock's. She might order scones and champagne. If she's broke, she could drive right back to Paramount and bang on the gate.

I went to the Florentine Gardens, to the Zanzibar Room, where a crew set up microphones, camera tracks, reflectors. I felt light, giggly, stomach-sick like I'd leaned over a high railing. I wasn't upset or sad that I'd missed my appointment. I felt surprised that I wasn't upset, and most of all, I felt relieved. I stepped over electrical cords and around the camera crew to where Granny sat at a far table.

"Dear God. Look who it is. Miles Abbott is frantic. He's called everywhere, the police. We're all searching. Sheryl, what have I done wrong? I try to help. I give you advice, but do you take it? Did you even look for new shoes? Like right now, I'm not sure you're listening. Sheryl?"

"You had my room searched. You kept me talking, and all the while someone was in my room throwing clothes."

"Of course I did. How do we know what you're hiding up there?"

"Who told you to do it?"

"Sheryl, Sheryl," he said. "I'd search rooms for any studio head, not just yours. You wouldn't believe what Wally Beery hides in his trailer." He patted my shoulder. "The good thing is, your room was okay. Now you scoot back to Paramount. There's my girl."

I kept walking to the stage door. I wasn't scooting to Paramount or anywhere else. I was done. Straight to the dorms, up the stairs, to my room and Madge's and Rosemary's. A line of clothes divided our half of the room from the Career Girls'. On our half, kicked-around clothes, drawers pushed to one side of our bed. Piles of organdy, appliqués, winter white. On their half, a highboy in the corner, hairpins, and a Career Girl flat on the bed.

I squeezed Lorraine's shoulder. "I need your help."

"Mine?"

"You're Lorraine, right?"

"Cree? What's up? What's the time?"

"Not time yet. Three hours until call. You're fine. How are you?"

"Okay. I guess. Sore. Why are you asking? What's wrong? Is it my mom? Oh, God. What's happened?"

"I hereby make you Bull Girl, Lorraine. There's your outfit."

"Why'd you throw it in the corner? I'm Bull Girl? Where's the horns? Why would you give up film time?"

"I won't explain, and no, nothing bad will happen. I don't want to be in the revue," I said. "I'll help you get ready." My next surprise was that she let me. I set Lorraine's hair with juice cans. We worked together to fix the bull hat strap. I rolled her hair on each side and let the rest fall in curls.

"If you're watching the show, you should dress up," she said. "Cameras will pan the audience."

"I might not watch the show. I'm invited to Ciro's." I looked at my clothes heap. Madge's blue dimity gown lay twisted on the bed. A hem of white sequins stuck up from the floor pile. Beside it, a pink chiffon sleeve made a puff. I tugged on the sleeve.

"I'll wear this one. The pink."

"Let me button you. What's on your back? Did you get stabbed?"

"Old scars." My gown had a chiffon train and lace on the bodice. I wanted to wrap the dress tight around me, I loved it so. "One more thing, Lorraine. Promise you'll do one thing."

"What's the thing?"

"Promise. A real promise, not a Hollywood one."

"I promise I'll do the thing."

"Throw these clothes away. Please. For me. Shove them in sacks and burn them. No, forget burning. Give them to Mexican hookers. I think they work Lexington and Vine. You can do that, walk up with some sacks of clothes and say, *here*."

"All the clothes? I like that skirt with the plaid."

"There's a matching jacket, it's lovely. Yes, all the clothes. Don't keep any. Don't try them on. Once you put them on, you'll break your promise, I know."

"Are the clothes jinxed?"

"Every one."

"Then why are you wearing that gown? Isn't the gown jinxed?"

"I'm already jinxed. So are the hookers."

"I don't get you. I mean, I never think about you at all, but right now, I don't get why you're throwing all these away. They're better than anything I've got, or any girl in the dorm. Aren't these your only clothes?"

"They're mine, and Madge's and Rosemary's. Do you see now why they're jinxed?"

"Who's Madge and Rosemary?"

"Roll each one in a ball and hand it to a hooker. You made an out-of-Hollywood promise."

"I hereby promise to Cree Girl that I'll take these gorgeous clothes and ball them up and throw them at hookers."

"Not just any hookers, right?"

"Mexican hookers on Lexington and Vine."

"Thank you. Thank you, Lorraine. How do I look?"

"I need to fix your mouth. Stand still. Don't eat your lipstick, it's so unbecoming. You should smoke instead. Claudette Colbert smokes red cigarettes, did you know? I heard everyone's doing it. I wonder where you buy them. Okay, look at me. Twirl so I see the skirt. Oh. You don't look like Cree Girl. You look . . . you look . . ."

"Like me, I hope."

"But why look like you? Who are you?"

Some day, a month from now, I'll be driving Madge's car down Hollywood Boulevard and I'll see Lorraine come out of the Gardens in a plaid skirt and jacket. She'll look great. She'll have kept a few clothes and shared some with the other Career Girl. They'll march around town like movie stars, like Gloria Swanson walking her skinny dog. Then I'll drive to Lexington and Vine, and all my hookers will line up in fabulous Irene designs, each one an original.

I took my pink gown to the Zanzibar.

CHAPTER 42

"Ah, oh," she thought, "here's the villain I've been
warned about." So she took to her heels.

—*Photoplay*, November 1940

The Gardens, bright and hot. Reflection screens, lighting cords
taped to the floor. Granny a beach ball between crew and staff.
Guests sweating, trying to eat beef. A director telling them, *Don't
eat yet, didn't I tell you not to eat*, and the steak's already cold. Joe
stood behind it all, arms crossed, near the kitchen swing door,
cigarette in his mouth, smoke making his eyes blink, his uniform
brown and pressed, his mouth smiling, his eyes seeing me, blink-
ing, his mouth in a frown. Joe could get away with Rose's murder.
I'd given up my chance to have him fixed. It was hard to ignore
him. The Zanzibar was crowded with guests and picadors.

I felt like Rosemary, the beauty who got eyes stuck on her from
door to hat check, Rosemary in pink; it must be how she'd felt
each day. Penny Harp in pink. Miss Harp, who swishes past a
murderer to the Zanzibar table with Marty Martin at one end and
the Robert Taylors at the other.

Stany sat by her husband, but it took me a while to see her. I
saw Bob Taylor and nobody else. And I couldn't breathe! Bob Taylor in a tuxedo, the most beautiful man in Hollywood.

"Look at you, Pen," Stany said. "Someone dipped you in white chocolate and colored you pink. You positively clash with the room." Stany wore gold lamé. She probably itched. "I was just telling Junior here, why, look at Pen, I thought she'd wear horns, and here she came as a pink marshmallow."

"I enjoy marshmallows," Bob said. He looked at me when he said it. At *me*. He stood.

"*Junior*," said Stany. "Pen, this is my husband. Sit away from him, on the other side. A little farther. There, that's fine. Aren't we cozy? Pen, order what you want, but we're leaving in one tiny minute. Are you coming with us? Don't spill on yourself. Chiffon's a nightmare to clean. Junior, light me a cigarette, *hmm?*"

"Why are you here?"

"Just for a drink," Bob said.

"Granny called us, all panicked," Stany said. "I hear someone didn't sign her contract."

Marty leaned across to me. "Where did you go today, Penny?"

"Nowhere. I went to see a doctor." Marty in a tuxedo was exactly like Marty in a lawyer suit. Nothing changed. He was Marty, and his fingernails were clean.

"Did your car stall? Was there an accident?"

"No, I'm fine."

"Then why? Why give up a chance? Look at these girls in here. Do you think any one of them wouldn't trade places with you?"

"Marty, are you still my lawyer?"

"No," he said, "not since the charges were dropped."

"Then shut up, will you?"

Stany said, "We're headed to Ciro's. It's a mess in this room. Are you coming?"

"I'll stay and root for the bull."

"Junior, drain your glass. Why the hell are *you* here?"

Stany didn't mean Junior. She meant Miles Abbott, behind me, his tie loose and his jacket unbuttoned. Around him, the sound crew bent boom mikes and tested sound.

"It's business," Abbott said. "Farm Girl forgot her appointment. She kept everyone waiting. *Everyone.*"

"I didn't forget," I said.

"Then what? You can't keep Adolph waiting. Adolph Zukor is everyone. You think you're a star already," Abbott said. "You think stars don't have rules."

"Penny knows better, don't you, Pen?"

"Stany, I'm not signing the contract."

"Oh, Penny. Penny. Here I thought we'd be twins. Junior, we've done our bit. I'm ready to leave. Grab my wrap. Marty, are you coming or not?"

"Meeting time," Abbott said. He pulled me away from the table, through crossed electrical cords and reflectors, picadors and Lorraine the bull, into the Zebra. Two bartenders served drinks.

"Dirty martini," he said. "And not that Mexican shit, either. With two olives, please."

"Gin fizz," I said.

"Who cares what you want? No," he said. He grabbed a bartender's sleeve. "Don't serve her anything. She's in trouble."

"Gin fizz," I said.

"You want to ruin me? Is that your plan? Me, what I do for the studio, important work I do for the studio?"

"I have no plans to ruin anyone. I'll shut my mouth."

"Damn you. Goddamn you. Why didn't you sign? What does it take?" The bartender slid a martini glass along the bar, two olives. Abbott swished the olives on their little stick, and then lifted them to his mouth. He sucked on the olives and talked through them, words mixed with liquor. "We had a whole crew waiting. Wardrobe, Wally and his team, those people can't run whenever you come strolling in. You cost us money, damn it. That's not how it works."

"Tell me about Madge's parents," I said.

Abbott rolled his olives and sucked. "It'll make a goddamn good war picture."

"I didn't get my drink."

"That's because you're nobody. Goddamn Mexican olives." He spat an olive pit into his hand and threw it. "Zukor's lined up Bette Davis to play the mom."

"You mean Madge's mom."

"Whoever. He got a hell of a trade from Warners."

"Bette Davis is too young for that role."

"Not in this story. Now Madge is ten, but precocious. A better fit for the storyline, and then there's the homecoming scene, mother sees daughter, the audience cries."

"So they're really out of Paris? They made it?"

"How do I know? Wait for the script, will you?"

"Did you kill Madge?"

"Did I—what?"

"Did you?" I said. "Did you kill Madge, push her off the deck?"

He laughed. He held his glass by the stem and lifted it like a toast.

"Madge worked for you," I said.

"And a hell of a job she did. I put her in your dorm to watch you, not help you. From what I heard, she was drunk and didn't need the push."

"And Rosemary? Did you kill her?"

"Just sign your goddamn contract, will you? I save these girls," Abbott said. "I don't have to. Not all studios extend this little benefit to Central Casting girls. What would those girls do with spare kids? Where would they go? Home to Nebraska? Who'd fucking talk to them if they're pregnant? I save their lives, and if I wanted to kill, I'd do it right now and make sure the whole room heard me."

"You were there," I said. "Oh, God. You were at the hospital on Halloween."

"Doing my job."

"For Bette Davis."

He slammed his glass on the bar. Glass broke and flew. He shouted at me over the orchestra. I don't remember what he said, except, "Fuck you. *Fuck* you, little nobody, little—" Something about Zukor, fuck Zukor, too, but I was walking away from the bar. I was so angry I shook, as angry as I'd been last night in Stany's car, my whole body mad. I had one more person to talk to.

Not Granny; fuck Granny and his *Hail the Bullfighters* film. I mean Joe, the guy I couldn't fix, murderer Joe, moonlighting as security to the film crew.

Not scary Joe, in the tin shed at Paramount by the spools of sharp wire. Not empty Joe, kicking Spencer Tracy. But at the Gardens? All those people? Film crew and lighting, singers? He'd be security Joe. I was stupid. I thought I'd find him and he'd yell because I'd crossed someone's mark. He'd push me to the back, out of camera angle. Then I'd ask him, and he'd tell me: *Who killed Rose, you or Abbott? Which one of you killed her because she wouldn't stop screaming?*

"Get out of the way," he said. "Don't you know you're on someone's mark? You're beautiful. I'm mad at you."

"You or Abbott, one of you killed her," I said. I yelled it across the Zanzibar. With everyone else yelling, too, only Joe understood. I walked through tables to the kitchen door. The tourists watched me and whispered. I was somebody. Who was I, in my pink chiffon? What was my name? Where had they seen me?

"Everyone's staring," Joe said.

"Who was it? On Halloween. You picked up Bette Davis from Hollywood Receiving. Abbott was there, too. Rosemary saw. She began screaming and wouldn't stop. You and Abbott, one of you had to kill her to shut her up. Who did it? Did you kill her, Joe?"

He grabbed my arm, fast. He pulled me through the kitchen, more noise and pots rattling. A cook smoking a cigar and stirring, stirring. Through the alley door, me tripping on pink, the skirt tearing at the doorframe, and we stood in the alley by the garbage cans and the dug-up dirt around Rose's grave. Trash and cold air. A wire garrote still leaning on garbage. He wasn't security Joe anymore. He had flat eyes.

"You listen," Joe said. "Rose was screaming. I didn't kill her. I could have. I really could have killed her, and I thought about it."

Down the alley, a guy on Santa Claus Lane fought with his girl—"Come on, you promised, it's *Christmas*"—and through the Gardens wall, far into the Zanzibar, the first notes of the bull song floated out. Film would roll, the headliner posed by the orchestra, dressed in picador gold, feeling her teeth with her tongue, testing smears of petroleum. Lorraine offstage, balancing the stupid bull hat, framed by Picador Girls. The lights would be *hot*. They'd cover the stage, dance floor, audience. Guests in the Zanzibar: *All this for a moving picture? Real movies aren't made like this.*

Joe in his Paramount brown, with me in the alley, said, "I didn't kill her. I didn't have to. I'm not a killer, Pen."

"You were supposed to pick up Bette Davis."

"Who told you? How do you know?"

"You pick up girls after their abortions. Don't deny it. I already know. Does Paramount pay you, or do you work for Abbott?"

"I work for the studio. Don't hate me, Pen. I couldn't stand if you hated me."

"Who do you work for tonight? Warners or Paramount? Do you need to stand guard in the Zanzibar, or are you a Hollywood beat cop, or are you working for Abbott?"

He pushed me to the building wall. My head hit the stucco. He put his hands on the wall; he stood close to me and caged me between his arms. My heart beat fast and my face was cold, the wall brittle against my head, the air icy between us, his breath cold, too. I'd been here before, pushed against stucco. I'd felt the dry peaks and swirls against my back, felt them rip and break and crumble when I'd slid down the wall.

Not Teddy tonight. Not Teddy. It was Joe.

"I didn't pick up Bette Davis. I couldn't."

"No, you had to kill Rose instead. Back up, Joe."

"Am I a killer? I helped you break into the autopsy files."

"You beat Spencer Tracy bloody."

"No, I didn't, remember? You never saw that. He fell. There must have been rock on the sidewalk, or he tripped."

"I know what I saw. Back up, Joe. Right now."

"You're not remembering the right way. You don't understand about Rosemary. Our idea was, I'd wait for her to calm down and then I'd untie her and fix everything, then take her home."

"Our?"

"Mr. Abbott and me, and that lawyer, Martin. He waited for Rosemary at the hospital, but once she started screaming, it was clear that she couldn't go with him. She had to go with me to be fixed."

"Marty was there?"

"I told you, she was screaming. Martin left. Mr. Abbott said, 'I'll take Miss Davis, you stop that girl screaming.'"

"You locked her in the tin shed."

"I was supposed to take her to your dorms but I couldn't, not like that. She wouldn't calm down. She kept screaming and pounding her fists, she didn't know where she was or who was taking her. I couldn't bring her to the dorms. I put her in the shed so she'd calm down. I didn't lock her in. I should have, but I didn't lock the shed. I didn't need to, because I'd tied her hands and feet. I just tied her so she'd calm down. She kept screaming, Pen. I had to hit her. I couldn't believe it. I thought, okay, I'll gag her and tie her up, and wait for her to calm down."

"She screamed when you brought her to the back lot?"

"I took her through a tunnel."

"I know the tunnel."

"I carried her. She wasn't heavy. I put my hand on her mouth."

"Then you could have let her go."

"No," he said. "She needed to talk to me, or to Mr. Abbott, so we knew she'd stay quiet. She hadn't been fixed yet. And I left her in the tin shed."

"She got loose. She bit off her own thumb to get out of those ropes. You killed her and buried her right here."

"I didn't kill her. Mr. Abbott got back and we went to the tin shed. We were going to fix her, that's all, and we saw blood! We saw blood, oh, God, it was sprayed all over, but no girl. I don't know what happened. Maybe she did kill herself. That's what the coroner says, and we should believe him."

"She buried herself, too? Why call me a murderess? Why tell me I'd get the gas chamber?"

"By then you were a murderess, don't you see? Detective Conejos thought you were, and it was a good story, and Mr. Abbott had to fix it somehow."

"I'm finished here," I said, and I put my hand on Joe's chest and shoved him. He moved a little and I saw his flat eyes, and felt his cold hands heavy by my neck.

"I didn't know about her thumb. I'm not a killer." His breath froze and cracked air between us. I was wrong. I said I'd been here before, the night Teddy pushed me against another wall in another town. The walls scraped my back the same way, ripped my dress just the same. But even as I was raped, it was always Teddy doing it. He'd never changed as he'd hit me, not like Joe. Against this wall, in this town, Joe was gone. He was two flat eyes, flat, heavy arms, no Joe inside, caging me to the wall. From the Zanzibar the headliner's refrain:

> *The mighty bull and the Mexican girl*
> *On the streets of Rialto at dawn*
> *The bull lowered his head*
> *Toward the brown girl and said*
> *If we live through today then we've won*

"She had to be fixed." His hands came to my neck, circled my neck, and tugged up. "Someone fixed her." He squeezed, hard. "Like this."

"Let go of my neck."

"Suicide," Joe said. "I tried to clean up the blood. You saw it, didn't you? In the shed, it's in the cement. I did what I could. On every little thing, nails and bolts and bolts of electric cord, under the tables, the ceiling. I had to scrub the ceiling!"

"Let go of me. Please, Joe."

He held my throat tight and rubbed my skin with his fingers. He was cleaning blood in the tin shed with Rose, and she bled beside him and he cleaned it up. He said he hadn't killed her, she was gone when he came back with Abbott, but he saw her now. Blood smeared her face, her body, the wall. Blood pulsed from her hand and neck. I saw her, too. I felt her throat close and seal. Her hands—my hands—pulled at cold wire. I beat the hard wall of Joe's chest. Behind us, in the Zanzibar, horns and drums grew. Picadors faced the bull.

"Do you believe me? It's the truth."

I couldn't answer. Joe's voice floated and sank through the Zanzibar's drums. I just hung. He opened his hands and I gasped, then slid down his chest to the dirt, limp.

Do you believe me?

"Pick her up. She's dead? Carry her."

"I didn't kill her." Joe's voice.

"Pick her up." The other voice.

Then I was lifted and carried, and Joe climbed the staircase that led to the dorm's back door, three floors up, where girls banged all the time but nobody let them in. Madge had stood on that deck once, looking at roofs over Hollywood Boulevard, before her neck broke on the stairs. Now Joe carried me up those stairs, he set me against that dorm door, and when I opened my eyes, all I saw was pink chiffon. My Irene gown. Then, through chiffon, klieg lights from the Palladium down the street, flashing gold and swaying. Then Joe at my side, and then, at the stair rail, Marty Martin.

"You can leave, Joe."

"I'm not leaving her."

"She's fine. She's with me."

"She's with *me,* and I'm not leaving."

"Are you nuts? Are you crazy? You nearly killed her, and anyone seeing her right now is going to know you nearly killed her, and do you want that? I'm trying to *fix* you, goddamn it, so leave!"

Joe crouched in front of me. Behind him, the kliegs outlined his head in gold. His cheekbones shone from the stage door opening, closing, opening, flashes of light on and off. He was beautiful. My hand lifted and touched his face.

"I wouldn't hurt you," he said. "You know that, right?"

I tried to nod. My throat hurt.

"Let Mr. Martin fix you. You know that, don't you? Mr. Martin will fix it."

Fix? What was there to fix? What had I done worth fixing? But Joe was beautiful, and the kliegs on Santa Claus Lane step-swayed, step-swayed, a halo, and light from the stage door lifted his cheeks high above me, and I nodded again and closed my eyes. When I opened them, it was Marty Martin, not Joe, in the glow of kliegs.

"Can you stand?" He didn't want an answer. He yanked my hair, and I stood. "Can you talk?"

"I . . . My throat's sore."

"Come to the railing."

"No."

He punched my face. A bone cracked above my eye, hot water pouring under my skin through my eye, cheek, mouth. I turned and beat on the dorm's back door like I'd beat on Joe's chest. Nobody answered this door, ever, we knew better, nothing good stood outside of it beating, wanting in. Nobody would answer, but I beat anyway.

Marty yelled. "You could have had two years. You could have shut your mouth. Do you know how much money it takes to live like these people? To dress like they do and go to their parties? Because I have to go to their parties. Do you know?"

"Let me in let me in let me in," I said.

"Yes, your friend Madge said that, too."

I stopped beating the door. My face pulsed, like being hit with a rock in the same place. Pulse. I turned to Marty. "What do you mean, Madge said that?" Pulse.

"When she stood there, just like you. She hit that door."

"Why did she hit the door?"

"Because I brought her here. Because you told her some wild story about Rosemary breaking into houses. And me a thief. You shouldn't have told her that. She thought I had helped your brother break into a house."

"You did."

"The night I dropped you off, I'd had enough. I parked down the street and went to the Gardens. I was waiting for you, it should have been you, but your friend Madge came out of the bar with quite a few things to say, and she'd say them to Mr. Zukor if I didn't help. I told her, why don't we climb these nice stairs and talk about it? And really, nothing could help find her parents. How could a lawyer do anything? How could I? How could Paramount? It's a movie studio."

It's a world, I thought.

"She kept threatening. What could I do?" He swung his arm toward the klieg lights. They swayed and crossed each other, the beams reaching so high they disappeared. They became their own galaxy. "Everyone out there," he said. "There's a whole *world.* They only know what we tell them."

You're a galaxy, I thought. "You killed Madge. You threw her down these stairs."

He punched my face, and I fell against the door. My left eye blurred; blood hit the insides of my cheeks and behind my eyes in hard slams. "Couldn't you just help her? Don't you hit me. Couldn't you write a letter, or call an embassy or something?"

"I deal with divorces."

"I believe you. Then you killed her."

"She fell." He grabbed my arm, and I slid toward the stairs. My face bled, my nose bled. Blood in my mouth. I slid in a little pool of my own blood.

"Why can't you listen? Rosemary, too, thinking I'd save her because Joe had tied her up in the shed. I followed Joe and Abbott to the tunnel, and they'd better be grateful I did. Abbott left, but where was Joe with Rosemary? They didn't come out, so I went in. I found her climbing the back wall. But she wouldn't shut up. Not screaming, not then. She'd gotten out of the wire Joe used to tie her, and the wire's right there, she bled everywhere, it was disgusting, took me who knows how long to find her thumb, and you know what she's saying?"

"You killed her. Oh, God, you killed Rose."

"She's yelling, 'Penny saw you.' What does that mean?"

Marty kicked me, and I hooked my free arm around a stair post. He kicked again.

"I can't have her yelling 'Penny,' and that I was part of some theft ring. I couldn't have Abbott come back and hear that story, no. I wrapped the wire around her neck. Joe had already used it to tie her up, and it was bloody already, wasn't it? She'd found a way to get out of the wire, hadn't she? With the work gloves right there. I had to stop her without cutting myself, didn't I? And if she told you what she was doing in Beverly Hills, and I know she did tell you about me, then I had to get to you. But I didn't know who you were. You were nothing. I could pick through the whole lot of you extras and never see you. Every one of you looks the same. But I knew you worked at the Gardens."

"You buried her here."

"It shut you up, didn't it? And I burned her clothes. Mine, too, and the gloves. I couldn't drag all that blood around. That's why studios keep incinerators."

"She didn't tell me about you. There was nothing to shut up." I balanced between the staircase and air, one leg sliding down, one leg swinging through nothing at all, my arm around the post but slipping a little each time my leg swung.

"Of course she didn't. I never met her. I had nothing to do with those break-ins." And his hand bunched, light from the stage door, lifting his fist, his arm winding up for a pitch, and I knew when his fist hit I'd sail over the edge, I'd lose, my arm flying from the post, I'd hit one stair then another. I knew because I saw it clear, through one eye. I saw his fist and the windup. He stood in hot light like we were on a sound stage. And the throaty, smoky, smooth, deep, fast and sharp voice:

"Go ahead, Marty. We're filming. Throw her off the balcony."

Marty looked down, and his fist stopped. On the ground, can lights angled up at us, and beneath the lights, tripods supported cameras. I heard the cameras sputter and wind, and Stany was there, too, hidden behind can lights, shouting directions. "Let's get it on film: Marty Martin, lawyer to the stars, commits murder. I'll make sure it's in every newsreel across the country. Anyone at a theater will see you throwing a poor Farm Girl off a balcony, three stories down. I'll add sound, you bastard. You want that on film, Marty? Go ahead."

"I'm trying to stop her from jumping," he said.

"That's not what the film will show. Go ahead. Stop her from jumping."

He looked back at me, his tuxedo perfect, bow tie splashed with my blood. He dropped his fist, then raised it. Here came the blow. I waited for his fist and for me to hit every stair like Madge had, to hear my neck bend and crack like Madge's had. She must have heard her own neck break. Now she floated by the stairs, with Rose. I hadn't seen them; I didn't have to. I loved them so much, I knew they were there. Film time. I waited for Marty's fist.

He didn't hit me. The can lights bleached his face. He turned to the railing, threw his fist over the railing, and his whole body followed.

CHAPTER 43

Clark Gable and Carole Lombard, one persistently hears, have never gotten over the idea of adopting one of their own and have recently been glimpsed in a certain home for homeless babies.

—*Photoplay*, November 1940

Granny gave me hot tea and had me sit at a booth in the Zebra. He gave me raw sirloin for my eye. Stany sat across from me and drank gin martinis.

"We were getting in my car outside the Gardens, and I saw Marty go back in," Stany said. "He looked sneaky, but he's always sneaky, so it wasn't that. He looked *convinced*, and I didn't like it. I didn't know what to do. Should I go to Ciro's? After all, I was throwing a party for my own husband. Should I follow Marty? I couldn't decide. I sent Bob to Ciro's. And I thought, *Penny needs me*. After all, you'd been so forthcoming about breaking into my house and nearly kidnapping my son.

"I arrived just in time. I saw Joe carry you up those stairs, and there was Marty, and I knew *that* wasn't going to end well, but if I ran up those stairs, he'd throw you off before I got there. I devised a plan." She downed her martini. She signaled the waitress by waving her glass in the air. Another martini.

"I didn't know he'd leap over the railing. What am I supposed to do with the film? Oh, my God." She gulped the new martini and waved her glass at the waitress. "I had a good plan. It saved your life."

She'd run through the Zebra to the Zanzibar Room. She'd gone for help and seen the film crew. She'd moved cameras and lights from the *Hail the Bullfighters* set. She'd brought the crew outside. They'd followed her and brought their equipment because she was Missy and she'd said, "Let's stop a murder or at least film it, by God," so they'd followed her and brought cameras, electrical cords, can lights, reflectors; and the light from the stage door opening, closing, opening wasn't just light, it was Stany moving them all into position before the can lights snapped on and there we were, my only moment on film.

"Granny's livid. I mean, he's madder than I've ever seen. I interrupted his filming, but I think it's for the best, because that poor girl in the horns was flat on her back with those spears dangling over her. Terrifying. I probably saved her life, too. Slide over my cigarettes."

"What about my face? I hurt. I can barely open my mouth."

"What about your face? I've never seen you look better. You look strong, battle-weary, you're—"

"An Amazon," I said.

"Let me drink to oblivion. Then we'll go see Dr. Ostrander. I lied, something strange is happening to your face. What's that dent in your cheek?"

"What will happen to Joe?"

"It's time for Joe to enlist, don't you think? He'll make a fine soldier. Paramount will be so very proud."

It's hard knowing the truth. The thing is, you can know the truth and nothing big changes. Marty strangled Rose, and he pushed Madge down three flights of stairs. I knew the truth about both of my friends, but nothing big changed. I could sit in the Zebra, and Stany could drink martinis, and everything around me—Hollywood, Stany, the studio—would all stay the same whether I knew the truth or a Hollywood story.

The change was small, inside of me. The change made me

scoot forward and wince and then kiss Stany's forehead. She looked down, into her martini glass. Her hair shone gray in the candlelight.

"I still have questions," she said.

"You told me not to ask questions."

"Yes, but it's different when you're me. My question is this: On Halloween night, why did Rosemary leave the emergency room? She got there safely. She'd had her hand checked. All she had to do was stay there and get stitches. Why did she leave? Oh, and my other question: Why did she scream when she saw Bette? She leaves the emergency room, sees Bette, and screams. Nobody ever screams when they see Bette. Okay, Joan Crawford screams, but that's all. I mean, Bette does have those massive eyes, but not worth screaming about."

"Have you ever been like Bette, leaving from a hospital side door?"

"We're not discussing your questions. We're discussing mine. Do you have the answers?"

"Stany, remember our lunch at the Pig 'n Whistle?"

"You had tuna fish," Stany said. "I'm getting you a martini so I can drink it. That way I'll line up two at a time."

"I had egg salad. You asked about Rose's baby. We talked about it in the Pig 'n Whistle. The baby got adopted."

"Of course it did. Otherwise, Rose couldn't have come to Hollywood. Who'd hire an unwed mother? Except Loretta Young. I keep forgetting about her and Clark Gable. And with that kid's ears, thank God for knit caps! But even Loretta had to adopt her own kid. People don't like unwed mothers."

"That's it, though," I said. "Rose wasn't giving up her baby. She wasn't planning to go to Hollywood or anywhere else. She wanted her baby, and she wanted to marry Will."

But Will didn't know Rose was pregnant. Neither had I, back then. Rose called me one day and said she was moving from Buena Park, and months later, when she came home, Aunt Lou was dead, her house sold, so Rose moved in with us. Will said, *Now let's get married,* and Rose looked at him like she'd forgotten his name.

And one day, when we sat under a huge, dying Washington navel and I told her I'd saved enough to move out, how I'd go to Hollywood and forget the scars on my back, she'd told me about her baby.

No, that's not exactly what happened. First she said she was going to Hollywood with me, that she'd find the money somewhere. She danced and danced in a seersucker skirt. I remember the dirt flying when she scuffed her feet. I was mad! I didn't want her to go with me. I was mad that she'd left Buena Park and come back, and I was mad that after my date with Teddy, she'd said, *You act like it's the worst that can happen.* Then she sat and got quiet, and told me about her baby.

She said her aunt sold the house to pay for her trip to Pomona, six months in a mothers' home. Seven hundred dollars plus chores. Rose said the birth was easy, too fast, she'd wanted to feel more pain. It was hardly worth being pregnant, she said, for two hours of bad cramps and a doctor saying, *Shut her up,* and twisting her insides with canning tongs. And why wrap the baby tight? She'd pulled off the blanket. If Aunt Lou could have lived to see. The nurse told her, *Lie back, stay here, but give me your baby.* So that's what Rose did.

She said the baby was sticky and warm, and she handed it off. At the window, sun cut the room into two long pieces through twill drapes. The table next to her bed held a vase with old sea foam and dried hydrangeas. The nurse carried out Rose's baby girl. When blood dried on Rose's hands, she wiped them clean because she knew there'd be more: years of blood from all the ways a girl can bleed, and she'd see it all. She wanted it all. The nurse never brought back the baby.

Where's my baby? she said.

Heavens, you're not married. A young girl like you. How can you raise a child?

Where's my baby? she said.

She came home different.

I know why Rose left the receiving hospital before Dr. Ostrander stitched her hand. The doctor was busy. Halloween night at the hospital, costumes and crying. He told the nurse to clean up Rose. The nurse—the one Madge and I talked to—she seemed nice, but Rose wouldn't notice. Rose had held a rag on her own cut hand for nearly an hour. Blood dried on her fingers and clothes. Shock, it's called. She'd see the nurse and her own bloody hands, and she'd know she wasn't in Hollywood. She was in Pomona. It doesn't matter that really she was in Hollywood and her daughter had been stolen from her arms almost two years before. It was Pomona to her, and grief picked her up, and she ran.

Outside, Rose would have leaned against the emergency room door. Let's say she leaned on the wall, where the door starts and leads to the room filled with hurt people, screaming people in costumes with blood fake and real. Let's say Rose can still hear those people, but she doesn't care. She's in shock. She's holding one wrist and scratching the cut on her thumb so it opens and drips. She's just seen a nurse like the one in Pomona, who smiled and seemed nice but lifted her baby from her arms. The worst that can happen. The baby-stealing nurse.

Our nurse in receiving is that same nurse to Rose. Outside the building, the wind hits Rose's face, and her hair is loose from its pins. Little whips of hair hit her cheeks. Little hard whips. And down the brick wall she sees another door swing and bang, and here comes Miles Abbott and Dr. Ostrander, *doctor*, holding a woman's arms. The woman limps like she's played *vaquero* and ridden a horse for five days. Rosemary knows that limp, and I do, too. It's the limp of something stolen.

Rose wouldn't shut up. She'd scream and scream, and in the wind, maybe her screams reached the woman, and maybe they didn't. Maybe Rose recognized Bette Davis, and maybe she didn't. Bette Davis could be any woman with that same limp.

She's not, though. She's Bette Davis. At the curb, Joe is waiting to drive home Miss Bette Davis, and at the curb, Marty is waiting for Miss Rosemary Brown. And Rose is screaming.

"This stinking world," Stany said. She lit a cigarette and sucked in hard. She flipped over one empty martini glass and slid its rim on top of the other. With my one eye swollen shut and the other eye watering from pain, the stacked glasses looked to me like a huge rose-cut diamond.

Stany blew a smoke ring at the diamond. "Does Conejos know?"

"I told him this afternoon."

"Conejos is nice. Handsome, in a round way. I do believe he's handsome. He'd make a good leading man if he lost fifty pounds. At the very least, he'll keep you away from my husband."

Picador Girls wandered in from the Zanzibar. I didn't know their picador names. I knew them as Indians: Apache, Lakota, Paiute, and a Paramount Wallflower who hated me. They crowded the bar with nothing to do, the shoot postponed.

"I suppose now you'll move back to the farm," Stany said. "And here we've just become friends. Who will be my friend now?"

"I know someone who'd make a great friend," I said. "I don't know her real name." I set my steak on the table, slid out, and walked to the bar. The girls at the bar stopped talking and watched me. They didn't care that my face was beat up, an eye swollen, dried blood in my nose. We didn't trust each other. We didn't know any real names or each other's real stories. Alive or dead, in Hollywood we were ghosts. I kicked off my Wallflower shoes. I leaned over and felt the blood pulse in my hurt face and reached under my chiffon; I picked up the shoes by their dirty heels, then held them out to the Wallflower. "You can have your shoes back."

She frowned. By candlelight, the shoes looked grimy and scuffed. They smelled. By daylight, they'd look worse. Both toes were stained purple, and one shoe had loose threads between the crepe sole and leather. Wallflower reached out one hand and took the shoes. She held them away from her fluffy picador skirt. "Why give them to me now? They're ruined."

"They're magic. See those stains? That's Spencer Tracy's dried blood. You'll have Spencer Tracy's blood on your feet."

"Spencer Tracy? You're lying."

"No. Look at me. I mean, really look at me. Look. Am I lying?"

"Yes. Probably. Maybe not," she said.

"You've got Spencer Tracy's blood on your shoes. With those

shoes you'll rule Hollywood. You'll wear Spencer Tracy all day. I'm telling you, those shoes are magic. Say, do you want to be hated? You want all these girls to talk about you, and leave the room when you come in, and forget to tell you things and maybe push you and misplace your callbacks and block your way during rehearsals?"

"Sure," she said.

"Come meet someone." I brought Wallflower to the booth to meet Stany.

CHAPTER 44

Bette Davis will appear soon in her stunning new triumph *The Great Lie*.

—*Photoplay* combined with *Movie Mirror*, May 1941

Marty Martin, Esq., fell accidentally from a staircase. I sat on my mom's front steps in Buena Park and read it in an old *Hollywood Reporter*. All Hollywood grieved; Joan Crawford said, "Hollywood has lost a friend, and I, personally, am sick with grief. He was a good lawyer." Nothing was said about the film Stany made of Marty's accident, and nothing was said about me. Just below that article, a short notice from MGM announced Spencer Tracy's return from a much-deserved secret vacation but didn't mention his split lip or seventeen stitches above his ear. Dr. Ostrander had had to shave half his head. At least I'd only needed three stitches, above my left eye.

On the third page, I read about Bette Davis's upcoming trade to Paramount for the picture *She Lost Them to Paris*. Production would start early summer.

> Miss Davis, having just returned from a short and much-deserved secret vacation, continues to shoot her current motion picture for Warner Brothers, *All This, and Heaven Too*.

"Can I sit?"

Teddy Marshall stood on the front walk in his deputy's uniform, hat tucked under one arm. I'd seen his car slowing on Grand, and my throat hadn't closed. I'd heard him walk up, and I hadn't bothered to watch. I was an Amazon now. Teddy seemed boring compared to me.

"Pen, can I sit?" Teddy used to look funny. He had a weird-angled tooth and hair we couldn't describe. He used to kiss me in the mock orange and cut my lip. In his uniform now, about three feet from my face, he could have been in the movies. A Cary Grant nose. He sat on the bottom stair. He leaned forward and set a long envelope on the steps, then set his hat on the envelope. "I had trouble finding you. I came here, then I went to Hollywood. Then I found out you'd come back here. I'm sorry about your face."

"Hmm."

"Your boss at the Gardens said some months back, you fell down a staircase. You don't look bad, except for that big scar."

"Ah."

"You could have been really hurt. Say, I heard about Will's arrest."

"What arrest? Now he's army."

"I am, too. Not army. I enlisted in the navy two weeks ago." He flicked a page of the *Reporter*. "You always liked to read."

"No, I didn't. I hated reading. You enlisted two weeks ago? Did you tell Will?"

"He knew I was leaving."

"It doesn't matter," I said.

"I guess not." He kept flicking the *Reporter*.

"Stop it," I said.

"Pen, I want to tell you something before I leave."

"What? That you raped me? I already know."

"I'm sorry you feel like that," he said. "But now I'm leaving, and I can't carry this secret, it's not fair."

"It's not a secret. You raped me."

"Pen, some things aren't about you. Can we go somewhere quieter?"

"Teddy. What's quieter than an orange grove?" Down Grand, people lined up for Mrs. Knott's fried chicken. Families yelled to each other: *Hey, how about that chicken?*

"Okay," Teddy said. "It's quiet enough. Where's Daisy and your mom? They okay?"

"Hmm," I said.

"Must be tough, living at home again."

"It's better than living in Hollywood. Teddy, why are you here? What are you telling me?"

"I'm telling you the rest of what happened. At least, I'm telling you what I know."

"So tell me."

"Okay. Don't cry, okay? Here goes. Just don't cry. Last fall Rosie came to see us, to see Will and me. She said you wouldn't miss her in Hollywood. She said she'd leave the Gardens for whole days and you never asked questions."

"Then I must not have cared, huh?"

"She came to see me and Will. She'd met some guy who'd give us a side job."

"To break into houses," I said.

"No. Absolutely not. We'd climb in and take some things. We never broke one thing, not until Rosie broke that window. But we, me and Will, we never robbed. These were rich people, Pen. Robbery doesn't happen to people like that, they don't even notice things gone! It's not like we stole from people in Buena Park."

"People in Beverly Hills aren't really real," I said.

"Yeah, like that. And you know how bad Will needed money, with you not here."

"If I'd stayed home, if I'd stayed right here on this porch, he wouldn't have had to do it," I said.

"Probably not, yeah. But it's not all your fault. Will also wanted Rosie back. He'd do anything for Rosie."

"Yes, it was her fault, too. What about you, Teddy? Will wanted Rose. What did you want?"

"I was trying to help, you know? Pen, do you have any iced tea?"

I jumped. I'd been picturing Stany's backyard, the base of a ladder, and now I was on my mom's front steps. I went into the kitchen and ran Teddy a glass of tap water. Back at the porch, I handed Teddy the glass. "You were all helping each other," I said.

"Exactly. And I never went in one house, not one."

"You helped pass out the stuff, guy to guy?"

"Me and Will drove his truck, too. Load and unload, that sort of thing. And the night Rosie died, I wasn't even there. Pen, you couldn't get me a simple glass of iced tea? What is this?" He raised the glass full of tap water.

"You didn't rob houses," I said. "You didn't break anything, you didn't go in. Why are you telling me? This isn't a secret. Where's your terrible secret?"

He leaned forward and set the glass on the step next to his hat. Then he shifted his hat and picked up the long envelope underneath. He held the envelope out to me.

"What?"

"This is it," he said. "This is the secret."

A long white envelope, probably taken from the sheriff's office downtown. Not stolen, though. Something thick and heavy and flexible inside. I opened the envelope and looked.

"Eight thousand dollars," Teddy said. "Will's share. His share of the—of our work. I didn't know what to do. Should I keep it? What if Will finds out? Should I hide it? But I'm enlisting, too, and what if something . . . something . . . well, what if the worst happens and Will comes home but I don't, what would he think of me? For God's sake, Pen, don't count it."

A big pause, Teddy breathing, and then: "Penny? Aw, god-damn it."

His shirt against my face felt crisp and warm, like Will's or my dad's might have, like a shirt freshly line-dried. He wasn't Teddy the bad date, he was a shirt that felt crisp on my face, and I'd needed a shirt. I didn't know until I pressed my face against it that I'd needed a crisp shirt. I cried for Rosemary and her lost daughter, and for Madge and her lost parents, and for my mother, whose son would be lost soon.

"I'm glad I told you," Teddy said. "I feel much better now."

We sat together and I cried, and we listened to the line of people shuffling toward fried chicken. A while later, Mom and Daisy came home. The second mom and the silent girl. My family. We watched Mom's old car putt down Grand and onto our gravel drive.

"Your mom doesn't like me," Teddy said. "See? She's glaring. I'll leave. Pen, when I'm wearing a sailor's cap and I'm on some ship getting bombed in the English Channel, can I write to you? Will you be my girl at home?"

"No," I said. "I will burn every letter you send."

He nodded. That was it. He stood up, put on his hat, and brushed at his spitty shirt.

Behind him, Mom swung open her car door and stepped out. "I only have two arms," she said to me, holding grocery bags. I stood and kicked the *Hollywood Reporter* out of the way and went to help her. When she handed off a bag, I squeezed her arm and kissed her on the cheek.

"I thought you were helping," she said, but she smiled when she said it.

Eight thousand dollars will hold us for a year, while we negotiate our land sale with Mr. Knott. We'll have time to decide what comes next. I like Riverside, Madge's hometown. The heat! In Riverside, sun burns the grass to brown threads. It's beautiful, though. Louis—Conejos—says he grew up in sun like that. I think Rose would have liked Riverside.

Rose, who got pregnant nearly three years ago and left home to hide it from Will and me. Rose, who gave her baby to a nurse. It's all I know. I don't think Will was the baby's father. She wouldn't have needed to leave home if the baby was Will's. They were planning to marry. Maybe she, too, had a bad date with Teddy, but I just don't know. Like Stany warned me, I still have questions. When I'd asked Dr. Ostrander which star had come out the hospital side door, he had a question, too: "Does it make a difference?"

Not to Rose. She would have screamed no matter who limped

out that door. The difference is Joe and Marty and Abbott and Dr. Ostrander. Abbott didn't hurt Rosemary, but he needed her quiet. And Dr. Ostrander, I like to think that when he found out about Rose, he felt bad. But behind him is the studio, and studios don't feel.

And Marty. A killer and thief and a pretty good lawyer. He was important in Hollywood. At the studio, when Stany and Marty listened to my story about Halloween, Marty had rubbed Stany's shoulders and knew what to say. He knew why she was upset. Hollywood needs those kinds of people. The greatest movie stars, the real ones, Bette Davis and Stany, aren't real at all. They need guys like Marty. Their stories have changed so many times that comfort is what moves them forward.

I forgave Rose for being a thief. She also lied, but I forgave her. I'd learned how grief makes us change, first mother to second mother, each of us changing in our own way, but none of it good. We need movies to remember what it was like before the grief. When Paramount released *The Lady Eve,* I went to a theater. I've seen the movie three times now, and I've got a secret: Preston didn't reshoot the wedding scene.

He meant to. I'm sure he cut what he could. Stany in Edith Head's gown and veil, pearls and pink gladiola, descending a staircase toward Hank. Behind Hank, all the guests at the wedding, and there—the foot and skirt nearly hidden, but there, and a hand—Rosemary on film.

Maybe it's me—I want to see Rose so badly I've made my own film. It runs alongside the real one. Here's a Wallflower, Career Girls, part of a Femme Fatale. But not me. Not Madge, either. And Rose steps to her mark, and Preston yells, and the film rolls, and we're not there. We've left Paramount, Madge and me. We're in her creaky Dodge on Route 18, driving to Riverside. *Drive fast,* Madge says. *We're nearly there, goddamn you, keep driving.* That's the film I want. That's the only film I'm willing to make.

ACKNOWLEDGMENTS

The following people and organizations assisted with research for my story. Thank you, with my gratitude, to the Buena Park Historical Society; Esotouric; Glynn Martin at the Los Angeles Police Historical Society; Knott's Berry Farm; Los Angeles Public Library; Margaret Herrick Library at the Academy of Motion Picture Arts and Sciences; Media History Digital Library; Newport Beach Public Library; Tom Sturges; UCLA Library Department of Special Collections, and curators of the Preston Sturges papers; and Melinda (Mindy) Brown at Paramount Pictures.

My deepest thanks to everyone who generously read and commented on the story or the writing: Shirley Barker, Kelly Berman, Cramer R. Cauthen, Kate Collins, Anthony Diaz, Amy Dominetta, Wendy Gates, Kelly Graves, Barbara Jaffe, Donald Maass, Jeanette McCann, Lorin Oberweger, Jennifer Peters, Lissa Price, John Roche, Joanne Steinmetz, and Brenda Windberg.

A sparkling thank you to my agent, Jennifer Udden, editor, Peter Senftleben, and the extraordinary team at Kensington, including my editor, Wendy McCurdy, copy chief, Tracy Marx, production editor, Paula Reedy, and copy editor, Linda Seed.